PENGUIN BOOKS
The Time Out Book of London Short Stories Volume 2

Nicholas Royle is the author of four novels – *Counterparts, Saxophone Dreams, The Matter of the Heart, The Director's Cut* – and more than a hundred short stories. He has edited eleven anthologies, including *The Time Out Book of New York Short Stories, The Time Out Book of Paris Short Stories* and two volumes of *Neonlit: Time Out Book of New Writing*. Fiction editor of neonlit.com, he also writes regularly for *Time Out*.

Praise for The Time Out Book of Paris Short Stories

'Enjoyably provocative' *Times*

'Splendidly evocative' *Glasgow Herald*

'Formidable!' *Guardian*

Praise for Neonlit: Time Out Book of New Writing Volume 2

'An excellent eclectica of short stories... I would urge all avid readers who enjoy a good yarn to spend some time in with this' *Pulp*, C4 TV

'Well edited... polished... plenty to satisfy all appetites' *New Statesman*

The Time Out Book of
London Short Stories
Volume 2

Edited by Nicholas Royle

PENGUIN BOOKS

PENGUIN BOOKS

Published by the Penguin Group
Penguin Books Ltd, 27 Wrights Lane, London W8 5TZ, England
Penguin Books USA Inc, 375 Hudson Street, New York, New York 10014, USA
Penguin Books Australia Ltd, Ringwood, Victoria, Australia
Penguin Books Canada Ltd, 10 Alcorn Avenue, Toronto, Ontario, Canada M4V 3B2
Penguin Books (NZ) Ltd, 182-190 Wairau Road, Auckland 10, New Zealand

Penguin Books Ltd, Registered Offices: Harmondsworth, Middlesex, England

First published in Great Britain by Penguin Books 2000
10 9 8 7 6 5 4 3 2 1

Printed in England by Clays Ltd, St Ives plc

Contents

For Charlie (born London, 1997)
& Bella (born London, 1999)

& to the memory of
Nigel Watts (1957-99)

The editor would like to thank the following:
Kate Ryan; Sahera Chohan, Sally Stokes, Mark Le Fanu,
Jonathan Coe; Peter Fiennes, Sarah Guy, Sophie Blacksell;
John Oakey, Kerri Miles, Max Jourdan;
Tamsin Shelton; RMC, CRW, GE.

Contributors

Born in 1968, **Rhonda Carrier** grew up in the Midlands. After living in London for several years, she recently gave up her job as an editor in order to live by the sea and write full time. Her short story in *Neonlit: Time Out Book of New Writing Volume 2* won the Jack Trevor Story Memorial Prize. She has recently completed a first novel, *Delta Rhythm*.

Robert Elms was born in north London in 1959. Widely published as a journalist and travel writer, he is the author of one novel, *In Search of the Crack*, and one work of non-fiction, *Spain – A Portrait After the General*. An experienced broadcaster on both radio and television, he presents BBC London Live's morning show five days a week.

Gareth Evans is a freelance arts writer based in London. He is currently co-editing *Rogue Transmissions: Explorations in Contemporary Culture*, to be published by Rebel Inc in 2001.

Christopher Fowler lives in London and runs a film company. His novels include *Roofworld*, *Darkest Day*, *Spanky*, *Psychoville*, *Disturbia*, *Soho Black* and *Calabash*. Among his collections are *City Jitters*, *Flesh Wounds* and *Sharper Knives*. Forthcoming are another collection, *The Devil in Me*, and a new novel, *Homeland*.

Maureen Freely, born in Neptune, New Jersey, in 1952, grew up in Istanbul. She now lives in Bath. Her novels include *Mother's Helper*, *The Stork Club*, *Under the Vulcania* and *The Other Rebecca*. She is a lecturer on the creative writing programme at the University of Warwick.

Esther Freud was born in 1963. She trained as an actress before writing her first novel, *Hideous Kinky*, in 1992, which was made into a film starring Kate Winslet. Her other novels are *Peerless Flats* (1993), *Gaglow* (1997) and *The Wild* (2000). She lives in London with her family.

Steve Grant is a writer and freelance journalist who lives in London.

Stewart Home was born in south London but has lived in the East End for the last fifteen years. His ninth novel, *69 Things to Do With a Dead Princess*, will be published by Rebel Inc in spring 2001.

Angelica Jacob was born in Prague in 1963. Her first novel, *Fermentation*, was published by Bloomsbury in 1997 and her second, *The Reflection*, by Deuticke in Vienna. Her short stories have appeared in several magazines, including *Frieze* and the *Erotic Review*. She is currently working on her third novel, *Homesick*.

Russell Celyn Jones is the author of *Soldiers and Innocents*, *Small Times*, *An Interference of Light* and *The Eros Hunter*. His new novel, *Surface Tension*, will be published in January 2001 by Abacus. A regular reviewer for the *Times,* he teaches at Warwick University and lives in London.

Christopher Kenworthy's first novel, *The Winter Inside*, is published by Serpent's Tail. A second, *Pilotage*, will follow in 2001. Born in Preston in 1968, he now lives in Western Australia. Having directed one short film, he is currently putting a second into production.

Reuben Lane lives in east London where he works as a cinema usher. His short stories have featured in *Random Factor*, *Does the Sun Rise Over Dagenham?* and *Pretext 1*. His first novel, *Throwing Stones at Jonathan*, was shortlisted for the Waterstone's/Mardi Gras Book Award 2000.

Toby Litt was born in Bedford in 1968. His first three books were *Adventures in Capitalism* (1996), *Beatniks* (1997) and *Corpsing* (2000).

Jacqueline Lucas's stories have appeared in *Ambit*, *em two*, *The Printer's Devil*, *Allnighter*, *Rites of Spring* and *neonlit.com*. She lives in London and is currently working on a novel and a video diary.

Paul J McAuley was born in 1955. He has worked as a researcher at various universities, including Oxford and UCLA, and was a lecturer in botany at St Andrews. Now a full-time writer, his novels include *Four Hundred Billion Stars*, *Fairyland* and *Shrine of Stars*. His latest novel, *The Secret of Life*, will be published in the UK by HarperCollins in January 2001. He lives in Islington, north London.

Born in south London in 1939, **Michael Moorcock** is the author of dozens of novels including, most recently, *King of the City*, described by its publisher as a sequel to *Mother London*. His next book will be a collection of stories, *London Bone*. Although he currently lives in Texas, his work still reflects his ongoing obsession with his home city.

Courttia Newland is the author of two novels, *The Scholar* and *Society Within*. Co-editor of *IC3: The Penguin Book of New Black Writing in Britain*, he has had stories published in numerous anthologies. He is currently working on a new novel, and a book of surreal short stories, including the one published here.

Kim Newman's novels include *The Night Mayor*, *Jago* and *Life's Lottery*, and among his collections are *The Original Dr Shade* and *Where the Bodies Are Buried*. His non-fiction includes *Nightmare Movies* and *Millennium Movies*. Born in Brixton, he lives in north London and is currently working on two new novels, *An English Ghost Story* and *Johnny Alucard*, and, with Eugene Byrne, a novel cycle entitled *The Matter of Britain*.

Geoff Nicholson is the author of thirteen novels, including *Bleeding London*, *Footsucker* and, most recently, *Bedlam Burning*. He lives in London and New York.

John O'Connell was born in 1972. He lives in London.

Kate Pemberton was born in 1972 and grew up in Bath. She now lives in London, writing, editing, teaching English and translating. Other stories have been published in recent issues of *Ambit*.

Chris Petit is a writer and film-maker. He is the author of *Robinson*, *The Psalm Killer* and *Back From the Dead*. His films include *Radio On* and *Chinese Boxes*, numerous documentaries and, as co-director with Iain Sinclair, *The Falconer* and *Asylum*. His contribution to this volume is an extract from a forthcoming novel, *The Hard Shoulder*.

Half-English and half-French, **Michèle Roberts** was born in 1949. She is the author of ten novels, among them *A Piece of the Night* (1978), *In the Red Kitchen* (1990), *Daughters of the House* (1992), *Flesh & Blood*

(1994) and *The Looking Glass* (2000), and one collection of short stories, *During Mother's Absence* (1993), in addition to poetry collections and a book of essays. She lives in London and Mayenne, France.

Leone Ross has published two novels – *All the Blood is Red* (1996) and *Orange Laughter* (1999). Her stories have appeared in the following anthologies: *Wild Women: Stories of Women on the Road* (1998), *Burning Words, Flaming Images* (1997) and *Dark Matter* (2000).

Iain Sinclair is the author of the novels *White Chappell, Scarlet Tracings*, *Downriver* and *Radon Daughters*, and a collection of short stories, *Slow Chocolate Autopsy*. His new novel, *Landor's Tower*, is due in spring 2001 from Granta Books, who will also be publish his forthcoming work, *O(r)bituary Trances: A Walk Around the M25*. In parallel with this, he is collaborating with Chris Petit on a film about the M25 for Channel 4.

Tamara Smith grew up in London and Los Angeles. She has worked as a copywriter and was the Live Literature Officer at the British Council and Arts Council. Since leaving full-time employment last year, she has worked as a documentary producer for Sky TV and as a journalist writing features. This is her first short story.

Born in 1968, **Marc Werner** has lived in Paris, Berlin and Brussels, and is now based in London. A previous story appeared in *The Time Out Book of Paris Short Stories*. He is working on a book about the application of Dalí's 'paranoiac critical method' to photography.

Conrad Williams spent the last six years working in London as a freelance journalist but has now left the capital to live on the Suffolk coast and write full time. He has adapted his first novel, *Head Injuries*, for Revolution Films and is currently writing a new novel, *Penetralia*, as well as a novel for teens, *The Autumn Manufacturer*.

Elizabeth Young was born in Lagos, Nigeria and brought up in Scotland until attending The Mount boarding school in York. She has degrees in American Literature and has published widely as a critic and arts journalist. Her second book, *Pandora's Handbag*, will appear in February 2001. She is married and lives in west London.

Introduction

Cities are breeding grounds for many things, above all narrative. Stories are everywhere around us, in the pubs and bars of Soho and outlying districts alike, in the cinemas, theatres, coffee shops and art galleries. Text gathers like intelligent dust in the abandoned buildings that await development along the canals and flyovers. Fiction rises up from the streets, from the most intensively visited tourist haunts to the narrowest, grimiest, most neglected alleyways. It springs from the memories of the city's residents and those who make a living in it. From the boneyards and hospitals, chat rooms and hotel suites. It begins with the writing on the wall. The stories that can be written about London – one of the world's greatest cities, perhaps *the* greatest – are endless. Here are twenty-nine of the freshest.

They (publishers, booksellers) say that short stories don't sell. You and I know this to be untrue. *The Time Out Book of London Short Stories*, edited by Maria Lexton, has sold steadily since 1993. The volumes of New York and Paris short stories have also sold well. They – along with the *Neonlit* anthologies – have introduced some exciting new voices to a wide readership, as well as featuring new work by some of the finest practitioners of the form.

Time Out remains committed to promoting and encouraging new and established talent in London. Not all of these writers live in the capital, but, in this book, it is manifestly their subject.

Nicholas Royle
London, August 2000

Mud man

Leone Ross

Matthew is his mother's little mud man. This is what she calls him when he is very small, growing to be tall in the hills of Port Antonio in Jamaica. She holds him to her breasts when they return from the banks of the Rio Grande. When Matthew's mother walks by the river, the fish cry. She watches the canoe men with the tourist women, slow-ripple waves filling her shallow eyes. Matthew's daddy was a canoe man, spending his days tripping on-off, on-off the six-inch-high rafts, his feet muddy to the ankle and white with it. Matthew doesn't know that his mother missed the smell of river mud in her bed until he came. Every day he follows her along the banks, playing in the mud until he is bored and white all over. Matthew's mother holds him close to her and breathes him in. Matthew doesn't know his daddy left with a tourist woman, even though the district gossips whisper it softly into the hills, tucking it around Matthew's mother's bed head, until her mattress fills with shame and cruel laughter. Matthew is like all the boys he knows. A mummy's boy because daddies are ghosts.

Matthew grows to be a squashy boy, so tall he gives the neighbours crick-cracked necks, as soft as the inside of a cocoa pod, his palms and soles pink like raw cocoa, his head shiny and deep brown like the dried cocoa beans strewn in his mother's back yard. She is proud of the deep rolls of fat in his sides, the wideness of his bright young eyes, and his child-bearing hips. He is tall and broad but he feels small when she tells him it is time for him to go to London, England. She tells him how kind his Auntie Susu is, how she will take care of him and show him how to smooth the magic of the great United Kingdom on to his elbows and forehead.

Aunt Susu is rubbed raw from work. She smells of white people's urine and pain and she walks with a bent back from scrubbing and tending people who hate her. She pushes a long sharp pin into the dreams that Matthew's mother packed in his red suitcase, along with the shining ackees and sand mangoes that the airport men take away. Aunt Susu sends Matthew to school and pats him on the head when he tells her that the people in London look at him as if a mongoose lives in his eyes. Matthew turns the pages of his schoolbooks, never seeing himself there, wondering about the way the girls call him names. At school he clings to the front gate and bows his head to all that look at him. Softness is the only gift he has to bring, and he sweeps the classroom in the morning for home-room teacher and picks small flowers from the spring breeze to leave on the desks of the white girls who look sad.

When the black girl arrives at school Matthew sees the fire in her belly from as far as twenty paces. He watches her walk through the school as if she is balancing on broken glass. He watches her erase the laughter in the faces of the boys who take Aunt Susu's nursing money, leaving the imprint of their delicate hands on his skin. The black girl's name is Marsha and she is hard as Matthew is soft. She takes one boy by a handful of his golden hair and spits in his face. Marsha is brave for Matthew and he loves her as much as his mother loved his father. Matthew has nothing to give her, but he murmurs fragrant Jamaican songs into her plaits. She has never heard songs like this. She calls him jungle bunny, this girl who is the same colour as him but has never seen green hills. She tells him stories of cold rain that makes no noise on the roof, and he tries to tell her what crickets sound like. They travel on the underground together, staring and giggling at women who kiss, watching rows of hands that disappear into newspapers. One day when Matthew is singing in Marsha's ear, a drunken man with dawn-sprung eyes tries to make the carriage join in. He tells the children they are beautiful. They are too afraid to smile, but they watch him sing a rousing solo, listening to the carriage people ignore him.

God is good to Matthew. He gets him a job as a conductor on the buses. God chuckles down from pulpits in churches, bleeding and rib-bound, as Matthew makes the money to marry Marsha. He cools Matthew's brow when people pinch their coins between finger and thumb, never touching Matthew's pink palms. Matthew likes his work. He sings as much as he can and always says thank you and please and have a nice day, young lady. Matthew sings the songs his mother taught him, wedges his hips between the shiny seats and brushes his head against the bus top. Matthew's customers complain that he cannot sing. They do not mean that. What they mean is that his songs are sad and that they cannot bear their homesickness. Matthew bows his head when he is told to stop singing, and his eyes are white mud.

When Matthew is twenty years old, Marsha gives him a pair of orange-shaped twins. She plucks them out of her body like a canoe man kicking off from the shallow shore and then wraps the baby fat they left behind around her like a womb. Matthew doesn't mind. The bed still creaks, like merry crickets at night, and he buys his wife clothes the colour of Port Antonio sunsets. Marsha is in charge of spanking even though she is careful for the social people not to know. Matthew is in charge of play fighting, of sitting in his children's beds at night, holding them and feeding them bottles of thick milk. Matthew is in charge of touch, as his children grow too heavy for his wife to hold. Matthew's family are fat as moons, and full of childish laughter.

Matthew's laughter stops three days after his children's eighth birthday. His son is David and his daughter is Susan, and they go to their first birthday party, with cake and chips and jelly and ice cream. Matthew cannot afford chips and cakes and rainbow ice cream, so his children must attend this party. The lady having the party promises that she will drive David and Susan home. Susan is a small puddle on the floor as she tells Matthew about the long walk back, about the electric lights that steamed into the sky and the tiny policeman who turned his back when they asked directions. She tells Matthew that David holds her hand very tight and says that a big star will guide them home. She tells Matthew that she saw the star and dropped David's hand. That cold hit her back when she turned to see her brother stumbling, too slow to escape the man who caught him and held him close.

Three months of questions pass and Matthew walks around his home, sweeping brittle pieces of Marsha into his arms. He reads the newspapers on the way to work and counts the missing children in the headlines, all colours, all shapes, little knees and feet all gone, missing, under the stars. He is promoted and takes a deep breath when his boss tells him he is the best boy at the depot. He watches the child that London left him.

Susan eats. She goes shopping with her mother and carries mountains of plantain to the tube station. In pretty parks she hop skips over dog shit while she sucks pints of blackcurrant juice. In chippies she swallows strings of sausages and at home she burns her mind on pots of chicken stew. Her pillows make way for delicate choux pastry. She listens to an Italian waiter call her *l'arancia bella*, the beautiful orange, as she pastes her eyelids closed with garlic butter.

One day Matthew is searching for the pieces of his wife under their new sofa, and a sparkling piece of her cheekbone speaks to him. She tells him that she is tired of fighting. She calls him a weak man, and then blinks into nothing. The rest of her is too busy stroking Susan's brow to notice. Matthew raises his head and watches his daughter stumble upstairs. It seems to him that she is walking through the sea, through sand, one slow foot after another. He asks her to tell him the story of David again. Two years have passed and Susan cannot remember it all. She stutters through the old tale but Matthew makes her tell it over and over, until she is screaming. Marsha saves her, turning burning eyes on her husband.

Matthew knows what to do. His mind is full of his boy, running through sand and sea, his heavy feet not quick enough to escape the man who held him. He looks at pictures of his son and remembers how David buried his face into his chest at sports day when they called him to the egg and spoon race. Matthew looks at the breadth of his own belly and knows that it is his fault.

Matthew visits pharmacies and bookstores and homeopaths. He flings away armfuls of dairy, carbohydrate and sugar, and all the time he sees David's feet become lighter, lighter, whizzing through the air, changing the past. Matthew dices carrots and celery and buys new clothes and sees his son drawing nearer. He speaks to Marsha in new tones, and she obeys. Matthew's family shrink. They practice slipping down plugholes, through telephone wires; they dance together on the head of a pin.

Matthew wakes up one day to the sound of Marsha opening the door to the police. He walks downstairs and sees his wife trying to fit their son inside her. David's eyes fill the kitchen, he cannot take them away from his sister, how tall she is, how slender. He pushes his mother into the stove and she bangs her leg against it; he slaps her. *You are not my mother*, he says, until the room echoes with it. Matthew falls to his knees and cries.

David has not been touched with tenderness for years, and it shows. He can run now, but he runs from those who love him and he hides in the toilet. He sits in the garden, ripping up the grass. Susan whispers to him, but he climbs a tree and sits there for three days, until she stops. The social worker talks about abuse and post-traumatic shock and time. Matthew knows he is running out of time. He goes to his son and tells him how much he loves him and how much he missed him.

David laughs. You don't look like my father, he says.

Matthew knows what to do. He must make it like it was. He asks Marsha to bake. Together they rebuild the house until its roof is marzipan, its windows are smoky with chocolate mist and its carpets are sticky toffee. Marsha makes dumplings and her hands drip with syrup. Susan gives up after-school drama club and painting and says no to her first dates, for there is only time to eat. Matthew does not buy new clothes; he allows his belly to flop over tailored trousers so that David will, once again, see the memories that kept him alive. The family grow fat as moons and try to laugh like children. Every day Matthew watches David's face for happiness, for recognition. David is as round as the rest, but still his eyes are crumpled pieces of paper. He spends his days and most of his nights away from his family, and comes home with strange piles of money, no note smaller than twenty.

One day Matthew climbs into bed with David when he is asleep. He has a glass of warm milk in his hand. David is still dreaming, but he rolls on his tummy and presents his haunches, like a small lion waiting for mounting. Matthew vomits across Susan's books. But I'm your father, he says to David. I wouldn't touch you like that. David wakes up and laughs. Everyone has urges, he says. I hear you at night with Mamma. I see the boys looking at Susan. Everybody touches me. Why not you?

Matthew is his mother's little mud man. This is what she calls him when he is very small, growing to be tall in the hills of Port Antonio in Jamaica. Matthew goes for a walk by the river, and the fish cry. He watches the tourist men with the tourist women, slow-ripple waves filling his shallow eyes. He buys something in a shop and goes home to his family late at night. David is not there.

He wakes his wife softly and then lies on top of her, so that she cannot spark and burn him. The knife that he has bought is a sharp one and it slices through flesh easily. Matthew trims the hair between her legs first, and then cuts deeply and neatly, singing into Marsha's cool ear. Matthew visits his daughter and does his work as fast as he can. He props Susan at the head of her bed and smiles at a job well done. He covers the bloody hole between her legs, and lays her down. She looks like she is dreaming.

Matthew slices onions and sweet peppers and seasons meat. He sets the table for one. He sits down and sharpens his knife. He can see his son in his mind, the men who touched him for so many years, and the men who still do. He tests the knife against his groin and readies himself for the pain. David can come home for dinner now. There will be nothing in his home to remind David of the past. Nothing at all.

The tango shift

Russell Celyn Jones

He got sent out that time by the station officer who could just as easily have picked on any of the three crews in the mess. Rees often thought about this piece of providential bad luck, obsessed over it even. It was near 23.00 when the ASO came off the phone and pointed randomly into the games room where they were playing pool. Rees was in his line of sight, as simple as that, and so went out into the night, navigating the ambulance for his partner, Alison.

The caller's coordinates was a place off St Martin's Lane and they crossed Waterloo Bridge from the south. From the bridge London always seemed more like a fictional setting than a real city, a honeycomb bathed in the light of a full moon hanging above St Paul's. In Covent Garden and on Long Acre the traffic created a parting for them. It was the only time when cars showed signs of being extensions of human consciousness, in the way they scuttled nervously towards the kerb at the sound of sirens and blue lights bouncing off the façades. His partner – a burnt-out primary school teacher in another life – drove at incredible speed and they got there just under five minutes from the time of the call.

Brydges Place was an alleyway off St Martin's Lane beside the English National Opera house and so narrow his shoulders brushed the walls on each side. It was unlit and smelled badly of urine, human waste. Rees thought it smelled like anger. There were sleeping bags in doorways. Their instinct was to check for signs of life, but no one was at home. When Alison rang a door bell Rees prepared himself for some gay pick-up bar or shag-and-suck emporium. Instead a rather luxurious dining club presented itself to them. Tiny book-lined rooms stacked one on top of the other in which jovial groups of people stopped eating and talking as these two anomalies clumped up the stairs, carrying respirator, I&I equipment and stretcher. They all looked terribly anxious to see Rees. The-bell-tolls-for-thee kind of thing.

The club manager directed them up to the top floor and to a woman lying on her back between cleared tables. Six or seven other people were clucking around her head. Rees caught the eye of one he thought looked most sober, a man in a tuxedo, and made sure he had his attention before asking him what had happened. He would not lift a finger until he was briefed. Paramedics in the past have gone up in a puff of smoke after touching casualties lying on live electricity cables.

The man in the tux didn't know what happened exactly. One minute she was talking and the next she had fallen off her chair and couldn't be revived. Rees checked her carotid. Her pulse was weak and her breathing shallow. There was no bleeding, but she was desperately white. With Alison's help he gently lifted her on to the stretcher.

Rees went in the back of the ambulance with the casualty while Alison radioed the crash unit at UCH. As they set keel for the hospital the woman's big opaline eyes flickered open, staring at Rees without curiosity. She was about thirty years old – his age. Rees figured that standing on her feet she would probably be an inch or two taller than him. Her black hair clung to her white face, her lips were painted red and he wondered what it would be like to kiss them. There was an endemic intimacy to this job, involving the touching of both the living and the dead, but it was more promiscuity than anything like love. The majority of the casualties they attended were old and frail, drunk and homeless. This woman was clearly from a different world and the more he thought about her otherness, the more his desire built.

They took her into the A&E through the ambulance bays, the route for blue-light front-line casualties, straight into the cubicles where a duty doctor was waiting. She revived on the trolley bed seconds after arriving. 'Can you hear me?' the doctor pronounced loudly. 'What's your name?'

'Laura.'

'What's your full name?'

'Where are we?'

'You're in hospital.'

'What happened?'

'Are you allergic to anything? Do you use insulin?'

'I get eczema. I get lonely. But I don't use insulin.' She was flirting with the doctor.

It seemed she had passed out, nothing more, a faint, a feint. She asked if she could be taken home.

Rees and Alison drove her home to her flat in Bayswater. Rees walked her inside the mansion block. With her keys he opened up the flat and led her into the living room with a hand under her arm. He noticed the hardback books on every wall, a baby Steinway piano, before sitting her down on a white leather sofa.

He asked her if she lived alone.

'That's a very personal question.'

'It's not intended to be personal.' Rees offered to make her tea.

'Do you do this often?'

'It's part of the service.'

'Silver Service.' She laughed at her own joke, more an intake of breath than a laugh, and Rees found himself attracted to her for the second time that night. She was aristocratic looking, what he imagined aristocratic to look like anyway, a cold-blooded English beauty that made him think of the stained glass in cathedrals. He could have happily meditated on her face for hours.

He found what he needed in the kitchen to make tea. As he kneeled beside her and placed the mug on the table she touched his lapels. 'I like men in uniform,' she smiled. 'You know who a man is in uniform.'

'What a man is, perhaps. Will you be OK if I go now?'

'Yes. And thank you very much. I don't meet such kind men where I work.'

'Where do you work?'

'In publishing… the men are all on the make.' She sighed dreamily, not yet quite back to where she was two hours ago. 'What a strange day it's been, that started with me working at home this morning, editing a new edition of Roland Barthes' *A Lover's Discourse*. I had a lovely lunch of oysters with one of my authors, John, boyfriend of my friend Peter. Maybe the oysters upset me? Tonight I collapsed over dinner. Now I'm home again with an ambulanceman making me tea.'

He got home at twenty minutes past midnight to his one-bedroom flat on the ninth floor of a high-rise block of council flats in London Fields. He walked into the flat without turning on any lamps and stared out into the night where a million flickering lights marked out a million souls trying to survive some received and impossible concept of life. He thought about Laura inhaling oysters with authors, and of her friends in the dining club in Brydges Place – none of whom knew how to revive her – and compared them to his own life resuscitating the sick and the dying like a human mechanic, day after day. And like

Laura they always professed such gratitude, which expired minutes later as soon as they felt better. If all people experienced a moment of near-fatality every day of their lives then Rees would be the most popular guy in town, instead of going home alone each night. He had come to London from a Welsh market town with high expectations, and spent eight years in solitary confinement.

Through the bare branches of a plane tree he saw in the adjacent block of flats a tenant restlessly circling her lair in the nude. Even from that distance her body looked healthy, bearing no wounds, burns, fractures. A piece of wonder, a vision. In the Ambulance Service they were taught there are two ways of dying: by stopping breathing or by a cessation of blood. Rees knew of a third: through sheer longing.

Several days passed and Rees was back at UCH with an RTA for the A&E and the assessment nurse gave him a letter from Laura. Rees balanced it in his palm as though weighing its significance. 'She delivered it in person, didn't know your name. But I guessed it was you, lover boy.'

Rees sat in the waiting room of the A&E, surrounded by a migratory community of the sick and injured, the walking wounded, and read Laura's letter.

> I had such a huge urge to contact you that I just ran out of the Dome Cafe where I am sitting to an Indian newsagent and managed to buy this paper and a nasty biro. Now I can tell you how much I feel. I feel like I've taken a long breath and am holding it in until I see you. I miss you in the pit of my stomach, that kind of physical missing which I've only known once before. Should I be saying these things? Is it too much? But it feels so good to me, so right, so full of possibility and I suppose natural, which seems like a little miracle. I feel very lucky. I've been listening to music all day and dancing in my flat, and thinking of you.

The letter ended on a enigmatic note. 'Coach and Horses in Soho, tomorrow night, 8pm?'

Rees was meant to be working that night, so called in sick. He got to Soho early and wandered up and down Old Compton Street for half an hour, not liking it very much. He was not used to seeing Soho in this way, on foot, couldn't understand what it was for. When he finally walked into the Coach and Horses he was five minutes late and couldn't see her among the crowds. His heart started to palpitate. As he squeezed through he spotted her sitting alone at the bar, giving him a look that seemed to pay out line. She kissed him on the lips and Rees had to turn his head away. He badly needed a drink and held a ten-pound note in his hand, waving it at the busy, preoccupied bar staff. A guy standing hopefully next to Laura said to Rees in a tense voice, 'You're a lucky guy.'

'I'd be even luckier if I could get a fucking drink.'

At that the guy visibly relaxed, his shoulders lost their stiffness because Rees's parodic remark had released him of the seriousness of his observation. And for Rees too. There was only so much of that true statement he could bear. He did feel lucky. Luck is fantastic. Until you lose it.

'No uniform tonight,' she observed. 'I'm disappointed.' He had come to meet her in full Sunday rig: grey suit, white shirt and half-brogues. He felt stupid suddenly.

'I don't even know your name,' she said.

'Rees.'

'Well, Rees, we are going dancing tonight.'

There was no choice in this decision, that much was clear. But it didn't matter to him. At that point it felt a kind of generosity to be led by her.

As they were leaving the Coach and Horses she said something about preserving life through dance and music that he didn't understand. By and by she added, 'I feel so safe with you. I mean, if I have an accident you'll know what to do.' It was the kind of declaration of self-possession that served only to make her more alluring to him.

On Brewer Street she directed him down some steps into a base-ment. It was slamming inside; people were dancing to Latin music. It was very hot and the air felt greased. She held Rees by the hand and around the back. And she *was* two inches taller than him. Her long legs gave length to her stride. As they moved she whispered in his ear over the loud tango music: 'Walk right front, left front. Progressive side step, right front, diagonal to centre, rock, right front, rock… back. Corte. Fallaway promenade, brush tap. That's it! You're doing the tango.'

This was news to him. 'The tango's what we call the solo shift in the ambulance service. No partner. *Pas de un*.' He got no response.

Rees was a good mover and was soon communicating with her, stealing time from one step to give a hovering effect to the next. The mechanics of movement evaporated until they floated on the music, promenading on air. Her head moved with her body, not against it. The way she held herself with arched back and joined to Rees at the waist, embodied something platonic, a love without physical pain, a universe without injury.

She was very persuasive as long as the music lasted. She had an atmosphere about her, defined in sinuous and sophisticated movement. She was dominant the whole time, uninhibited, exotic and dramatic.

After a busy hour her lipstick had faded, her hair fell lank and beads of sweat glistened in her eyebrows.

They didn't sleep together on that first night, each going home in separate taxis. But when Rees arrived in his flat there was a message from her on his answering machine:

> I want to know you in ways nobody else does. Like a well-used map, the folds worn down and smooth, the corners curled, marks suggesting routes followed and yet still places not visited, still surprises, still untouched parts. Oh I miss you already. I wish you were in my bed with me now, your taut, muscular, compassionate... Listen, I bought some tickets for a concert yesterday and want you to come. I pray you won't be working and that you'll be able to. Do you like Scriabin? Please say yes. Bye bye. Much love...

After he listened to her message (twice) another, fainter sound started to impinge. His neighbour was tapping on the adjoining wall. Mr Blackmore was an old blind man who lived alone, who sometimes called upon Rees's good nature to help him out. Rees had his own key to Mr Blackmore's flat and, as late as it was, he went next door to see what help he could offer.

The flat was dark and a creeping fruity staleness clung to the curtains, furniture. The old man was reclining in an armchair with a blanket on his lap, in front of a one-bar electric fire. The TV was on, even though he couldn't see it. His silvered hands were wrapped around a chipped tea mug and it occurred to Rees that it must have been a long time since something hot was in there. He told Rees to sit beside him and began to tell the same story Rees had before, about how he fought against the Germans for a whole week in a wheat field whitened by the sun that gradually turned red with the blood of thousands of soldiers.

Rees didn't want to hear any of this. It was now 1.30 in the morning. He decided to sabotage the old man's story with one of his own,

about the time he witnessed a fatal accident. He saw plenty of acci-
dents, of course, but always five minutes after they went off. The girl
was about twenty years old, cycling in a billowing skirt and blouse, on
her way to meet friends, or family, or going to the pictures. She was
in her life. Everything was fine. Then in the next moment it was all
over. A bus had crushed her against a parked van. Rees stopped the
car he was driving and ran to help. But the girl was dead, her skull had
caved in and she was lying on the road where she'd fallen, her eyes
staring sideways to the site of the fracture. Cerebrospinal fluid seeped
out of her eyes like pink tears.

With the telling of their stories they cancelled each other out and
sat in silence in the room that was illuminated only by the flickering
TV, and Rees wondered if he'd be sitting alone in thirty years still
telling the same story to anyone who'd listen.

The concert was in Duke's Hall, at the Royal Academy of Music. As
they waited for it to begin Laura asked Rees about his day.

'What happened in my day is best left inside my head,' he replied.

'Have you seen many people die?'

He began to tell her a story that he thought she wanted to hear, about
a butcher he saved on Tuesday who had severed his femoral artery with
a cleaver, and her eyes clouded over. He stopped talking mid-sentence
and she didn't seem to notice. He didn't mind. Telling war stories was
not an affection-building exercise. She had little experience of the
world, had really only herself, a quality that charmed him.

The concert was of Scriabin's Piano Sonata No 9. Rees had an ear
for music, although he had never heard this piece before, with its three
harmonic atmospheres. The black mass the Russian pianist played
without any cheap Shakespearean imagery. His pianissimo nuanced the
dark passions, the emotion poisoned by love. It was a dark performance
but creative also, a conflict of the lyrical and the provocative. Principal
contrasts. His interpretation was expansive, swinging from those dark
masses to streaming light, to love yearning, flying and swimming. His
phrasing was aromatic. Many pianists don't have dramatic range or
depth, they only have piano. But this Russian seemed to know what
he wanted to make before he got to the piano and didn't so much play
the music as release it. He rode the piano like a horse, with his back
arched, hands straight in front of him.

That night he and Laura slept together at her flat. Naked, she was thin and pale as a birch tree. Her long legs wrapped around his. At first she was uncommitted, vague, before finding the right rhythm as though they were dancing the tango. The mechanics of movement evaporated, they promenaded on air.

Afterwards she smoked in bed and told him she'd only had one relationship in her life and nothing else had really come up to it in terms of meaning. She asked him about his childhood, as if there could be some connection between romantic love and childhood. So he talked about growing up next to the sea until she interrupted him to say that the sea had no hold on her, that she couldn't even swim, adding, 'I was a Caesarean birth. Maybe that has something to do with it.'

Rees dug out a photograph from inside his wallet, of his parents and three siblings as small children; a family that had gone different ways, drifting through divorces, seeking opposing geographical identities. The last time he'd seen any of them was eight years ago.

Laura looked at the photograph as though suffering from great weariness. He made a few more single-shot revelations about his family before she got out of bed, wrapped herself in a robe and went to take a shower.

After that night of the concert Laura's interest in Rees dried up. He would come home from work to no messages on his answerphone. There were no letters waiting for him at UCH. He called her flat and got her answerphone. He called her at work and her secretary said she'd tell Laura to call him. But she didn't.

After a week passed he went round uninvited to her flat. It was ten in the morning on a cold winter's day. She was only just out of bed and reluctant to let him into the flat. He pleaded with her. 'I need to know what you feel about me. Saying something can't be worse than saying nothing.'

'You always ask me what I'm feeling,' she replied angrily, even though it wasn't true. She let him inside.

They sat on the same white leather sofa where he'd brought her after her 'accident'. She sat with him, but apart, her back against the wall. 'So you want an explanation?' she said. 'About what?'

'About where you have gone.'

'Look, you were kind to me when I was sick. But it's not enough. It's not enough to sustain a relationship.'

'I never thought it was.'

'I don't think I can continue seeing you.'

'You once described meeting me as a little miracle.'

Laura said nothing. She just stared at him with a hint of a smile.

'Please don't end this. Give me a chance. I can love, I know how to love. I beg you.'

The faint smile on her face vanished completely. She looked sickly pale as if what he was asking was abusive. Her eyes turned black and cold as a lake. 'We don't have enough in common, Rees.'

'Not enough in common?' he repeated. 'What do you mean?'

'Well, for instance, we went to that concert and I felt I couldn't talk to you about it afterwards, about Scriabin, that you wouldn't understand.'

Then she laughed, that characteristic intake of breath, as though there was nothing inside for her to let out. She stood and went to the mirror to look at her face, turning her head to each side. He stared at her collection of contemporary hardback literary novels and wondered if the life experiences of writers that went into the making of such books ever touched her, *hurt* her. She was taste only, he thought, as a way of protecting himself now, like some pianists are piano only. Her letters to him, the messages left on his answerphone were fictions.

'Damn it to hell,' she said at the mirror. 'I'm getting eczema again.'

A month later he was riding to an incident with Alison. They took Regent's Street at speed. These minutes before arriving at the scene of an incident were always good to Rees, a few minutes of existential calm.

On this occasion Alison undid all that.

'Rees, I've got to ask. You've been a shell for weeks. You're like, dead. What went wrong with your book editor?'

'I failed to respond to a concert we went to.'

Then Alison said something quite fine. 'Me and my husband, it's become what it is because of a shared struggle. How strong can love ever be based on entertainments? You don't belong to such women.'

They arrived at a nightclub where an explosion had occurred. It was a major incident and they were the first of the emergency services to arrive. That meant Rees would have to be incident officer. He grew a skin immediately in preparation for what he had to do for these people spilling into the road, bleeding and crying, calling out for their mothers, husbands, brothers, wives.

Swim

Kate Pemberton

I go to the women's bathing pond on the heath when summer hits London in the stomach. I like joining the tradition of women breast-stroking through cold water towards the trees which hang down low on all sides. I like not being able to touch the bottom, except for the soft mud at the far end which takes my momentary footprints. And I like best the way it feels afterwards, eating ice cream, flip-flopping back along dusty paths, my skin blending from cold to warm. That's when I'm in love with the heath – the way you can see the city shining in the heat, the air above it bent with the fumes of traffic hidden in the grooves of the streets, and yet smell sweet dry grass and hear crickets cracking on all sides. Turn 180 degrees and you see nothing but dark-headed trees on Highgate Hill, orange roofs baking and the bleached copper dome of St Joseph's Retreat. That's when you can imagine you're on the edge of a magic city – that it stops there and becomes instant countryside for ever. That's where a man approached me and said he could see my aura like sun's rays fanning out of me. 'You're standing underneath a silver tree,' he said, 'and gifts are falling from it onto your head.' And that's where I first saw Jule and time zigzagged out a day for us, in the middle of the relentless heat, a day that had no connection with life before or since.

After swimming I had come up a narrow path across the grass under the kites to the top of the hill, where I stopped and breathed in the view with my eyes shut for a while. Then I turned down towards the tennis courts to go back home. I was staying in the attic of a school friend's house that year. She was away travelling and her parents were happy for a little extra money and the odd bit of company at meal times. On the way down the hill I noticed the feel of my dress, the only thing I was wearing, just one layer of thin fabric against me, my swimming costume rolled up in a damp towel, cool under my arm, raising tiny bumps across my skin. There was a skipping feeling inside my chest, which turned into a surge of coldness like a lift dropping. The criss-crossing of the slopes together with the straight up and down of the trees held me steady and caused from all sides a rush of possibilities, as if I could do all things all at once, it would just happen to me easily. I thought I would be able to carry on walking on the horizontal as the path and all the people dipped down beneath my feet. I started searching in the eyes of those walking past me for some recognition of the way I was feeling, but no one looked at me, except Jule. His looking brought me to a natural stop and he stopped too, a few feet away from me, and I could hear a voice saying my name, 'Hannah, hello! All right?' And I was pulling my gaze away from Jule's and down a bit and suddenly there was Lennie, a girl I knew from the bar where we both worked, and she was saying, 'This is Jule, at last you get to meet him.' And he was quietly saying, 'No, not just a figment of her imagination,' and she hit him playfully. 'Good to meet you finally,' I said, and couldn't make myself shake his hand. He didn't reach for my hand either, and I was looking anywhere but his eyes, which I knew were fixed on me. How could anyone stand so still? Lennie was asking me when my next shift was and then saying that they had to go or they'd miss their film. 'See you soon,' I said to her, taking big steps backwards down the path. I heard Jule say goodbye as I turned away and I said it back, but facing forwards, to the person walking up towards me.

I don't think I had his face right in my head that night. I took a bottle of wine onto the roof where my friend and I had spent hours as children and where later, behind the massive chimney stack, we had smoked our first joint. It was rolled from the curly strings of bananas which had been dried ritualistically along the top of her radiator then mixed with old tobacco, and it cut the back of our throats and made our eyes spin. I looked down into the garden below at the tree standing in the centre of a patio made from concentric rings of bricks, and then I looked towards the heath, a few streets across, stretching away over its 800 acres, green turned to grey in the night. Jule was standing there on the path in the dark exactly where I'd last seen him, staring towards the house, knowing I was on this roof, being able to see everything I was doing, and not just now but later as I undressed for bed and as I fell asleep.

The next day I walked down the front steps, between the pots of geraniums blazing red on either side, and along Grove Terrace where the pansies in their oval beds were gossiping about me again. Today I was going swimming at the Lido. I liked the Lido because of the depth, the perverse coldness and the diving board which was only for men, children and me. I was planning to spend all day there and had with me my straw mat, edged with fraying pink cotton, a book to write in and a book to read, and a string bag with clacking wooden handles which had stuffed into it my towel and a brown paper bag of cherries. Jule was everywhere, choosing fruit on the pavement, driving past in various cars, recycling bottles, whizzing by on a bicycle. I got to the pool and laid out my mat before lifting off my dress and walking straight to the diving board. As usual the men stood back for me, the same men or different men each time I never knew, and watched me pace along the board, jump once and arch into the pool. Under the water sound expanded in my ears and ballooned around my head. I found the flat surface of the bottom, rough but painted over many times, and swam along it. I hadn't taken enough breath before I'd dived and had to push quickly to the surface, coming up almost on the other side where Jule was sitting at the top of the steps, watching me. His short hair was glossed black with water and sunlight, his eyes were shining. I dived back under, turned sharply and swam away. When I got out he had gone.

I lay back on my mat, propped up on my elbows, letting the sun dry me, watching the parade of men each trying to form some kind of shape while diving from the board. Such a hard place, sharp concrete edges to crack your head, light glaring off pale blue brickwork, people glaring at each other openly as if the heat had burnt off inhibitions. My head was aching from the cold water and mistimed breathing and suddenly I didn't want to stay there. Jule came out of the café and down the steps carrying two orange Calippos out in front of him like he was divining for more water. I looked away but this one came and sat beside me, holding out one of the Calippos.

'We met yesterday,' he said smiling, his eyebrows raised in surprise. 'Hannah, right?'

'Yes, and you're Jule,' I said almost as a question, narrowing my eyes as if in an effort to remember the name I'd been hearing all morning. 'Is Lennie here?'

He sat down cross-legged beside me. 'No, no, she's working today I think.' I took one of the ice lollies from him and ripped off its foil top with much more concentration than was needed because I didn't know where else to look.

'You look like you're set up here for the day.' He glanced at the things which I had begun pointlessly taking out of my bag with my free hand and arranging round me.

'Yes I was going to stay but I think I want to find somewhere a bit cooler.'

'Oh right, I was going to go to the Italian garden, over on the other side of the heath.' He was watching the divers on the board but turned to look at me. 'Do you want to come?'

'OK,' I nodded, a swivelling sensation in my stomach, 'I haven't been over there for ages.' Suddenly we had hours together ahead of us. We were quiet for a few minutes taking it in, watching the pool, until Jule said, 'Are you going back in?'

'No, I'm all dry now.'

'We could go then.'

I packed everything back into my bag and watched him go to the other end of the pool to roll up his towel. Jule. It was like when you learn a new word and then come across it the very next day, and you wonder how you never noticed it before, never even needed it. We stepped around the sunbathers towards each other but had to separate again to exit through the clanking turnstiles of our respective changing rooms. Apart from the towel under his arm Jule had nothing with him and walked in long steps, with his hands in his shorts pockets. We kept trying to look at each other while we were talking, but his fast pace made it difficult, so mostly we just looked ahead, walking unnaturally far apart. We headed up towards the hill where we'd met the day before. The sun was at its highest point above us as we came over the top. We didn't stop to look at the view but carried on towards the wooded area on the other side. As we went into the shadows under the first trees a pack of dogs of all different breeds came bounding towards us like some advert for dog food, and veered to left and right to get by. Their two walkers strolled behind them with fistfuls of leads.

'We're going to pass my favourite place in a minute,' I said, 'the mound with the pine trees on it – I've always wanted to sleep the night there.'

'The one like an island?' he said. And then we saw it, ringed with a stern wrought-iron fence, then benches facing outwards, and then the green grass sea.

It was getting steadily hotter as we carried on towards the west side of the heath but we didn't slow down. Jule kept pulling leaves off the bushes, folding them carefully, ripping along the creases and then scattering the small squares and triangles. We didn't stop on the bridge over Viaduct Pond but I could see the lily leaves, like paint palettes, spread just under the surface of the water. The soil was beginning to turn sandy when I saw the butterflies. The first ones were pale yellow brimstones, at least ten of them, like flying primroses fluttering about our ears to get past. A little further along the path was a cloud of cabbage whites, whipping around each other in constant figure eights. I had never seen so many, even in the butterfly farm where I'd asked the assistant if they killed the specimens on sale in the shop. 'They are bred for that purpose,' she'd said coldly. And I thought as well of the beach in Norfolk crusted with ladybirds along the shoreline one summer, thousands of them washed up and standing out red against the black seaweed, crawling over its swollen, goosebumped pods. I was telling Jule all this as we came up through the gorse bushes towards the stand of leaning pines by the road.

'Smell one of the flowers. Don't prick yourself,' he said, waving towards the gorse. 'Can you smell it? They smell of Nice biscuits.' I could see some women washing clothes in the lake down to my left, then stretching them across the yellow bushes, to dry infused with the scent of burnt vanilla and coconut oil.

We went down the road past Jack Straw's Castle to the lane that led to the Hill garden. I felt exhausted from all the walking and the heat and we lay down on the grass in the shade of a laurel bush below the ornamental pond.

'I love it here,' he said. 'It's like no one really knows about it.'

We had done enough talking on the way to allow us a little silence now, and I closed my eyes for a moment. When I opened them he was looking at me. He quickly rolled out his towel saying, 'You'd been to the Lido yesterday as well, hadn't you? I saw your towel.'

'No, I'd been to the women's pond.'

'Oh right,' he said, sounding confused and trying to stop himself grinning at the same time. I began eating cherries but soon stopped because I was too embarrassed to spit the pips. It must have been about lunchtime and I was hungry and needed something to drink but we had only just arrived. Now that we were finally here neither of us was quite sure what to do, so I closed my eyes again, listening to the buzz of the garden.

Swim

When I woke up I found myself looking at Jule, asleep on his front beside me. I watched his face for a while and then sat up. My head throbbed from sleep and dehydration and I couldn't get my thoughts into any pattern. My eyes weren't registering colours properly and all the yellows and greens around me had merged into one. I touched Jule's arm to wake him. 'Can we go and get some food from somewhere?' I asked.

I found it hard to get my bearings as we went towards the steps of the pergola. My feet kept hitting the ground too quickly and there was darkness in the corners of my eyes. We wandered along the walkway under the wisteria and roses, Jule telling me how the structure had been built high with earth dug out of tube tunnels. We went down the spiral steps at the far end and took a well-trodden path that I thought led to the road. Instead it went steeply up a sudden slope between some trees, got narrower, twisted back on itself and ended in a tiny clearing like a room. The ground was littered with tickets, flattened into the cracked earth. There was a wooden crate lying down and one propped against a tree. The tickets were many colours under our feet, bright blue, purple, red, hundreds of them, shiny, with corners ripped off and silver insides, and as our sight adjusted to the darkness of the place we saw that they were condom wrappers. That's when Jule first took my hand, quite naturally, and led back the way we had come, scuffing wrappers off the soles of his trainers.

Getting back onto the road proved to be a problem and soon we weren't sure which direction to aim for. One small path would intersect with another, which would split into two more, until we realised that, not for the first time, we had come full circle. I was alarmingly dizzy now, my head thumping in a steady beat, everywhere the sour milk smell of neck-high cow parsley. Jule suggested that we rested until I was feeling better. We knelt down facing each other under a huge elm tree and he took both of my hands and bent his head down so he could look properly into my eyes. 'I'm sorry,' I said. I felt like I was ruining everything. 'I'll feel better in a minute.' He leant forward slowly and kissed my cheekbone, right next to my eye, then lay down and looked into the tree. The thumping in my head descended beat by beat until it was coming from somewhere inside my chest. I couldn't stop looking at Jule's mouth and was just beginning to bend towards him when he sat up suddenly. 'I think we should go – I've remembered a good way to get back.'

'What is it?'

'Nothing, come on, let's go.' He was pulling me up. 'You need water, it's this heat, you're dehydrated.' His voice sounded strained and he was pale. I looked above to where Jule had been staring but he was pulling me away and I thought maybe I wasn't seeing straight. I'd got up really quickly and hexagons were floating across my eyes diagonally from right to left. I saw the feet first because I was directly underneath the body, which was more of a skeleton, stretched over with skin like thin leather, hanging from a chain on a high branch and swaying almost weightless in the breeze. But then we were out from underneath the tree and moving fast away, and looking back I couldn't see anything in the branches. I lurched forward to be sick, but nothing came. 'You've got sunstroke,' Jule said, his arms around my shoulders, helping me to keep walking.

It was the noise of the fair that took us back to the main part of the heath. The breeze was getting quite strong now, cooling me down and bringing with it music from a barrel organ on the upper fairground. We followed the sound to an avenue of stalls and crowds of people. We found a place selling square cartons of salty cockles and whelks spiked with wooden splints, and dark brown toffee apples stuck upside down in rows on blackened trays. Donkeys were being tugged around with children on their backs. Along the central path were green and gold swing boats, a helter-skelter like a tiny lighthouse and a coconut shy where men with sleeves rolled up were failing to knock the stubborn coconuts off their stands into the sawdust. Further down we came to a shabby gypsy caravan, a curtain pulled across the doorway and a sign leaning against one of the wheels saying 'Cross my palm with silver' in swirling letters.

'What do you reckon?' Jule said, trying to look through the gap at the side of the curtain. 'I'm going in.' He put one foot on the wheel and heaved himself up. 'Stay here, I won't be a minute,' he said, and pulled the curtain round him. I glimpsed a red glow from inside and a flickering of candles. Somewhere nuts were being roasted and I thought I'd have time to go and find them.

When I came back the curtain was hooked to one side and the caravan was empty. I stayed where I was for ages, waiting for Jule. The sun was going down and people were leaving. I felt a heaviness over my shoulders as if I could hardly hold myself up any longer. After a while the fortune teller came back and before I could ask her about Jule she looked directly into my eyes and said 'How was it?'

'How was what?'

'The journey here.'

I didn't know how to answer. Her eyes were glinting at me from beneath her head scarf, the coins hanging from her ears were shivering. 'It's not trivial,' she said, tilting her head to one side. 'You're just beginning to see that now.' And as she said it I realised that the unfamiliar heavy feeling that had taken over my entire body was loneliness. My throat felt thick and closed and my eyes were stinging from holding down tears. 'When he saw you weren't here he went that way,' the woman said, pointing back towards the swing boats, in the direction I was already running.

I ran all round the fairground, behind the stalls, up onto the road and back, much further than I should have run, but I couldn't find Jule anywhere. Eventually I crouched down, my back against a fallen tree, to get my breath back. There was an acid taste on my tongue and I couldn't stop the tears slipping out of my eyes and lining up along my jaw. The heat which had been in the air around me all day was now gathering beneath my skin. I was waiting for Jule to come walking towards me, just like he had at the Lido. All I had to do to make it happen was think about it hard enough, but it didn't work. The light was leaving the ground, the green of the trees was deepening, the stall owners had packed up and gone home. I could hear the squeaks of bats above me and began to see them flicking around, black in the white sky. 'He's not going to come,' I said to them, and in saying it out loud I understood why.

I knew where I had to get to but wasn't sure which path would lead there quickest. I felt so small under the trees of the now empty heath and scanned constantly from side to side and sometimes back the way I had come, checking that I really was alone. The paths had turned into tunnels in the dark, holding down the sharp smell of wild garlic and amplifying the twitching of birds in the branches. I had too far to go to run all the way but walked as fast as I could manage, my string bag swinging like a pendulum beside me, pulling me along. I came out onto the bridge over Viaduct Pond more quickly than expected and let myself start running, laughing as I recognised the path ahead which would lead straight into the wide open meadow. There was that skipping inside me again and then the lift dropping and the land dipping down beneath my feet because I was so close now and because I knew what was going to happen when I got there.

I could see Jule from quite a way off, sitting cross-legged like he had done on my mat that morning, right at the top of the mound under the silhouetted pine trees. I raced across the flattened grass with my arms out wide to take in all the space that swept down ahead of me to the island. I slowed down as I got closer, not wanting to let Jule know I was there. The railings came up to my ribs, but in one place, next to a bench, some spikes had been snapped off leaving a gap where I could put my foot. Before jumping over I read the inscription on the bench, 'Take one day, rest a while and pretend the world is just for you.' Jule had his towel spread out on the ground over the long pine needles and flat scales of bark. He heard me coming up the slope towards him and turned round smiling. 'You took your time,' he managed to say before the back of his head was in my hands and I was kissing him.

All night under the trees we listened to many things; each other's breathing, the fizzing of pine needles, fir cones not much bigger than dice falling to the ground. We heard the creaking trunks, bent like question marks against the sky above us, and the constant waves of some vast and ancient ocean, rolling up and down the shore, pulling us in and out of sleep.

Rainy day boys

Christopher Fowler

There aren't many moments in life when you can point and say
with certainty that something got decided, but this is about one of
those moments. It involved a friendship, a city and a death. Davis and
I were the friends. London was the city. And the death – well, that
was probably the part that got things decided.

It was a wet Sunday afternoon in November, the kind of day that
never gets light or dries out. The sky was low and sulphurous, an evil-
tempered shade of sienna that had everyone running to find cover.
King's Cross was bathed in the sort of light you see in old paintings of
a biblical nature, where hapless mortals take up a tiny fraction of the
canvas and jagged lightning cleaves the heavens. On such a day the area's
residents look dirty and depressed, as though they've been deserted
by their gods and left to die. Even the pigeons, huddled on damaged
stumps in the eaves of St Pancras, look suicidal. King's Cross is for
transients; it isn't a spot to stop. It isn't for saying, 'Oh, let's have a cup
of coffee and wander about for a while.' In this part of town you keep
on the move if you know what's good for you. Not a refreshing place.
It's incapable of regenerating itself, let alone anyone who visits it.

And yet.

I always think that London looks best on a day of rain. The houses
and streets slink back into proportion. Traffic diminishes, pavements
reflect, structures of glass and steel dull down in shame so that neglected
stone buildings can emerge from the gloom like safe harbours.

London in the rain.

Trees and hedges drip. Rich greens and browns predominate. The
Thames flattens. Railway arches exude a strange childhood smell, like old
cinemas. Coffee bar windows steam over. Bookstores and rummagey junk
shops beckon. Interior lives are illuminated from the streets. It's a time for
thinking and dreaming. A time when I usually attempt to clean my flat.

I had been trying to reach the streaks of dirt smeared along the top
window in the lounge with a tomato cane, on the end of which was
tied a Windolene-soaked J-Cloth. I thought the rain would help to

keep the cloth wet. The frame was stuck because its sash-cords had seized up, and it had been painted over about a hundred and fifty times. When I raised the bottom pane it covered the one above, rendering cleaning impossible. I had broken three canes so far, my jeans were soaked and the window remained dirty. The thought of tackling the job from the outside on a dry day up a ladder never crossed my mind. I didn't possess the capacity for that kind of deductive reasoning.

I lived on the second floor of a council block off York Way, a part of King's Cross so architecturally decimated by railways, roads and canals that Camden Council, having destroyed everything of interest that the Blitz hadn't removed (including one of London's most loved landmarks, the Euston Portico), was clutching at straws by decreeing the area's gas holders to be of aesthetic merit. In a city where Knightsbridge airing-cupboards were selling for half a million, King's Cross was still pretty cheap. To survive in the area I had to breathe in the shuddering filth from a million gridlocked vehicles. I had to tack my way along canal towpaths between tramps who sang at the sky, while the bloated bodies of river rats bobbed past in a miasma of polystyrene pellets. I had to regularly pull my wallet back from the palsied hands of inept pick-pockets. I had to skirt the grey-faced junkies who built their nests out-side McDonald's like big bedraggled pigeons, and remember to walk on the other side of the road during gang confrontations (rival factions of schoolchildren divided by territory, ethnicity and haircuts). Then I had to barter access rights to my flat with two local whores who brought new meaning to the term 'oldest profession'.

I wasn't much safer at home, either; my next-door neighbour reg-ularly got drunk and threw items of furniture over the balcony in fits of self-loathing. The people in the flat below (five shifty-looking young men in tracksuit bottoms and jackets with grey cotton hoods) were, I suspected, not a family unit but drug dealers; they received visits around the clock from people who never stayed longer than five minutes. And the danger didn't end there, because Battle Bridge House was built so close to the railway lines there was always the possibility that the front carriages of the 17.45 to Barnsley might jump the signals, flinging com-muters in all directions, and end up embedded in my bedroom wall.

When you think about an area in architectural detail, certain images spring to mind. Holland Park has sedate redbrick villas, Lisson Grove has leafy LCC forecourts, St John's Wood has plexiglass balconies, but all I see when I think of King's Cross is a sturdy drain-fed weed push-ing its way through brickwork halfway up a wet tunnel wall. The only things that live here do so because they're hardy.

Despite all this, I liked King's Cross. Too much of the city had been colonised by decaf-latte television producers dropping their homunculi off at school in Sahara Land-Cruisers. Fulham, Putney and Hampstead had long since become no-go areas, but now the disease was so wide-spread that even Deptford probably had a Starbucks. Every Saturday morning I walked down to the paper shop, under the dripping rail-way arches, past the Beverly Hills Hair Salon (which had about as much to do with Beverly Hills as Sid James), past the sad plaque marking the spot where a fifteen-year-old boy had been brutally stabbed to death, past stupefied clubbers returning home from Bagley's Warehouse and northern lads in thin summer jackets looking for B&B accommodation, past all kinds of life, seeing everything but taking care to touch as little as possible. I don't interfere. I'm too much of a dreamer. I don't see things as they really are.

I was a few days away from turning thirty. From the age of five until my hormones kicked in I had been a child actor, starring mostly in commercials, the son of a single stage mother. I'd attended Anna Scher's drama school in Islington, and had been accepted by the RADA, to end up, after a lengthy period of unemployment, in the stage version of Disney's *Beauty and the Beast*. Annoyed by the fact that I had under-gone years of tortuous classical training in order to play a dancing spoon in Tottenham Court Road, I had ignored my fellow performers' cries of 'at least it's work' and violated my contract, drifting away from the acting profession altogether. I was now employed by a replacement car-parts company under one of the area's many arches. In my spare time I was trying to write The Screenplay, but I'd been stuck on page seven for about two years. On my days off I sat on my stool by the window in my flat, half-heartedly waiting for a big break and a per-fect partner to come along, but meanwhile I sold exhaust pipes and dated a girl who had first come to my attention soaping the ariel of my boss's van in the Chicago Car Wash two doors down.

On this particularly sodden Sunday afternoon I abandoned my window-cleaning exercise to sit with my elbows on damp jeans staring out at the rain, hypnotised by my own inactivity. I was vaguely thinking about my script when I became aware of a buzzing noise.

'Thanks a lot, Jake. It's chucking it down out there. Didn't you hear me ringing?' Davis stamped his feet on the mat and shook water everywhere. The little hair he had left was plastered to his head. He gave me a beady look. 'Lend a hand with this.' He dragged a tall, heavy-looking cardboard box in through the door and thumped it down. Something inside clanged dully.

I went over to the box and poked it with the toe of my trainer. 'The bell's packed up. Where are your keys?'

'You want to get that fixed, I'm soaked. In my other jacket.'

'There's a towel somewhere. What's in the box?'

'Look at the state of this place. If you don't mind me saying so, you are living in the most disgusting area in the whole of London.'

'I like King's Cross. And I do mind you saying so. I believe in psychic geography. It's a place of great mystery.'

'The only mystery is why you stay here.'

'You wouldn't understand.' I cleared a patch of condensation on the window. 'Did you know the whole area used to be called Battle Bridge, after the road that crossed over the River Fleet? It was where Boadicea fought against Paulinus. The Roman generals rode on elephants up Goods Way.'

'Yeah, I know, she turned into a hare and escaped. We did it at school. There's nothing mystical about it, just a load of bollocks to cover up the fact that the English lost.'

'It doesn't matter whether it happened exactly like that,' I replied hotly, 'it's the significance of the events occurring on this ground that's important. It affects everything. There are centuries of conflict and deception all around us. Thieves and murderers used to lie in wait for their victims –'

'They still do,' Davis retorted.

'– and as Boadicea was buried just up the road, they decided to reduce the area's notoriety by changing its name to Boadicea's Cross, which became St George's Cross, then King's Cross.' I warmed to the subject. It was a bit of a hobby with me. 'After the Great Fire of London, it was the only place where Neapolitan cress grew. It was picked by the Pinder of Wakefield himself. Then George IV marked the junction of its six roads with a huge octagonal building of white stone that housed a pub, a police station and a camera obscura. The dustheaps of Victorian London grew here, and pigs fed on mountains of horse bones. The Russians bought the dustheaps to rebuild Moscow after the French invasion.

The Pandemonium Company bought the flattened cinder-ground for their theatre, the Royal Clarence, and it became a practice-spot for acrobats and clowns. Later they opened a healing spring near the small-pox hospital called St Chad's Well, and people came from all over the country to drink the waters and promenade in the gardens. See, it's all paradox; warriors and clowns, pestilence and healing waters, kings and cut-throats, cities and bone-mounds. Typical London. Every time you think you see it, it slips away from you. It's a view of the world from an acute angle. The picture keeps changing...'

I could feel Davis staring at me. 'Thanks very much for the lecture. You know what I think? You're going round the twist. You want to stop thinking so hard and get out more. Breathe some fresh air. Get yourself sorted. Have a tidy up for a start.'

I glanced back at the crinkled piles of comics and the dirty crockery stacked on top of the gas fire. 'I know where everything is.'

'Then you must have psychic powers. You could get a job with the Egyptian government, locating antiquities. We'll have to clear a space.' He pulled the top of the box toward me.

'What's in it?'

'Birthday present. Happy thirty.'

Davis was thirty-four, and liked to give me the benefit of his advice, even though most of it was inaccurate or useless. He was always perfectly groomed, and even at the weekends dressed as though he was just about to go out to dinner. His clothes looked as though they had never been worn before, unlike mine, which looked like they had been worn by several people at once.

Davis and I were friends in that odd urban way in which people find themselves drifting into the circle of each other's company for no particular reason. We certainly didn't have much in common. Looking back, it was a relationship that allowed our weaknesses to flourish in a faintly disastrous symbiosis. Davis was a surly bundle of complaints and grudges. His attitude stemmed from the fact that he was a dot.com workaholic who had uniquely managed to lose his company money while everyone else appeared to grow rich. He trusted no one and was desperate to succeed, but the more desperately he tried, the less he succeeded. He had never forgiven himself for being bamboozled out of an IT business partnership, and he had never absolved his girlfriend Erica for leaving him just as he was about to suggest getting engaged, which shows how little he understood her. An aura of bitterness radiated from him like flu germs.

Davis was staying at my place while his own apartment was being redecorated. He wasn't thrilled about the arrangement but it was convenient for his office, which was situated in a featureless block behind Liverpool Street Station. His own flat was a pristine loft conversion in Primrose Hill, where the streets had a pre-war look that reminded me of the locations for old Ealing films, except that the pubs were full of coke-addled television executives on mobile phones instead of beery cockneys with Woodbines behind their ears.

Davis's flat was filled with state-of-the-art technology. He could communicate instantly with anyone in the world, but the only calls he ever received were from computer companies updating him about software or people trying to sell him dormer windows. He chased after girls who didn't even bother to pretend liking him, and had virtually no friends. In the days after Erica upped stumps and returned to the Disillusioned Single Women's pavilion, we would sprawl in Davis's creepily immaculate lounge and multi-task our leisure time, rolling post-pub joints, downloading smut from the Internet, thrashing PlayStation race-cars and staring at trailer-trash TV shows about stupid fat people driving the wrong way up Miami freeways.

Since Davis had moved in with me, we had refined this process of mental ossification to include sitting all night nursing pints in the Hoop and Grapes, and having the kind of peculiar conversations you only bother with when you're truly bored. After three weeks passed drifting in this state of mutual dysfunction, we realised that we were getting on each other's nerves, and something had to give.

'I suppose you want to see inside,' said Davis. He dropped the other end of the box on the floor and pulled out a number of chromium-plated rods. 'It's a home gym.'

'For me? I don't need a gym.'

'Of course you do. You're falling to bits. You walk down to the shop when you're out of snouts, and that's about it. 'Twenty Kensitas and a *Daily Mirror*, please.' Stop on the landing to get your breath back. That's not exercise. You'll have your first heart attack before you're forty.'

'I don't think they make Kensitas any more.' I wandered into the kitchen to find the kettle. 'If you're going to stay here you could do some washing up occasionally.'

'You want to be fit like me, mate. I go to the gym four times a week. Nearly kill myself. Veins standing out in my temples, heart hammering, dizzy spells. Does me the world of good. Six hundred quid a year it costs me. You'll save a bloody fortune.'

'I don't go now, so I'm already saving a fortune. Just think of all the things I don't do, and add up all the money I'm saving. No sky-diving, no polo, no water-skiing, no trying to book tables at The Ivy, there's loads saved right there.'

'We can put this up in half an hour. I've got the brackets. Ten minutes a day and you'll be as perky as a cat in a sack. Birds'll be falling over you with their tongues hanging out.'

'That's an attractive image.'

'Trust me, the only way you'll get more pussy is to go for gender reassignment.'

It was useless to argue. Davis was already emptying various bolts and hinges out of the box. I filled two Cornish pottery mugs with tea and sat cross-legged on the floor. 'You know how to put this together, then?'

'It can't be hard, can it?'

'No instruction book. Knocked off, is it?'

'It belonged to someone at work. He doesn't need it any more. He's in a coma.'

In addition to the brackets there were cables, pulleys and two red plastic cushions mounted on squares of plywood. 'Butterfly press,' Davis explained, 'needs to go against a load-bearing wall. You got a hammer-drill?'

'I've got a hand-drill.'

'That's no good, we need a Black & Decker. Can't you borrow one?'

So, against my better judgement, I went next door to ask Mr Gorridge. My neighbour was a retired teacher and a solitary drinker. I sublet my flat from him, and owed him quite a bit of back-rent, but he never made a fuss about it. He resembled his old school nickname, Porridge, with masses of frizzy grey hair and kaftany brown clothes that appeared to be fashioned from knitted rope. He had African masks and crocheted mandalas hanging in his kitchen window, taught yoga at an adult education college, and spent his evenings getting pissed to old Hawkwind albums. He only ever had one visitor, his daughter Holly, a smart-looking financial services consultant in her late twenties, although it beat me how she could allow her father to live in such a dump. Gorridge was pleasant enough and kept his distance, which was fine with me. There were three main types of resident in our building: people who were infringing the law in some way, and who kept to themselves so much that you wouldn't know if they were dead or if they had been arrested, families whose appalling public rows held the entire block in thrall, and loners who you occasionally saw creeping up staircases with plastic bags full of bottles. I had Gorridge down in the latter category.

For once, when he opened the door he wasn't paralytic, but his frizzy hair was flat on one side and sticking up on the other, so he must have been sleeping. He left me on the step while he went to get his drill. Something inside smelled awful. I peered around the front door. His hall floor was covered in linoleum. I hadn't seen lino in years. It was exactly the shade you get when you mix every plasticine colour together. The lights were hung with those huge dusty paper globes that were once the staple fixture of every student flat in London.

'You will let me have it back, won't you?' he called, dragging miles of tangled flex into the hall. 'You can come in and have a drink if you like.'

'I won't stop, thanks.' I caught myself feeling sorry for him, and made a mental note to be more friendly at some point in the future, just not this century.

It took over two hours just to assemble the butterfly press and its counterweights. 'This is a support wall,' explained Davis, knocking on the plaster. 'You want to put a hole here,' he drew a cross with a felt-tip pen about three feet from the floor, 'and here.' He put his ear against the wall and tapped it with his index finger. 'OK, give me the drill. We can get this fitted together and working in no time, then go over the Hoop and Grapes for a pint.'

But we weren't destined to reach the pub.

I realised that we didn't have any drill bits. The logical thing would have been to go next door and ask Gorridge if he had any, but by then Davis had come up with an alternative plan. He said we should knock a nail into the wall, extract it, then screw the first of the bolts into the hole we had made. I rooted through the paltry contents of my tool box, and came up with a single six-inch masonry nail and a pathetically small hammer.

'What's that for, cracking toffee?' he scoffed. 'Haven't you got anything bigger?'

'Hang on a minute.' I came back from the hall with a sledgehammer the workmen had left behind when they'd demolished one of the concrete staircases in the building's courtyard.

'Christ on a bike. Just don't miss.' Davis gingerly held the nail over its cross. I drew the sledgehammer back as far as I could, then swung it down. There was an explosion of filthy plaster as it smashed a hole clean through the wall to my neighbour's flat. In the ensuing silence I stared at the splintered crater as plaster dust settled in my hair. Davis appeared unconcerned. He pressed his face against the hole and tried to see inside. 'That wasn't a supporting wall. It's been subdivided.' He dug out a Kleenex and blew his nose. 'So much for co-operative housing. It's another Ronan Point. I wonder where the nail went.'

I knew Gorridge would be knocking on my door at any minute. He had complained several times in the past when Davis had cranked up my CD player in order to hear some obscure stereo effect on one of his Moby albums. I decided to get the jump on Gorridge by apologising first, so I left Davis complaining about the poor quality of my walls and ventured across the balcony. I hadn't decided what I was going to say, but after trying the doorbell a few times and receiving no answer, I figured he must have gone out. I was about to walk away when I noticed that his front door was ajar.

I stepped into the hall. The horrible smell that had assailed me earlier intensified. On my right was the kitchen, where something gurgled in a pot on the cooker. The lounge lay directly in front of me. I reached the doorway and saw a tablelamp on its side, the shade broken, the bulb lighting one corner of the room. Nuggets of glass crunched in the carpet. I had an ominous feeling that we had caused something bad to happen.

Gorridge was lying in the gloom with his face buried in a putty-coloured sofa. The cushions beneath him were soaked red. He had fallen forward on his knees, apparently from a position beside the hole we had made in the wall, and my six-inch nail was sticking out of the back of his head. I could see the gleaming end of it poking through his hair. I only looked at him for a second, but I knew the sight would stay with me for a lifetime. Panic crowded in and I galloped back to Davis, fighting to catch my breath.

'You'd better come and see,' I managed. Before he could ask questions, I grabbed his arm and pulled him outside. Checking that there was no one else on the balcony, I re-entered Gorridge's flat with Davis in tow.

'God, what's that awful smell?' asked Davis, 'What's he doing, boiling a cat?' He headed off into the kitchen and checked the saucepan on the cooker. 'This has gone dry. Looks like sock casserole. Lucky it didn't catch fire. Why hasn't he turned it off?'

By way of an answer, I pulled Davis toward the Lounge of Death.

'Blimey, so that's where the nail went. What a mess.'

'Is that all you can say?' I screamed.

'I need a fag.' He pulled out a cigarette and lit it from the lighter on Gorridge's coffee table.

'We've killed him!' I yelled. 'He was a yoga instructor!'

'What the hell's that got to do with it?'

'He did yoga. He sits against the wall with his legs folded and meditates. Meditates with his head against the wall.'

'Well, he reached Nirvana this time.' Davis leaned in for a closer look and exhaled.

'Don't blow smoke over him!'

'Why not, he's dead, isn't he?'

I was incandescent with panic. 'You've left your fingerprints on the lighter. And on the table. And – everywhere.'

'Yeah, but who cares? I mean, you're the one who killed him.'

'What?' I shrieked.

'You were holding the hammer, mate.'

'It was an accident. You know that.' I thrust an accusing finger at Davis. 'You told me it was a support wall. Everything you ever tell me is wrong. What are we going to do? We can't just leave him here.'

'I'm not going to drag him down the corridor wrapped in a carpet, if that's what you mean.'

'We'll have to call the police.'

'Forget it. I'm not being beaten into a confession by a bunch of uniformed monkeys. Think what it would do to my career. And you – you've got a motive. You owe him money.'

He had a point. Gorridge's daughter apparently took care of his finances; the old teacher had once confided to me that he was hopeless with money. Which meant that there was a Living Gorridge who knew about my debt.

'Wait a minute, his front door was ajar. Someone else could have crept in, killed him and left.'

'And they shifted the blame to you by inserting your nail into his head. Bit unlikely, don't you think?'

The smell from the kitchen and the oppressiveness of Gorridge's lounge was making me feel sick. 'I have to get out of here,' I swallowed, moving back into the hall. I was about to go on to the balcony when I heard the boys from the flat below coming up the stairwell. 'Shit, we can't let them see us.' I grabbed Davis and pushed him back. Once they had bounced past we crept out of the flat, just as Gorridge's neighbour Mrs Lynch opened her front door.

'Oh hello, Jake, how are you?' she asked, pulling her rainhood tightly around her perm.

'Fine thank you,' I mumbled.

'Someone reported my Sean for keeping pets in his bedroom,' she explained, as if in response to an enquiry on my part. 'I let them out of their cages. He's ever so upset, but it seemed the kindest thing to do. Now I'm worried that they might breed, so don't be alarmed if you see anything running about. They'll probably get eaten by something from the canal. Have you been to see Mr Gorridge? Is he all right?' She tried to look back through the door that I was hastily pulling shut behind me. 'Only there was a crash earlier and I thought he might have fallen over.'

'No, he's fine,' I lied, 'never better, fantastic in fact.'

'Perhaps I should look in and see if he wants anything from the shops. Save him going out in this awful weather, with his legs.'

'No, he's got everything he needs, I've just checked, weeks of shopping in, he doesn't need to go out for ages if he doesn't want to, he's feeling a bit whacked and having a lie-down –' Davis jabbed me in the ribs, and I snapped my mouth shut.

'Well.' She looked at both of us indecisively, then looked at Gorridge's closed front door. 'So. I'd better be getting on.'

'Great,' I hissed at Davis as we hustled back into my hall, 'she can place me in my neighbour's flat at the time of his death, and you pulled the front door shut so we can't get back in and wipe our prints, wonderful.'

'I don't know why you're obsessing about fingerprints. Your nail is sticking out of the back of his head.'

'I shouldn't be worrying at all, should I? I've got nothing to hide. I should just tell the truth, say that it was an unfortunate accident. I can't be held responsible, surely?'

'Surely.' He mimicked my pronunciation. 'No wonder you've never been able to hold down a real job. People would walk all over you.'

'Acting was a real job,' I said indignantly.

'Acting is not a job, it's just showing off. It's for people who can't grow up.'

'It's a respectable adult profession.'

'Oh yeah? You were a spoon.'

'A *dancing* spoon. I stepped in for Mark a couple of times when he was off sick.'

'And what was he?'

'A candlestick.'

'The résumé just keeps getting better, doesn't it? You could have played the contents of an entire kitchen drawer and you still wouldn't have found any employment other than a car exhaust shop.'

'I like where I work. And I'm writing a screenplay.'

'Oh yes, the famous *screenplay*. How is that coming along, by the way?'

'It's not at the moment.'

'Stalled again? It can't be writer's block, because you haven't actually written anything yet, have you?'

I was tempted to point out a few of the glitches in Davis's career, the bankrupted mobile phone company, the on-line services nobody wanted, the lousy investments, the failed entrepreneurial bids, but what was the point? I headed for the kitchen.

'Now what are you doing?'

'I'm going to put the kettle on. I need a cup of tea. I have to concentrate my mind.'

We stood in the kitchen waiting for the contents of the teapot to brew, watching the rain stream down the window, the trains drawing into the station below, the umbrellas of commuters opening like sinister black flowers.

'He might lie there undiscovered for days,' Davis pointed out.

'No, his daughter comes around...' I was chewing my thumbnail, and had made it bleed.

'When?'

My stomach twisted. 'Um, Sundays.'

'Today? What time?'

I looked at the kitchen clock. 'In about half an hour.'

'Then we have to get the body out before she finds it and calls the police.'

'How? I shut the front door.'

'The hole.' David darted back into the lounge. 'Maybe we can pull him through the hole you made in the wall.'

'Will you stop saying I made the hole? I didn't want a sodding home gym in the first place.'

The shattered centre of the crater in the lounge wall was only about an inch across, and when I tried to peer through it I couldn't see anything. It would mean tearing down a sizeable chunk of the room.

'You want to hit it really hard with the sledgehammer. You want to –'

'Will you stop saying "I want to" all the time? I don't want to do any of it.'

'You want to go to jail?'

'No. But the hammer.' I studied it anxiously. 'The neighbours will complain about the noise.'

'They'll complain a lot more if they find out you murdered him. "He was a quiet bloke, always kept to himself, didn't seem like a nutter." That's what they'll say when they're interviewed on the news.'

'You think this is my fault for living here. Like it couldn't happen in Primrose Hill.'

'You're right it couldn't, because my neighbours aren't vile old hippies.'

'No, they're advertising executives who park their mountain tanks in handicapped spaces while they're making dinner reservations at fucking Granita.'

'I don't know what you've got against the middle classes,' said Davis. 'I've never seen this bitter side of you before.'

I tried to stay calm. 'I hope he didn't feel anything. If he was meditating, his mind was probably on a different plane. I wonder what was going through his head.'

'Your six-inch nail.'

'That's it, I'm going out for some air,' I said. 'If you touch my wall, I'll kill you.'

I found a raincoat and opened the front door, but got no further than the balcony. A black Mercedes Kompressor had pulled into one of the parking spaces below. It was the car Holly drove. She was early. I ducked back into the hall.

'Now what?'

'His daughter's here.'

'Well, you'll have to go downstairs and stop her from coming up.'

'I can't do that.'

'You've got to send her away, Jake. You want to go to jail?'

'Stop saying that.'

'Then stop her.'

He shoved me out on to the balcony, and after a moment of hopping about in indecision I ran to the stairwell. Hearing Holly slam her car door and bip-bip the alarm, I stuck my head over the staircase wall. She was as sleek and beautiful as her car, dressed in a charcoal-grey business suit and a white blouse, blonde hair tied back, a slimline leather briefcase in one hand. I looked like I'd been in some kind of explosion. I didn't have the authority to impede her progress. If she'd seen me in the street she would probably have given me 50p. I ran back and knocked on my front door. Davis eventually answered and peered around it as if expecting Jehovah's witnesses. 'What is it now?'

'I can't talk to her.'

'Oh, for God's sake. One simple thing. How can you let a woman intimidate you?'

'Fine, if you're so good with women, you do it.'

'I don't even live here.'

This was costing us time. Holly had reached the top of the stairwell.

'She's coming, she's coming, let me in.' I shoved against the door. Davis shoved back.

'You stay out there and send her away.'

'This is my flat!'

'No, it's his flat, and you owed him money and you killed him by driving a six-inch nail into his skull, so you'd better stall his daughter, otherwise she'll find the body and call the police and they'll dance on your face with their stupid boots until you tell them everything, and I'll lose my job and the precious scrap of dignity I've been able to muster in the last ten years, and you'll be sent to Holloway and the convicts will find out you were a spoon and they'll gang-rape you, all because you can't remember how to strike up a conversation with a bird.'

'Hang on, Holloway's a women's prison.'

'Brixton, then.'

I pushed hard against the door, whacking Davis back against the wall. 'Davis, I've had it with you always telling me what to do. Let her find the body. I'll make a clean breast of it because it's the decent thing – the moral thing – and if they ask me how come I was hammering nails into the wall I'll tell them the truth, that it was your bright idea in the first place –'

I heard a key turn in the lock next door and realised we were too late to do anything. Davis was seething, leaping about in anger and hissing like a pressure cooker. 'You *fuckwit!*' he fizzed. He hurled himself back into the lounge and threw his hands over his ears. 'Any second now she's going to start screaming the place down!'

And we waited. We hovered near the hole, listening without daring to hear, but there was nothing, no sound at all.

'What's going on?' Davis whispered after several minutes had elapsed.

'I don't know, she must have seen him by now.' I crept away toward the kitchen.

'Where are you going?' Davis hissed.

'I didn't finish my tea.'

'Bloody hell, how can you think of tea at a time like this, your freedom is about to come to an end. It'll be cold by now, make a fresh one.'

'Freedom's an illusion,' I told him, looking for my Cornish pottery mug. 'I tell people I'm an actor but I'm not, I sell car exhausts. I say I'm writing a screenplay but I've written nothing at all, and even if I did it would probably be utter rubbish. You tell everyone you're a financial director but you work in a phone centre making cold-calls. You think you're charming but people hate you even before they've met you. It's all a load of self-deluding bollocks because everyone wants to look as successful as – that.' I pointed out of my window at the billboard opposite. The poster hoarding showed Christian Bale in *American Psycho*.

'Then what do you really want to do?' asked Davis.

'I'd like to work in the Museum of London, just as a guard or something, just to be near the exhibits. I've read millions of books. I know tons of history. You only remember the things that interest you. That's why I kept forgetting the words to "Be Our Guest".'

'You haven't even got the qualifications to be a museum guard, mate. Look at the way you live, in this collapsing dump of a flat –'

'It wasn't in a state of collapse before you arrived. But even if it was,

I'd like it, because that's the beauty of living here, we can all do what we like, and the difference between you and me is that I'm basically content to be like this, and you're not.'

'What, happy with your lot, are you?'

'Er, yes,' I faltered.

'Content to shag that dog who works in the car wash?'

'Yes, and she's not a dog, she's great, she's a dish, and she's gonna run away with this spoon.'

'Go on then, enjoy your crappy little life.'

'Thanks, I will. It twists you up inside to see people having fun, doesn't it?'

'You're about to be done for murder. I hardly think it qualifies as fun.'

If Davis and I had been married, we would have gone on like this for the next thirty years before one of us died. By now twenty minutes had passed since Holly had entered her father's flat.

'Listen.'

I heard Gorridge's front door open and close. Davis ran back into the passage and tried to see through the fluted glass of the hall window. 'She's going back out. What's the deal here?'

'Maybe she called the rozzers and she's going to meet them downstairs.'

'Do you see any police?'

I ducked into the front room and pulled back the curtains, but she had already passed by. We gave her a minute to reach the stairwell, shot back out on to the balcony and looked over the wall. Holly was dragging a black binliner across the car park. She unlocked the Mercedes, hauled the bag into the boot and then drove off. Silence fell once more, broken only by the patter of flooded gutters.

'Right,' said Davis, 'I've had enough of this. I'm going through the wall.'

He used the handle of the sledgehammer to prise off a three-foot panel of plasterboard. Beyond this was a six-inch gap filled with mouse droppings, then the wall of the next flat. 'You can go first, seeing as you caused this.' He cracked the panel back on the far side, and shoved me through. I snagged my sweater on the damaged wooden struts, and tore my way through into Gorridge's lounge.

'Well,' called Davis, 'how is he?'

'I don't know,' I replied.

'For God's sake. How does he look?'

'It's hard to tell.'

'What do you mean?'

'He's not here.'

'What do you mean, not here?'

'Gone.'

'Yes, I understand the words, I just don't see how he could have gone.'

'Come through and see for yourself.'

'Not in these strides. Go around and open the door.'

Gorridge's body had disappeared, the table lamp had been placed upright and the stained cushions had been removed from the sofa. Holly had apparently hidden her father's corpse and covered up for us – but why?

'She took the cushions out in the binliner, but what the hell did she do with the body? She couldn't have taken it out of the flat.'

We searched the place room by room. We checked under the bed and inside the airing cupboard. David even emptied out Gorridge's Hoover bag hunting for clues. Everywhere we looked we found Rioja bottles and underpants, but no Gorridge.

'There's nowhere else she could have put him,' said Davis. 'Unless she slipped out with him earlier and you didn't hear her.'

'I don't think she just "slipped out" carrying her dead father. What, you think she managed to manhandle him down to the rubbish chute?'

'Oh my God.'

We dashed out on to the balcony and yanked open the chute, but couldn't see anything. 'Try the floor below,' Davis suggested. Taking the stairs two at a time, I swung around the bend in the staircase and crashed straight into Holly Gorridge.

'Well, you're in a hurry,' she said, righting herself and pushing her hair behind her ears. I had never seen her close up. Big green eyes, cheeky smile, astonishingly attractive. A future life together flashed before my eyes; courtship, engagement, betrothal, procreation, maturity, dotage, this domestic fantasy disrupted only by the knowledge that Holly would probably not be keen on marrying her father's assassin.

'Have you got my money?' she asked cheerfully.

I tried to look puzzled and innocent. 'What do you mean?'

'You owe my father three months' rent.'

She had a nerve to start going after her old man's outstanding debtors before his body was even cold, but perhaps that was how she managed to keep a good job in the City.

'Um, I can pop around with it in the morning? Will he be in?'

'No, he won't.'

'What about the day after tomorrow?'

'He won't be there then, either. You can give the money to me.'

She's playing it very cool, I thought. She carried a sense of inner strength. Outer strength, too, if she could clear up the Lounge of Death and stash Gorridge somewhere in just under twenty minutes.

'You can give me a cheque if you like.'

'I can do that,' I countered. 'Shall I make it out to your father?'

'No, make it out to me.'

It suddenly crossed my mind that she might not be above a little blackmail. 'If I do, can I ask you something, just out of scientific curiosity?'

Holly tilted her head to one side and, for the first time, smiled at me a little. 'All right then. Go ahead and ask.'

'What did you do with the old man?'

When I returned to my flat, I found Davis sitting on the stool by the rainy window with his head in his hands. He looked sheepish and miserable. 'I'm sorry I left you to deal with Gorridge's daughter. I just couldn't do it. I knew I'd seen her somewhere before. She drinks in a bar in Primrose Hill. I tried to pick her up once and she just gave me a look.'

'What kind of look?'

'The worst kind.'

'What did she tell you?'

'Oh, not much. I think it was my fault.'

'What do you mean?'

'I got it all wrong. I mean, I didn't see what I thought I saw. You know how things look —'

'What the *shagging fuck* are you talking about?'

'Gorridge was drunk. He'd dropped his bottle of Rioja and passed out on the couch. He was already face down when my nail shot through the wall and lodged in his hair. Holly roused her old man and sent him off to her place while she cleared up the mess.'

'You mean the yoga and everything? We put ourselves through all that for nothing?'

'There was no harm done. Except to the wall.'

'Well, it defeats me.' He slumped down on the stool and stared gloomily into the goods yards. 'I just can't get to grips with things.'

'What things?' I asked.

'Oh, fuck it, everything. All of this.' His fingers marked a forlorn trail on the glass. 'When I was a kid we lived in the suburbs, near Orpington. I never remember it raining, but now it rains all the time. Nothing ever used to change. No one went anywhere. No one did anything more than tend their gardens and go to the seaside in the summer. I *suppose* it was boring. Now I'm stuck here and everything changes all the time. You should see the people I have to work with. They look about eleven years old. They seem to cope all right. Well, I admit defeat. I can't get a fucking handle on it.'

'I wouldn't worry. Not many people can.'

'Then why doesn't it bother you?'

'I guess I like where I live, Davis. Nothing stops here for very long. Railways, roads, rivers, people whizzing back and forth, buildings spring up and get knocked down. You can be among all this and still not making any difference to the world. You can go unnoticed, like a blur on an old photograph. That's OK, I don't need to make my mark, I just want to be happy.'

Davis rested his forehead against the window and sighed. 'Maybe I should move home. Perhaps going back is the only way I'll count for something.'

A feeling of melancholy settled over us. I was sorry that Davis felt so driven to succeed, and sad because I knew we had moved too far apart to remain friends. 'I'll put the kettle on.' I patted him awkwardly on the back.

'It's already boiled once. I was waiting for you.' Davis rose from the stool and brightened up a bit. 'Have we got any biscuits?'

We walked down to the Hoop and Grapes, but weren't in the mood to stay for long. On the way back we stopped in Liverpool Road and watched something shifting beneath the lamplight. It was a small animal of some kind, creeping out from under a rain-beaten bush. At first I thought it must be a cat. Then it hopped on to the glistening pavement.

'The rats around here are certainly getting bigger.'

'No, it's a rabbit,' said Davis, amazed. 'Right here in town.'

'Mrs Lynch said she had to get rid of her son's pets,' I reminded him. 'She was worried they might breed.'

'Maybe it's a hare.' Davis smiled ruefully. 'Maybe it's Boadicea.'

'That's the spirit.' I smiled back.

'I think I'm going to go home, Jake. I'll come by for my stuff.'

'Sure thing, Davis. Whenever you like.'

'I wonder if it'll ever stop raining.'

'Oh, I suppose so.'

We solemnly shook hands and walked off in opposite directions. When I got back to the flat, I turned on my computer and set to work.

I completely forgot to give Gorridge his cheque. He came by a few evenings later to complain about the damage we had done to the wall, but I'd remembered to buy some Rioja, so he left a happy man.

Even at night, you can hear everything moving on.

The man on the Clapham omnibus

Kim Newman

Throat clogged with sulphurous filth, Orlando clung to a skinny lamp-post and coughed out his lungs. Stinging, liquid ropes hung from his mouth and nose; he shook them away, and wiped the last snail-tracks on his coat cuff. God Almighty knew, worse was on his clothes. The harder he ran, the more fog he inhaled, which forced him to stop and noisily purge his chest. It was as good as shouting 'Come on and get me' to the conductors. There were three uniforms, and he did not doubt they wanted to do him harm, certainly grievous, probably fatal.

He looked up at the eye-blue lamp-flame, piss-green in the sick-yellow murk. His eyes smarted, and crossed when the fore horn of his too-large tricorn hat dipped into his vision. London fog wasn't proper weather, but air-borne industrial waste from the tanneries, factories and processing plants along the Thames. The famous pea-soup was so heavy with flammable by-products that spontaneous combustions of the atmosphere were common. When the yellow tide rose to the level of the burning gas-lamps, whole streets could go up in a swift puff of flame: cats burned hairless, faces blacked for music hall minstrel turns, buildings dusted with soot. Just now, that might be a mercy.

His ears were rat-sharp, as well they might be. All too often he needed eight or nine senses to get out of scrapes like this. He listened for footsteps, the clank of ticket machines, the creak of boot- and strap-leather. The conductors might not be interested in a ninepenny fare to Streatham Hill, but they had the full London Transport kit. Now he thought of it, the gear was too new, too mint. And what were the chances of three random busmen being white? Next time he was tempted to rely on public transport, he would get a minicab and flip for the fare with his two-headed sovereign.

The conductors were near. He wondered if there were a manhole in the road nearby. If possible, he wanted to avoid the sewers.

The labyrinth below the city had its own particular dangers. Even this far south of Hampstead, the Black Swine ruled the tunnels. Their forefathers had gone underground two centuries back, and piggy generations had bred away from the light, subsisting on human ordure and carrion, developing fearsome tusks, wrought-iron hides and extra-sensitive snouts. Those eyeless pork-goliaths could fetch off a good-sized workman and render him to bones in minutes. It was rumoured they picked late-night drunks from platforms along the Jubilee Line Extension. Orlando was small enough to pass for a boy if a recruiting sergeant was about. His wrists and ankles twisted the wrong way, and his back had a kink that came whenever, as now, he was forced to exert himself. He was not up for a tussle with mutant man-killer pigs.

A shrill whistle cut through the fog. The first few notes of 'Champagne Supernova'. Another whistle answered, further off, carrying on the tune, strangling the notes.

They were triangulating on him.

Orlando was determined not to be killed by Oasis fans. It would be too much bleeding embarrassment. Manchester was a spent force, still occupied by the Army of the South-East. Just after the reunification, he had been up North with a carpet-bag full of Abbey Road acetates, but few fortunes were to be made on the club scene for anyone with his accent.

He controlled his racking cough and stood still. He had taken care to practise the trick of slipping into the fog, becoming one with the night.

Ordinary bus conductors would never have found him. These fellows, however, had fog-skills of their own. Since the Civil War, a lot of dangerous people were milling in with the general citizenry.

Even before he saw the vaguest shape in the fog, a peaked cap and broad shoulders, Orlando heard footfalls. Good boots – too good for a ticket-puncher – on cobbles.

He thought of shinning up the lamp-post. If there was an overhanging roof, he might scramble up and down valleys of slick slates. Being small, light and crooked was an advantage up among the chimney pots.

But they were on him.

A long knife sliced across his coat, ripping the shirt-ruffle at his throat, cutting through the strap of his pannier-like satchel. Hands tore the satchel away from him. Nothing was in it he couldn't afford to lose: a roll of snide cup tie tickets that'd pass in indifferent light, a bundle of French postcards manufactured in Romford, half of one of Bellamy's pork pies, pirated wire recordings of the last two weeks' worth of *Mrs Dale's Diary*.

A hard face emerged from the gloom. One eye was clouded, yellow as the fog.

'I didn't see nothing,' Orlando said.

'Anything,' the man corrected. 'You didn't see anything.'

Yellow-Eye didn't speak like a busman. His tone was more like a wireless announcer, correct and superior.

Orlando nodded, agreeing with him.

But he had seen the man on the bus. And the conductor knew he had seen him, had recognised – as anyone would – the face, and was asking himself questions.

Orlando wished he could burn out that segment of his past, touch a lit cigarette to his memory of the face as he could if it were printed in a newspaper.

It was no use.

Hands took his arms. The other conductors.

He had a two-shot pistolet holstered in the small of his back, a pig-knife in his boot, brass-knucks in his coat pocket, a pepper spray in his trouser pocket, a straight razor in the concealed partition of his satchel and a loop of cheesewire inside his hat. All useless now.

Hands frisked him, professionally. They found everything.

'Evidently, we have a charming character on our hands,' said Yellow-Eye. 'His real paper is in the sufficiently outlandish name of Orlando Boldt, Esquire, but he feels the need to port far less convincing fall-backs in the names of Aloysius Stonecarver, Brendan Two Roses, and, ah, Righteous Pilgrim Furie. Makes things easier all round, I think. This singular fellow would appear to be an entire krewe of double-desperate men.'

'I know my rights,' said Orlando.

'I'm sure you do, Goodman Boldt. As should all public-spirited citizens.'

Orlando thought fast, but got nowhere: he had to pretend to be stupider than he was, stupider than his captors knew him to be, to go along with the game in the hope a hole would turn up, a hole he could slip through. Away from these three, he knew where to go, who to see. If he made a big enough noise, he'd save his life, make such a fuss that he would himself become insignificant. Then, other folk could do the threatening, fighting, wounding and dying.

'I want a brief,' he spluttered. 'I can explain.'

Yellow-Eye laughed, nastily. 'I'm not a policeman, I'm a bus conductor.'

'And I've got three arses,' Orlando replied.

He knew Yellow-Eye would hit him and that he'd be good at it, know where to land the blow. Orlando clenched his gut and closed his thighs, but the conductor chopped him across the throat.

His Adam's apple crunched and he spouted phlegmy spittle over Yellow-Eye's uniform chest. He doubled over, all his weight dragging off-balance the conductor who had his arms pinned.

The knife was there again, at his face.

'Three against one,' said a new voice. 'Scarcely sporting.'

The new man spoke like Yellow-Eye, precisely and with an officer's command. Maybe it was the shaking his skull had just had, but to Orlando the man sounded like deliverance, voice resounding off the stones of the nearest buildings.

The third conductor, the one who had searched him, took a pistol out of his change-bag and there was a shot.

Orlando's sensitive ears rang.

The shot had come not from the third conductor, who was looking surprised, a splash of blood dead-square in his chest, but from the new man. A swirl of the fog had combusted from the spark and Orlando saw a black-browed face lit yellow as by a stage magician's flare. He didn't know the man personally, but recognised him. During the Civil War, his face had been famous, often appearing in the illustrated press. There were ballads and broadsheets about his deeds. These last few years, the face was less often seen than the name heard.

Lytton. Captain James Lytton.

He had made some hard choices. Orlando understood Lytton hadn't turned up to collect his medals at the War's end. The rumour mill had him out west somewhere, camping with the hippies at Glastonbury or communing with Arthur at Tintagel.

Now he was here, somewhere just north of Clapham Common, an avenger with a pistol. Orlando made a poor maiden in distress, but this was still like a cover engraving of any number of Andy McNab's *Ninepenny Marvel*. The ruffians, the victim, the gunman emerging from the fog. It was the sort of situation Orlando associated with Dr Shade, the penumbral outlaw adventurer whom the editors of the *Halfpenny Wonder* and *Union Jack Weekly* had sworn was real. The scene lacked only a faithful hound.

Conductor-in-chief Yellow-Eye made a motion to slit Orlando's throat and get it over with. Lytton fired again, and the knife-hand vanished into red, gritty mist that went all over Orlando's face and shirt. The blade blasted into the distance, and clattered against a wall.

Yellow-Eye didn't make a sound, though the blood was squeezed out of his lips and into his eyes. With his left (remaining) hand, he reached behind his back, for a holster. Lytton didn't bother with a warning shot, and put his next ball in the man's head, settling his clouded-eye problem once and for all. For a heartbeat, Orlando thought even that wouldn't stop the artist formerly known as Yellow-Eye, now liable to be tagged briefly as Red-Socket. The conductor-in-chief jerked backward, but continued to draw his own pistol, bringing it round, aiming the long barrel generally at the Captain. Then he crumpled.

The third conductor still had a grip on Orlando's arms. He swivelled and held Orlando up, using him as a shield.

Lytton stepped forward, gun raised. The fog seemed to part to make way for him. A tall man, he wore a long motorcyclist's coat and a broad-brimmed hat. His bootfalls were heavy. His eyes glinted, even through the fog.

The surviving conductor backed away, dragging Orlando, but collided with the lamp-post. He dropped Orlando and scarpered into the fog.

Orlando twisted as he fell, jamming his hands against cobbles, feeling the impact in his wrists and elbows. He sat, and found Lytton knelt over him.

'Nothing broken?' the Captain asked, like a doctor. His long-barrelled six-shot revolver was still drawn and cocked.

Orlando checked himself and shook his head. He wasn't really in much worse shape than usual.

Lytton nodded towards the two dead men.

'I'd heard the Lord Mayor Elect took a tough line on fare dodgers, but this seems excessive.'

Whistles sounded, nearby. The sort that never failed to scrape Orlando's nerves. Police whistles.

'It'd probably be for the best if we moved on,' Lytton said.

Orlando agreed with him.

One of the Lord Mayor Elect's most popular campaign promises was revision of draconian licensing laws that had come as a relief in the latter stages of the Civil War. Even pubs forced to close at half past ten of an

evening had been welcomed after a spell of brutally enforced tem-
perance. Lord Protector John Minor, desperately trying to sustain the
coalition, had committed himself to the experiment to gain the support of one of the more obnoxious Puritan factions. Actually, Pro-
hibition had been a magic time for Orlando; touting for the shebeens
that mushroomed into existence, he'd been in the gravy. The stew of
ill-advised moral heavy-handedness had thrown up more than a few
black economy millionaires.

Until the Assembly passed the new raft of London laws, every street
in the city still had its illegal after-hours grogshop or lock-in, but all
were wary of new faces. It'd probably be an even worse idea to show
himself where he was known. The conductor who had fled knew
Orlando's name and too many of his Sunday best aliases. Yellow-Eye
had sneered at his forged papers, but they were of the highest quality.
The conductor-in-chief must have had an eye for snide, a skill hardly
picked up to cope with a wave of counterfeit bus passes. He had every
reason to believe the people the conductors worked for could get the
word out faster than a town crier or a Newgate pamphleteer.

So hiding in a boozer was out. And a fancy house – of which there
were several within easy distance – was a worse idea. Drunks might be
too sozzled to remember to sell you out, but a tart always sniffed potential profit and had no concept of loyalty. Orlando's Mum, who worked
under the nom de slut of Fifi la Française, had repeatedly informed on
his Dad, who went by the slightly too-giveaway handle Burglar Bill
Boldt, sending him away to Pentonville for long stretches to pocket
the escalating reward money. She even nagged the old man to go
for quality blags so the Judas purse on him would swell enough to be
worth the claiming. They were retired to Hove now; Mum was still
at it, grassing on Dad for fiddling his pension claims.

Orlando and Lytton walked across Clapham Common, wading
through a knee-high fog pool that soaked trouser-cuffs and would
eventually eat through boots.

Where to go?

Orlando's crib in Streatham would be blown. The Captain was newly
arrived in the city, and had yet to secure lodgings for the night.

It was best to keep walking.

He volunteered no explanation of the contretemps with the conductors. The Captain must be wondering if he had not intervened on

the wrong side. Orlando could make no claim to good character and his assailants were uniforms, deporting themselves as if empowered to give him a hard time.

That face. The man on the bus.

Orlando still didn't have an idea what the business was all about, but knew it was momentous.

Police whistles shrilled again, in the distance. There were disturbances at the edge of the Common. With luck, the peelers would turn up enough citizens unwilling to explain their presence to keep them busy until morning.

A gent in a natty cutaway coat hobbled past at top speed, trews around his knees, dickybird waving like a broken spigot, shrieking in what Orlando recognised as Welsh. Taffs were all cracked, from coal dust and lava bread. Without discussion, Lytton and Orlando stopped walking and stepped close to tall bushes, swirling fog cloaking around them. A whistle sounded close by, and a fat plod galumphed past, nipple-head hat wobbling, truncheon out at the ready. He gained on the Welshman and launched himself with a roar, bearing his quarry into the thick of the fog.

Beyond their sight, a severe beating took place. By the sound of it, more constables pitched up to help the queer-bashing. One lovingly whistled the theme to *Dixon of Dock Green* to cover yelps and thumps. The bastards always did that. Anyone who thought community coppers were really like George Dixon on the wireless was in for a nasty surprise. The Lord Mayor Elect had promised yet another inquiry into corruption at the Met, and word on the street was that he might actually mean it.

The hapless perv was dragged off by the rozzers, whining 'Don't you know who I am, boyos?' between truncheon taps. Then, the commotion was over. The fog was thick all around, and they were far enough from gaslight for yellow to seem sludgy gray. In a natural hollow, Orlando and Lytton were surrounded by bushes: a fine site for an assignation or an assassination.

'Now,' said Lytton. 'What is this all about?'

Orlando shrugged.

Lytton turned and walked away, disappearing completely.

Terror rose. Orlando had been abandoned.

'Wait,' he shouted. 'I saw something I shouldn't. Something important.'

He looked into the dark and saw nothing.

'Go on,' said Lytton.

Orlando jumped, at being addressed by an invisible presence. He couldn't even work out where Lytton was standing.

'I caught a bloody bus. It was marked "Not in Service", but I didn't notice. I had, ahem, been drinking, in celebration of a tidy bit of business and, not to mince words, was fairly bladdered. It was a good old Routemaster, with the open platform at the back. None of your OMOV bollocks. I found it at a traffic light, and climbed aboard. The bus had three conductors, and one particular passenger. Unwilling, I'd say. He was handcuffed to a hanging-strap and drugged to the eyeballs. When I got on, the conductors were seeing to the prisoner. A leather mask was being fitted over his face, like a bondage hood. It had been taken off because Old Yellow-Eye was afraid he had choked on his tongue, but they were satisfied he was just zonked and were fitting the thing on again. I saw this man's face, and I recognised it. Just as I recognised your face, Captain Lytton.'

'Who was this unfortunate?'

Orlando thought a moment. 'Not yet. I have to think hard before I say. But, besides the conductors, three other men were on the bus. I knew them too. Those names I will give you. Strawjack Crowe, Geodfroy Arachnid, Truro Daine.'

Lytton's face appeared. 'A fine collection of rogues.'

'The Prime Minister's Spy-Master, the disgraced High Elder of the Sect of Diana, and the worst criminal in London. Not exactly the sort of folk you expect to find on the last bus to Streatham Hill.'

'If those three have common interests, it'd be a sorry day for the city.'

'Believe me, that's true,' said Orlando.

'Still, I hadn't planned on biding long here. I'd advise you get out too, especially if they know your name.'

Orlando's insides knotted. Leave London! He'd tried that once, and would not be going down that sad road any time in the near future, no matter what. Beyond the city limits, wearing socks made you unspeakably posh and they sweetened the tea with cat's piss.

Besides, he would never be safe. Strawjack Crowe, a pox-cheeked Puritan who had been master of the Lord Protector's Secret Police, ruled the Star Chamber of the Parliament of the Marches, the central agency entrusted by the new Prime Minister with overall command of all police forces, civil militias and honour guards in the country. Famous for having his own son flogged in public for singing on a Sunday, Crowe was the most frighteningly efficient enemy of harmless pleasure England had ever seen. His power – mandated by the Prime Minister of the Marches, not the London Assembly – was on the rise even within the city.

And, if there was a place in these islands beyond Crowe's reach, it would still be within the grasp of Truro Daine, Emperor of the Underworld, the 'Cromwell of Crime'. They said the fog itself worked for Daine, whose initial riverside powerbase was so permanently thick with the stuff he could no longer breathe fresh air or see clearly without the murk. He lived in rooms especially pumped full of fog and, on the bus, had been taking draughts through a breathing mask which left a yellow triangle around his mouth and nose.

'You're in this too,' Orlando said. 'The conductor found out my name, but he must have known your face.'

Lytton held his chin, and conceded the point.

'I'm sorry, Captain, but we're on the bus together, as it were, until we get to the depot. Between them, Crowe and Daine can have every man against us. Even Arachnid has followers, and he's a standing joke among his own sect, let alone real people. Think of it: coppers, crooks, Dianaheads – all against us. Eyes in the fog. They expect us to run, to try and get out of the city, to head for the walls. The gates will be double- and triple-guarded. Hunting dogs will be loose in the greenbelt. They'll be searching the trains and coaches. Our only hope is to stay in the smoke, to scare up some friends.'

'We have no friends.'

Orlando understood. 'Maybe not, but we can find allies. Have you heard of the Diogenes Club?'

Lytton nodded. He accepted casually that Orlando could drop the name of an institution which was supposedly unknown to the general public.

'They were supposed to be broken up, as a condition of the reunification,' Orlando said. 'It's part of the Prime Minister's programme of recovery, but the Parliament of the Marches is out there in the sticks, hopping like a bunch of ravers between New Towns and the fens. What the PM says in some jumped-up Women's Institute Hall doesn't mean a fly's fart in London. The Diogenes Club is in Pall Mall. Would you wager that some of its members still take an interest in matters of state?'

'In the War, I ran ops for Diogenes,' Lytton admitted.

'Didn't we all?'

Lytton looked at him, really taking him in for the first time. Orlando knew he wasn't impressive, wasn't tall, didn't sound like the BBC. But sometimes blending in was more important than standing out.

'Pall Mall, eh? There's Battersea, the Thames, Belgravia, the Palace and Green Park between here and there. Quite a stroll in the best of times. We'd best shift ourselves, Goodman Boldt.'

'Just what I was going to say.'

By dawn, they had made it to the Thames, and stood on Chelsea Reach. Day brought light but not clarity. The fog was thicker and yellower than school custard. Back in his crib, Orlando had a selection of stylish breathing masks – but he'd neglected to bring any of them out. His perennially troublesome lungs gave him gyp. He clocked Lytton noticing the blood in his hankie after he had a good old Frank Bough.

They'd kept out of the way of trouble, staying off main thorough-fares, avoiding all other early-morning folk. Orlando, *A–Z* imprinted on his brain from birth, knew the city in a way that made a black cabbie with a headful of Knowledge seem like a Geordie wandering out of Victoria coach station for the first time and wondering where his wallet had gone. Lytton let him lead and Orlando had a little puff of pride, understanding the Captain judged him sound in this area of expertise, and was prepared to entrust him with his life.

'Battersea, Albert or Chelsea?' Orlando asked. 'Maybe Vauxhall, if you fancy a bit of a hike.'

Lytton considered. They were closest to the Chelsea Bridge. Beyond the fog-wall that hung over the river was the Chelsea Embankment. Orlando was antsy about the Chelsea Bridge just now, perhaps because there was a Bus Depot attached to the approach road. He still half-thought London Transport was in on this whole thing with the Three Villains, fighting the Lord Mayor Elect's policies on low fares and public ownership.

They looked up at the span of the bridge. Vague shapes stood idling. Orlando made out the tithead shape of a bobby's helmet on one of them, but the other fellows wore tricorns like his.

'They'll have all the bridges guarded,' said Lytton. 'Damn, I hadn't expected them to be this fast.'

'We can hardly swim across.'

Orlando was worried when Lytton didn't immediately agree with him. Because of his back and limbs, he could barely do a width in the Lambeth Baths. And the Thames was definitely not fit for human immersion. Trapped in the Sargasso of detergent scum that drifted slowly by the Reach were dead cats, clumps of raw sewage, a myriad partial clay pipes and an amazing amount of assorted jetsam. A faceless grandfather clock bobbed past, a raft for a large, red-eyed rat. More than a few unwary folk of Orlando's acquaintance had taken a last dip in these waters.

'No, but we can make an effort to be unpredictable.'

'You're hoping for a small boat we can, ah…'

'Requisition? Not necessarily. What do you weigh?'

Orlando didn't know. His only scale was a wonky jeweller's cast-off.

'About nine stone, I'd think. And I'm fourteen. Together, we're not too heavy.'

'I'm not going in the river.'

Lytton shuddered. 'No fear of that.'

Nearby was a pier, gated and locked at this hour. Lytton took out an impressive Swiss Army implement and unfolded a blade. He started working on the hinges of the tall gates.

'What's behind those that you want?'

'Nothing,' Lytton said. 'I want the gates themselves.'

The makeshift raft drifted out on to the river, dubious liquids sloshing over the edges. Orlando's tummy was distinctly roiling, from the stench as much as the movement. God didn't mean for him to live on water, which is why He had built many fine bridges over His favoured river. It took nervous minutes to get beyond the clogged banks, but when the current caught them, the board whirled out, not towards the opposite bank but along the Thames, seaward. They had a couple of planks for oars, but Lytton wouldn't let Orlando use them yet. They lay quiet on the raft as it passed under the Chelsea Bridge. The knot of fellows up above were harassing early foot-commuters like licensed footpads.

'Someone on the river,' shouted a voice.

Lytton mouthed a swear word.

Orlando cringed and reconsidered his aversion to sliding off the raft and into the water. The worst of the filth was along the banks, not in mid-stream.

'You there, halt,' said a bobby. 'In the name of the law.'

'Bugger that,' said a rougher voice.

There was a blast and a plop. It wasn't a warning shot, but inaccurate marksmanship. The next rifle-shot blew a spouting hole in the raft.

Lytton was on one knee, pistol up, sighting carefully. He judged their sluggish drift and the upward angle, probably the wind.

He fired twice.

The policeman's helmet flew off and the rifleman's shoulder came bloodily apart.

A fusillade, mostly cobbles but with a few wild shots mixed in, came down on the river, raining into the water where the raft had been. Orlando paddled furiously now, wrestling with the board as the river tried to take it away from him.

The bridge receded into the fog. There was a glint, off the glass of a scope. Lytton fired at it, and someone whirled away from a broken implement.

'There'll be another krewe on Vauxhall Bridge,' Lytton said. 'We've got to make it to the other side.'

'You could help by paddling. I'm just tiddling us round in a circle.'

Lytton holstered his pistol, and took up a plank.

A flare rose from the bridge, spurting through the fog, and exploded like a Guy Fawkes rocket. Orlando wondered how many eyes were up for the signal.

Paddling faster, they could see the other embankment now.

'Where are we?' Lytton asked.

'Pimlico,' Orlando said, heart sinking. 'Not a good place to strike land.'

The raft nudged shingles, scraped through another drift of muck, and fetched up somewhere under the Grosvenor Road.

Orlando was pleased to get his shaky knees on to dry land, even here.

'Come on,' Lytton said, hauling him upright, 'hurry along.'

Orlando allowed himself to be dragged into the worst borough in London for the likes of him.

They passed under a lamp-post. Reeking feet knocked Orlando's hat off. He scrambled around on the cobbles for it.

'What's that?' Lytton asked.

They looked up. The corpse had been dangling for a few weeks and the deader's face probably hadn't been much in the first place. A neatly printed sign was pinned to the chest, in the style of a special offer in a greengrocer's window. 'Sturdy Beggar.' The hanged man's coat pockets were stuffed with rolled-up copies of the *Big Issue*.

'Neighbourhood Watch,' spat Orlando. 'It's the borough's Short Sharp Shock policy.'

They hurried on, away from the ghastly reminder.

Pimlico, in loose alliance with Westminster and Lambeth, was a law unto itself. The Lord Mayor Elect was holding talks with the councillors of these districts, to bring them back into the Assembly. Orlando thought the tinpot dictators, imposing their 'emergency regulations' years after the emergency, would not easily give up power.

Now, with what he knew, that was all open for argument.

'You two there,' said someone. 'Passports, please.'

A patrol emerged around them, like an ambush. Soldier suits and deckchair attendant hats, flintlock side-arms and butcher-knives.

Even if Orlando still had his papers, none of them would be of any use. He'd never been sent down for anything serious, but Pimlico operated Zero Tolerance. A few parking tickets or a drunk and disorderly earned a stripe from the cat. With Orlando's sheet, he was due for a hoist up the nearest lamp-post.

Lytton made no move to produce any document.

'Passports,' repeated the Watchman, a short, balding, brush-moustached bank manager-type. None of his fellows was especially hard, but they had the numbers. One was a tubby woman, with Diana hair and white robes. She carried a clockwork-powered prod, crackling with blue electricity. Flounces of multicoloured ribbon were pinned to their breasts with badges that emblazoned their post-codes.

'They won't have any,' said a taller man, with a deeper voice.

He didn't have NW insignia, and wore no council ribbons. He reminded Orlando of the conductor-in-chief, but where Yellow-Eye's face had been hard but bland this man was black-browed and hollow-cheeked, a skull coated with papier mâché. His eyes were like bullet-holes.

'Good morning, James,' the new man said to Lytton.

Orlando realised Lytton was tense, hand close to his pistol.

'Hello, Stryng,' he said.

'I didn't realise we were scouting for you,' said Stryng. He had a slightly recessive 'r', which should have sounded silly but didn't.

'I'd have demanded a bigger purse if I'd known there was challenge involved. They only told me about your crookback pet.'

'Really, there are procedures,' said the NW jobsworth.

'Shut up, little man,' said Stryng. The petty Watchman swallowed it, but went red. His mates muttered at the breach of discipline. The Dianahead raised her prod like a magic wand.

'This is Captain James Lytton,' said Stryng. 'My old CO at the Siege of Manchester. He got a Victoria Cross. And I got a dishonourable. You wouldn't credit how close things came to being the other way round.'

'Lieutenant Rutland Stryng,' said Lytton. 'You were lucky to get off with a dishonourable discharge.'

'You voted for the blindfold, didn't you? Well, we all make mistakes.'

Stryng drew a serious pistol, a Webley. Lytton let him, which surprised Orlando. Stryng didn't fire, as Lytton must have known.

'I'm disappointed,' said Stryng. 'It seems your reputation for sharp reflexes is exaggerated. When it comes down to it, you're a snail-fingered slowcoach.'

Lytton tapped his left hip, drawing Stryng's attention, and slapped away Stryng's gun-barrel with his right hand, twisting the pistol out of the Lieutenant's grip and tossing it into the street. Then, he drew his own pistol and pointed it at Stryng's surprised face.

Stryng whistled, unevenly. A drip of sweat ran from under his feather-brimmed hat and into his eye.

'So, you are swift. Pity it isn't loaded.'

'Yes,' said Lytton. 'Isn't it?'

Counting, Orlando realised the Captain had shot his six and not reloaded. Always a mistake to go about without spare ammo.

He smashed Stryng across the side of the head with the heavy barrel, raising a red welt.

'Run,' he shouted.

Stryng tried to grab Lytton's shoulders but the Captain heaved him off, throwing him against the NW krewe. Stryng landed on the plump Dianahead, who charged her shock prod full into his arse. He yelled as blue light arced all around.

Orlando didn't need to be told twice.

He was running. And Lytton was catching up fast.

★

They were in Greencoat Place, coming up to the kink of Greycoat Place, into Artillery Row and Victoria Street. Even in dire panic, with street-signs obscured by fog, Orlando knew that much. St James's Park wasn't far off, and the Mall.

Though he'd never been inside the building, he knew the Diogenes Club. It was an unobtrusive establishment, with the most modest of brass plates. Orlando had exaggerated a smidge when he told Lytton he had run ops for the Club during the Civil War. In those troubled times, there had been opportunities, and he'd found agents of the Diogenes Club by far the best people to pass on any information that came his way. They paid better than the police or parliament, and could protect you from the likes of Truro Daine or the Traffic Wardens. At least, that had once been the case. Now that the Lord Mayor Elect and the Prime Minister had agreed the faithful dogs had had their day, Orlando didn't know what to expect.

Since their tangle with the Pimlico Watch and Rutland Stryng, Lytton had said nothing. Orlando wondered if he was professionally shamed to have fired his gun empty. Obviously, there was unsettled business between the Captain and the former Lieutenant. Orlando didn't understand the honour of the service thing, but then again he had ducked conscription through his feet and a week's soap diet.

It was mid-morning. Hardy Londoners were on the streets around Victoria Station, swarming to Whitehall and Westminster. They wore fog-breather faceplates with dangling elephant's trunk filters, topped off with bowler hats. Everyone had a furled umbrella, most containing flick-blades as insurance against road agents or persistent spare change extortionists. Unmasked, Orlando and Lytton stood out among civil servants and office workers.

They crossed Victoria Road and made their way to St James's Park through backstreets. The fog was less thick in the park, but chill mist rose from the duck-pond. It was a foolhardy soul indeed who stepped off Birdcage Walk and walked on the grass. The grounds had controversially been declared sacred to Diana by Geoffroy Arachnid, and his sect sent patrols out to keep the paths virginally untrodden, though word from the Palace was that the sanctification of the Martyr Princess was highly unofficial. Frequent punch-ups took place between the Household Guard and the Dianaheads, skirmishing over rotting floral tributes left at the Palace gates, which the Guards liked to dump in the pond.

'We'll use the bridge,' said Lytton.

They could see it, rising over the pond. A favoured duck-feeding spot, it was festooned with wreaths in the shape of land-mines and tank traps. Orlando wouldn't have been surprised to learn they were genuinely booby-trapped.

'Whatever you say, Captain.'

They strolled to the bridge. As usual, Orlando felt itchy with grass and dirt under his shoes. It was too much like being cast out of the city, crawling into the sticks where the cat-eaters and the sheep-worriers ruled. When the Countryside Alliance had tried to besiege the capital, he'd seen the shotgun-toting yokels at their worst, staging fox-hunts through the streets of New Malden, setting their hounds on London folk, destroying food stores by sending in diseased ferrets. The Lord Mayor Elect-to-be had rallied disparate Watches and Guards to see off the yokels, halting the green tide at Traps Lane, throwing back at the CA their own slogan, 'Get orff moi laand!' For that alone, he would have had Orlando's vote – if Orlando had wanted to volunteer an address and register on the rolls, which as it happens wasn't convenient.

The humpbacked bridge was hung with Diana-face tributes. Hundreds of identical smiles and sparkle-eyes. Lytton eased a triffid-sized arrangement of white chrysanthemums out of the way and set foot on the bridge. He crossed over, and Orlando followed, uncomfortable. It was as if all the dead eyes were on him. He often profaned the Sacred Name with oaths like 'Di's diminishing braincells!', 'Diana's spew!' and 'Di's diet!' As the star of *The Sinful Milkman*, a one-reel flicker produced for private audiences, he had upset an ingénue by ad-libbing the immortal line, 'You be Princess Di, and I'll be the Naughty French Coroner'. Now, superstitious terror gripped him. The Princess was reputed to be a vengeful soul, unforgiving of her most casual enemies.

He made it off the bridge, and heaved a sigh.

'That wasn't so hard.'

A flock of ducks swarmed off the waters of the pond and surged at their ankles, stabbing with bills, quacking in fury. They were used to fare more substantial than bread-shreds, and all had mad Diana eyes.

Orlando and Lytton ran away, hardly heroes.

The windows of the Diogenes Club were boarded. No one stood guard at the front door. Orlando was afraid they'd come too late, and the Club was abandoned, its members packed off to the provinces.

Clearly, the institution's many enemies were in the ascendant.

Lytton opened the door and stepped inside. Orlando followed. The lobby was deserted, a strew of old periodicals over the scuffed marble floor. Light patches stood out on dark walls where portraits had hung. A half-disassembled field-gun gathered dust in the corner, under a torn Mayoral election poster.

Orlando found a bell-pull, which he yanked. A distant tinkle sounded, the giggle of an idiot angel. Scouting this level, he found only locked doors. Ahead stood the main stairs. The secret business of the Diogenes Club was conducted on the upper floors; off the lobby were only the chambers that most resembled an old-fashioned gentlemen's club.

'Come on, I know the way.'

Lytton mounted the stairs. Orlando was getting used to the Captain's way of moving. Apparently casual and at ease, but always with an underlying tension, alert to potential threat.

The first-floor landing was heavily carpeted. White corpse outlines marred the red plush, and darker patches suggested they weren't just a ghoulish decoration. There had been fighting here, during one of the attempted coups.

'Who's there?' came a voice. 'Who's there, blast you!'

A doorway that should have contained a stout oak door was hung with multicoloured love beads. The unmistakable, dead-sweet smell of kif wafted through the rippling curtain. Low Indian music was playing, not the filmi-filmi rot from flock-wallpaper curry-houses but classical sitar.

Taking out a knife, Lytton parted the curtain. He went through, beckoning Orlando to follow.

The room was a wreck, lit by an open fireplace where the red embers of former furniture burned and a three-foot-tall lava lamp in the shape of Dan Dare's rocket. On a Sultanate pile of tasselled cushions sprawled a very thin man, his long tumble of ringlets coal-dark, his moustache and eyebrows black threaded with white. He wore a candy-striped swallowtail coat, orange velvet knee-britches, hand-painted Constable landscape waistcoat and silver-buckled, stack-heeled Clark's shoes. A froth of cherry-crimson cravat bubbled out from his diamond-pointed collar.

In his hand was the mouthpiece of a hookah, which bubbled beside him. On the bare floorboards by his cushions were an ice-bucket jammed with bottles of champagne and a Derry & Tom's hamper of preserves and game-meats.

'Richard Jeperson,' said Lytton.

'Who's that fellow?' asked the foppish stoner, hand-shading his unfocused eyes. He was high as a kite. 'Isn't it Cap'n Lytton, Hero of Harpendon, Saviour of St Albans? War's over, don't ch'know. Don't have to take any more orders. Country's reunited, parliaments devolved. Big celebratory confab coming up at the Dome, peace and love and hugs and harmony all round. For the lion shall lay down with the lamb, the yokel will shake hands with the city gent, and the Scouser will snog the Scot. Hurrah hurrah huzzah hoolay!'

Jeperson overbalanced on the cushions and sprawled, dropping his hookah-pipe. He reached for it and Lytton kindly stepped on his hand.

'I think you've had enough, Jeperson.'

'Do you really? I probably agree with you. But it's not been an easy decade, has it? Just look at the old place. I'm the only one left, you know. The others have all gone, to the Lord Mayor Elect or the bloody Prime Minister. My girl Vanessa upped and joined the Libertarian Demagogues. What do you think of that, eh? Dratted shame. When it all fell apart, I was chairman of the Ruling Cabal of the Diogenes Club, heir to the sainted Beauregard and the underrated Withrop. I thought I ought to stay, just in case. We're only here because the old country needs us from time to time, and we don't mind getting our fingers dirty. Well, not much.'

Orlando couldn't make out Lytton's expression. Getting on that bus had transported him to an alternative reality where everyone knew more than he did, except for that one vital thing only he knew. He could only hope to understand the iceberg-tip of every conversation.

'You're needed again, Jeperson.'

Steel sparked in Jeperson's eye.

'I trust your judgement, Lytton. It's a shameful waste, but would you kindly sober me?'

'All right.'

Lytton took his boot off Jeperson's hand and let the man get to his knees. Jeperson looked up like a supplicant, and spread his arms. Lytton plucked two champagne bottles out of the ice-bucket, and popped the corks with his thumbs. They ricocheted against the ceiling.

'Mind the clobber, would you. It's a new suit.'

Lytton emptied frothing, icy bubbly over Jeperson's head. The man roared and shook his head, splashing the wallpaper as his hair whipped the champagne off.

'Now,' said Jeperson, leaping up, lassitude washed away, 'there's a stash of Colombia's second finest product about somewhere. A serious caffeine infusion is called for. See if you can scout out the coffee-pot, young fellow. A shame to put the last of the Victorian silver into the grate, but this is, as usual, an emergency.'

Orlando found the pot and Jeperson came up with a tin of brown ground. The Master of the Diogenes Club set about making the strongest, thickest, best coffee Orlando had ever tasted. A single swallow made his heart contract like a bruised fist.

'Lytton, what is all this about? And who is this ill-made little fellow?'

'This is Orlando Boldt. And he has something to tell you.'

'Then, tell me he must. Noble Orlando, spiel away.'

He felt compelled to look both ways, as if there might be concealed listeners. Lytton and Jeperson gave subliminal nods of approval.

'I just wanted to catch a bus,' he began.

'Arachnid, I don't take seriously,' said Jeperson. 'Not since the *News of the Screws* exposé of his fling with the buxom orange-seller. Even the Diana devouts are embarrassed by a clown like that. And Pea-Soup Daine's a jumped-up criminal, whose unusual personal habits hardly make him more interesting than the average Maltese crime boss of Soho or Heathen Chinee tong-master of Limehouse. But Deacon Crowe's the worst man in England, a festering sore in the government who works the Prime Minister like a Punch and Judy Man works a glove puppet. Not that Strawjack'd appreciate the comparison, for he's vowed to slap a ban on such disgraceful violent entertainments. Mr Punch, apparently, is a disastrous role model for the kiddiewinks. The ruin you see around you is at least three-fourths the work of Strawjack Crowe, who has personally been dismantling all that stands in the way of his iron vision of an England chained to the pews. Did you know that when he was Overseer of Liverpool, he had the Cavern Club fire-bombed? I'm not surprised to discover he associates with such low people as Arachnid and Daine, but he'll be thinking all the while of how to get shot of them.'

Orlando had only told Jeperson as much as he had told Lytton. Now he came to it, he still didn't know if he should say any more. Would he be safer if the secret were shared? Or might he still be able to cut a deal with Crowe, to stay out of the way until whatever was in the off-ing had come to fruition. The England Jeperson described might look askance at the likes of Goodman Orlando Boldt, but more prohibi-tions meant more black markets. Strawjack Crowe wanted bans on Britpop, chocolate humbugs, pet cats, tobacco, all spirituous liquors, Windmill girls, bingo and lotteries, spices and relishes, Sunday foot-ball, street-vendors of all kinds, the wireless after nine o'clock and any live music. Fortunes could be made in a world like that, where the most God-fearing citizen would be the slave of some harmless pursuit reclassified as an illicit vice.

'Go on, Orlando,' said Lytton. 'Tell it all. Who was this prisoner?'

There had been a beseeching in the man's eyes, a plea for help from this accidental co-passenger. Orlando had been trying not to remember it.

He could not lie to himself. Crowe's Britain would be briefly a paradise, but he wouldn't last long. He'd be ear-clipped, face-branded, cat-lashed and finally hung at Tyburn and put on show down at Execution Docks. Rotting corpses dangling in cages would be just about the only entertainment Strawjack Crowe would still permit.

'Whittington,' he said.

'The Lord Mayor Elect?' queried Jeperson. 'Impossible. This close to the Mayor-Making Ceremony at the Dome and the formal treaty with the Parliament of the Marches, he's in public practically all the day and night long.'

'It was him,' Orlando insisted. 'I've seen Whittington before, up close. I was in New Malden when he saw off the sheep-worriers. He can't be mistaken for anyone.'

Jeperson didn't argue any more.

Orlando was almost afraid about that. He was hoping that the man could come out with an explanation. The bus had been carrying a group of celebrity lookalikes to the Gaiety Theatre for a contest, and 'Whittington' was being nobbled by his stage rivals.

'You will pardon me,' said the Master of the Diogenes Club.

They were in a meeting room, which had obviously been abandoned in haste. Filing cabinets had their drawers pulled out and were full of the ash of destroyed documents. Jeperson swept the upright cradle phone off the table and tossed it into a corner, but dug out a canvas bag with a field telephone. He hooked the thing up to a wall-jack and cranked the handle. Then he dialled a number and turned away from them, walking into a corner and huddling to have a conversation.

Orlando looked at Lytton.

Now the secret was out, things should be different between them. Ideally, they could both leave, go their separate ways. Whatever the big picture was, it was Jeperson's business, an affair of state.

Orlando had good tips on the dogs. And a shipment of poppers coming in on a freighter from Spain. He had favours to collect, debts to pay, pots to stir and doxies to duck. He wanted to get back to his life, where Watchmen and coppers didn't like him much but weren't ordered to kill him on sight.

Lytton had reloaded his gun and filled all the loops on his ammo belt, out of the Diogenes Club's stash. Otherwise, he was no different. He wasn't tired and he wasn't excited.

Jeperson hung up.

'The Lord Mayor Elect has cancelled all his appointments until the Mayor-Making, pleading a sore throat. But he is very much in evidence, shaking hands and nodding.'

'It's not him,' said Orlando.

'No,' Jeperson agreed. 'It's not.'

'What's Crowe up to?' asked Lytton.

'Who can know? He's the type who has five different plans going at once, weaving in and out of each other. Just like me, in fact. After the Mayor-Making, the Lord Mayor will be the only real balance in the country. A strong capital means that the Parliament of the Marches will settle in Oxford or somewhere, and be able to ratify treaties with the Welsh, the Scots and the Cornish. If London were to, say, fall apart, then there would be another civil war, a short and brutal one. Crowe might want to puppet-master the Lord Mayor as well as the Prime Minister, keeping his hands up Punch and Judy as it were, maintaining the squabble as a distraction. He's got Arachnid in the mix to call on the Dianaheads, who are fanatics by nature and could well go Puritan, and he needs Daine and all his krewes – down to your old comrade-in-arms Rutland Stryng, Captain – on the street to apply the brute force he needs. Then again, he could intend something as blunt as having the "Mayor" discovered in the Savoy in bed with a Page 3 girl and

Julian Clary, hoping for an orchestrated outburst of public morality which will end in him accepting a mass call, untroubled by the messy business of an electoral mandate, to become the new Lord Protector.'

'Three days,' said Lytton.

Orlando missed the point.

'You are right, Captain.' Jeperson evidently didn't. 'The Doppelgänger Elect will show up at the Dome, for the Mayor-Making and the Ratification of the Treaty. Whatever Crowe is planning, that shindig is crucial.'

This was too huge to cope with.

Jeperson played with a quill, tapping the nib against his front teeth. He had shrugged off any drug daze, and was thinking faster than any man Orlando had ever known, and that included the most celebrated duckers and divers in the riskiest businesses in town.

'We must find the true Lord Mayor Elect. They can't ferry him around in a bus for ever, and if they were going to all the trouble of trussing him up they won't just have killed him and fed the body to the swine in the sewers. He'll be clapped up in a dungeon somewhere, head wrapped in that BDSM hood you mentioned. Probably haven't got everything they need out of the poor blighter yet. I voted for him, you know. He was the only candidate with a grasp of public transport. That's what keeps a great city alive. The Diogenes Club is not what it was, and we can no longer call on our renowned network of agents or the favour of those in high places. We have been repudiated by everyone we served, the Parliament, the Assembly, the Crown. But we are not abandoned, not alone. Besides we three, there are others we can call on. A little battered perhaps, but aren't we all?'

'"We three"?'

Jeperson raised hawk-wing eyebrows. It had not occurred to him that Orlando might want to leave.

'For self-preservation, if nothing else,' said Jeperson.

'Stryng's a head-collector,' said Lytton, impersonally. 'If there's a purse on you, he'll keep trying for it. Even if there isn't, he'll have to take you down to keep his standing in the community. He's never lost a quarry yet; if you become "the one that got away", his career hits a major setback. Your only chance for safety is to see this through.'

Orlando remembered the bullet-hole eyes of Rutland Stryng.

The field-telephone rang; Jeperson answered it, listened, thanked, and hung up.

'By the way, you're both wanted for murder,' he said.

'The conductors?' asked Lytton.

'No, they'll have been shadow folk, spirited away to unmarked graves without so much as a telegram to the wives. You two are sought for severe questioning in connection with the extermination of an entire patrol of the Pimlico Neighbourhood Watch. Shot the lot of 'em dead, including some dotty Dianahead whose mug is all over the *Standard*, along with glowering portraits of the desperate fiends. There are ballads on the street already about the dastardly deed.'

'Stryng,' said Lytton.

Jeperson shrugged and said, 'Looks like you're in with us, Goodman Boldt.'

Orlando saw no other way out of it. Damnation.

Jeperson produced a black book out of a concealed drawer.

'I must have neglected to incinerate this. Quel domage!'

With a long forefinger, he turned the pages.

'Dead, dead, dead, inactive, dead, retired, turned traitor, found Diana, incarcerated... all our favourite tools seem to be unavailable... two more deads, another retired, "head-hunted by the Yankees", ugh! Inactive, permanently hospitalised, dead, ah-hah, here's your name, Goodman Boldt. Still at the crib in Streatham, I'll wager? Under the name of McTavish? Didn't think anyone knew that, did you? Dead, dead... a possibility. Richard Lionheart "Pitbull" Brittan. Frightfully thick, but patriotic. Remarkable in some ways. I'd prefer not to use him, but it seems we can't be choosy. Dead, inactive, imprisoned, circus freak... this is fairly tiresome, isn't it?'

Orlando had heard of 'Pitbull' Brittan. Seven feet tall, muscles like oak, a real have-a-go hero. In fact, Orlando had once been an errand boy for a gent by the name of Skinner, whose dope ring this Brittan had single-handedly smashed. The fellow was an amateur, and tended to run off the leash. Orlando wouldn't have bet on him against Lytton, let alone someone like Stryng.

Jeperson came up with and rejected a few more outlandish names, Buck Breakfast, 'Corporal Punishment' (the Right Wing Tory super-hero), Constant Drache, Harald Kleindeinst. There were even a few women on the list: Mimsy Mountmain, Jenny Godgift. Orlando knew who some of these people were and had vaguely heard of others. A couple came as complete surprises, since he'd have sworn them to be crooked through and through and not even remotely reliable. Then, Jeperson shut the book.

'Should have burned it, after all. Less depressing.'

'So we're stuffed?' Orlando said.

'Stuffed-ish, rather. There are the usual channels, the police and the law courts and dull fellows like that. The likes of which you must have to deal with on a depressingly regular basis, Goodman Boldt. Then, there are the extraordinary channels, essentially us and them – the Diogenes Club and other Secret Organisations, and the conspirators we find ourselves facing. Unevenly matched at present, but still a game we can all play and understand.'

Orlando was getting fed up with the lectures.

'And after the usual channels and the extraordinary channels, things get pretty hairy. That's when we have to send up the Black Rocket.'

Lytton's hands became fists and he drew in his breath.

That reaction told Orlando more than he knew.

'Desperate times, Captain,' said Jeperson, 'desperate remedies.'

'Excuse me, but "the Black Rocket"? I've never heard of him.'

'It's not a him, it's a signal. On the roof. It's been there for years, never fired. But it's been maintained. It's a last resort.'

'He can't still be alive,' said Lytton.

Jeperson shrugged.

'Who are you talking about?'

'Shade,' said Lytton.

'The one and only, the original, accept no substitutes,' said Jeperson.

'Doctor Shade?'

They had to be spoofing him. The man, if Dr Shade were a man, was a myth, like Spring-Heel'd Jack, the Rat King or the Monk of Mitre Square, like the angel chariots the yokels said made crop circles. Dr Shade had never been real, even if he had been seen over the years; he came from an old wireless serial, hundreds of comic papers, a music hall illusionist act. All the stories Orlando had heard of him were just stories.

'Let's go up to the roof,' said Jeperson.

The fog was thin up here, the air almost breathable. Orlando saw the hulks of the taller buildings rising from yellow-ochre swamp, rooftops like islands, spires like masts. Over to the north, the BBC's weather dirigible was gliding through clouds.

Jeperson expertly dismantled a fake pigeon-coop, tossing aside decoy birds. A sleek, razor-finned dart, about four feet long, stood upright, supported by a wicker gantry. Jeperson unsheathed a length of twisted blue touch-paper and checked that it was dry.

'All in order,' he said, producing a silver box of lucifers. He struck one and lit the paper. 'We should get out of the way,' he said. 'Probably should have mentioned that earlier. This has never been fired before, so I don't know how forceful the blast is likely to be.'

The paper fizzed and burned.

Orlando, Lytton and Jeperson backed away.

Infernal flame spurted from the rocket's fundament, belching thick black smoke in a radius of ten feet. For seconds, Orlando thought the firework was going to explode before taking off, but it rose slowly from the gantry, farted out another flower of fire – and an invisible cloud of heat which washed over them – and streaked upwards. The BBC's dirigible should be grateful not to be in the way.

'Lord God Almighty,' said Jeperson. 'It really is black.'

The rocket left a thick trail. It seemed not to be smoke, but actual black flame, which Orlando had never seen before and couldn't understand.

High above the city, the rocket exploded, leaving a black cloud shaped vaguely like a skull.

'Someone will have seen that,' said Jeperson. 'Let's hope the Good Doctor is in.'

'Good?' queried Lytton.

'Figure of speech, old fellow.'

Half the stories of Dr Shade had him as a heroic saviour, but the rest had him as a fiend incarnate. Orlando worried that the man might be both.

They waited, and nothing happened. A faint disappointment, but not unexpected. It wasn't as if they were summoning a demon from Hell; if Dr Shade was real, he had to live somewhere, and would take a while to get to the Diogenes Club. He might be in the bath, or something. Or listening to *The Archers*.

'Look,' said Lytton, pointing towards the Palace of Westminster, at St Stephen's Tower. There, Benjamin Vulliamy's clock – named after the bell that used to hang in the tower, Big Ben – kept time in sync with the Royal Observatory. Until now.

'The clock-face,' Lytton elaborated.

The hands of Big Ben spun too swiftly, like a watch being set. The chimes, imitating those of St Mary's church in Cambridge, sounded. The notes were familiar, but there was a different quality, a strength, to the bell-chimes. It was as if Orlando were hearing them for the first time.

'Of course,' said Jeperson. 'Where else would the Shadow-Lair be?'

The hands of all the faces stood straight up. A bell sounded twelve midnight, in the middle of the morning. The black skull in the sky came apart and spread, like a carpet of night, over the city.

The nearest face of the clock irised open, and a buzzing black metal insect emerged, hovering momentarily over the Palace, doubtless attracting the interest of Assemblymen and their hangers-on, then came straight towards the Diogenes Club. The insect was an autogiro, its shrouded black blades whipping through the fog-trails.

As it neared, Orlando saw the vehicle's passenger.

A man all in black: a cloak-like gloss-black coat over jet-black surgeon's vestments, beetle-black goggles under a matt-black broad-brimmed felt hat. He seemed to carry blackness with him like an aura, absorbing all imaginable light.

Jeperson whistled. Orlando suppressed an urge to run away.

The autogiro touched down on the roof. Dr Shade flowed off its saddle-like seat. His boots made no sound on the shingle, his clothes didn't rustle. He seemed to glide towards them.

Orlando's heart was ice. He was grateful for the Doctor's goggles, for he dreaded to think what this man's – this creature's – eyes might be like.

'Richard Jeperson,' said the Master of the Diogenes Club, extending a very white-looking hand towards the black figure. 'As you must have gathered from our deployment of the Black Rocket, things have come to a pretty pass.'

Dr Shade said nothing but a thought-groove appeared in his brows, between goggles and hat-brim. He took Jeperson's hand in his black leather glove. His mouth was a thin white line which gave nothing away.

'It falls, I'm afraid, to us,' continued Jeperson, 'to save a man, the city, the country. All that is enlightened and clear and decent has failed. Now, we must turn to the dark, the night, the shade.'

The black figure gave nothing away.

'I know you,' said Dr Shade. His human voice sounded artificial, as if the sounds of the Big Ben chimes were scrambled and processed to make words. 'I know you all three. Richard Jeperson, of the Ruling Cabal. Captain James Lytton. Goodman Orlando Boldt.'

Absolute terror clawed at Orlando: this walking embodiment of night knew his name, probably his address and every rotten thing he'd ever done. If he got off this roof alive, he'd become a Sally Army singer.

'I understand the situation. I have been observing it all.'

'You know?' said Lytton, in disbelief. 'Why haven't you done anything about it?'

Dr Shade showed empty hands.

'Nothing escapes my ken, but it would be a wearisome task to prevent all evil. In the past, my methods have proved unpopular. Too often, society wishes for an evil to continue, even to thrive. Even now, many might deem good the conspiracy you stand against, and consider you – an indulgent decadent, a bloody-handed warrior and a denizen of the lowest stratum of the city – of the Devil's Party.'

'Enough,' snapped Lytton. 'Will you help us, yes or no?'

'All you have to do is ask, and accept the consequences.'

Lytton was given pause. He stood as tall as the Doctor, and was less awed by the man inside the blackness. Beside Lytton, it was clear – as it was not if Orlando looked away – that the Doctor was a man, that there was someone inside the costume. Was this the same Dr Shade whose exploits Orlando had read of in *British Pluck* as a shaver? Or some new inheritor of the name and role? It was impossible to guess the Doctor's age.

'I ask,' said Jeperson. 'I am prepared.'

'All of you?'

'Yes,' said Lytton. 'I ask too.'

Dr Shade looked into Lytton's eyes, and nodded. Then he swivelled and looked at Orlando. The eyes behind the goggles were faintly visible, burning with a black light beyond ordinary black, a violet so rich it was poison.

'You have to say it,' Jeperson said.

Once let loose, what would Dr Shade not do?

Orlando remembered the Man on the Clapham Omnibus, and all he had promised for the city. And that he was wanted for a hanging offence.

He swallowed. 'All very well, lads, but what's in it for me?'

'I let you live,' said Lytton.

Orlando's hands were trembling.

'No fair, guv. Look at you, you're all great men, part of the big story. I'm not. I'm what Dark-Doc said, "a denizen of the lowest stratum of the city". I don't want too much law and order, just as I don't want too much blood and thunder. I've gone against my gut and done my duty, by coming here, by telling you what I saw. I could have sold the information, you know. All over the show. I could have been owed favours by Daine, which would open doors for me. I've dodged the gallows before, and can do it again. No, I've already played your game. It's time for me to pack up and go home, to let you get on with rescuing the princess and restoring democracy or whatever it is you people get off on. I'm not stopping you, but I'm not being a part of it either. I'm not being Squire to any Noble Knight.'

Dr Shade said nothing, made no argument. He turned towards his autogiro.

Lytton's eyes blazed fury. Jeperson was aghast, unable to understand Orlando's point.

Dr Shade slid on to the saddle, and checked switches. The blades lazily began to revolve, which made tall men like Lytton and Jeperson duck.

As he completed the start-up protocol, Dr Shade looked a last time at Orlando. His goggles were transparent, it seemed. Twin ultra-black beams shone through.

Orlando's tricorn was whipped from his head by bladewash and skipped over the side of the roof, spinning like a plate.

An abyss opened in his heart. It was not imposed on him, but came from within. He made a choice, a hard choice.

'I ask,' he said, squeaking. 'I ask Dr Shade to help.'

Relief and dread commingled. His trick knees were knocking. He still didn't know if what he had just done was for the best, or even for the right. But he had done it, and he would stand by it.

The blades of the autogiro slowed to a halt.

'Very well,' said Dr Shade. 'Let us consider our course of action.'

Two nights later, Orlando rowed a small boat through Traitors' Gate. At least, he was confident it was the gate he was passing through. Night and fog made it impossible to confirm that by his eyes.

Dr Shade, in one of his habitual mysterious pronouncements, had said they would find the true Lord Mayor Elect where the fog was thickest. The BBC Home Service, with its roving dirigible, reported that the pea-soup was unusually concentrated around the Tower of London. Further enquiries, as Jeperson pestered his few remaining government contacts, revealed that Strawjack Crowe had recently taken over the public commission on the administration of the Tower, instituting a purge of the Yeoman Warders and bringing in a new breed of beefeater. Bush telegraph had it that these fellows were not the Puritans one might expect, but double-dyed ruffians of the sort most associated with the fog's master, Truro Daine.

The Doctor was up in the air somewhere, ravens flapping around his whirlybird. Jeperson was leading a cadre of Diogenes loyalists along the riverbanks. But it had fallen to Orlando and Lytton to make covert approach to the Tower from the Thames itself. This was not the first time he had been on the river at night, rowing with muffled oars. Much of the black economy was conducted this way, in midnight exchanges between boats floating between the ships at dock.

Orlando was disguised with an enormous false beard and a Yeoman Warder uniform that hung loose on him, while Lytton wore an executioner's hood, doublet and tights. The fog was so thick here that dressing up as anything was beside the point, but Jeperson had insisted the full resources of the Diogenes Club's fancy dress department be called upon. Lytton even carried a headsman's axe, with a wicked half-moon blade.

'Who goes there?' boomed a voice.

'Good men and true,' responded Orlando.

For a queasy second, he was sure Jeperson's sources had secured the wrong passwords.

'Pass, good men and true.'

'That we will,' he muttered, and rowed harder.

The tooth-like projections of the raised portcullis loomed through the fog. Lytton had to duck as the boat passed under the spears and through the mouth-like gate. The river was high.

Under his hood, Lytton wore a breather. Orlando had to rely on nose-plugs and goggles.

Orlando put his oars up and they drifted into the sunken courtyard. Stone walls rose all around, enclosing and containing. A hefty beefeater awaited at the mooring-quay, face red as his tunic.

'What's all this? There've been no orders.'

Orlando waved an oilskin packet.

'Most confidential,' he said. 'From the top. It's about Little Ease.'

The beefeater stiffened at the phrase. Another victory for Dr Shade's mysterious intelligence sources. Little Ease was the oldest, smallest cell in the Tower – a four-foot-square stone cube in which it was impossible to stand or lie comfortably. At present, it was home to a masked man.

Orlando hopped out of the boat, and Lytton climbed carefully on to the stone dock, hefting his axe. The warder looked at the black-edged packet and the executioner, and shrugged as if he had been expecting this all along.

'We've a pole ready for his head, sirrah,' he said.

'Good man,' Orlando commented.

Up close, he recognised the warder. Benjamin Crude, a cut-purse and battery man from Cheapside. His uniform didn't fit either. The last Orlando heard, Crude was working for Truro Daine, duffing up club DJs for protection money.

Crude led the way into the Tower, a thousand-year-old fortress keep of Caen limestone, Kentish ragstone and baked Thames mud. Braziers burned in the corridors at regular intervals, but this was an impossible place to warm. Through his shoe-soles, Orlando felt icy flags. The black walls were wet. The fires were yellowish, fog-coloured. Threads of fog hung up to knee-height, like mustard gas.

Orlando's cheek tickled as spirit gum gave way. He slapped his face, sticking his beard back with little more than sweat. Crude turned and looked at him.

'Mosquito,' he said. 'Bastards.'

The beefeater accepted it.

'We're to be quick about this,' Orlando said. 'Whip him out sharpish and into the boat, then off to the chopping block.'

Crude held the sealed packet, which he hadn't yet examined. Inside were authentic-looking orders, full of the correct code-words and euphemisms. The envelope was even impregnated with gunpowder for instant disposal. A touch of a lucifer, and all the evidence was gone – just the way Crowe and Daine liked it.

'I'll have to get confirmation over the phone,' said Crude. 'There's one by the cell.'

Orlando bit a mouthful of beard.

By the door of Little Ease, a cupboard-like hatch, stood two more warders, otherwise Oisin Murphy-Lawless, the three-fingered Kentish Town safecracker, and Con Williams, the Hoxton Bruiser (Undefeated By Fair Means or Foul). Crude unsealed the orders, looked them over by the light of a sconced electric bulb, then went to a stand and began the business of putting a phone call through channels.

Orlando was sure his beard was coming off.

'Lovely weather, eh, lads?' he ventured.

Murphy-Lawless looked at him as if he were scum, which was at least comfortingly familiar. The Irishman was famous as the worst karaoke performer in north London: his rendition of 'I Met Her in the Garden Where the Praties Grow' could clear out the Assembly Rooms before he got to the chorus. The Bruiser's gently vacant smile didn't waver. His brains were so scrambled that little got through to him; you could saw his leg off and he wouldn't remember to feel pain until after he'd tied you in a hitch-knot and pulled you so tight your eyes popped out.

Lytton heaved his axe from one shoulder to the other.

Orlando wondered when the Captain would move.

'Daine is coming down,' said Crude.

'Better tidy up before he gets here,' Orlando suggested, nodding at the 'orders'.

Crude accepted the idea and fished a fag-lighter out of a pouch under his bloomers. Behind his fog-goggles, Orlando shut his eyes.

Flame touched the packet and the whole thing went up in a noxious magnesium flare that burned light even through Orlando's goggles and eyelids.

The three beefeaters coughed and stumbled. Opening his eyes, Orlando saw them flailing, the door guards reaching for pikes, and got out of the way.

Lytton held the axe like a golfclub and swung it through a powerful arc. The blade lodged in the door of Little Ease, splitting it in two. He pried it out and chopped again, smashing the thick, solid wood to fragments and splinters.

Crude had a pistol out, but lost it when Orlando noosed cheesewire around his wrist. The envelope was on the floor, still burning brightly enough to leave squiggles in vision. The blinded warders hammered away at each other, yelling. Murphy-Lawless was screaming in pain, which was easier on the ears than his 'She Sits Among the Cabbages and Peas'. Orlando had never lost betting on the Hoxton Bruiser, and would've laid money on him right now had he not been busy with other concerns.

People were coming.

No one crawled out of Little Ease. Lytton nodded his hooded head at the open door, shrugging apologetically. He was too broad of shoulder to go in there.

Orlando went on his hands and knees, ripping his tights open on splinters, and looked into the cell. He hoped the prisoner wasn't chained.

'Come on out, Your Worship,' he shouted.

A shape moved inside. The fizzing fire lit up the squalid interior of the cell. A ragged man, recognisable by the bondage hood Orlando had seen on the bus in Clapham, shrank in abject terror.

'We're rescuers, sirrah,' Orlando said, not even convincing himself. 'Shift your arse.'

The prisoner made no move, pressing himself against the far stone wall.

Orlando tore off his bloody beard, taking strips of his skin with it. He showed his face.

'Remember me?'

Whittington did and crawled out of the cell. He tried to stand, but his limbs wouldn't work. Orlando knew how that felt. He took hold of the man and hauled him upright. The hood prevented him from making any sound beyond a muffled grunt. He wore the remains of a smart-ish business suit, fouled by captivity. If Strawjack Crowe could see the Lord Mayor Elect, he'd have clapped him in jug again as an unsightly vagrant.

Lytton kept Crude down with the blunt end of his axe.

Suddenly, the weather was indoors. The corridor filled with serious fog.

A shape came through the murk, clanking.

Truro Daine wore some kind of armoured diving suit, with an apparatus on its back that produced fog, which fed into his helmet – the face-plate showed yellow features and eyes – and belched out into the atmosphere. It was the foulest fog Orlando had ever known, making his nose and eyes sting and water even through plugs and goggles. He found himself clinging to Whittington for support, which had not been the idea.

'You will all die,' croaked Daine, through a voice-box.

With Daine, fog-masked, was a familiar man in a Puritan coat and feathered hat. Rutland Stryng, the murderer. He raised a pistol and drew a bead. Orlando knew this would happen. Before he died, he'd probably be tortured.

Lytton kicked Crude away and swung his axe again.

Stryng shifted swiftly but Daine, bulky and encumbered, couldn't move as fast. The axe whispered past his head, glancing off an iron shoulder-pad and striking sparks from the wall. Daine staggered under the blow but didn't seem hurt. Orlando saw Lytton had cut through the tubes of his fog-making device. Coils of foul smoke poured forth from the severed ends. Daine thrashed about in the corridor, drowning in clean air.

Orlando knew it was time to retreat and dragged the freed prisoner away.

A shot was fired, wildly. Stryng.

Lytton tossed his axe back at the Yeomen and ran. The three of them made it to the jetty and the boat. Shouts and confusion were all around.

Orlando and Lytton rowed, bunched up ridiculously side-by-side on the bobbing boat, taking an oar each. Orlando heard vast grating and clanking. The spiked gate was coming down. He saw the sharp points touch disturbed waters.

'Nothing else for it,' said Lytton. 'Hold tight, everyone.'

The Captain threw himself to one side, leaving go of his oar. The boat capsized and Orlando found himself under water, his head in the bubble of trapped air, clinging to the bench he had been sitting on.

The upturned wooden hull jammed against the descending gate-points. A spear-tip punched through and grazed Orlando's forehead. Water rose as air escaped and he got a throatful. His noseplugs were uncomfortably jammed into his nostrils, but at least the goggles meant he could vaguely see under water.

He let go of the bench and kicked his way under the gate-points, swimming through Traitors' Gate. Lytton was behind him, moving easily and powerfully through the water, dragging the Lord Mayor Elect. From the depths, Orlando saw lights streaking above, and made for them.

After what seemed like hours, he broke the surface of the river. His lungs felt as if they had been torn apart from the insides and his heart hammered like a clockwork blacksmith under a tight deadline. He was probably infected with a combination of awful diseases.

The Tower was under attack from the sky and the riverbank. Incendiaries rained down from the dark. Volleys fired from entrenched positions. Dr Shade and Richard Jeperson were distracting the Yeoman Warders.

Orlando found Lytton and Whittington, thrashing to stay afloat. Lytton had shaken off his headsman's hood, but the Lord Mayor Elect was still strapped into his mask.

'Let's get out of the water,' Lytton suggested.

'Yes,' agreed Orlando, 'let's.'

The Fire Brigade had turned up at the Diogenes Club a good ten minutes before the blaze started, and kept the public back while they squirted burning oil through the upstairs windows. Jeperson had been prepared to abandon the Pall Mall site, just as Dr Shade could no longer return to his clockwork cocoon inside Big Ben. Orlando understood three men had been killed tampering with the device, cut apart by the booby traps the Doctor had installed over the years.

They were all fugitives, now. An entire charity school in Muswell Hill had undergone Recovered Memory Therapy and alleged Richard Jeperson had been molesting them, with black candles and Satanic robes, since infancy. The Prime Minister had cheerfully re-opened the enquiry into the Siege of Manchester, with a view to stripping Lytton of his VC and shifting the blame for the unfortunate events away from Rutland Stryng. Jeperson was now of the opinion that the PM was completely the creature of Strawjack Crowe, grinning like a Cheshire Cat as his supposed hatchet man gave him orders. The Parliament of the Marches was still intent on withholding the franchise from anyone but home-owners of proven British parentage.

Orlando nestled uncomfortably between stiff mannequins of Neville Heath and Neall Cream, in a vault under the Madame Tussaud's Chamber of Horrors. Here, less memorable murderers – whose infamy never matched that of Crippen or Jack the Ripper – were shunted for a while, before removal to Wookey Hole. The enemy hadn't tracked them to this cramped lair, which was one of Shade's fall-backs.

The Lord Mayor Elect sat in a bath-chair salvaged from the home of John Reginald Halliday Christie, while an attractively mousy woman named Miss Rhodes, skirt daringly cut above her ankles, snipped the clasps and catches on his bondage hood with a pair of dressmaker's scissors. Miss Rhodes was one of the Diogenes Club loyalists who had responded to Jeperson's general alert, which meant she probably knew seven ways to end a man's life with one slip of the scissors.

Lytton, Jeperson and Dr Shade stood to one side, heads bowed by the low brickwork ceiling. Orlando noticed they tended to hang together, though Lytton was still wary of the Doctor. Close to the shadow man, Lytton and Jeperson tended to be touched with his darkness, almost pulled in. The Doctor believed in radical surgery, which was always uncomfortable.

'There now,' said Miss Rhodes.

The leather mask was loose.

What if Orlando had been wrong? What if the hood came away to disclose not Lord Mayor Elect Whittington but some dire stranger who'd deservedly been clapped into the lowest, darkest dungeon in the kingdom?

It didn't. The Lord Mayor Elect blinked, blinded even in the gloom. Dr Shade stepped in, and examined Whittington's face, holding up a finger and asking the man to focus. Orlando found it strange that this dark-shrouded avenger could also act like a proper doctor.

The Lord Mayor Elect looked as if he had passed from the hands of one malevolent conspiracy into another. Orlando understood how he might feel that way, surrounded by wax murderers and real-live creatures of the night.

'Sirrah, I'm Richard Jeperson, late of the Diogenes Club.'

'What day is it?' asked the Lord Mayor Elect. 'How long was I locked away?'

It was not the first question Orlando would have asked, but he wasn't a politician.

Jeperson understood. 'It's only been three days. The Mayor-Making is not until this evening. We shall get you to the Dome on time.'

Whittington indicated his filthy clothes.

'I'm not dressed for it.'

'You have the pick of a store of fine, if sombre suits. I hope it doesn't discomfit you that they were all previously worn by murderers. You look to be about the same size as the Brides in the Bath fellow, and he was reckoned a spiffy dresser.'

'Fair enough.'

At the end of it, Orlando was back where he was supposed to be, in the crowd.

The Dome, that giant cow-pat in Greenwich, was tarted up like Christmas, New Year's Eve, Trooping the Colour, Derby Day, a Boyzone Ritual Suicide Concert, a Savoy Opera and the Cup Final rolled into one. A thousand miles of flags, ten thousand tons of statuary and a million candles of electric light, and all on a colossal scale. From a distance, the Dome looked like the aftermath of an air disaster featuring a collision between titanic angel chariots; from inside, it was impossible to know where to look, with such a wealth of detail and decor that many of the crowd were struck with the fits characteristic of the Stendhal Syndrome. It was a promised land for pickpockets, programme sellers, souvenir manufacturers and fly-by-night food and beverage merchants.

Each delegation arrived in choreographed splendour: the Scots in a skirl of bagpipes and with Sean Connery at their head; the Welsh with a male-voice choir and a dancing troupe of pretty leek-hatted Blodwyns; the Cornish in full tin armour, their Royals in blue body-paint. The Prime Minister was backed up by a cross-party collection of Members of Parliament, in identical shiny, tight, bright suits, with identical shiny, tight, bright smiley-faces. Stark-vestmented Puritans among the MPs acted like sergeants among raw recruits, snapping orders and inflicting instant punishments for infractions.

The business of the evening was the Mayor-Making, with the Queen confirming Whittington or the Nearest Offer in position as duly elected Lord Mayor of London, Convener of the City Assembly and Chief Constable of the Metropolitan Police. Then, it was to be the first official action of the new Lord Mayor to ratify the treaty that would bring the smoke – along with the jocks, taffs and pasties – back into the country-wide administration of the Parliament of the Marches. To get all the parties to the table, the Prime Minister had made so many concessions that the overall power of his government was reduced in essence to an advisory capacity. And a good job too, Orlando thought, looking at the waxy-faced, fire-eyed PM. The man's constant smile, snide in every sense of the term, reminded him of the murderers' mugs in Tussaud's back-up Chamber of Horrors.

In among the general populace, mostly overawed to be inside such a giant structure and in the presence of so many VIPs, Orlando picked up on the tensions of the moment. There were a lot of peelers, uniformed and otherwise, and even more unofficial hard-nuts. Among the Puritans, forming a guard for Strawjack Crowe, was Rutland Stryng, his Webley slung in a holster on the front of his broad belt. Stryng's eyes ranged constantly over the crowd, and Orlando took care not to be wherever they were directed.

One wrong word from the platform, and…

The Dome was a famous folly, which the various factions who had gained momentary power during the Civil War blamed on each other. It contained exhibitions in celebration of British achievement, mounted tattily at a point when the country's main achievement was tearing itself apart. The project had been initiated in a time of plenty and allotted a vastly bloated budget, but its construction had dragged on, interrupted by the worst of the fighting, and had been rushed to completion, years after the deadline, by the Prime Minister's order that everything be done on the cheap. One reason for the crowd tension was the possibility that the whole structure would collapse on itself. Every brickie and plasterer in the land had charged double-overtime on this scam, at a time when they were really needed to rebuild the towns and cities more or less levelled by battles. They had still done a dodgy job Orlando's DIY-crazed Uncle Fred would have laughed at.

He saw Miss Rhodes, dolled up significantly, wearing a straw hat with a 'Votes for Women' band. He hoped she still had her scissors. Jeperson had salted the crowd with his own people, but so many agents of so many factions were here that Orlando wondered if any real people had slipped in by mistake.

The lights dimmed, and Strawjack Crowe took the stage.

No official business could be conducted in the land until prayer had been given, which was how Crowe managed to get top billing at any ceremony. Even the wireless weather forecast had to start with a lengthy blessing.

'Lord God's Will be done in this Kingdom,' pronounced Crowe, in tones suitable for a public execution. 'Obedience to His design is Our Lot, lest we be cast down into the Burning Pit of Chaos.'

Then Elaine Paige sang 'Amazing Grace'. Crowe glared from the wings, like a man who knew he would in the morning have the power to ban all singing of any sort for ever.

The Prime Minister bounced on stage, smile cutting into his cheeks, and greeted the Lord Mayor Elect with a hearty hug and a pumping handshake.

From back here, Orlando couldn't tell if it was the real Whittington. If so, it was a miracle he didn't try to throttle the PM.

Then Ben Elton did five minutes of inoffensive jokes about father-hood and fridges. People looked in their programmes to see if it was permitted to laugh.

The Queen descended from the eaves on a Peter Pan harness, look-ing radiantly furious in white. She was spotlit against a three-storey image of the Sainted Diana, and the National Anthem quickly segued into Elton John's 'Hymn to a Princess'. Among the ranks of dignitaries on stage, Geodfroy Arachnid sent out a million watts of smug hypocrisy.

The Archbishop of London and a couple of pages came on stage, with the Lord Mayor's ceremonial robes and chains. The Archbish muttered something that wasn't sufficiently amplified, and the kids weighed the Lord Mayor Elect down with the full kit, which he assumed. The Queen hung the chain of office around the man's neck.

'Now,' said Crowe, 'Lord Mayor Whittington has an announcement.'

The new-made Lord Mayor took a wireless-mike, and declared that the London Assembly was dissolved and subordinated to the Parliament of the Marches, and that the military might of the capital was at the disposal of the Prime Minister for the subjugation of the rebellious provinces.

Sean Connery growled, and five rugby players in Metropolitan Police uniforms jumped on him. Orlando thought that the Scotsman had been scalped, but it was just his rug falling off.

The Lord Mayor continued to outline a programme which included the appointment of three Puritans as the city's Entertainments Licensing Commission; the recriminalisation of buggery, gaming and mendicancy; the contracting-out of public transport, policing and health services to private enterprise or charity; and the replacement of the Monarch with a theological figurehead known as the Pontiff of Diana.

Ben Elton laughed, and Rutland Stryng shock-prodded him into catatonia.

The Lord Mayor ordered the Welsh delegates to turn out their pockets and give back the silverware.

Orlando was certain this wasn't Whittington.

The Prime Minister beamed fit to bust his tummy-buttons, and Strawjack Crowe whispered orders to his cadre of Puritan heavies. Ripples of discontent spread through the crowd, but any protests were stifled by Puritans with hammers, Dianaheads with lamé garrotes or policemen with shock-prods.

Orlando saw Miss Rhodes punched in the midriff by a Puritan Elder who upbraided her as a vile strumpet of Babylon, citing the disgusting shortness of her skirt. He tore off her hat and stamped on it.

'Now, now,' said the PM. 'All's fair. This was voted on. We must respect the will of the people.'

'What people?' someone shouted.

'Our people,' said the PM. 'We know best. It's very encouraging Mr Whittington has recognised that. Now, I think it would be super if we could all join in prayer. Let us look up to Heaven with thanks for His guidance.'

The roof of the Dome ruptured.

Everyone did look up.

A blinding streak shot down at the stage, and smote the Lord Mayor. His robes burned in an instant, his face and flesh melted like wax. His still-standing skeleton was a blackened armature of wire and clockwork.

The burning Mayor began his speech again, stuttering.

'He's artificial,' came a shout. 'He's a clockwork waxwork!'

A black shape came down through the hole in the roof. Dr Shade's autogiro. The Doctor hovered beneath banks of lights, casting a thousand stark shadows on the stage and the crowd. The electric cannon that had blasted the automaton was good for only one charge at a time, so a half-dozen other weapons came into play. The autogiro spat projectiles and darts from an assortment of black tubes, while spraying out liquids that turned in mid-air into sticky nets.

Burning holes burst across the giant Diana portrait. Black smoke-bombs exploded inside the Dome. The Prime Minister's smile froze, but Crowe was jumping around, giving orders.

Following Dr Shade's autogiro came a rain of men in fatigues, abseiling down to the stage. Jeperson's people.

Dr Shade zoomed about, crashing through a giant papier mâché butterfly, hurling fiery darts with accuracy. Orlando saw Geodfroy Arachnid, who was sighting a blow-pipe at the Queen, speared off his tiered seat. He was stuck to the giant Diana-mouth, which seemed to suck him through into limbo as the image tore.

There was panic and brawling all around.

Orlando hid under an overturned whelk stall. Rough hands pulled him out, and he found himself looking up close at the angry face of Rutland Stryng.

'I remember you,' he said. 'This is all your fault.'

'You're a professional, aren't you?'

Stryng nodded.

'No more pay packets,' Orlando said.

On stage, Strawjack Crowe was jittering, a thousand shadow-darts in his face and torso. Strange little hypodermic needles stuck in and emptied into the bloodstream. Orlando didn't like to think what the Doctor had filled them with.

'You don't have a bounty here,' Orlando said.

'I agree. But I have a hostage.'

'There's always that.'

Stryng's Webley was at Orlando's temple.

'Rutland Stryng,' came a shout.

Across the floor strode Captain Lytton.

'Here's where we find out,' muttered Stryng.

Without letting go of his hold on Orlando's throat, Stryng turned, sliding as much of his body behind Orlando as possible, extending his arm to fire. Lytton reached for his side-arm.

A shot roared past Orlando's ear.

Lytton stood still, as if shocked. Orlando, deafened, thought the whole mêlée had gone silent.

Then Stryng let him go.

Lytton holstered his pistol. Orlando looked over his shoulder and saw Stryng had taken a ball in the forehead. His knees gave out and he fell.

Noise rushed back into Orlando's head.

When the real Whittington appeared, everyone was grateful. The Prime Minister sweated gallons as he denied knowledge of the substitution. The Queen looked stern and pleased at once, posing in front of the still-burning Diana face. The Archbishop dug out the hot chain of office from the trashed automaton and handed it over.

Dr Shade disappeared into the night, leaving a great many fires and not a few deserving casualties. Orlando still didn't understand the shadowman, and had an unsettled feeling that his cure could be far worse than the disease a few years down the line. The city owed its continued independence, probably its continued existence, to a creature far beyond human notions of right and wrong. From now on, as in dark times long ago, the shade was upon London, and would be a final court of appeal for the desperate and the high-minded. And Orlando had asked him back.

Jeperson, in Union Jack tunic and boots, was in charge of rounding up the few reliable coppers and restoring order. He got everyone calm until Whittington could get on stage and apologise for the poor show. The true Lord Mayor made his real speech, which was greeted with cheers.

Orlando got out of the Dome.

He found Lytton, walking away.

'Thanks, Captain,' he said.

Lytton shrugged. 'Had to be done.'

'I think you clipped my ear.'

Lytton examined the wound.

'Your looks aren't spoiled.'

'Where are you going?'

Lytton looked away from the Dome, and said, 'Somewhere green. What about you?'

Orlando thought of slate and stone, tarmac and brick, shingle and concrete. And the shadow that had fallen upon the city.

'Green, ugh,' he said. 'Give me somewhere grey any day.'

The bodyguards

Esther Freud

Kate gripped the phone, pressing the receiver so hard against her ear it hurt. Lizzie's voice was urgent at the other end, describing the axe, the tip of it, how frightened she was when it slammed into her door.

'Where are you now?' Kate asked.

'At work.' Lizzie started to cry. 'I don't want to go home.'

'Well, you mustn't. Don't see him again. Just don't.'

Lizzie snuffled. 'Can I come round to you? Stay with you for a few days?'

'Of course.' Kate was still bristling. 'Yes,' she said, more softly, remembering Lizzie was coming to her for help. 'I'll be here. Just come whenever you can.'

Kate sat on the sofa, cradling the phone, wondering who she could ring now to pass on the gory news.

Kate lived alone in Belgravia at the far end of a narrow, cobbled mews. It was a tiny flat above a garage, where her father had lived before moving to Hong Kong. The flat looked dazzling when you first went in, all buttermilk and white, but as soon as you sat down on the ruined sofa and felt the icy breeze through the patio doors you realised the thin matt paint was an illusion and underneath everything was dilapidated and damp.

On one side of Kate there lived a chauffeur whose employer never seemed to need him to go out. Sometimes he'd stand for hours, polishing his dun-coloured car, hoping and waiting for his telephone to ring. Once Kate admired the car. She reached out to stroke the silver figure pirouetting on its nose, and before the man could warn her, before he could stop her hand, the little dancing model had shattered the air with an alarm. 'It's in case anybody steals it,' the chauffeur explained, and they watched as the figure spiralled down into a hole. On the other side of Kate the flat was empty, although the garage underneath was used for storing cars, and occasionally a bodyguard from the house owned by the Crown Prince of Kuwait would surreptitiously open the door and slip inside. The Crown Prince's bodyguards had assumed an

86

intimate relationship with Kate. They worked in shifts, manning the mouth of the mews twenty-four hours, seven days a week, so that Kate had to pass them every time she ventured in or out. At first they'd simply nodded to her, but soon they were exchanging muted greetings and now, only three months after moving in, they seemed to feel quite free to comment openly on every aspect of her life. Right from the start they'd taken against Edward. They raised their eyebrows at him, shaking their heads as if to say, 'What can you expect, Kate? What can you expect from life if you hitch up with a hopeless lot like him?' Kate didn't care. She was in love. She loved Edward's freckled hands, his red gold hair, the way he stretched out his long lean body in front of the gas fire. He read poetry to her and quoted lines from plays, and although he was himself from Macclesfield, he'd discovered secret parts of London, offering them up to Kate like jewels. He'd taken her to the Electric Cinema, where they signed petitions to stop it being closed, and early one morning he'd shaken her awake so that they could go to New Covent Garden and buy a box of flowers. They'd filled her flat with narcissi, white with orange frills, and the smell of the hundred bunches was so overwhelming they had to walk up to Hyde Park for air.

Lizzie arrived just after six, looking all powdery and soft. She was the prettiest girl Kate knew, without ever being beautiful, and she had the extraordinary ability to light up the colour of her clothes. Everything she wore always looked startling, as if the juxtaposition of her straw-berry hair brightened even the denim of a pair of jeans. Sometimes Kate sat and watched her as if she were a child, the fluffiness of her, the little wrinkled dents already furrowing her brow. But today her eyes were red from crying, her nose widened and sore. 'But where did he get the axe?' Kate asked, wanting to hear again how Dan had smashed it into the wood of her locked door. Lizzie smiled, despite herself, and told her how Dan sometimes used to wander out into the streets of Kilburn and find old furniture to chop up for a fire.

Kate ran a bath for Lizzie. Normally she would have stayed with her, chatting to her, watching as her pink shoulders slipped under the foam, but she felt strangely awed by her friend's experience, and didn't trust herself not to stare at the flowering green bruises that marked her legs and arms. Instead she went into the spare room and shook the blankets out over the bed. She was glad Lizzie had come to her for shelter.

Glad to feel sorry for someone else for a change, and she thought of the moment Edward had turned around and told her he couldn't pretend to be in love for a moment more. She'd stood and stared at him, pain clutching at her heart, and she thought how really he must hate her if he was prepared to let her walk past the bodyguards alone.

'When's Edward back anyway?' Lizzie asked as she leant into the bathroom with towels, and Kate closed her eyes against the lie and said it was probably next Sunday. Or the Sunday after that.

The next morning the bodyguards were waiting, smiling, wanting to be introduced to Kate's new friend. Lizzie blushed and smiled and chatted sweetly to them and Kate's heart sank to think that now they would all be bound together on even more intimate terms. 'We'll be late,' Kate urged her, afraid that they might tell, and pulling her out of the admiring throng they hurried round the creamy crescent and up towards the tube.

That afternoon Kate walked into Soho. She bought fresh pasta and homemade sauce, and as she wandered along Berwick Street she started planning what she would give Lizzie for desert. She even bought flowers, tulips, already drooping at the stem, and she caught a bus on Piccadilly, hoping to get home first. But when she did arrive there was a message on the answerphone saying Lizzie was going out with friends. She'd see her later, and if she was very late, she'd try not to wake her up when she came in. Kate felt stupidly disappointed. She stood beside the phone, biting her lip, and then it rang again, and hopeful suddenly Kate jumped to get it.

Kate was reading in bed when she heard the key turning in the lock. Lizzie looked flushed as if she had been running, and Kate thought she should warn her how the cobbles of the mews bit into your heels. 'Your Mum rang,' she said instead. 'Dan's been phoning there all day.'

Lizzie flushed a little and then went pale.

'It's all right.' Kate stretched a hand out to her. 'He'll never find you here.'

Lizzie nodded. She looked intently serious for a moment as if she was going to cry.

'You can sleep in here with me,' Kate said, moving over in the double bed, and Lizzie began to slip off her jeans. 'It's lucky Edward's away,' she said, and Kate breathed in her talcum powder scent, the city night-time smell of her still lingering on her hair. 'Goodnight,' they said, and laughing at the sound of their own voices so close together on the pillows, they turned and tried to hold themselves from falling towards each other in the bed.

Lizzie was in the bathroom, smiling, her face gleaming and made up. She had on a soft blue T-shirt and white trousers, and Kate understood what it must be like to be her mother, far away in Hampshire, unable to accept her little girl could love a man like Dan.

Kate sat up in bed. 'Tonight,' she said, 'let's us go out.'

Lizzie looked troubled. She was brushing her lion hair, twisting it round into a ponytail, catching the stray strands with a scarf.

'Mmm…' Lizzie looked unsure.

'It's all right,' Kate soothed her, 'we won't go anywhere near Kilburn. We could even eat right round the corner from here.'

On the way to the tube they talked about the escalating dangers of London. How eventually there would be nowhere safe to go. They couldn't go to Kilburn, obviously, and Kate had had two regrettable affairs in Kentish Town, which meant if she wanted to visit anyone in Archway she had to go right up to Jack Straw's Castle and across to Highgate through the Heath. Chelsea was out of bounds for Lizzie because of some man she'd once met in a club, and now, Kate thought, if she wanted to avoid Edward she must never cross the Thames at Vauxhall Bridge.

'See you later, then.' They kissed under the vaulted tunnel, before darting on to separate platforms for their trains.

Kate couldn't really avoid Vauxhall. She had a dentist there and a childhood friend at Camberwell School of Art. Sometimes she made detours past Edward's house, glancing up at the long front room he rented, and once, late at night, she stopped the taxi she was taking home and rang his bell. She stood there, trembling, spurred on by the engine rumbling behind, and when no one came to answer she felt flooded with misery and relief. That night she couldn't face the bodyguards, the way they peered into her face to see if she'd been crying, patting her shoulders and telling her 'There there', and so she made the taxi driver pull right into the mews and drop her at her door. They always resented it, the extra effort of trying to turn around, and sometimes to show how much they'd been inconvenienced they accelerated hard and reversed all the way out.

That afternoon Lizzie called from work to say she'd been asked to stay on late. She'd get something at a wine bar, quickly, and then just carry on. 'Can they do that?' Kate was outraged. 'Make you work late without warning?' But Lizzie said she really didn't mind. 'I'll see you, then,' she said breezily, and Kate got up to put a potato in the oven, wondering how she'd fill the time till it was baked.

'You know, one of those bodyguards is quite dishy,' Lizzie called from the bottom of the stairs, and Kate woke up with a start. She'd been sleeping on the sofa and one of the broken springs had jammed into her back. 'They've asked us to go out one night, for a drink.'

Kate looked at her to see if she was joking.

'It might be quite fun.' Lizzie put her head on one side. 'There are some funny old pubs round here. Some of them with restaurants.'

'Maybe,' Kate said, but it made her squirm to think of sitting with the bodyguards, pressed in against their quilted jackets, the fake fur fringes of their hoods, the redness of their knuckles, how well she knew them, how well they knew her.

'I suppose it's different for me.' Lizzie did a little skip, and then she frowned beseechingly. 'But Edward is away?'

Kate picked up the cold remainder of her baked potato, and scraped it into the bin beside the sink.

'I'm not sure,' she said, and she gave a little sniff.

'I think it could be fun,' and Lizzie sailed away into the bathroom to get washed.

'He's stopped calling.' It was Lizzie's mother. Her voice was low and frightened as if she was being watched.

'Is that good or bad?'

'What if she's seeing him again? If he's caught her coming out of work? What if…'

'No, no.' Kate had to stop her. 'It's over. Lizzie says she doesn't want anything to do with him any more.' Kate didn't know how much she knew. If she'd seen the evidence of the slaps and cuffs and mental torture Dan had inflicted on Lizzie before he picked up the axe.

Lizzie's mother sighed. 'I hope you're right.'

'I am. Don't worry, really,' and it cheered her up to give such sound advice.

Now, whenever Kate approached the arched mouth of the mews, the bodyguards seemed to strike up awkward poses, lounging against walls, smoking, shifting their legs and arms. 'Where's your friend, then? Deserted us, has she?' And they grinned at her, their mouths out of control. 'So we're off on a date, are we? Really, we can't wait.'

Kate thought of reporting them to the Crown Prince of Kuwait. Surely they couldn't be protecting him if they spent all their time harassing girls, but when she stopped to ask if there was anyone in, the bodyguard, the one Lizzie said was attractive, looked surprised and said the Crown Prince lived in Kuwait and only came to London a few days a year. He pointed out the gold leaf on the railings and explained how much each one was worth, and Kate understood it wasn't the man himself they were protecting, but the doorstep and the railings of his house.

'I've been invited away for the weekend by my boss.' Lizzie started laughing. 'Don't get the wrong idea. My boss is a woman.' There were lots of girls from the office going, but until then they hadn't thought to ask Lizzie because usually she was with Dan. 'It's some sort of golf hotel,' she laughed again, and she said she'd be back on Sunday.

'It's just strange.' Lizzie's mother whispered when she rang. 'Until this week she never had any time for those other girls at work.'

On Sunday Kate got up early and went to Brick Lane. It was drizzling and still dark and she felt foolish when she realised she was so early most of the stalls hadn't been set up. It was worse, she decided as she poked through curtains, worse being left alone by Lizzie, worse even than when Edward had told her not to phone. 'I just miss you,' she had said. 'Miss talking to you.' And after a long silence Edward had said there was really nothing he could say. They stayed like that, almost as if to prove it, until eventually, very carefully, Kate put down the phone.

The next night Kate didn't bother hurrying home. Instead she went to meet some friends at a tapas bar in Camberwell. She'd booked the place herself and the evening was a torture. Each time the door swung open she'd been unable to stop herself from glancing round, and once when she saw the stoop of a familiar shoulder, her heart had almost overturned. To cover up her agitation she'd been bright eyed and alive, and when they parted, her friends had congratulated her on her high spirits. 'God,' they'd said when they hugged her, 'you look so well.'

It was dark when she got home. The mews looked empty, and she stepped gingerly in, hoping to slip through without being seen.

'You've got a visitor,' a voice called out of the shadow, and as she turned she saw the red tips of two cigarettes. 'An unexpected guest.'

Kate felt her body startle, and she remembered suddenly that Edward had never given back his key. She rushed over the cobbles, not caring if she ruined her shoes, and it was true, there was a light on. As she pushed open the door a man stepped out of the kitchen. He looked down at her, smiling, his eyes ridiculously blue.

Kate shrank back against the door. 'It's all right.' Lizzie was beside her. 'It's all right, it's only Dan.'

'Lizzie's been so upset about deceiving you.' Dan stepped forward. 'She was crying about it all weekend.'

'At the golf hotel?' Kate asked, and then she realised her mistake.

'We've talked things over,' Lizzie said, 'and we've both decided it's the best thing if I move back in with Dan.'

Kate stood looking at them, remembering the way she'd laughed at Lizzie's Mum.

'He says he's sorry. Really sorry.' And they stood together, holding hands, smiling convincingly at Kate.

'I'm sorry not to have been more honest with you.' Lizzie gave her a soft and scented hug. 'But thanks for having me to stay. It meant the world, it really did.'

Kate stood in the doorway, watching them walk away along the mews. The bodyguards nodded to them and raised their hands to wave, and Kate thought she saw them smile indulgently as the happy couple turned out into the street.

Didn't I (blow your mind this time)

Stewart Home

I thought I clocked a store detective watching me. I knew something wasn't right. She was a hefty young blonde dressed down in a tight black T-shirt and short black skirt with ragged black tights. Exactly the type of hop-head I find attractive and that a bunch of motherfucking hip capitalists would employ as a secret weapon against shrinkage. I was rifling my way through the soul section of the central London flagship store of a well-known record chain and she was glancing back to see if I was squinting back to see if she was peeping back at me. I had a fistful of Booker T & the MGs albums in my hand – *Hip Hug Her, And Now, Doin' Our Thing, Up Tight, Play the Hip Hits*. Thinking about it now, perhaps my confusion stemmed not so much from my interest in men with organs, as from an ongoing puzzlement over whether the MGs' biggest hit, 'Green Onions', would have been such a huge smash if it had gone out using the British English term for this vegetable – spring onions – rather than the more alluring American English variant. In a similar groove, I can remember being extremely perplexed when I came across references to eggplant in American hard-boiled crime novels as a teenager, and it wasn't until years later that I discovered this was the American English term for aubergine.

I tried to stay calm and act like a legitimate shopper by grabbing a copy of *Soul Serenade: The Best of Willie Mitchell*. Retaining my composure wasn't easy when the CD in question claimed to be the first comprehensive collection of works from the famed Memphis producer, arranger, bandleader, trumpeter and composer. This assertion was obviously a complete bluff since I already possessed a Willie Mitchell selection CD in the Hi Records Masters series. I also had a two-LPs-on-one-CD set by Mitchell comprised of *Ooh Baby, You Turn Me On* and *Live at the Royal*. It should go without saying that Mitchell was to Hi Records what Booker T & the MGs were to Stax. As well as backing the likes of Al Green and Syl Johnson, Mitchell turned out numerous cookin' instrumentals under his own name, on which he played the organ as well as the trumpet – so perhaps I should have compared him to the Mar-Kays rather than the MGs. That said, I'm not ashamed to admit I was having difficulty focusing my mind on music matters with the hefty blonde store detective lurking at the periphery of my vision.

I'd looked for Wynder K Frog under 'F' and I almost lost my cool when I couldn't find the organist – Colchester's answer to Booker T Jones – under 'K' or 'W' either. I only retained possession of my mind by grabbing an album of Billy Preston organ instrumentals from the 'P' section. The long player was endlessly reissued under different titles with the track order switched around. The copy in my hand was titled *King of the Road* but I had an earlier version of the CD at home that had gone out as *Billy's Bag*. I took several deep breaths, eyed the hefty blonde with a mixture of lust and fear, then headed up to the classical music section on the top floor of the store. I expected the well-stacked beauty to follow me, but she was apparently locked into the soul section. Cackling hysterically, I placed the Booker T & the MGs CDs I'd got from downstairs amongst recordings of John Cage works for prepared piano. I was distraught when I discovered there were no Cornelius Cardew albums in the store. Instead I placed *The Best of Willie Mitchell* amongst a selection of recordings of George Henry Crumb's *Twelve Fantasy Pieces after the Zodiac for Amplified Piano*. Then I made my way over to the Glenn Gould CDs and placed *King of the Road* by Billy Preston in with them. Having grabbed a whole bunch of Gould renditions of Bach, I made my way back to the soul CDs.

The hefty blonde moved her arse – and it was a beautiful arse: full, firm and round as Jennifer Lopez's in *Out of Sight* – to the reggae section when she saw me return. I slipped the Glenn Gould albums in where I'd removed CDs by Booker T & the MGs, Willie Mitchell and Billy Preston, then legged it into the street. I made my way to another flagship record shop and as the hefty blonde followed me without attempting to catch up, I realised she couldn't possibly be a store detective. When I saw her removing a customer-response card from inside a Don Bryant CD, I clapped a hand on her shoulder. The girl nearly jumped out of her skin but calmed down as I assured her everything was going to be all right. Once her tits stopped jiggling, Melissa – for that was her name – agreed that we should retire to a nearby drinking establishment. Over beers I explained my tactics for speeding up the process of cultural cross-fertilisation by switching top-drawer classical piano CDs with soulful organ instrumentals in order to break down the rigidly segmented commodification of culture promoted by record shops.

My ultimate plan was to turn people on to a wide variety of sounds and simultaneously extend Pierre Bourdieu's purely sociological critique of the culture industry into the realm of the political by developing the concept of fictive social capital. I wanted to create a freaky crossover between academic research into social stratification and the type of psychedelic Bordiguism promoted by ultra-leftists like Jacques Camatte. Melissa explained that she spent her days stealing the customer-response cards from soul and reggae CDs. She'd fill these in, giving the names and addresses of those prominent right-wingers listed in *Who's Who*. Melissa was one classy bitch – and unfortunately not nearly as submissive as I'd have liked. Melissa might have gone in for tight T-shirts and short skirts, but that didn't stop her from seeing women's liberation as an integral part of proletarian revolution. Fucking with the minds of patriarchs and racists was merely one of a number of concrete steps Melissa had undertaken with the ultimate aim of overthrowing the state. In the final analysis we had a lot in common, right down to a perverse liking for kitsch records by Sinitta and the Spice Girls. So I never have been able to work out why Melissa wouldn't fuck me.

Gone to earth

John O'Connell

It all started on the 7.28 Thameslink train from Herne Hill to King's Cross. I'd lived in Herne Hill for over a year, so it was a train I knew well, though you had to choose your moment if you wanted to reach your destination even remotely composed. On weekday mornings it's a total no-go area, a kind of mobile Black Hole of Calcutta. But this was a Sunday, and the novelty of being able to breathe without gagging made the journey almost pleasurable.

I was on the way to meet my friend Bill, who lived in a particularly inaccessible part of Stoke Newington. We were medical students at UCL. Buses scare me (my therapist has the details) and I can't afford cabs, even minicabs, so Bill was going to pick me up at King's Cross in his mum's car and drive me back to his house, where we were going to revise for a bit, then get stoned and watch his new *Bagpuss* video.

The train stopped at Elephant & Castle and a couple got on. He was broad and bulky. She was gangly-tall, with cropped hair which fluffed out at the back like escaped stuffing. Their bags smacked against the seats as they panted up the aisle. They stopped right in front of me.

'Here?' said the man.

'Yeah,' said the woman.

They made audibly heavy weather of pushing their luggage on to the overhead shelf. Christ, I thought, it's only Thameslink. What's all this about? Nobody stores luggage on the overhead shelves of Thameslink trains any more than they use the toilets. Aren't these people familiar with the Great Unspoken Protocol of Thameslink travel?

Seated now, the woman pulled a mobile phone out of her jacket pocket and dialled an eleven-digit number. A few tense seconds followed while she waited to be connected. Then, quite suddenly, she shrieked: 'Dave!'

('Is he there?' asked her partner, this evidence notwithstanding.)

'We're on the train.'

('Ask him where he wants us to meet him.')

The woman, to the man, crossly: 'Shhhhh.'

('I'm only trying to...')

'Yeah, that sounds fine. Yeah.'

('Is he going to pick us up?')

'Will you fucking shut up?' To Dave: 'No, not you, sweet. Tom. He's doing his usual trick.'

A pause. Dave was telling the woman something.

'OK, well we'll just sort of hang around outside the station.'

('What are you arranging?')

'Dave, I've got to go. See you soon. Bye.' To Tom: 'Why do you do that? Why? You know I hate it.'

'Do what?'

'What you just did. Interrupt me when I'm talking.'

'Because you always forget the point of the conversation. You forget to ask the crucial questions.'

'I didn't need to ask questions. It was obvious why I was phoning.'

This shut Tom up for about twenty seconds. Then he said: 'It doesn't matter whether you asked the questions or not. That's not the issue. The issue is the fact that I expected you not to ask the questions. Why was that, do you think?'

'I don't know, do I? Jesus, Tom, you are so full of shit.' She sighed. 'We're going to have a nice holiday, OK? I am not going to let you mess this holiday up.'

'Nat,' said Tom softly, bringing his hand up to touch her shoulder. 'Natalie. I'm sorry.'

Tom and Natalie. Natalie and Tom. I wondered how long they'd been together. Four years? Five? Five. That final 'I'm sorry' from Tom was revealing. They argue a lot, I decided. Too much. So much that they've been practising 'closing down' arguments before they become full-scale seismic seizures of rage and frustration. That's what my ex-girlfriend Sam and I tried to do. It didn't work very well for us.

Natalie and Tom fell silent. Settling back, I skimmed the contents of my book, a set text called *Blood Diseases: An Introduction*: pernicious anaemia; simple anaemia; anaemia after haemorrhage. But my attention wandered. It drifted, on an inexorable undertow of nosiness, back to my neighbours, specifically Tom's rather abstract remark: 'The issue is the fact that I expected you not to ask the questions.'

Maybe he was right. Maybe that was the issue.

Outside, the morning mist parted on a curve of tumbledown shops

– teeth no one could be bothered to extract, rotting painlessly in the shadow of a damp-stained tower block. I don't know about you, but I average around one epiphany a day, and that Sunday's hit me just then, just as I was trying on my Socially Concerned face (forehead scrunched, lips lightly sucked in). That Sunday's epiphany went something like this: I really fancied Natalie.

I couldn't stop myself smiling. It felt great, fancying Natalie. I don't fancy people very often, so being able to narrow my focus to that degree, to be able to say, categorically, 'Yes, I fancy that woman' was tremendously... can I use the word 'enabling'? Well then, enabling. Enabling is what it was.

Hang on, though: what did she look like exactly? Infatuation couldn't begin in earnest till I'd built up a full mental picture. Peering at her through the gap between the seats wasn't yielding much. I'd got a vague sense of her profile from the reflection in the window, but that was hardly substantial, hardly worth filing away for future reflection. No, it was all doomed. Unless...

Unless I got up and went to the toilet. Perfect.

There was only one problem: no one, and I mean no one, goes to the toilet on Thameslink trains. I mean, there *are* toilets. Toilets exist. But by common consensus, they're not for public use. They're just there, loitering like paedophiles around a primary school in a contractual-obligation, stale-piss-and-sodden-clumps-of-old-*Sun*s-open-at-page-three kind of way.

Obviously, I wasn't actually going to go to the toilet. I was going to wander vacantly through a few carriages, down to where the buffet car would have been were this a train worth travelling on, then swagger back, beaming with faked relief. There was a slight risk Natalie would think I was weird, but she hadn't known the overhead-rack rule so was, on balance, unlikely to know the toilet one.

I tidied my belongings away to deter thieves. Books and personal stereo in bag (to be taken with me); empty wallet files and newspaper scattered around (to mark my territory). Speed was essential. We'd be at King's Cross, where I'd judged Natalie and Tom were most likely to alight, in about four minutes.

I edged out into the aisle, then walked casually towards the sliding door, hands in pockets, front teeth resting lightly on lower lip. As I passed the couple, I turned my head 180 degrees to the right to look at them, just for an instant. Tom, eyes shut, was resting his head on Natalie's shoulder while she stared disconsolately (I thought) into space. But the merest fraction of a second after I'd gauged the scene, disaster struck. Natalie looked up and met my gaze, returning it with equal force and clarity. Then she did something which chilled me to the core; mortified me so deeply, I thought I might collapse there and then.

She winked at me.

Struggling to regain composure – pretending, in fact, that nothing in the least untoward had happened – I kept on walking, on and on for what seemed like miles, until I reached the toilet.

It smelt horrible. There was piss all over the seat, all over the floor, but I decided to spend the rest of the journey there anyway to avoid the embarrassment of walking past the couple again. I didn't have long to wait: within seconds, the guard's announcement that the train would shortly be arriving at King's Cross boomed into the cubicle. I tore down the carriage like a greyhound with a tartrazine allergy. If I went fast enough, maybe Natalie wouldn't register that I'd passed her.

Shit! They were getting ready to get off too. In fact, they were blocking the aisle, which meant I had to push past them with a soft 'Excuse me'. Could this be done? It could. Phew. Heart pounding, I scooped my belongings into my bag and raced for the door.

I left the train before them feeling jittery and light-headed, then walked briskly out into the precinct by the taxi rank where all the prostitutes and dealers collect. I couldn't see Bill. I couldn't see Bill's car. There was a phone booth. I dragged its door open in time to see Tom and Natalie emerge from the ticket hall stooped with luggage. I lifted the receiver. No dialling tone. The little LCD display was blank. Oh dear.

What if Bill had forgotten I was coming? Had I told him the right train?

It was then that I remembered the mobile phone – the source of the couple's intriguing argument. Maybe I should stop being so neurotic and just ask them directly if I could borrow it? After all, she had winked at me. She'd made what my father would have called an overture. And she did look a bit like Jenny Agutter.

Bag slung casually over shoulder, I wandered down to the kerb where the couple were standing, waiting for the mysterious Dave. I got a better look at them and was amazed by how little they resembled the photofits in my head. Natalie's hair was dark blonde rather than brown, and her features were flatter and neater than I remembered. Height: around five foot eight. She was wearing a tight-fitting pale-blue T-shirt and khaki combat trousers; her snub nose and domed forehead lent her a piquant, slightly forbidding demureness.

Tom, on the other hand, looked a baffling jumble of threatening and stupid. His clothes – baggy corduroys and a green jumper with a thick red line across the front – were far too shambling for his clenched, up-for-it demeanour. He looked like he'd been dressed by someone else, in sale-rail Gap.

Steeling myself, I approached them. 'Hello,' I said. 'I was on the train with you, sitting behind you actually, and I couldn't help noticing you had a mobile phone.' The words came out crisp and clear, give or take a few prep-school inflections. 'It's just that the payphone over there is broken and my friend said he'd be here to meet me and he isn't and…'

'Yes,' said Natalie. 'Of course.' She fished in the side pocket of her rucksack and brought out the mobile. Out of the corner of my eye, I saw Tom pacing about in a circle a few feet away. He was grinning with a sort of slit-eyed, don't-mind-me smugness. Shit. So they *had* noticed me. They thought I was weird. Worse than that, I'd become their private joke – a sort of post-row bonding implement.

I dialled Bill's number in brutal stabs. Answer, you bastard.

'Hello?'

'Bill. It's me, Paul. I'm on a mobile.'

'Well done.'

'Where are you?'

'Shit, you're not at King's Cross already?'

'Look,' I heard myself say, 'don't worry. I'll get a taxi.'

'No no no. Don't be stupid. Give me half an hour.'

'Half an hour?'

'Maybe a bit more.'

'Christ. Are you mid-wank or something?'

'Well,' he said, apparently intrigued by the question, 'I'm watching a Stephen Poliakoff film. So I suppose technically I am, yes. Can you really not get a bus?'

'I hate buses. People get stabbed and die on buses.'

'Only occasionally.'

'How much is a cab?'

'Dunno. A tenner?'

'A tenner! That's half my weekly food budget.'

'I'll pay half.'

'Yeah, right. Like you paid half for those Meltdown tickets.'

I was cross with myself for not insisting that Bill pick me up. Why did I always capitulate like that? Why did people always assume I wouldn't mind if they let me down?

'Hello?' Natalie was calling. 'Can we have our phone back please?'

'Oh. Yeah. Yeah, of course. Sorry.' I slunk across to where Natalie was sitting on her rucksack and handed her the tiny device. She smiled. Her skin looked thin and papery. There was a trace of eczema around her eyes.

'Is your friend on his way?'

I couldn't decide how to answer. Should I lie? No. No need. You're never going to see these people again. Let your misfortune feed their joke. 'No,' I said. 'There's been a bit of a problem. I'm going to have to get a cab, I think.'

She smiled again. She had a lovely smile. 'Great,' she said. 'Actually,' she seemed happy to make conversation, 'we're waiting for a friend ourselves. Not that he's showing any sign of turning up!'

She folded her arms over her chest and started craning her neck in a figure of eight.

Then Tom said: 'Why don't you get a ride with us? There's loads of room in the car.'

'Yeah!' Natalie seemed to like the idea. 'Where are you headed?'

'Stoke Newington.'

She almost whooped. 'Great! Us too.' This was far, far too good to be true. 'Do you know Linsbergh Road?' I shook my head. 'No. Neither do we. It's next to a church or something…' I tried to place her voice. It was neutral-posh, with a distant trace of… Manchester? 'I'm Natalie. This' – she pointed – 'is Tom.' Tom waved cordially. 'And you are?'

'Oh,' I started, taken aback by the speed of events. 'I'm Paul.' I smiled and extended a hand. 'Paul Simon.'

'So,' called Dave from the driving seat. 'You must have had a bit of a rough time at school with a name like yours.'

'Yes,' I said.

'You must have had people coming up to you all the time going, "Look! There goes rhymin' Simon!"'

'Yes,' I said.

'People really rated *Graceland*, didn't they? Not me. I prefer the early ones. "Me and Julio Down by the Schoolyard". Or "Kodachrome" – that's a brilliant song. "Kodachro-*oo-oooome…*"'

Dave even *looked* annoying, with his bush of dense, white-blond curls. White eyebrows, too. He couldn't be more than twenty-five, yet he'd already acquired the bone-crushing handshake of someone much older, as well as an obsession with eye contact. He was screaming his opinions at the windscreen. 'There ought to be a support network for people who share names with famous people.' A lorry thundered past, sending a gust of wind through the open window. He swerved to the left.

'Dave!' barked Natalie, who was next to me in the back. Tom, in the front passenger seat, had the belt pulled taut against his chest.

Dave flinched. 'Sorry.'

'Music?' asked Tom. There was already a tape in the stereo; it protruded from the dashboard like a plastic tongue. Reading the silence as assent, he pushed it in. The chunky, choppy sound of Boston's 'More Than a Feeling' filled the car. Natalie groaned; the others chuckled. I sort of smiled awkwardly.

It was then that Natalie groaned again. Looking back, I remember thinking that that was a bit odd, a bit of an excessive response, even to Boston. But I didn't say anything.

About five minutes passed.

The car turned a corner. I gripped the seat to stop myself sliding into Natalie. There was a strong, rancid smell coming from somewhere, tinged with the usual vehicular waft of petrol, exhaust fumes and warm plastic. I didn't feel so great. One glance at Natalie, though, and my own nausea contracted with a snap. She looked terrible. Her face was a bright neon white. Her arms, which she was hugging to her chest as if to squeeze out some terrible pain from inside her, were mottled and covered in goosebumps. Christ, I thought, they're junkies. Just my fucking luck.

'Er,' I said. 'Tom.'

No response. I tried again. 'Tom! Dave! TOM!'

Tom turned and saw. 'Oh shit,' he said. 'Dave, pull over.'

'What? Why?'

'We need the manual. Natalie's fading.'

'Fading?' I shrieked, adrenalin-bold. 'She's *dying* by the looks of things.'

Tom swung round. 'Look, I know we've only just met, and I don't mean to be rude, but I'm going to have to ask you to stay out of this.'

'But I'm a medical student,' I said.

'And?'

'We need to call an ambulance.'

'No we don't.'

'I should check her pulse, all the same.'

This seemed to touch a nerve. 'No!' shouted Tom and Dave in unison.

As Dave pulled over, Tom rifled through the glove compartment, flinging travel sweet tins and empty cassette boxes on to the floor. I sneaked a momentary feel of Natalie's pulse, my fingers creeping across the seat to where her left arm rested on her thigh. Her skin was hard and cold. I lifted the underside of her wrist in search of a vein. Nothing – not the slightest vibration.

The music stopped as the engine died. Tom flicked through a small, black, leather-bound book. 'There's got to be somewhere near here,' he said.

'The Whittington isn't far,' I said.

'I'm not looking for a hospital.'

Dave piped up. 'There's a pub in Crouch End I remember using once, though its levels were pretty low. Still, in an emergency...'

But Tom seemed to have found what he was looking for. 'St Joseph's. That'll do. Keep on this road.'

We drove for what seemed like hours, far too fast for the narrow, hazardous streets. As the engine whined (Dave rarely moved out of third gear) and the sky turned black with rain, I began to imagine the worst. Tom and Dave were psychopaths, I decided. Psychopaths who had killed Natalie, maybe with some kind of slow-release poison, and were looking for somewhere to dump her body. They would then have no choice but to kill me, the sole witness, as well. There was even a sense in which such a fate was my due; deserved punishment for breaching that oldest of parental axioms: *don't accept lifts from strangers.*

Natalie was getting whiter, if that was possible. Odder still, there were times when she seemed to be almost transparent. Every five seconds or so, a line like TV static rippled all the way down her body, starting at her head. As it moved, the dogtooth pattern of the seat-cover became visible through her.

We turned right into a street called Lisson Mews, Tom and Dave leaning attentively into the windscreen; next to me, Natalie's undulating form became slowly less substantial. There were only about ten houses in the street. At the far end, next to a tatty-looking church, was a ruddy-bricked Victorian building which had been converted into a primary school; a sign outside read 'St Joseph's C of E'.

'There's a playground round the back,' said Tom. 'Park as near as you can. We don't want to be seen.'

'It's Sunday,' said Dave. 'There shouldn't be anyone around.'

I'd have felt happier if there'd been someone around to notice something. As it was, the whole street felt deserted. Tom and Dave carried Natalie across to the centre of the playground. I stayed in the car. The best policy, I decided, was to be blankly, unquestioningly passive and observe carefully, in case the police had tricksy questions for me later.

Dave had parked just in front of the playground gate, thus accidentally granting me a clear view of whatever he and Tom were doing. I watched as they rested Natalie gently on the tarmac; then Tom stood back a little while Dave remained crouched, supporting the base of Natalie's head with his hands.

And then it began. It was like watching a time-lapse film of a severely dehydrated plant after it had been placed in a jug of water. There was something unsettlingly natural about it, and suddenly I knew that if it hadn't been for my presence and the burden of my intervention, they would have approached the task even more casually, even more like a routine trip to a petrol station.

It took about a minute in all. At the end, Natalie raised herself into a squatting position, then stood up straight, just like that. She didn't seem to need any time to recuperate. The trio approached the car silently, sternly, Natalie rubbing her arm as if to ward off muscle cramp. She looked completely normal. Her skin was no longer papery and pale, but rosy and supple. Her eyes were bright and alert. She slid into the back seat next to me. Nobody said anything. Nobody even looked at me. It was as if they'd forgotten I was there.

The Caravaggio room

Reuben Lane

The weirdest kinds of truth.

Mary's cloak that shining deep-pitched blue of the Mediterranean Sea.

The floor covered in the debris of naked muscled soldier bodies going grey and stiff with rigor mortis; gold flagons, upturned chairs and yellow-pink peaches escaped from a smashed bowl.

We are full of shock. Extricate – snip along the lines and remove from my head. We'd all be the monster if we had the nerve – if we had nothing left to lose. Milosevic launching missiles into the hills. Splinters from the cross snagging in the flesh of our shoulder.

The green flock walls of the Caravaggio room. Two women push the doors open and enter – just behind them a young man. The women start with the opposite wall – clockwise – *David and Goliath* – the young man separates and begins on my side – *The Supper at Emmaus* – anti-clockwise. He turns in a strange ballet of hesitant loops. Looking from the pictures over his shoulder – he stops and stares – a frozen half-second straight at me – our eyes sending out hooks that catch and pull taut. Pale stonewashed jeans. Black and cream Nikes. A long blue canvas jacket. He's about twenty, no more. He lingers along the Caravaggios – doubling back when he reaches the far end, back to the centre of the room where he sits on one of the polished oak benches – angled so we can dart quick glances at one another. His is a gentle aura. He turns to look behind him and I realise the two women in the background are his mother and sister. He flashes me a final look and then walks with them out of the room – into the darker green – his limbs reluctant as if they are moving through oil. I follow him through to the entrance gallery – the walls decked with huge scenes from the Napoleonic wars – charging blue tunics and thousands of horses.

He sits in one of the brown leather armchairs next to his sister – his legs sprawled out in front of him. When his sister gets up to go through the swing doors to the Orazio Gentileschi room he speaks to his mother and peels away on his own. I follow him to the top of the stairs. He's asking about the acoustiguides – his voice is deep – an accent, perhaps East European. I walk to the bottom of the stone steps – standing looking back up at him. He's clocked my gaze and he nervously crosses, picks up a leaflet – the face of Cardinal Wolsey – and walks diagonally down the stairs, almost touching me as he passes – waits a moment and then walks up the side stairs into the Gallery shop. He flicks through the books, the poster rack – checking on my geography every now and then. On the left cheekbone of his face there's a big red spot.

He rejoins his mother and sister and I wander like a private detective after them – lurking one room behind – my eyes greased – a precision radar.

This story simmers away to nothing. The mother sees me watching her boy and cottons on – I feel like a filthy old perv. At ten to six the voice over the tannoy announces the National Gallery is about to close. I follow them out of the main entrance. I stand leaning against the balustrade and I feel as if I'm a tourist too, seeing this scene for the first time – the dirty rainy grandeur of Trafalgar Square – Big Ben – the trundling double decker buses – the hordes of people. The sister takes her brother's photo. The boy's buzzing – here's another completely new world. I follow a hundred feet behind as they walk briskly up towards Leicester Square – almost tripping over them as they double back – and I try to melt into the crowd – but the mother's seen me – and I realise I'll have to give this game up or she'll freak that I'm stalking them.

Umbrellas and police cars. My heart still trapped, doing a faster dance. Out into the evening. Tea and a chocolate brownie in Pret a Manger. Another London story retracing itself – a vanishing trick – as if these incidents never were – as if my abandoned imaginings could never have come to anything.

His name is Louis.

'What – like Donald Duck's nephew – Huey, Louis and... what's the third one called?'

I find myself blabbering on like this.

Louis sits the other side of the sofa. His feet tucked up into a semi-lotus. Blue and grey climbing socks. His Nikes unlaced and abandoned on the carpet. Newly washed clothes smelling vaguely of marzipan.

In the gallery we stood elbow to elbow in front of Titian's portrait of a young Florentine merchant. I dropped my guide on the floor. He bent to pick it up and give it to me. 'No,' I whispered. 'You keep it.' Just as his mother and sister entered the room. And I split away.

This morning the phone rang at 9.30.

'Hello,' said his deep accented voice. 'This is the man from yesterday.'

He gave me the name and address of the hotel he was staying at: 'Come as soon as you can.'

'But your family ?'

'It's OK – they've gone out shopping for the day.'

We stare at each other. Two glasses of white wine from a bottle in the minibar fridge stand on the back of the sofa.

It's a big luxurious room. A hotel behind Piccadilly. There is a copy of *Steppenwolf* on the table. I ask if he's reading it. And he says: 'No – it's my sister's.'

Watching his mouth, I undo my top shirt button.

He watches. He takes a sip of wine – and then like a reflection in a mirror slightly delayed he moves his right hand to his shirt collar and undoes the top button too.

I wait for half a minute – the sound of a fluttering pigeon on the windowsill outside – and then I lean across and undo his next shirt button. Twigging the game, the edges of his lips rise and he lifts out his hand and loosens my second button – a finger touching my sternum.

A rolling in the pit of my stomach like sea sickness. It somehow makes it better when I see his fingers are shaking.

'How old are you?' I was thinking, riding my bike here, I'd better get that in before he asks.

'Eighteen. And you?'

Whether to shave a couple of years off – throw a few shovelfuls of dirt into the gulf between us? Fuck – he was born in the 1980s.

'Twenty-eight.' A lie of mathematics – four multiplied by seven instead of eight.

'Will you kiss me?' It's a plea. And as I kneel on the sofa and seal his lips over mine – as I watch his eyelids closing and his eyes herky jerky under the skin – as I clamp my teeth over his tongue and suck hard – both of us grow calm. His hand wraps itself around the back of my neck. One moment I'm in charge, the next he is – a sureness come from adolescent longing.

We undress each other one garment at a time – like flunkeys clearing the table after an elaborate banquet – from clothes to body.

Louis stands in the middle of the room on the Persian rug – a nervous chuckle as he bats down his blood-hard penis with the palm of his hand. I watch him – tender tall body – the slight swell of puppy fat that still hangs on his stomach – long legs – the cloud of fair pubic hair – dark blackened nipples. Zones of his body like sirens calling for the touch of my hands, the firm bite of my mouth.

'Louis – who are you anyway? Where do you come from? Do you have a boyfriend, a girlfriend – anyone back home?'

He looks puzzled.

'Are you going to fuck me? I have condoms. Look – here.' He tips open the lid of his suitcase and feels in the side pocket and withdraws a single Durex in its foil wrapper.

I get up off the sofa – putting a finger under the elastic of my underpants and tugging them off – a ritual made illicit by the morning sunshine glancing in through the long windows. I cradle one arm around Louis's shoulders – my hand smoothing down his back over the velvet skin and the notches of his vertebrae – coming to rest on the ledge of his hip. I lick in long slow strips the side of his neck. My prick pressed hard against his thigh sticky like cuckoo spit.

Louis's body rests in mine. However I move my hands or shift my weight against him it feels like a perfect fit. His kisses are long – like one urgent question melting into the next – a whole string of them needing answers. His mouth and hands travelling fast all over me. I stand in front of him and for a moment hold his eagerness at arm's length – looking Louis's body up and down – making a list of all the places I'll show him in London.

I cup a hand under his bollocks as I sink my teeth around his nipple – lapping at it with the tip of my tongue. I press and rub the muscle that runs from the base of his balls to his arse. Louis suddenly tenses and through gritted teeth lets out a strangled 'No' – the veins in his held-back neck standing out like thick cords. His sperm floods against my stomach. I press in against him to catch it all.

Louis looks down – for a second embarrassed – breathing in the seaweed smell of sex. He twists around to reach for the box of paper handkerchiefs by the copy of *Steppenwolf* on the table.

'Don't.' I pull him back around. He watches as I put the palm of my hand in the gluey pool on my stomach and then transfer and rub the stickiness over on to his chest, over my chest; a streak across my face – over my cheeks – then his face – like war paint.

He smiles.

'Your sister. Does *she* know?'

When I was eighteen, my sister, who is a year and a half younger than me, seemed to be having a wild time – a string of horny confident boys she'd go skateboarding and flirt with out in the street in the evenings – Milo and Danny and Ivan. And one night her name appeared in two-foot letters in white paint on the wall opposite after the words IVAN FUCKED. Someone tried to wash the graffiti off but it remained ghostlike and still decipherable if you stopped long enough to figure it out – on the bricks – for ever afterwards. When I eventually told her I was gay she said she'd known it for years. 'You and I – we have the same taste in men,' she said.

Louis's sister wore a long brown leather coat and had a love-filled smile when she was taking her brother's photo outside the pillared entranceway to the gallery yesterday. Suddenly I remember a story by Thomas Mann where he sees a brother and sister standing above him on a balcony – and becomes infatuated with their beauty – their individual beauty made more intoxicating by their close proximity to one another.

'No,' says Louis with a shaking voice. 'No one knows.'

His heart drums on the thin layer of skin between his second and third ribs. I place two fingers on this frenetic beat.

'It's OK.' I keep on whispering it as I pull him into me – our skins melding – our two bodies crushing up against each other – taking up a smaller and smaller volume of space. 'It's OK.' Deep down aching that this is all I want him to remember – to take with him from London back home to Budapest. 'It's OK.'

You're growing up and a lot of it is simply luck – into whose hands you should fall. I remember Saturdays going up to the West End on the number 3 bus, aged ten and eleven – sitting in public toilet cubicles reading the graffiti – mesmerised and terrified. Big cock needs sucking. Make date. Meet here. Gouged into the chipboard walls – wherever I looked – felt-tip drawings of disembodied penises. These caverns of fevered desire stinking of piss and ammonia. Men with flickering eyes who would watch me from the urinals as I washed my hands and dried them under the hot-air blower. For years this was my only gay reality – the only possible envelope. Like some smutty Pandora's box. NO LOITERING. Colluding with what the herd imagines. Until I could grow up and escape the fear. The fear engineered to keep me from going queer. 'How queer,' my grandmother used to say when she was puzzled – and my sister and I would burst out laughing. John Inman in *Are You Being Served?*: 'Oooh, everything's coming down in the Men's Underwear Department today. Isn't that *queer*, Mrs Slocombe?'

Louis and I lie on his bed; his head sideways, my thigh his pillow. The sheets like a chaos of broken ice. Our muscles singing with exhaustion. 'Let's try everything,' Louis had said. And so like result-hungry scientists we worked our way through a list of erotic experiments. Tracing every inch of the other's body with eyes, fingers and tongues. Tender fucking as Big Ben chimed away the quarter hours. The spirit of Hermann Hesse keeping watch over us from the pages of his sister's dog-eared paperback.

On television Bill Clinton tells America to 'wake up' after two teenage students walked into their school in Colorado and started a massacre to celebrate Hitler's birthday – before shooting themselves. He says that American children should be given lessons in 'conflict resolution'. The next item on the news – Clinton and Blair are having talks in Washington about committing ground troops in Serbia.

One hand around my knee – with his other Louis flicks the remote control to MTV.

Perhaps our highest purpose is the search for love.

Physical desire like an ink-stain that runs in the wash.

I'd like to stay all afternoon and evening in this room, Louis and I exchanging snippets of our lives – binding them together – this place and time – like a capsule of memory that we'll be able to look back on down the far-flung corridors of the future. Two bodies that we'll excavate when we're old men.

Tomorrow – I'm thinking – I'll ring in sick at work. Then I'll come and meet Louis and walk up with him through Chinatown to Soho – have a pot of tea; share a strawberry millefeuille in the upper room at Maison Bertaux – our forks cutting through the cream and pastry from opposite sides of the table. Then along to Sir John Soane's Museum on Lincoln's Inn Fields – I'll take Louis down to the cold

eerie cellar with its Ancient Egyptian sarcophagus and stolen stones –
then back up to the picture room where the warder will fold out the
wood panels to show him – my hand resting on his shoulder – the
paintings and drawings concealed inside the wall.

We have to travel; we have to see the world.

Louis and I under the shower soaping each other's flesh – under arms,
between toes, under the foreskin, up the crevice of the arse – rubbing
shampoo into the other's hair. The tiny tablet of hotel soap slips
between his hands and mine as we wash each other clean. The soft
lint of the white towels embroidered with the name of the hotel –
pummel each other dry.

Louis breaks the silence as he pulls on his jeans: 'What's his name?'

'Who?'

'Your boyfriend.'

'Who said I have a boyfriend?'

'You do – I know. What's his name?'

I button my shirt looking in the mirror. Louis's wet fringe falls across
his face as he looks down to buckle his belt.

'Garcia. His name's Garcia.'

Bits of me break off. How many lives can you fit into one lifetime?

Louis's mother and sister climb off the bus at the traffic lights at
Piccadilly Circus. His sister puts her shopping bags between her feet
and snaps a photo of Eros. 'Let's go back to the hotel,' says her mother
in Hungarian.

Late at night in bed Garcia and I sit up drinking our mugs of camomile
tea. 'Look,' I say – reaching out for my knapsack on the floor: 'I've got
a new story to read to you.'

Reverse evolution

Angelica Jacob

Yesterday, Jack left.

I heard the door close and fifteen minutes later a pigeon slammed into the window. When I went on to the balcony its body was laid on the ground. I picked it up and its neck flopped to one side. Its eyes were glassy and black and a small trickle of a brownish, grey liquid spilled from its beak. I put the pigeon in a plastic carrier bag and unceremoniously dumped the bag in a bin.

Almost immediately it started to rain; a grey, London drizzle, a ghostly mist of water and smog. I retired indoors and noticed a blister of paint above the sink in the kitchen. The blister was approximately one foot in diameter and three inches wide. The paint bulged and when I punctured it with a knife, liquid spilled down the wall. There was a leak in the ceiling; I could see the crack, hear the drip, drip of the water.

My chest and my stomach began to go funny – my fingers and toes, even my skin, but the greatest distress lay behind each of my eyes. When I peered out of the window the city looked bleak. The previous night the whole place had glittered. Jack and I had walked back, hand in hand through the crowds. The sky was lit with thousands of stars, the lights on the Telecom Tower flashed on and off; fluorescent reds, greens and fabulous yellows. Soho was lit up like a large Spandex box. Theatreland glimmered with shiny black cabs. Even the Limelight and the Hippodrome looked halfway decent. Everywhere heaved with hot, eager faces. The air smelled of popcorn, hotdogs and onions and, above everything else, the moon had glittered and shone.

But now, as I stood by my window, grey clouds smothered the buildings. They were lidding everything down, a chiaroscuro of ill health and shadow. My breath shallowed out; a panicky feeling spread through my veins.

I boiled the kettle, but immediately burnt myself on the steam. When I screamed my voice echoed through each room of the flat. It turned into hundreds of voices, each one quieter than the last. Then the last voice faded and silence took over. I buried my head in my hands, tried to block out what wasn't there. But the silence persisted. It was softer than silk, sleeker than poison.

I tried to make a small breakfast. I fetched an apple and a melon from the wooden bowl on the sideboard, but every piece, all the peaches and plums, the apples and oranges were rimed with green mould. My eyes locked on to this sight. For a time I watched as the mould crept over a three-day-old lemon. The mould threw out spores and the spores wove white webs. They planted themselves under the skin of the fruit, creating a thread-mass of roots. When I picked up the melon, its skin collapsed; tiny decompositions of flesh clung to my fingers. The smell was astringent, and when I tried slicing the bad half away, the knife slipped in my hand. The wound was deep; my skin flapped back exposing red muscle.

The rain continued and with it the grey, indistinct light. I dressed and found a hole in my sleeve. The sweater, a gift from my sister, was falling apart. The yarn unravelled and when I pulled at a thread the stitches vanished. What was once cloth was now nothing more than string in my hand; it trailed on the floor and with my teeth I broke the thread off, chucked it into the bin alongside the pigeon, then switched on the TV.

I liked watching the news, but unfortunately I'd missed the main broadcast. Instead I was forced to watch a chef explaining how to dissect a raw chicken. The carcass looked cold; it was trussed by its legs with two rubber bands. A close-up of the skin revealed the holes out of which the feathers were plucked, after which the chef bent back a leg and showed how to cut through the joint where the bone met the muscle. This was the softest area, the point of least resistance, packed as it was with cartilage and delicate, marrowy substances. He dismantled both legs, then slipped his knife through each breast, after which he prised them away from the bone, slicing and dicing until nothing remained but small cubes of jelly-white flesh.

The sight made me shudder; to see the chef's eyes glinting so brightly. To see his large claw-like hands ripping the bird, cold limb from cold limb. Soon the flesh would be eaten. It would disappear and later the remnants excreted and flushed down the toilet.

I turned my back on the TV, picked up my brush and drew it over my head. Clumps of hair drifted on to the floor and, when I started to cry, my tears dissolved amongst the white, linen sheets. I brushed

my cheek with my hand and an eyelash caught on my fingertip. I blew
the eyelash away, but I had no wish to make, leastways nothing of any
great consequence.

Instead I returned to the window and watched the sun slide down
the sky as if a yoke and an egg white were gradually separating. London
looked so old and decrepit. It was encrusted with dog shit, knee-deep
in rubbish. I knew there were beautiful buildings around, but all I could
see was Centrepoint tower and, despite the fact I lived bang in the
centre, I felt peripheral, surplus to requirements, like a piece of flotsam
washed up by a tide.

I decided the best thing to do was visit my cousin. She (her name
was Martine) would know what to do. She had such a practical side
to her nature. She was the kind of girl who made things out of paper,
out of old bottles and string and bits of tin foil. She kept a gallon of
glue in her hall cupboard, she had sixteen pairs of scissors and she also
had a wide circle of friends, unlike the loose, fragmentary relationships
I tended to nurture. Besides, I needed to clear my head and the fresh
air would do me some good.

In the dwindling half-light I walked down Greek Street. A cloud of
pigeons peeled themselves off the pavement and rattled over the
rooftops while a flat, grey wind rubbed at my face. It was relentless,
as if it had been blowing since before time began, since twenty-five
million moons ago; ripping and crushing and wiping away. Pulverising
the earth till nothing but deathly grey flakes blew through the dark.

I passed by the Lounge, which was empty. I walked down Old
Compton Street, which was littered with beer cans. On the corner a
dark, sharp-boned girl sat in a booth. A neon sign flashed above her,
the red and blue tubes forming the words, Magnificent Love Show. I
read them twice over. They rattled me like a barbaric nurse slapping
my face, after which I glanced down at the girl and noticed how unhap-
piness pitted her skin, corroding her face in a way no acid could possibly manage, and I turned around and headed for Beak Street. I stopped
to admire a flimsy silk dress. It was red with strands of pale grey down
each voluptuous sleeve. Seconds later two boys ran past. They threw
a brick at the window and the sound shattered my eardrums. It was
high-pitched, sharper than nails, and the glass exploded. Tiny fragments
caught in my hair. The sky was cutting me up, unspooling, slicing me
into raw chunks of meat. The dress collapsed; the hollow arms fell

about in pale tatters and I slunk down a side alley. I was afraid the police might think that *I* had broken the window, that *I* was the cause of this senseless destruction.

I caught a bus into Leyton and when I alighted walked towards my cousin's new house. She lived in the suburbs, those neat streets and square, redbrick houses with flat metal-rimmed windows and shabby back gardens. When I glanced up, the clouds began to unravel. Each crease slowly disintegrated; millions of atoms flattened the pavements and lengthened the roads, after which more rain hit my face. It was a seamless sheet of grey water – a cascade, a cataract that raked down the sides of the buildings, filled the gutters, till all the houses were lost in a sluice.

When I reached my cousin's, she greeted me with a hug. Her arms wrapped around me and crushed down on my ribcage. She ruffled my hair and though I heard what she said, the words made no sense. Instead they slipped from her lips like wreaths of grey smoke and an invisible wall started growing between us.

She led me through to the living room and sat bright-eyed, surrounded by photos of her husband (Benny) and three, beautiful children (Charlie, Vicky and Liz) while I sat in the shadow, shrouded and grim.

My cousin laughed, she nodded, she giggled, and I knew almost immediately she couldn't feel what I felt. She couldn't see what I saw; for instance the way the rubber plants that stood in the corner of this well-ordered room began to unfurl. Or the manner in which the curtains unwove and spooled over the back of my chair. The patterns they made were unnerving. Mites gnawed at her furniture. I touched a table, and the table collapsed. I watched an armchair transformed into sawdust.

My cousin stood up. She made a pot of fresh coffee and I seem to remember the cups were bright blue. She talked about Vicky's new brace and Charlie's exam results, while I mentioned something about the world falling apart and she quietly muttered the word 'backbone' then hastily placed a packet of biscuits between us. When I dropped my coffee cup on the floor, my cousin suggested that I pick up the pieces. I knelt down and gingerly collected the shards one by one. Small splinters dug into my knees. They entered my bloodstream and my veins started to crackle. In the bathroom a bar of soap slipped from my hands, shattering a bottle of olive shampoo. The liquid leaked over the sink, streaked the toilet, and when I left my cousin's, I saw she was still mopping my blood off the floor.

I went on with my walk, drifted down one street after another. The landscape was more like a waiting room; grubby walls, obsolete posters, people staring down at their feet in the hope that something might happen. My legs wobbled, tears blinded my eyes and when I bumped into a woman I saw a small child wrapped in her arms. I thought it would be nice to stroke this child's cheek, but the second I touched it, the child started to scream and these screams rang out louder than church bells. The woman muttered something under her breath. She stared at me as if I was some verminous life form and I hurried away and took shelter inside Leyton bus station.

There was a large group of people milling around, all pushing and shoving each other. It seemed everyone wanted to get on to a bus, everyone needed to leave this area as quickly as possible. Their panic alerted me. Suddenly I wanted to be on board too. I fought with a young man for a seat. He scratched my arm with his briefcase, but finally I secured my position and he was removed from the vehicle. As we pulled out, I saw him standing in a doorway. He was hitting a woman with his clenched fists.

The bus took the main road back towards the centre of town. We passed by a garage and several charity shops: Save the Children, Help the Aged. We trundled over a flyover, down the Mile End Road, past Queen Mary College, Whitechapel, the diseased-looking London Hospital, above which a helicopter hovered like an over-sized fly. Then we drove over the flyover again and I wondered if anyone else noticed that we were going in circles, covering the same ground, over and over. I also wondered if they could see how, on either side of the street, the grey-looking trees were covered in gangrene. They were mottled and stained, slimy and wet, and the trees bore no leaves. Their branches clacked together like bones.

When we came to a bus stop a couple of women alighted. Then the vehicle started up again and, as we drove round a corner, I saw a building consumed in a cloud of white smoke. The man sitting opposite asked for a cigarette, but when I looked for my bag I realised I must have left it behind at my cousin's. Panic gripped hold of me. Everything was inside that bag: money, keys, the last gift Jack had given me, as well as my identification papers. I let out a terrified wail. I banged my hand on the window and at the next stop the driver made me alight from the bus. He said I was pond life. He didn't want 'my sort' on his bus.

I was standing close to the Thames. I saw a young couple walking hand in hand down a thin concrete path. I shouted, but neither one heard. They were too busy staring into each other's eyes and I hated them for it. I hated the way she kissed him and the way he kissed her. I hated the dumb smile over her face; the smile that said, 'If you kiss me then I'll be yours for ever. This is the road that leads straight to paradise.'

I turned my back on the couple and hurriedly walked down some steps, then on to a narrow strip of mud, but the mud kept collapsing under my feet. There were various objects scattered across it: oil drums, shopping trolleys, an old leather boot. The river swelled and slapped against the sides of the drums. It was gnawing and mining under the city.

I remembered a picnic on the banks of this river two years ago. The same river, but a different scenario. Jack and I had visited Hampton Court Palace. We'd brought cold chicken, hard-boiled eggs, three fresh oranges wrapped up in tissue. I remembered dabbling my feet in the water, feeding ducks, watching peacocks drift over green lawns, the pleasure boats sailing merrily down towards Greenwich. Jack was hardly real during this time; he was still just a word, but a word that kept me awake night after night, made me dance down the streets, made me buy huge bunches of flowers. On Guy Fawkes we walked through Regent's Park; we watched sprays of fireworks light up the sky, listened to wolves and lions communing. We visited St Paul's and made love in the Whispering Gallery. We sat by the Sphinx eating strawberry ice creams, heady with ardour and riddled with love.

These memories tore at my throat while above me seagulls clattered their wings and a grey scum swilled round my shoes. My tongue withered inside my mouth. I lowered my head and listened to the slow suck of the mud.

On the opposite side of the river the warehouses were chewed up and rotten. I knew for a fact there were hundreds of holes deep inside them: vents, fissures, wells, vacuums. I could hear the emptiness booming within, and far downwind the lone sound of a foghorn against a backdrop of sirens.

The rain and the clouds made me dizzy, and between gulping back tears and trying to breathe, I threw up in my hands. Regular secretions of phlegm mixed with foamy pink vomit spewed from my mouth. It seeped through my fingers, slicker than oil, after which the river thankfully washed it away.

I hitched a lift. I told the driver I needed to get back to the centre, but as soon as he started the engine, I knew I was travelling in the wrong direction. Each building we passed was less familiar than the building before. I wanted to shut my eyes, to curl into a ball and fall fast asleep. After ten minutes I told the driver to stop and when I stepped out of his car he drove away without saying goodbye. I wandered down street after street searching for someone to talk to. My footsteps were distant, muffled by the sound of the rain.

I watched two grey vans, but the moment I saw them, they collided into each other. The metal fractured and buckled like plasticine. The windscreens frosted and a body was abruptly propelled over a bonnet. Steam snaked into the air in great plumes; blood started to irrigate the shiny black tarmac.

I crossed to the far side of the road and snow began falling. When I saw a church I walked towards it and pushed open the door. It was only when I was seated on one of the pews that I realised the ceiling was missing. Instead of plaster and brickwork, stars were scattered over the roof, tiny pinpricks of light that appeared to grow fainter the longer I stared.

I crawled under the pew, but the snow wound its way round my feet; a white yarn like pearls which dwindled and melted the moment I touched them. I felt lonely, dark, inconsolable, and when I started to cry, the tears froze my lashes. A terrible world of cold and destruction tore at my throat. The ice cramped my stomach and I walked out of the church and away from this district.

Once, a long time ago, London had seemed like a ballroom, a fairground, like a magical place where love could be pulled out of a hat like a floppy-eared rabbit. I remembered the swish of the traffic, the bright-coloured cars, the swirl of bookshops, cinemas, art galleries and beautiful restaurants in whose sparkling interiors I dined out with Jack. Even the place names sounded like fairy tales: Crystal Palace, Knightsbridge, The Angel, King's Road. Now, in the blink of an eye, everything was reduced to the bone. It was The Cut, World's End, Hanger Lane, the Hungerford Bridge and Duff Street.

Reverse evolution

In the distance a bonfire crackled. It had been built in a skip and I walked towards it and for a time was warmed by its flames. I threw a log into the centre and watched the bark blister and melt before turning to ash. Then a spark caught my shoe and in turn my shoe smouldered till a small hole appeared. I had no choice but to take the shoe off, then discard it amongst the rest of the rubbish.

My teeth chatterred and, in an attempt to keep warm, I lay down in a park where a gust of decomposing leaves drifted over my body. The rotting vegetation clung to my skin, but I didn't brush it away. Instead a bird hopped down – a blackbird, a sparrow, a vulture? I couldn't tell which, but it fixed me with a glittering eye, then quietly pecked at my fingers as though they were worms.

I looked round for a sign that would lead me back home. One said that dogs weren't allowed to foul on the paths. Another that it was forbidden to walk on the grass. A third was in the shape of a map. I stared at it for a long time. I stared at an arrow with the words 'You Are Here' confidently printed in black underneath.

My bones ached; each nerve seemed torn in two, and the sinews between each of the nerves, and the synapses between each of the sinews.

If I'd poured acid over my body, I doubt I'd have felt more pain, if I'd taken a knife to my wrists, or set light to myself with matches and petrol. I was famine and murder and earthquake and suicide. I was the same tune as the small shards of glass, as the scraps of paper, the bones, the ashes and the broken black bottles.

I left the park and continued to walk. I clambered over a mass of barbed wire, instinctively knowing that this was a place of No Entry; the ground was scattered with old fridges and rust-ridden cookers, caravans, car tyres, window frames, yesterday's news and odd bits of metal twisted into the most inorganic of shapes. When I prodded what looked like a mattress, the whole thing gave way. The bulk was a putrefying mass of cabbage, cardboard and maggots. My hands were blue and burning with cold. My hair was nothing but a shroud of mud.

I slithered and crawled until I reached the edge of this wasteland. In the distance, mile-high cranes and long black trucks glittered and hummed. Their lights scored the earth, their brakes screeched, their large metal mouths opened and yawned. There were mountains of refuse higher than tower blocks. There was mile upon mile of rotting food, vegetation and shit, in fact a decomposition of all that was human mixed together with rats. I watched one in particular gnawing a carcass. It was making a nest from the bones, then a second joined in the fun, and a third and a fourth, the size of small dogs.

I crawled to the edge of a crater like the spineless creature I was. Over the past couple of hours my body had grown soft. It was now the texture of putty, the consistency of blancmange. I stared down at the crater which was five miles wide and at least twice as deep. A bomb might have caused it, a meteorite falling to earth, like you see in those films where whole worlds are wiped out, where the universe spins out of control and arc-shaped clouds disperse tons of white debris.

I looked down at my hands, which no longer worked, and my legs, which no longer moved. The snowflakes turned grey. Each reticulation of ice, each foreign particle was like a piece of my body. They fell around and beneath me, tattered and broken and I knew that neither the ground, nor the sky, nor the feel of my pulse could hold me down or stop me from shaking.

I struggled to catch hold of my breath, to gain equilibrium. I was breaking apart, after which I felt myself fall.

When I hit the ground a rock punctured my lung and one of my ribs ripped through my chest. There was a sudden soft wheezing as my stomach collapsed. I scrunched into a ball, shrunk to the molecular level of enzymes, to the size and number of blood cells, to corpuscles, organelles, platelets… to the electrical waves of my broken, dead heart. There wasn't a place on the Earth lower than this. There wasn't a single moment of warmth or relief. I'd reached rock bottom and no one, *no one* (neither my sister, nor cousin, nor friends, nor acquaintances) could convince me that this wasn't the truth. A slug crawled on the ground near where I lay.

I'm not exaggerating when I tell you that its cold, gummy body was as insignificant, as characterless as my own. Every link to the future was irrevocably broken and crushed.

Portions

Steve Grant

We had a nice exchange, the Asian woman and I, as she bumped and barged me in the shop, the corner shop which was cramped and permanently crowded and designed so that it was wide where it should be long and vice versa. 'It's all right, love, I used to push one of those,' I said cheerily, pointing at her chair and the invisible kid cocooned in artificial fibre. And I did, as Peg and I would travel remorselessly against the wind, all those years ago, in Tooting; and Peg would jump up and down and curse because the bus conductor wouldn't wait as we tried to fold the thing up and gather our shopping. And Jake's face, fiercely red and indignant in the pushchair.

The Asian woman smiled, and it's good to get a smile these days on the Harrow Road, where everyone looks so wet and blistered and ravaged and alone, where men stumble and women cringe as if their first greeting might be their last. And schoolgirls drink out of the can. And I felt good, like a puppy had licked me, and I watched her backside as she shuffled off into the gloom, and I thought, as it was a Rollover Wednesday, if I don't win the Lottery then I hope it's you. And I thought: it's because you, Adrian Murphy, hold the drink so well, because you have just had seven pints of Fosters lager and lime, well actually six because I'd stopped off at the Neald Arms on the way back from the doctor's and there they serve Carlsberg. Of course I should have been working, on a novel, planning a desk-top conspiracy, typing up some flavour-of-the-month-type interview, which I really hate because you have to listen to the sound of your own voice, your ingratiation, your mock-heroic guffaws, and every time I do that I want to be sick.

I never want to be sick on the booze. Not any more. I drink bottles of the stuff, I drink Scotch and vodka, bottles, the cheap stuff, £6.99 a throw, on an empty stomach, and if the doc knew, she'd have me committed. Because of all the drugs I take, the nifedipine, the atenolol, the hypovase, the lithium, the imdur, the aldactone, the zopoclone, the insulin, which is in fact called human insulatard but which used to come from a pig. Drugs for nearly every part of my body. And she'd say, with her bonny, chubby, blonde-bobbed Geordie face leaning towards me like she cared, 'Mr Murphy, why are you trying to kill yourself?' And I would reply that we only had ten minutes after all, and that if I really wanted to kill myself I could just swallow or inject all the pharmaceuticals she prescribes for me on a regular basis. Anyway, half of London's trying to kill themselves these days, doc, honest. They just can't find their way to the river. Why is that, she'll wonder, given that in Mozambique they are doing everything they can to stay alive, hanging on to the helicopters like it was *Apocalypse Now*, Les Afriques Très Plucky. And what about Chechnya, she'll wonder, who would want to live in a shithole like that, but they do, they go back. And no, you can't have any more sleeping pills just yet, Mr Murphy. Try sleeping with the window open, try a brisk walk, and have you ever thought of a good book? And cut out all that fried food.

Lately, I've found myself in the pub more often than I'd like to admit. Like every day. And I don't go there for the company, oh no, my local is a decided alco-hole, where they don't serve food, where the gents is always out of order, and where they run out of crisps, peanuts and cigarettes three weeks out of four. The only thing that works is the golf machine. The regulars organise golf tournaments (first prize £20); they crowd around the machine like it was the eighteenth at Turnbury. The daytime crowd: unemployed Chelsea-supporting skinheads, pasty-faced drunks living off their wives, baleful pensioners, shrill-voiced Welsh whores, lots of Irish, one of whom approached me the other day and asked if I had a place to stay. Cheeky cunt. I sit in a far corner and read the *Standard* or stare at the wall. I have nothing to say to these people, although I am such a feature these days that some of them nod in my direction, inform me of the result of some televised horse race and try to summon the barmaid for me when she's out of eye contact, which is almost permanently, the pious Catholic teetotal bitch. One of them calls me Bigfoot.

Occasionally a decent-looking woman comes in, from the nearby college, or one of the firms on the main road. She'll actually be alone, be fit-looking, drink pints and smoke fags, and I will think that it's like being young again and she must be a goer or at least of independent spirit and sexual charity and sometimes I will walk up, because they always sit near me, being that it's the non-tossers' area of the main bar. But mostly I don't bother because I'm so old now, and so impotent, and I think I may smell bad, and I haven't changed my sheets for ages and they are full of joint burns and stains of various description. And what's the point, because she'll probably tell me to sod off or, worse, take a few pints off me and then leave.

A few days ago I went to Swallows, my regular massage haunt, because they had this new girl there from Italy who was supposedly eighteen years old. Apparently there's almost been a queue down Camden Road. Anyway, this girl is supposed to be called Oleanna, only when I get there she's called Tina and she's twenty. Which is all right, a relief. Because I was a bit worried about her being called Oleanna, because that's the name of a play by David Mamet about this mad feminist who fucks up her teacher's life and I think maybe she's a plant, because they hardly ever use their real names, maybe she's got a hidden camera, which is all the rage these days, maybe she's doing a series for Channel 4. Actually, the girls reckon she's Albanian. Anyway, when I get there, Geri, who I see a lot, is on the door. Geri is great, she's thirty-eight and anorexic and has had more pricks than a second-hand dartboard, but she gives the best blow job in town (think of your favourite heroin fix, multiply it by a zillion and you're nowhere close). She doesn't worry about condoms if you pay extra (strictly for the oral and no swallowing), and is a very likeable and clever woman who's lived with a Triad and swum representatively. (This is getting a bit irresponsible, isn't it? So, a few quick messages. Fight AIDS. Smoking kills. OK?)

Geri has a son, Clifford, who's hyperactive, and a Chinese partner with an unpronounceable name, Wong is at the end of it, and she's having problems with accommodation because her partner is an illegal immigrant, and I often bring presents for her boy and check on her progress. Geri is saying, 'This is Adrian, he's one of our regulars, he's a very nice man, Tina,' and she turns to me and says, 'Isn't Tina beautiful, Ade? She looks like one of the Corrs.' I don't know what she means, what is the Corrs, is it that American beer? True, Tina is very attractive, and very young, younger than both my kids, but we'll leave that, cos it's not the same thing, but the problem is that she doesn't speak a word of English. Well, she does know two words, 'Money' and 'No'. Wouldn't let me go down on her, so I left, only it took me at least twenty minutes to explain to her that I'm not interested in a Milanese, or is it Tiranese, ice maiden who looks like she's just reluctantly kissed someone's arse. When I get out, Geri's saying how Tina's really upset and everyone else has gone out with a smirk and is there something wrong, and she hands me a half-smoked spliff, and I tell her the problem. Then I see the look on Geri's face, and she's trying to hide it, because she's a professional, but I know what she's thinking: You never go down on me, do you, you fucking jam rag? And she's right, I don't. Because she's thirty-eight and she's had more pricks than a Victorian pin cushion. Sadly, she's just not cunnilingually compatible. And for the first time in a while, I actually feel seedy.

I'm at home trying to boil some water in a large saucepan, which is filmed with minestrone soup and isn't very good with tea. The phone rings. It's a rare occurrence these days, my few remaining friends having decided that I can ring them, and that I'm not really worth bothering with anyway, because I never go out any more in the evenings and don't see the point of rehearsing my current decline again over a bottle of cheap or pretentious plonk.

It's Mary, once about as close as they get, but now a blur of first nights and press screenings and late-night meals where she would always spot something wrong with the food and get us a discount. Mary teaches drama and has rung up to say that she is off to Toledo to see some art exhibition with Joaquim, who's gay and writes architecture books that cost £100 for a living.

'What, that cunt?'

'Don't you mean prick, Adrian?' Mary doesn't like the word 'cunt' and constantly substitutes the word 'prick', which doesn't do it, frankly. Mary travels a lot in her work, and when she isn't travelling on work she is travelling for pleasure, rooting out the bargains in the superior sorts of travel agents even though she's been round the world at least eight times already. Every two years, Mary turns down some foreign millionaire who wants to whisk her off into the sunlight. She wants to be independent. But she's pushing fifty now, and she sometimes worries about dying alone. We don't discuss it. If it happens to me, which it almost certainly will, unless I collapse with the big one during a match at Wembley, I muse that the chances of me being found in less than a fortnight are pretty remote.

'You've got to get yourself together,' chirps Mary. 'You're a mess, you've got joint burns in every shirt, your upper lip is dark brown, you've got these strange marks on your trousers. You're a leper. Somebody has got to tell you.'

All through my decline from grace, Mary had been proffering the same sort of advice. 'You are committing professional suicide.' 'You should stop seeing those hookers.' 'You need to lose weight, here's a diet.' She used to think I was sensitive, but sadness is the unacceptable face of sensitivity; and black depression, depression that makes you stand rooted to the spot for hours unable to speak or open your eyes, depression that roots you to your mattress and makes putting on your trousers simply impossible, well that merely sucks.

'Is the lithium working yet?'

'Not really. It's making my skin dry.'

'Has it made you dopey?'

'Hard to say.'

'Well, stop drinking with it, it's dangerous.'

Mary and I started to fall out when she pulled a cigarette out of my mouth in Joe Allen's. There were people I knew in there.

'Every time you want to smoke, think of me,' Mary said.

I replied, 'Every time I think of you, I want to smoke.'

OK, so her dad died of a smoking-related disease, she reads the *Observer*, etc. I've never hit a woman but I came close.

'I'll send you a postcard from Toledo.'

'Great.'

'And stay off those drugs and those fucking women. They are wrecking what's left of your life.'

'Exactly.'

'You'll never work again, you know.'

'I know. Goodbye.'

'Goodbye.' Pause. 'You're a waste of space, Ade. I'm sorry to have to say it.'

Anyway, a week or so after, Geri rings me about some new skunk she's acquired and we arrange to meet the following day in King's Cross, owing to the fact that she's not working at Swallows for six days on account of her son being ill with chickenpox and her Chinese illegal immigrant common-law husband being 'totally fucking useless'. Which suits me cos I don't want to wait, and then she tells me about this old boy, a judge she insists, who likes to be crapped on and then have the stuff rubbed into his body, which nearly causes vomitus, and how the other night the showers broke down so he was stuck in the cubicle for hours. Shocking from a place which I took to be a sexual-fluids-only establishment. And it's not spacious. You can bump into anyone there, and the noise travels as well, given that all the cubicles seem to have been built from balsa wood. So how come I've never smelt it? Do they have a private wing for this kind of thing? Personally speaking, I've never been a slap, wallop and bash sort of a chap. I know that the Greeks who frequent the place seem to be no-nonsense merchants for whom foreplay might as well be Thermopylae, but I like to pretend there's romance about the place.

Certainly there's jealousy. Like young Clerise the other day, when Geri's down the chippy, telling me how Geri's husband is a 'real dirty bastard' and likes to eat crab lice and actually encourages her to catch them off the punters so he can turn them into some Oriental dish of dishes. I don't like this, but Clerise's laughter shimmers up and down the corridor. She's twenty-five and blonde and perfect except for a slight rash on her right cheek, which thankfully isn't related to her profession and which makes her sensitive and tender, touching it when she thinks you're not looking and even asking if it bothers you. How could it when she is so exquisite, even in a daft Santa Claus outfit with white fur trim, a freckled cabbage patch of skin her own mortal, grace-saving Achilles heel?

Clerise – her real name is Joan, according to a tax envelope sticking out of her bag – didn't want to work at Tesco's. And, like most of the girls, she likes a good time, which means drink, fags and dope but more pointedly ecstasy and crack cocaine. Clerise doesn't have any kids, and in that she's a minority, but instead she pays heavily for the upkeep of a succession of motor cars, fostered on her but soon dispatched into the night wrecked in both body and spirit. They are crashed, they are towed away, they are broken into by black youths who take her gloves and spare clothes but leave her Simon and Garfunkel tape. At present, she is forced to cab it back to Hackney, where she lives with her nan, who thinks she's a temp currently working for Royal Assurance. Which is a trek, and means that she sometimes slopes off early, which pisses off the owner, Madame Big. And she lights her twelfth spliff of the day and tells me that Mariana, the Dublin girl, currently has a boyfriend who likes fucking in the back of cabs and how he pays the driver fifty quid to drive round London for an hour or so with them at it like the clappers in the back seat. Typical London cab, I muse. You can fuck but you can't smoke.

Then Clerise tells me a joke. She's good at jokes, better at jokes than sex. Clerise is beautiful, and a sad but almost infallible rule of life and the sex game is that the better you look the less you have to try. Maybe why she is better at receiving pleasure than giving it, better at coming than going. She loves head, but demands you wear a condom (always with her the condom) over your tongue, which seems a small insurance. I find the rubber has a habit of slipping off just before she starts to arch and informs me in that breathy re-educated Essex Girl voice 'I'm gonna come so quick'. I know it's indefensible but it's not as indefensible as taking the condom off before you fuck someone, which is easier than it sounds. And I don't fuck, haven't for years, so I reckon I'm safe, well as safe as it ever gets. Certainly I'm no Freddie Mercury, no Kenny Everett, who was as hard to get as a Big Mac. Clerise is just uptight because she's a working girl, it's like safety in the workplace to her, next she'll be putting johnnies on her clients' fingers. By the way, did anyone ever tell you that condoms are fun? Condoms are like peace at an execution. Safe sex? My arse. So to speak. Safe sex? Tell that to Anne Boleyn.

The joke. A little girl goes into a shop, which claims to sell every flavour of ice cream known to mankind. So the little girl hands over her 50 pence and orders a bacon and egg sundae. It comes and she says: 'I can taste the bacon, but where's the egg?' And the vendor says: 'Well, lick the other side.' And then she orders a fish and chip lolly and she says: 'I can taste the chips but where's the fish?' And the guy again replies: 'Well, lick the other side.' Then she gets a pie and mash sundae. She is not impressed. 'This tastes like shit!' she cries. 'Well,' says the ice cream man, 'lick the other side.'

'Hang on,' Clerise says, 'I've got another one. Stevie Wonder gives this press conference and a journalist asks him was it tough growing up blind. Stevie says, yeah, but it could have been worse, I could be black.'

Sometimes I can hang out at Swallows for hours. The main frequenters of these places, despite what London's married women pretend to think, are young, well-off, employed, married businessmen. Or *do* they think? Maybe they suss out that London, which naturally has more massage parlours than any place in the country, many of them soon to be legalised by the Mayor's office, is awash with cheating men. Men who do it not because they're desperate, but because they have the money, are bored, think that they can, and feel that the wife or partner is a big disappointment in the sack. Sometimes I ride a bus and go home and think about how miserable London really is, and I feel like a pyrrhic victory. Only they don't serve them where I drink. All that shame and deceit can make a single man feel all flossy and glossy like a big dog in an advert.

It's ten am in the local, and there is a coffin lying along the bar. The coffin belongs to John Casey. Casey was a regular who made the mistake of forgetting his house keys when he arrived for an afternoon session. Leaving the pub at 4.30pm and being unable to locate said keys on returning to his home nearby, he tried to alert his family, wife Moira and children Liam and Shane, who had decided to take in a late afternoon showing of Tim Burton's decapitation marathon, *Sleepy Hollow*, at Whiteleys. Failing to summon any assistance, Casey shinned up the drainpipe, fell, being somewhat inebriated, and died. In a pool of blood.

Hence the tribute. I am here on sufferance, having been dragged here by my cleaner Jimmy. Jimmy is an alcoholic, hence his closeness to Casey, who was also an alcoholic, but unlike Jimmy never had the chance of a recovery programme, having expired in the process of convincing himself that he didn't have a problem, that his life was perfectly normal, apart from the occasional memory lapse. Casey's lapse of memory was fortunately traced to a medical condition, fortunate for his widow who picked up the insurance, though it was barely enough to cover the cost of the funeral. The medical condition was the result of the other stroke of ill fortune that struck Casey in the last of his thirty-seven years. Jimmy and Casey would spend some time together in the bookies, just round the corner from the local, a place of vigorous activity and high-tech finery. Casey was in the habit of winding up the punters by screaming with glee at the climax of every dog and horse race. Jimmy would encourage him to elaborate this act by making small talk with Big Doris at the Pay Out window and rattling the sides of his Beer Drinker's Wallet ('Only opens when the pub does') to give the impression that he's collecting. The upshot of this is that a group of extremely tough and unsophisticated navvies in the area to dig up the pavement in front of the post office are convinced that Casey is an infallible punter and decide to follow him and rob him one day when he's on his own. What's more, when they discover that Casey's pockets contain 49 pence, a comb and a prescription for Calpurid foot lotion, they give him a right good hammering and one of them finishes with a glancing blow to the temple from his size thirteen Doc Martens. Semi-coma-concussion job. Casey couldn't remember a thing.

Anyway, at least we are not going to the funeral. This is just a quick paying of respects, made possible by the landlord's generosity and the inexpensive placation of the Plod. The problem is that Jimmy made enemies when he was a drinker, and he is now among them. And Jimmy has brought me along in order to ensure that he doesn't meet with any harm, and that he stays off the booze, which he does and has done for almost a year, which strikes me as something wonderful as I gaze along the labels on the spirits bottles, and look at all that alluring artwork and liquid transparency. And compare that to the fellow mourners who all look very Kray-on-the-piss-like. I have seen Jimmy, seen him from the pub itself, seen him walk past the place and look in and grit his teeth and walk on. And I think that this is magnificent. And when he comes round to clean we have a spliff and talk about things and he says he's thought about suicide a hundred times but he knows he would fuck it up, and I remember when he was on four bottles of vodka and fourteen cans of Special Brew a day and how I came back and caught him trying to clean the back window from the outside, hanging backwards from the hips and sinking fast. What were my obligations as an admittedly cash-in-hand employer and generous with it, I wondered. He has lots of kids by various women. None of them speak to him on a regular basis.

The problem is that Jimmy's sobriety has not made him any the less temperate. Oh no. He is a sort of Jack the Hat, fond of winding up west London villains with his own distinctive brand of Scouse candour. As we stood up and milled around the coffin, which had to be out by midday and this being about 11.15, the eyeballing soon established itself, Jimmy being the object of affliction, so to speak, of a group of cockney nasties from Earls Court, the eldest of whom has been regaling his compadres with his determination to give up smoking as it's 'at least two fucking big bags of groceries a week'.

Jimmy whispers to me that there has unfortunately been pre-sobriety verbal fisticuffs with some of these gentlemen, the source of the trouble being the Irish Peace Process, and, Jimmy being from a staunch Protestant Liverpool background, the detail being Jimmy's declaration that the nuns let his mother die of the cancer. Anyway, I have to leave. Have to meet Geri at King's Cross, pick up my drugs. I'm English, folks, it's not my problem. It isn't my problem, honest. And I'm not being symbolic here. This is a real pub in a real part of north-west London, run by the Irish and therefore by no one. But I have to leave. These people can inflict real and serious damage. They talk openly of things which cannot be endured. They are like the end of disease, blindness, decapitated limbs, coma, they are people who will not be escaped. Unless you slope out.

'I gotta go, Jimmy.' I had him against the door to the gents which says G......T and is riddled like a dartboard. 'You caaan't,' he's croaking and squealing, and I can't work out whether he's telling me that I can't leave him, or that I am a cunt for doing so. And just then, one of these Gloucester Road Paddies comes over, all scrubbed up and looking like a bag of carrots in his orange off-the-peg-once-fitted-doesn't-now suit. 'Jimmy, I thought they banned ya from here, ya dirty little cunt.' 'Dat's right,' offers McGuinness the landlord, 'banned him for nothing at all to do with his drinking, as well.' Realising we are talking about the offence Jimmy has given to the nun and that noble institution across the water that has never caught on in London thanks to the good offices of more than one monarch. 'Coming to the funeral, Jimmy, the twist-ed little cuntshite that you are?' another asks. I am ignored by all. Except Jimmy, who is grabbing my sleeve, more scared, if this is in any way believable, of going back on the drink than he is of being battered half to death. How can a man be so unpopular with his peers? And it's not as if any of them know or like me, nor am I in any way reassured by my cleaner's assurance that they will not lay a finger on me or mine because they respect my 'booklarnin'. Apparently the atmosphere is now tense, tense by the standards of the local being pre-Gunfight at the OK Corral big match warm-up tense, the tragedy being that the pub is a women-free zone, that this is a special little get-together numbering no more than a dozen by which we can pay our last respects to a man who, from what I can discern, which is not very much admittedly, as without the women being present it is very much a non-verbal-communication zone, nobody had much to say for in the first place. Apart from, that is, he died in the way of duty, in a roundabout sense.

'Doesn't anybody in this place like you, Jimmy?'

'Fuck 'em. Fuck 'em.' He's waving his can of Irn Bru around, spilling it. He's sober. The only one. I ask him does he know that you can get low-calorie Irn Bru now, which frankly seems to me like the end of civilisation as we know it but is good for diabetics.

'Biopseee, man,' he starts moaning. 'Biopsee, biopsee.' Jimmy had to have a liver biopsy recently, last week, Wednesday, but they cancelled it. They told him it was because of the risk it might entail, but that's obviously bollocks, obviously another NHS cancellation, which now has Jimmy convinced that he is the possessor of an organ that would be sent back were it ever to be served in a café on Kilburn High Road.

It turns out that the Borgia feud that has been festering at the local concerns nothing less than the public bar bible itself, the *Sun*. One late morning when Jimmy was still sober enough to read, he had taken a copy of the newspaper from an empty bar stool. But the bar stool was not empty, oh no, it was the settling place of one Big John Connelly, who was in the men's room dusting himself down after another night of random carnage on the byways of Willesden. Jimmy was standing at the counter checking the football scores, as he was very partial to the bet where you bet on one side to be leading at half-time and the other to be winning at the end. And he was noting that there were two of these results and why the fuck had he not got out of bed on the Saturday and studied up the form, the answer being that he was having to go to a special meeting with his fifteen-year-old estranged son Darren's probation officer's psychiatric nurse. And that was when Big John Connelly reappeared, a retired criminal and one-time site foreman who actually did resemble a gnarled and mud-cased potato that had been stuffed into a boiler suit and a ginormous pair of wellies, and a Michigan State football jacket and a hard hat which he never took off even in the local, so many enemies had he made in the many years since he left Galway Bay.

Three things are known about Connelly: he has the most fearsome Alsatian bitch in London, a genuinely psychopathic animal on which he dotes, and against which he will not hear a word, but which has been known to empty the local in seconds and which Jimmy says would 'bite off your left leg and beat you to death with it as soon as fucking snarl at you'. He first signed on in 1948 when the dole thing started, and he was fresh out of the army, dishonourably discharged for selling petrol to the enemy. Being no fool he put down as his trade or profession 'trapeze artist' and spent the next three years in bed. He did three years for trying to kill a Muslim, who owed him money, with a hatchet. He had a gun but there were no bullets, as he found out when he pushed it against the poor man's head and pulled the trigger repeatedly. He should have done five, but several surprise defence witnesses managed to cast doubt on the Muslim's character, which was impeccable. Apart from his tendency to make disastrous choices when in debt.

Connelly, seeing that Jimmy was reading his *Sun*, took hold of Jimmy by the arse of his jeans and flipped him over to the other side of the bar and told him to start serving Big John for free. And nobody minded, not even Patrick the landlord, who laughed at everything. Big John, on reclaiming his *Sun*, had placed it atop the bar stool and sat down on top of it so fiercely that it was squashed as flat as a newspaper could get.

'Ah, John, it's a terrible thing to be doing to Richard Littlejohn,' quipped Pat the Landlord.

'And those page three girlies,' said Malone the Unemployable looking up from his Bloody Mary.

'And you can't see me pissing from here, John,' snarled Jimmy, who had nipped down to the cellar and done something unspeakable to the Guinness. That was the reason the argument turned into a local feud among the local's regulars. Jimmy had pissed in the Guinness. And there was a free *Mirror* on a table by the jukebox all the time.

King's Cross. Geri will be on time, but I am an hour early. She tells me to wait by one of the bus stops at the front of the station, that she will see me when she arrives in her car, with the drugs, which will keep me going for a week or more and which she gets at the drop of a hat from some spiv on the estate in Finchley where she lives. Geri wants to move home because her husband Wong is subject to lots of racial abuse. Being unable to speak English, he can't understand most of it but has started to get the message. The council are not interested because she doesn't have enough points, although her son does have 'behavioural problems', apparently, but whose doesn't? I took my son to see *Henry V* at the Regent's Park Open Air Theatre and during the speech about closing the wall up with our English dead and basically duffing up Froggy, there was a downpour and the entire English army buggered off stage left. This had a profound effect on him, a distrust of authority, which led inevitably to the school shrink after he had set fire to the school changing rooms. That day I felt proud of Jake. Even though I had spent two hours being paid to listen to some Hollywood actor banging on about his cocaine addiction and his car crashes and his paternity suits and the thousands of dames who wanted to suck his shrivelled and circumcised schlong, and how when he received his second Oscar – second, mind – he felt an enormous wave of ill will from the academy and he realised he had no friends and I had to sit there and cringe and not say that my son had just set fire to the school dressing room and there were fire engines and he would have to be up before the psycho-beak for ever after and I didn't give a fuck about his fucking cocaine fucking cunt overdose except that it should HAVE KILLED HIM!!! And it was an actor, Shakespeare, who screwed up my son. And he screwed me up too because they made me play Peasblossom the fairy at a decidedly impressionable age, and in fact that fucking Shakespeare has got a lot to answer for, as have bloody actors from Hollywood who don't know they are fucking born, which MEANS YOU!! But instead I asked: 'So I suppose this latest project has been a particular challenge for you?'

There are places in the world where you do not want to be stranded for an hour, even in daylight, waiting to pick up drugs from a prostitute, not even one who teaches horse-riding in her spare time. King's Cross is one of them. God, I used to work here when I first arrived in London in 1970. For a month only, I worked for a celebrated left-wing journal in a rickety, rat-infected and -infested, three-floor slum, until one of my older trad-jazz enthusiast friends arrived from Salford and started talking loudly in the foyer about 'that coon with the banjo that's died'. He meant Jimi Hendrix. Non-violent hippies have a simple solution when they feel the need for violence. They give you bad acid and then they sack you. But this place was strictly beards, beer and Marxism: so I just got the sack.

Now in those days, King's Cross was no beauty spot. Lorries piled into the Gray's Inn Road traffic system like drunken fans turning up late for the game, the exhaust fumes and the noise were constant and disgusting and with the mainline station it had its fair share of litter and trouble, especially when the Scots came down for the Wembley showdown. But it wasn't like this: ordure stacked against every available support, dripping boxes, discarded Tampax, rat-chewed burgers, killer syringes, greasy chips lain in cardboard boxes like air-crash victims, the indestructible condom, the dolls and bottles opened and broken. The people simply the cast of a year's worth of *Panorama*s, *Newsnight* specials and *Cutting Edge*s. There are fewer whores than there used to be in the 1980s but now they look a lot rougher, and they fight with their pimps in the doorways and outside the station. I've been waiting fifteen min-utes and I've already encountered two acts of violence: two Glasgow

winos trying to land a punch between them and almost failing, in
Burger King, and a junkie being rolled into a sheet by two extremely
large cops. I cross the road and enter this amusement arcade, but it's
full of Malays and they look extremely threatening, especially the ones
in the basement on the pool table. I leave and exchange words with a
crone dressed like she's a survivor of Stalingrad but with a heavy Irish
brogue and she thrusts a handful of these lucky-heather sprigs in my
face. I point out that she is not the best advertisement for her product
but that if she wins the Rollover on Saturday we'll do business.

I cross the road again, sit in one of the bus shelters and am immediately offered a can of Tennant's by the chap sprawled to my right. What
to do. I am desperate for a drink but he must have something disgusting, like Weil's disease or something. He tells me that he used to be a
fireman and one day he came home from work to find that his house
had burned down with his wife and two kids inside it; he turned round,
he says, and never went back. This is a précis, the way he tells it it's
much longer and interrupted by random vomiting. I am sceptical but
say nothing. He puts a hand into a filthy gabardine and shows me a
newspaper cutting, a paper from Scotland, Inverness. A story and a
picture of a smouldering terraced house. That's a long way to travel.
Did he ever think about suicide, I ask. 'What do you think I'm doing
now?' he murmurs, polishing the top of the can.

Suddenly I can see Geri striding towards me with her supposedly
sick but actually rather robust six-year-old son in tow. She's carrying
him but he looks too big, and he's struggling, and she looks extremely
pissed off. Where have you fucking well been sort of stuff. The council
are a bunch of cunts sort of stuff. The council have offered her a place
that is two hours from her son's school, and are telling her that the
only alternative is for her to rent privately, which is expensive given
that her partner Mr Wong is unable to work.

'Why can't I meet a rich bloke? All the other girls do. All I ever
meet are losers like you. Christ, I could have gone to the States with
that guy. Florida. He was facking loaded, and what do I do? I blow
him out. I'm a cunt. Clifford, come here, stop messing about with the
seat, babe.'

We are sitting in Geri's car, a Vauxhall something, I don't know, I
don't drive, and she hands over the packet of Benson and Hedges with
the bag inside and I give her three £20 notes and we are parked in a

side street by the station and I cannot believe that this is my life now. And sometimes I feel like I'm married to Geri, and am having an affair with Clerise on the side. Because Clerise and Geri often share shifts at Swallows and I can't see one of them while the other is there because it upsets them, and causes friction and jealousy.

(And when I went to the Brewer's Droop clinic, and they said I couldn't have Viagra but did qualify for the course of injections, when the doctor referred to my partner I had to remind him that I had the two, that my days with enthusiastic amateurs were over. Cheeky bastard then asked if I could see my own penis. To which I replied in my best Hancockian, 'See it, mush, it's lifting it above my head that's the tricky part', after which he reassured me that the question referred only to the size of my beer gut. I didn't have it done though. I can't face a future where a romantic exchange includes the likes of 'Open another bottle of Pinot Grigio, darling, while I nip off to the lav and inject myself in the knob'.)

'The place got worked over last night.' Geri's tense and picking at the steering wheel. Clifford, who I notice doesn't look Chinese at all, is duffing up a plastic dinosaur. She's wearing a Matthew Robinson sarong and a long scarf that she's got doubled up boa constrictor style with a muffler-type configuration around her neck. She pulls it down to reveal a crop of ugly-looking blue and grey choke marks. She suddenly reminds me of Stephen Tyler. Two black guys robbed the Swallows and beat up Janine and May the receptionist with coshes, and tried to throttle Geri when she tried to stop them nicking her mobile phone. 'They're fucking Somalis,' she thinks but isn't sure. The boss, Madame Big, doesn't provide any kind of protection but this has happened twice now and they are going to install CCTV. The cops have been round, she says. They're sweet, but the best way of catching the guys is if they strike again. It's a soft touch: straight in, bash the girls, nick the cash box and all the bags and anything out of the pockets, and scarper.

'I want to get out of this fucking racket, Ade,' she moans, but she's hurting and sweating and getting honked at by other drivers and she sticks an arm out and gives a V-sign and the kid in the back is trying to get out of the car and somebody's definitely farted, one way or another. I sit there looking at my rocks in the open cigarette packet, and I know she is going to bring up the subject of selling her story to a tabloid and so I make an excuse and kiss her on the cheek and run away as fast as I can, which is pretty slow. 'I would rather sell babies,' I hear her grunt just as Clifford is sick on the back seat.

In the *Mirror* today, there's a story about a man who was beaten up outside a club in Manchester so badly that his own son didn't recognise him. He got depressed, couldn't work, and hanged himself on the day he was due to be evicted. Only twenty-one. And the men who disfigured him got three months and laughed their way down to the cells. It was an argument about queue-jumping and he was with his wife. Six against one. He must have been trying to impress her. Poor, silly sod.

Last week it was a depressed accountant from Cheltenham who jumped off Beachy Head, where mum and dad used to take me when I was a kid, 580 feet and quite a way from Cheltenham. That should do it, but what if you don't land on your head? Same issue, sixteen-year-old girl worried about exams and a school bully takes an overdose of paracetamol which kills her but not until fifteen days have elapsed, after liver failure, and lots of agony. These are stories that stay. The man from Salford in his mid-forties who had four pints and got breathalysed and because he knew he would lose his job took himself up to the country near Alderley Edge and gassed himself with the exhaust. Left four kids and a widow. The single mother who cradled her baby as she jumped from the fourteenth floor, the abandoned gran who couldn't stand the noise and put a bag over her head. The farmer who shot himself in North Wales, one of seventy-one such suicides in the last year apparently, sick of months of worry and sleeplessness, unable to feed his flock or enjoy the view. Curiously these stories tend to appear next to the classified double-page spread about loan repayment, debt management, easy access to cash, don't worry if you're a financial cripple, we'll help. Sorry, no tenants.

Millennium.

Clerise is round. Funny how she knows whenever I've got the drugs, but I suppose Geri would have told her in that honour-among-whores way that they have. Clerise is so into partying, as she calls it, that reality almost ceases to impinge, making me wonder how she can find the address, and the right doorbell, and get up the stairs without falling up them. Not that she will encounter anything sobering at the top of

them. I don't make any effort any more. I don't even clean the cigarette butts out of the bog, empty the big straw basket of its rotting baltis,
its sour bottle cocktail, its creeping essence of old joint ash. My joint-
burn situation is now so bad that I'm too ashamed to take my skivvies
to the Asian laundromat next door. I dump them in the street and go
to M&S for replacements but come back with Cumberland sausages
or a bottle of vodka. I have to see a bloke about a job next week but
what will I fucking wear?

I do the business with Clerise as soon as poss. She's a stunning girl
apart from that rash, and despite her permanent daze she loves being
pleasured, which is good for a man to know, although there are still
some who don't even care. But because she's in a permanent daze the
pleasure doesn't register for long. And she's got a confession to make,
having to get it off her chest and knowing, thinking, that I'll be discreet, because she thinks, says, I'm a nice guy and that I care, which I
don't really know that I do any more, that the guys who smashed up
Swallows and beat up Geri and Janine were friends of her boyfriend,
well, in fact, were led by her boyfriend. Clerise's boyfriend is news to
me. She's not a great earbender and I'd assumed she was free and independent, unlike most of the girls who are usually dragging some useless piece of male trash around behind them. Usually something that
drinks their money and then them.

Winston is a fuck-up. According to Clerise he was christened Winston
Churchill by his post-war mom and pop as a tribute to the country to
which they had emigrated in 1946 and to its war leader, the Churchills
from Barbados not only being staunch Britophiles but having distinguished themselves in the wartime armed forces, he as a sergeant in
the Royal Signals, she as a radio operator stationed in Leeds. Apparently
Winston was a charming child, a real beam off the melon. Then he got
stopped by the police in Luton, where he grew up, and the police did
not take too kindly to it when Winston gave his name. As one of them
asked him: 'What's a nigger cunt like you doing with the name of the
man who defeated Nazism?' They beat him badly, and they beat his
mate who said that his name was Harold Macmillan, because he didn't
know Winston's surname and assumed he was taking the piss, which
he wasn't officer, man, no way. They didn't beat Winston's other friend,
though, who was white and just had to look on. It wasn't the first time,
but it was by far the worst. And it made Winston bitter. He'd always

been a bit of a thief. Winston used to work in the supermarket on the estate, stacking shelves and freezers after hours, and smuggle food out inside his clothes, frozen food, just stroll past the owner, a fat ras clat man, a pussy. One day the shop got robbed and they suspected Winston and he got the sack, so he went back and smashed all the windows and then he took nothing. Fat raas man, he been robbing those people blind for years, he done make me clean up dog puke on my first day, dog puke, he done laugh at ma name.

Clerise doesn't know what to do about Winston, who some years along the road has turned into a bit of a Bill Sykes, has been incarcerated by Her Majesty on three occasions, the last for a period of three years. It is quite clear to me that Clerise is scared of this guy, scared in an I-can't-leave-him kind of a way.

'I'm gonna end up in the river,' she moans, sitting on my sofa with its two bald arms and the stains on both sides, and I think I don't care but I should and Elvis is singing 'Peace in the Valley' on the stereo at the end of the room, and it empties both of us. The doorbell rings and it's Jimmy. Normally he's very cagey when I've got company, offers to disembowel himself on the spot, but now he's clambering up the stairs, crazed, I imagine, by some bodily reaction to the sudden cessation of alcoholic hostilities. The barrage of booze. He's jittery, barely nods at Clerise and starts going on about how he could do wonders for the flat and how it's got so much space and light, not like his poxy little council diphole, and he wants to put shelves in for the CDs and tapes, and I tell him that it ain't gonna happen, that I have no discernible future, and that he will be the tenant very soon. And he snarls 'Fuck off!' and starts rolling a spliff, despite which Clerise signals that she is leaving and that I can see her in seven days and that she wants paying. Which I do. Seventy quid.

Lou Reed's 'A Perfect Day' is playing in the portable CD player perched on top of the sound system. Jimmy tells me how he tore up a bet he had for a football match because he didn't realise that ninety minutes included time added on and so he's lost £40, only he hasn't because he's torn up the slip and put it in the bin under his desk in the kitchen, and his son Darren, his oldest, almost normal, is staying with him at the pres, and has retrieved the bits and stuck them together with super-glue, so it's legal. Apparently Darren turning up at the local with his mum in tow, one of the four women to whom Jimmy is CSA-wedded for life, saved Jimmy from a good pasting on the day of the funeral. He hasn't even asked me where I went.

Jimmy has just been to his AA meeting and complains that he is now expected to go on another AA weekend away, this time to Skegness, and how it's a complete ripoff, the bar stocked full of overpriced non-alcoholic beverages like Red Bull and Purdey's, even more expensive than they are in the supermarket where I met that Asian lady and causing bad vibes among the AA's lost tribe of twitching pledged.

'And at Southend they had on a fuckin tart who sang "Cigareets and Whisky and Wild Wild Women" at the top of her voice,' he says, pawing at my books, which he wants to clean so badly, one by one. Jimmy says he has been contemplating the Suicide again, on account that he can't sleep, at all, not for days, and he had thought seriously about rigging up a noose on his staircase, 'because it's too fuckin' small to swing a cat in', but he decided he wants to clean my flat instead.

Clerise isn't happy about Jimmy's presence. I think she's figured him as a woman-beater, which he is, and it's not much of a defence to point out that when Jimmy has hit a woman the woman in question has invariably hit him back three times as hard. He's also wired. But when you get to know him, well, he's a real gin and tonic. What with the insomnia, the alcoholism, the child support, the tax man, the women, the kids, the tiny council flat where his downstairs neighbours regularly spend their nights boiling goat's heads, suicide is an attractive option, but instead he has acquired a PC and is learning computer skills at a day centre, to add to his skills as a carpenter, plumber, painter, plasterer, window cleaner, seaman – 'I was in New York when I was sixteen, you know, I'm not a cunt.' In fact, this is a man who should put us all to shame and who has been driven to drink, but not, never, despair, by dark forces in this city where you can't sleep for the sound of flushing toilets.

My son Jake calls and asks if he can come round, as he's now in his final year at college and only goes in on Fridays and is at a loose end the rest of the time. I try making excuses because though I love Jake like a son, the flat is in a complete mess, worse than normal, on account of how Jimmy has gone berserk over the goat's head business and threatened his Somali neighbours with a baseball bat and been committed under Section Two of the Mental Health Act. His son Darren has been very supportive, though. It's brought them together and he's been round with some clothes and money because the bastards just took him away in a van or ambulance, two cops, a social worker with a club foot, his GP, and a consultant psychiatrist in, dig this, a white fucking suit. Anyway, Jimmy's incarceration has robbed me of the world's greatest cleaner. Jimmy is not one of those chaps who comes round, hoovers the same square yard of carpet for an hour, steals your Derek and the Dominoes CD and then shoots up in your toilet. He can produce order out of chaos. He will stay all day if necessary. Now, without him, the flat is a hovel. How will I ever be able to sell it, when the time comes, as it inevitably will, for me to move my impoverished, pensionless arse out? Jake has heard all this before and explains wearily that any flat in west London is saleable for the space alone. But that isn't the reason. I know he's worried about me and he's twenty and he's getting very serious, like so many of his generation, who have it so hard. We walk by the canal, a very fetching stretch, green and tidy, the water looking as wholesome as a French painting, the light on it making us blink. Jake has girl trouble. I offer advice but I come across like a reluctant salesman, because I've really none to give. I have flashes, of Jake having to clear out my flat, of Jake coming to identify my body, which is too smashed or bloated with water to identify. That he's stuck at home with me, Steptoe-style, into his thirties, his life almost done, me some dribbling kipper well out of his mind. Bankruptcy. Blindness. Amputation. Never getting more than three balls on the Lottery.

A pair of Rottweilers menace us, their perky owner, QPR shirt and rolled up *Guardian*, turns up five minutes after his brutes do, and I get very angry and tell him that I hope they fucking eat him and his *Guardian*, and Jake looks worried and earnest, like I've seen him look before, like Darren is no doubt feeling about Jimmy, burned-out fathers cannibalising their kids. When you're a slut, true love is hard to bear. A bouquet of wild flowers, tightly knotted with string, floats by at improbable speed. I think of his mother, Peg, like in the Steely Dan song, who loved flowers so much. All the good things. We go back to the flat, drink beer, watch a video, don't tidy up. No more cuddles then.

Clerise and Geri and I decide to visit Jimmy in the bin. It's not the bin really, it's the psychiatric wing of a large west London teaching hospital. But it's where they put the sectioned and the suicidal and

the mildly to not very mildly at all violent, and they have plastic cut-
lery and can't smoke in their room or shut their doors or leave the
ward except with a nurse and if they're deemed fit enough. Jimmy is
eating his dinner with a fat man dressed in a Hugo Boss T-shirt, a baseball cap and a massive pair of trousers, which don't quite fit his stomach
and on to which he has recently peed.

Jimmy declares: 'That clock just struck thirteen.'

'Did it fuck,' says an Irishman called Mac, looking doubtfully into
his curried lamb.

'Don't talk to me about clocks,' moans Barry. We notice he is eating
and smoking at the same time. 'Timex owe me eight thousand quid.'

Jimmy snarls back. And he's only been here a week. 'You're mental,
do you know that, Barry? You shouldn't be here. You should be in
fuckin BROADMOOR!'

Irish Mac butts in, draped in a blanket and a Paul Smith shirt, thin as
custard and with fingers the colour of Marmite: 'At least he doesn't
think it's just struck thirteen, you stupid cunt.'

Barry has started filling in his meal-card for the following week.
He's being ticked off by a young Malaysian nurse, ticked off for ticking every single box. Barry has a whale of an eating disorder. 'There
aren't enough portions, that's why,' he murmurs in his schoolboy's
voice. 'I want portions, nursey, I want portions.'

It was getting cold. They'd turned the heating off. A nurse told us
that the patients only complained if the tea was late. Apparently all the
designer gear was courtesy of some philanthropic record producer
who'd had a bad drugs habit and started eating boot polish. When we'd
gone, we found that Geri's purse had been nicked, probably by Barry,
who Jimmy had told us was a complete klepto and even stole the
umbrella and handbag from his own mother and his similarly rotund
girlfriend. He did in fact thrust a petition to the Queen into Clerise's
hands as we left because she'd come in her temping gear and he thought
she was a lawyer. Clerise wasn't amused. Times are hard now that
Winston's been banged up on remand and has been threatening
vengeance, fingering her as the grass. It wasn't, of course. It was me.

Jimmy already has a feud going with Irish Mac, who they picked up
off the street where he was raving and cursing and praying to the Lord.
Irish Mac is literate, educated, but Pope-crazed. He tried to stab Jimmy
in the showers once, with a half-pair of scissors. And when Jimmy had

the shits one morning he couldn't get into the toilet and they had to knock down the door, the nurses, and there was Irish Mac kneeling in front of the sink, stark-bollock naked and covered in his own shit, praying to the Virgin Mary. 'He's got half a fucking lung. Dead by Christmas, cardboard guttersnipe!' Jimmy snarls, revealing a pinkness of face. Jimmy looks like a pirate. A jailed pirate. He's been told it's schizophrenia. It's not good. He's ashamed of what his kids will say, especially Darren, almost normal, and that his four common-law wives will take the piss and put it around. And what's he going to do about Mr Azeer's Lottery ticket, referring to our local grocer, not the one where I met the Asian woman, another one, whose Lottery needs he takes care of, because Mr Azeer is a Muslim and doesn't believe in gambling? He's looking at me, but I say, Jimmy, I can't commit. I was supposed to see a bloke about a job and I turned up so drunk that he said no on the spot, that's the kind of life I lead. Geri, who doesn't even know the little Scouse prick, pipes in that she can do it in her motor. She's trying to be positive, bounteous. She has kicked Wong out and is talking about Australia. Later we all watch telly for a while in the common room. The telly is covered with hi-tech shatterproof glass and is showing a BBC magazine item on the current marital difficulties of Mr and Mrs Jonathan Ross. I find it hard not to sympathise. 'Will ya look at the tits on that!' screams a black patient called Darius, who is massive and magnificent in a doughboy sort of way and has never been the same since he beat up two CID officers who were terrorising him, when he was fourteen. He looks twenty-one but is in fact thirty-two, which may explain the Bob Marley music slithering out of his headset. Back on TV, a large, comely blonde lady I recognise as the novelist Fay Weldon is being interviewed by a young blonde presenter about a literary prize, and a thin, bearded fellow dressed only in a pair of pink briefs shouts, 'Mother and daughter! Which one would you fuck first?' and then headbutts the screen.

Then Darius tells how he went with a white prostitute who rubbed him with a vibrator and made his balls tingle-an-at. The parents of a manic-depressive teenager cringe. Not before time, it's time to go. Jimmy wants fags. We'll bring him fags. Why, asks Jimmy, do the government keep putting up the price of fags, when the people who smoke them are invariably hard-up, mad or stressed to buggery, like his common-law Sheryll who's got three kids by different blokes, Jimmy included, and doesn't have two brass farthings to rub together and is on forty a day? Cheap fags, Armaggedons or something, I couldn't make it out, which are even worse for her health than Bensons or Marlboro Lights. I reply that it's because the government is promoting a healthy lifestyle for the nation, to which Jimmy replies who wants to live till they're eighty-four so they can piss in a flowerpot in some geriatric home, and who is going to pay for it all, and who is going to provide all the NHS care and pensions, and surely heavy smokers (and drinkers, come to that) deserve a fucking government subsidy? And when he gets out he is going straight back on the piss. And can we also bring him a bottle of Bells? And he wants locking up. Apparently.

Later, back at my gaff, I try to go down on Clerise but she's put a Tampax in and either has forgotten because of the drugs or can't be bothered to tell me, and I see the white string sticking out between excellent alabaster legs and I cough and she says 'I'm OK on the out-side' and I have a shufty but she's not OK, she stinks like a butcher's counter. It all gets rather embarrassing after that: she blows me with a johnny on but I can't get hard, never can, and it keeps slipping off and she starts on about how my knob's too small for the condom and I can hear the neighbours laughing because the sound-proofing in this place is non-existent. I find myself shouting up at the ceiling, 'She didn't say my cock was small, she said it was small without a condom, I mean small without a hard-on. On it. I mean my dick's normal when it's hard!' It goes dead quiet. I bet that lot slam their door tomorrow morning.

That night I have a nightmare. That I'm Irish Mac, that I'm thin and shoeless and grey-bearded and Marmite-fingered. And I'm in a shop doorway, the Asian shop where I met the Asian lady, and I'm alone and cold and reaching out to black space. Then the Asian lady comes past, and she takes me home, and she feeds me and shaves me and intro-duces me to her well-behaved, well-scrubbed children, and the chil-dren include Jake, and I tell her that this one is my boy, and she says gently that, no, he has been adopted. He's been taken into care. Because it is better that way.

Then Clerise and Geri arrive and fit a black bag over my head until I can't breathe. And I wake up, and the angina's come back. I reach for the spray but I sneeze and blow the contents of an ashtray into my face. It's still early. I need something.

Unhaunted

Toby Litt

I first met Chloe online – in the *UK Women* chat room of gay.com.
When we logged on that night, neither of us was using our real name.
She had chosen to call herself Chloe, although her real name was
Monica. (Something I didn't learn until later.)

A few days later, I – who had previously masqueraded as '70s Disco
Queen 'Agneta' – changed my monicker to 'Daphne'.

Daphne and Chloe. We were a cybercouple, of sorts.

Chloe was witty, well read, intelligent and seemed genuinely com-
passionate towards other women and their problems. (How wrong
about a person can one be?)

Over the course of a week, we began to 'private' each other more and
more – going off into a separate chat room accessible only to ourselves.

One all-nighter led to another, and – a week or so later – we were
making arrangements to meet up at the Candy Bar, London's biggest
bar for gay women, along with a few more of the regulars from *UK
Women*.

Come the night, and I had dolled but, so I hoped, not tarted myself
up.

(Chloe later said that she'd seen I was up for it right from the off.
When I asked her, *What gave the game away?* Chloe said, *Oh, come on.
Just... everything. You were working so hard at seeming casual, it was untrue.*)

Chloe wasn't like I'd imagined her. Perhaps the gentility of her on-
line name had misled me: I'd expected someone a little less brash,
someone a bit quiet. Someone like me.

Chloe was certainly *not* quiet. She was the first of our group to
become openly pissed; but, once pissed, she seemed to remain perfectly
in control. I admired this. I slur after a glass and chuck up midway
through the second bottle.

Yet when she got up to go to the loo, there was a hint about Chloe
of debutante-learning-to-walk-with-volume-of-Debrett's-balanced-
on-her-noddle. I found this very endearing.

Plus the fact she was just gorgeous.

When we moved on to a restaurant, I manoeuvred myself into the seat next to Chloe.

For the rest of the evening we ignored the other *UK Women* completely.

To be honest, I lost interest in anything but Chloe the moment I felt her hand touching my knee.

I don't know which emotion, embarrassment or delight, eventually won out, but the intensity of their battle lit me up like the Disney Store on Xmas Eve.

This – this under-table touching – was the kind of thing I wouldn't have let anyone else do. But Chloe was a girl for whom one automatically made exceptions.

I was starting to think this might be really serious. In the loos, I said her name to myself in the mirror, and watched myself blush.

One firm rule of mine has always been *no sex on a first date*. (This isn't anything to do with being some kind of lesbian-variety Rules Girl. It's just, if a girl gets into the habit of showing too much interest too early on, she can end up with an impressive collection of stalkers. Clinginess is endemic out there.) And this wasn't even a first date. Yet somehow Chloe and I found ourselves in a taxi (nothing more than kissing *there*, of course). In my kitchen. My sitting room. Bedroom. We were laughing, kissing, undressing, fucking.

Chloe's public brashness continued – she dared things I'd *never* have done, outside of a long-standing relationship.

(I've certainly never known someone make *quite* such a beeline for my arse.)

It was all good stuff, though: I hadn't had decent sex in months.

Chloe stayed the night, and the night seemed very short.

Over breakfast, I tried to hold back from any mention of the future.

I needn't have worried. Chloe simply barged her way into my life. She said she'd outstayed her welcome with some scary Australian dykes down in Earl's Court. Could she, perhaps, stay at mine for a few days? Just until she'd sorted somewhere permanent out for herself.

At the time I felt a nigglet of worry. How had Chloe ended up without a permanent place to stay? Had she jumped out of this last one, or was she booted?

She had, or she said she had, a perfectly stable job in magazine publishing. But when I asked her about it, she was vague as *Vogue*.

Whatever, I ignored my doubts.

I said, *Yes*.

Chloe taxied over to Earl's Court and, two hours later, taxied back.

Somehow, without really planning or wanting it, I'd ended up with a full-time, live-in partner.

I don't really want to go into the day-to-day details of our three months four days together. The memories aren't pleasant, and least of all the pleasant ones.

We got on pretty well most of the time – at least, I *thought* we did.

I may not be the most perceptive person in the world, but I have a fairly well-developed sense of impending catastrophe. (I should have, given the sheer quantity of catastrophes that seem to impend themselves in my direction.)

Right from the start, Chloe took *everything* for granted. Most astonishingly, she took it for granted that I was in love with her.

And because she seemed so confident about this, and because I didn't have a moment to stop and consider it coldly, I too began to take it for granted.

I *must* love Chloe, my illogical logic said, otherwise I wouldn't be letting her live just another week and then *just* another week more in my flat. Rent free.

That it (this 'love') was truly out of character, for me, cautious me, seemed only to make it all the more deeply true.

Looking back, I can see now that I thought and believed it rather than felt it.

As for what Chloe felt, I really have no idea.

Of course, even on that first evening – after she'd arrived back from Earl's Court with her single suitcase – she did *say* she loved me.

But it wasn't quite that simple. What she actually said, every time but one (which I'll come to) was, 'I love you, babes.'

Perhaps it was the last message sent out by my depleted catastrophe-sensors, but something told me that the 'babes' wasn't entirely sincere. Or, maybe (though this I hardly dared think) that the 'babes' was the only part of Chloe's declaration that was sincere.

If we'd been going out for ages, and it had developed as one of the rhythms of our relationship, the verbal tics and tricks of passion turned affection, drama become devotion, then I could have believed in 'babes'.

As things stood, I always heard it as a catchy jingle – coming just at the wrong moment: right at the highest, most swellingest point of the rhapsody that I'd been waiting years to hear.

There were other jingles. I can hear them clearly now. At the time, however, they tended to be subsumed in the jazzy syncopations of Chloe's... I don't know how else to put it – of Chloe's *Chloe-ness*.

Right from day one, she was jealous of any time I spent away from her. She disguised this, not very cleverly but efficiently enough, as mock-jealousy. (At this point, cleverness, with my self-delusion in full effect, was hardly required.)

She began to wear my clothes. Not only comfy leggings and baggy sweaters, *that* I could understand. But my best underwear, and *all* the time. When I called her on it, she had an explanation ready, willing and able: 'I like to feel you next to me, babes.'

However, when I tried to put on a pair of *her* tights, she told me straight out they didn't suit. *No Trespassing* couldn't have been flagged up any clearer.

It took a couple of months for these little pixelated pixels to assemble themselves into anything approaching a full picture. (I doubt I have that even now.)

Something else which didn't help was Chloe's continued devotion to gay.com. She paid the chat rooms almost hourly visits – on *her* laptop, maybe, but on *my* phone bill. (And, quite often, when she could have been talking to me instead. Face-to-face. Or not talking – kissing.) She claimed she just wanted to keep up with old friends. But eventually I began to suspect that the parasite was on the lookout for another host organism. (I wasn't thinking about her in quite those terms, yet. She was still my infuriating Chloca-Chlola – leaving the showerhead dripping, clipping her toenails on to the living room carpet.)

About halfway through the third month, 'I love you, babes' metamorphosed into the even less convincing 'Love ya, babes'.

I had started to suspect that Chloe wasn't going in to work any more. She always got out of bed later than I did, and never seemed to bring her job worries home with her. (Sometimes I felt I brought nothing else back with me. Not even a pay packet.)

One day, premenstrual and needing little further excuse to give in to my suspicions, I pulled a sickie.

It was mid-morning by the time I got back to my flat.

During the tube journey, I had imagined myself catching Chloe going down on another *UK Woman*. This, your standard-issue betrayal, would have been crushing, but not exactly unforeseen.

What I *didn't* expect to find, when I rushed in the front door, giving her no time to escape, was Chloe, sitting at the kitchen table, blithely naked, eating an apple and reciting extracts from my diary into a Dictaphone.

The *main* reason this surprised me was that I kept my diary in a passworded file in my laptop. Chloe, so far as I remembered, hadn't been given even a hint of my diary's existence. Since she moved in, I'd been very careful: writing my diary entries on my desktop computer during breaks at work, e-mailing them back to myself at the end of the day. From there, once I'd downloaded them, I copied and pasted them straight into the passworded file. Even at the point of our greatest intimacy, I'd never let Chloe watch me collect my e-mail.

She turned to me very coldly as I stood there in the doorway. 'Home early?' she said. 'Not feeling well, babes?'

It was as if I'd lifted up the lovely mossy rock of her personality to see all the spiders and cockroaches wriggling and crawling about underneath.

'It took me two weeks to work out the password,' she said.

(My password, which I'd recently changed, was 'Pepsi'. This was a reference to my nickname for her: Chloca-Chlola.)

'Very witty,' she said.

Chloe, in her caught-out insolence, was more attractive than I'd ever seen her before. She was a completely different person. Not brash at all – calculating, in total control. Even her face looked different: longer, more defined.

'You have one hour to pack,' I said.

'Jesus,' she said. 'I don't need *that* long.'

I stood over her in the bedroom – intending to prevent her from stealing anything that belonged to me.

(As if, having taken my privacy, there was anything else *left*.)

Her new icy persona showed no crack. She packed as efficiently as a nurse boxing up the few bedside belongings of someone dead during the nightshift.

'Goodbye,' Chloe said, when she'd picked up her suitcase. 'I enjoyed it. Really, I did. I was hoping it could last – what? – at least another month.'

'Get out,' I said.

I followed her to the door and shut it behind her.

It was only then that I realised I'd forgotten to get my flat keys back.

For a moment I considered running out after her into the street. Demanding the keys.

But I knew, given the state I was in, I couldn't.

I felt that I couldn't physically speak another word to her. Honestly, I would have preferred to have died.

Stupidly, I didn't change the locks.

There was something about not doing this that was a kind of dare – a dare to myself.

Chloe was out of my life, and I was glad about that. But I didn't want to appear to *myself* as anything like the cold callous person she had revealed herself to be.

It was as if, instead, I wanted my old self, the more trusting person I'd been before I met her, to let themselves back into my flat through the slightly insecure door.

That wasn't, of course, what happened.

The first things I noticed were hardly 'things' at all. Each of them, in itself, seemed so infinitesimal – just one more speck of dust in the Hoover bag of existence – that I would most likely never have noticed them, had they not possessed one notable quality: meaning. Yet I even managed, to begin with, to ignore this, as well.

Chloe, as I think I mentioned earlier, had always left the showerhead dripping slightly. The longer our relationship went on, the more I asked her *please* not to do this – and the more infuriating became her failure to comply. After she left, I assumed – without really thinking about it – that the showerhead would never drip again.

But oh no.

The first time I found it dripping, I assumed that I had just, subconsciously, picked up this slovenly habit of Chloe's myself.

I made a mental note always to screw the tap up as tight as a brand-new jar of Marmite.

And nothing changed.

The fourth time I came back from work to find the showerhead sputtering every other second, I began to suspect that someone else had been in the shower that day. And not, of course, just any someone.

Arguments between Chloe and me had always started over domestic issues.

I was the Maid, she Lady Muck.

The things I noticed began as little annoyances, little imperfections, little messes. But, as they accumulated and their meaningfulness became harder and harder to ignore, I started to believe they were really something else: little messages.

And all of them said exactly the same thing: 'I'm not really gone. You may try to convince yourself that I am. But I'm as *here* as when I was here.'

The living room carpet became infested with toenail clippings. My jewellery box turned into a chaos of broken links and lost earrings.

One day I came home to find a single, greasy plate in the washing-up bowl; the next, the duvet turned back and the pillow dented. A week later, the phone was off the hook – beeping like crazy.

The phone wasn't the only crazy thing. Rather than think logically, act sensibly, and change the locks, I decided to do something else – something bizarre.

I began to leave notes for Chloe to find when she snuck back into the flat.

If the messes were her messages to me, then these notes were my messages back.

Some of the notes were your average Post-It, and these I left on the fridge door; others were little slivers of paper that I slipped in between the pages of books, under pillows, behind ornaments.

In them, I said the worst things about her that I could imagine.

They weren't really even *to* her – in order to make them as hurtful as possible, I used to imagine what I'd most fear hearing *her* say to *me*.

None of the notes disappeared. Nothing *that* dramatic occurred. Yet always, when I came home, the folds in them seemed a little less firm, and their orientation (not their position) on the kitchen table seemed to have changed.

One might put this down to the paper untensing, or to slight draughts, but right from the first day of the first note, I knew: Chloe and I were communicating again.

A dialogue, of sorts, began.

If I left something really offensive for her, she'd leave me something disgusting in return.

For example, the day I left a note calling her a selfish cunt, I found a recently used tampon in my linen drawer.

The next day, my note said I hoped she died alone; her response was to leave the toilet full of unflushed pee.

But when, a week or so later, I found a feather on the doormat, I left Chloe a sincere and rather blubby thank-you.

That evening, I returned home to find the TV on and *Breakfast at Tiffany's* being shown.

She must still love me, I thought – for about ten seconds.

I became almost glad that I'd let her keep the keys. (It was *let her* now; I'd completely forgotten about *been too cowardly to demand them back*.)

This was about three weeks after she left.

Perhaps a reconciliation was possible.

After Chloe moved out, I returned to gay.com – mainly as a means of talking out some of my anxiety and self-loathing.

Since the break-up, I'd been a complete wreck.

The others were very sympathetic. They saved my life by putting up with hour-upon-hour of maudlin badly typed drivel. I changed my online name to Dumpling.

Chloe seemed to have disappeared off the scene completely. Perhaps, having fucked me over so completely, she no longer felt able to cruise the other *UK Women*.

They all took my side. Chloe was the 'bfh' – bitch from hell.

No one seemed to have seen her or heard anything from her in person since that night at the Candy Bar.

I continued writing notes, about one a day, their hatefulness slowly decreasing.

It was about a month later that one of the *UK Women* regulars appeared in the chat room. I'll call her Medusa.

She didn't hang around. First thing she did was say she had something important to tell me.

We privated each other, in a chat room called *What?*, and it came straight out: *Chloe is dead*.

It was either someone who didn't like me, playing a gross prank. Or it was Chloe herself, logging on in this other woman's name, just to fuck me around a bit more… Or, perhaps, it was really true.

Whichever, I was grateful for being alone, at home, with only my laptop as witness.

I asked Medusa a couple of things she would know that Chloe definitely wouldn't – things that had been discussed by the *UK Women* before Chloe came on the scene. She convinced me fairly quickly that she was who she said she was.

My next question was coldly factual. I was crying.

When?

Two weeks ago.

How?

Hit by a motorbike crossing the road.

How do you know?

I was with her. She was my lover.

Your lover?

She moved in to mine after she moved out of yours.

Why didn't you tell me before?

She didn't want you to know where she was.

No. I guess not. Why didn't you tell me for so long about her being dead?

Grief.

Sorry.

Sorry.

Superstitiously, I had the locks changed the very next day.

I don't know why – perhaps I was trying to keep the idea out: the idea that, all this time (one whole month) I'd thought it was Chloe letting herself back into my flat, invading the smallest peripheries of my life, using tiny things to tell me huge things, and all this time it had been nothing but my own preoccupation with her.

I didn't want her to have disappeared from my life as completely as she seemed to have done; and neither did I want entirely to have vanished from her life.

Changing the locks didn't seem to help.

Two weeks later, and the shower still dripped when I came home, the bed seemed to have been lain in, the plates got dirty and moved about by themselves.

This time, though, I couldn't avoid the knowledge that it was me creating these things that were hardly things.

The mess-messages were mine; the meaningfulness, mine also.

Out of guilt and confusion, I was madly tricking myself into thinking myself mad.

This seemed to reach a climax a few days ago, when I began writing notes again.

But this time the notes weren't addressed to Chloe (or 'you bitch' as I'd mostly called her), they were to myself, and they were painfully simple.

For the most part, they read: 'Leave me alone. Please. Just leave me alone.'

My thing

Robert Elms

Other kids needed coat-hangers and Red Rovers, but not me. Sneaking into the Odeon (or was it the Gaumont? It's such a long time ago), on a Monday or Thursday evening was a very valuable skill, worth much more than the few new pence you saved by prising open the exit doors with a wire hanger, nicked from your mum's wonky melamine wardrobe. It meant as much kudos round our way as a Fred Perry shirt, proper Levis and a pair of Adidas or Gola, rather than the two bob Tesco bombers some poor sods had to sport. Almost as much as a reggae record on import pre, with no centre, the kind Lee Davis's big brother always carried in plain white cardboard sleeves in a big black box.

A talent at manipulating a bit of bent wire so that it hooked around the bar, thereby releasing the doors, thereby allowing a mob of cropped urchins in casual wear to go running in, whooping and dodging their way through the trailers, was a kind of community service, and a badge of rank. The kids who had the wherewithall, the necessary manipulative skills and the bottle, were little heroes. I could never do it, too fiddly. And besides, that was a job for leaders and I was always the quiet sort, the kid you didn't notice. If I really wanted to see a movie, rather than just invade one with my little mob of Herberts, I'd go on my own, in the afternoon usually, in which case I never needed to surreptitiously open any doors. I'd just stroll in.

The same goes for transport. If we fancied a day out and about. Up the Cross perhaps, to play the machines in the arcade by the Kentucky, or the lank men who invariably hung around them looking for chicken that wasn't fried but fresh. Teasing poor nonces was always a particularly popular team sport when our lot were Rovered up. Or maybe we'd hop on a 19 into Soho, to absorb the cool and pretend we were buying records in Groove on Frith Street, where the portly old lady who owned the shop knitted like an executioner and dispatched a startling wisdom about the latest jazz funk tunes. More likely we'd end up playing run-outs in the British Museum, getting chased by fat wheezy blokes in peaked caps and scaring each other with tales of mummies' curses and the like on the way back on the top of a 52 bus. This was where the Red Rovers came into their own, passports to limitless summer days of leaping on and off moving running boards and very minor collective delinquency. I'd buy them too, just to be part of the crew, but I never actually needed to.

On my Jack, when I could make the most of my abilities, I'd make fantastic journeys. But then this little business of mine has meant that I've always been alone. A secret that can't ever be shared and all that. Believe me, I've wanted to tell people, especially when I was younger and I first learnt how to do this thing. More accurately, I suppose I wanted to show them, because no one would believe me if I just told them. But I know I can't, so I live with that. And I live well, very well.

The tubes were even easier, in that they required far less concentration than the buses, where there was a conductor up and down the stairs looking for fares all the time. Most of the time I didn't even bother making any effort at the start of a ride on the tube; no one was going to stop you for not buying a ticket on the way down. I'd just stroll unchallenged past the booth, staffed – if at all – by a man who didn't give a toss. These were very didn't-give-a-toss times, which meant that just about everybody took liberties. Just about everybody bunked the fares on the underground back then, because they could, like salivating dogs and their bollocks. I mean, how often did you see an inspector on the trains? It was a positive invitation to ride the subterranean rails gratis. But also, everybody I knew bunked the fares, because that extra bit of dough always came in handy. I think it's very important to point out that less is only more if you've got loads to start with. For the rest of us more is more.

At the other end of the line, when I'd reached my stop, I just needed to turn it on for a minute or so and sail past, all insouciant and smiling at myself. Well, after I'd finished anyway. While I was doing it, my thing, so to speak, I couldn't have afforded a smile; that would have given the game away instantly. But once I was out into daylight, bowling down Jermyn Street in search of a bit of natty gear or maybe dodging the crowds heading up to the Arsenal, well, then I'd grin. That tunnel you have to walk through at Finsbury Park, that was always a brilliant place for a bit of a bowl and a good gurn to yourself in acknowledgement of a job well done. Especially if you were on your way to whoop the

Sheens. I'd whistle sometimes too, just to enjoy the echo. Believe me, you'd smile and blow a tune if you knew how to do what I can do.

My absolute favourite free journey was getting out at Green Park (if they hadn't closed Down Street, that would have been even better) and floating around all those hushed and lovely private galleries. Of course, I went to the Tate and the National and all that, but for me the big institutions with their red ropes and school parties and tutting old biddies up from the Home Counties couldn't compare with the little discreet Mayfair places. What I liked about them so much was the very fact that you could conceivably pull out a cheque book and buy these wondrous works. It was always an amazing thrill. I don't want to sound perverted, but it was almost a sexual rush for me, the wanton sensuality of seeing this gorgeous thing in such an intimate place, a Miró for instance, or even better a Barbara Hepworth, and it could just possibly, if you've done well enough, be yours to keep. I've told you already I do well, but I don't often keep and I don't buy, I sell.

In those days, though, I didn't do anything of the sort. I took a tube up west just to see. For many years I was a passive admirer of the fine arts. I can still vividly recall the first time I stood in front of a canvas, real close up so that you can smell the paint and the prices, so that you can almost climb inside the mind – or whatever bit of the artist it is he puts into his work – well, believe me, I was knocked over. The only way I can describe it is to say that it was better than first hearing Lonnie Liston Smith sublimely soaring above a club, out of your nut on speed. Or possibly even seeing Charlie George nutmeg some lumpen oaf in front of the North Bank, then do it again, just because that's the sort of man he is. I was filled with culture.

Looking back now, I don't know why it took me so long to actually deal in the art market, given that I had so many opportunities. I think it was probably some kind of residual class thing. I mean, people from my particular estate, people whose mum worked on the cosmetics counter in Woolworth's on the Holloway Road, and paid for their gaudy furniture with Provident cheques, didn't get involved in art. Well, except for Tretchikov and his ethnic ladies. My mum had the African one. I shouldn't really be ashamed of that, but it does make me wince a little. Even if I had come home with a proper picture for her back then, she wouldn't have got it, would she? Can you really see my mother with a Francis Bacon hanging in the front parlour?

My thing

I could have done it as well. With my talent I wasted so many opportunities, so many beautiful pieces I could have cared for, for a while.
Living in a city like this there's countless chances, so many levels on
which to operate. But there was a kind of cultural apartheid at work
back then. We stuck with our areas of connoisseurship and they with
theirs. It doesn't seem to be like that any more, I sit at a dinner party
in some loft thing in Clerkenwell with a load of luvvies or literary
types and discuss Tapies or Basquiat with my accent, and nobody bats
an eye.

And what's more, these days it works both ways. People in Clerkenwell
lofts who have masters degrees in semiotics and holidays in Zanzibar
think they know a bit about football. All because they've sat a couple
of times in the East Stand with their agent and raved about the innate
geometry of Emmanuel Petit's runs or some such bollocks. It does make
me laugh. I don't suppose they've ever had to become suddenly invisible on a rainy night in SE21 or face the wrath of a frothing Millwall
Neanderthal with a carpet layer's shiv in his hand. To think, all that time
I could have owned works that would make their ears bleed with envy
and I never even considered it. Still, you can't be greedy, I've definitely
learnt that you mustn't be greedy.

Anyway, then they introduced those barriers, those pincer machines
which catch your trousers if you're not careful, and that particular game
was up. I can't remember what year it was when they automated the
ticket collection at our stop on the Northern line, but I can certainly
recall the consternation it caused. Believe me, people were outraged.
Their inalienable right to defraud London Transport had been taken
away and they were severely vexed. One boy I know broke two front
teeth doing a kind of western roll over the barriers and was convinced
he could sue LT for the damage they had caused to his embouchure.
I told him that since Fosby had introduced the flop nobody did the
western roll, or the scissors jump come to that, any more, but he
didn't laugh. He couldn't really, not with his mouth in that state.

Me, well, I knew that little wheeze was now over. You cannot possibly do what I do to a machine. It's all about getting inside the head of
a human being, using your personality on theirs. I have to switch on my
charisma, turn it up to full volume and then invert it. You know the
way that you instantly notice some people when they walk into a room,
well, it's kind of the exact opposite of that. And machines definitely

don't respond to mind games. Besides, I was well past needing to save money on tube fares by that stage. I wasn't collecting art yet, but just about anything else you can think of acquiring and flogging.

The pictures came later. It's always been pictures. Not just because they're easier to work than, say, sculpture, although I admit it would be fairly tough to move around a Henry Moore, as much as I'd like to – his extraordinary spatial awareness fascinates me. He did do some little ones, and there's maquettes and everything, so it wouldn't be impossible, but somehow pictures were my first love and my first lark, and they're what I've stuck to. And besides, it's where the big money is; little pictures by the big figures, that's my speciality. And modernists only, I don't touch anything pre about 1880, 1890. It just isn't my area of expertise. I mean, as much as I love, say, Goya, I wouldn't feel confident. And besides, the old masters are all in museums and I've already told you I don't much like museums.

As for contemporary work, well, I have to admit I have real trouble getting excited by amateur hour videos and excrement and household objects. I realise that makes me sound a bit old fogeyish, and that's the last impression I want to leave you with, but surely you have to accept a lot of it is nonsense. I guess that if you looked back on any era, many of the artists working at the time were pretty poor, it's only the very good ones who last. I mean, look at the sentimental drivel the Holland Park school produced back in those days; this current Hoxton mob are certainly better than them. Damien Hirst is clearly a big talent. I've met him a few times in Groucho's and that, he's a wild one all right. But a clever one. I'm sure I'll be asked to get involved in one of his sooner or later, but as I said it would have to be a spot painting, which are my particular favourites, or one of the splash ones. I can't see me sneaking a shark on to the tube, can you?

Actually, these days I very rarely travel on the tube at all, and I haven't been on a bus in, well, it must be eight or nine years, maybe even longer. I don't think they even do Red Rovers any more, do they? I still think of myself as a bit of a tubist though, I can still recite the entire Northern line, from Edgware to Morden, both branches. I still love Leslie Green's stations, those ones with the maroon tiles, they are London for me. Russell Square tube station in the drizzle, that's my town. I still like movies too, especially in the afternoon, only now I pay to go in. I can afford to, thank you.

The keeper of the Rothenstein tomb

Iain Sinclair

Men were sick, women pregnant; Norton kept on walking. This was the form his mania took, hammering for hours at a time, out there beyond the traces of the Roman wall. He could no longer enter the city, the density of surveillance undid him, leeched his energies. Instead, he played the canary, fluttering around the rim of the affected area, interested to discover at what point he would go down. Norton was stone crazy, written out. If he stopped moving, so he believed, the treadmill would grind to a halt, buildings would topple, ancient streams would rise to the surface, the Walbrook, the Fleet, the Tyburn; the Wall would crumble back into dust and the demons of greed, paranoia, corruption would escape.

Hoxton hurt. Clerkenwell was a reservoir of self-images, a lake of shimmering paper reflections. Through dusty picture-windows, he drank the deep blues of photographed water. He found a surrogate calm in secondhand greenery, private parks and landscaped gardens reproduced on stiff white card. Idylls no thicker than a spray of varnish. Cabinets of naked strangers stared back at him.

Poetry was accessed from boards outside newsagents' shops, the ones that summarised what was happening in a tactful arrangement of upper-case lettering: BLIND BEGGAR SOLD. He loved these messages, covert dispatches produced for his eyes only. They were like transcripts taken down, hot, from a psychic wire service. In the towers of Hawksmoor churches and derelict end-of-terrace houses, waiting for demolition, were spies and watchers who tapped in their reports. BLIND BEGGAR SOLD. This was all that was left of pure information; lean, spare, pertinent. Norton aspired to, but never achieved, the style of these anonymous masters with their calligraphic half-haikus. BLIND BEGGAR SOLD.

His spirits lifted. The oasis of Bunhill Fields, the effigy of John Bunyan with grass growing from his sockets, hadn't lost its resonance; the stone-cistern monument of the woman was tap'd for the dropsy.

He looked forward, literally – previewing streetscapes in a rush of single-frame images – to his breakfast with the only woman in London who would still commission a story. The only one generous enough to humour his affliction, his curse, this compulsion to repeat himself, do the police and all other citizens in the *same* voice; to tell it and keep telling it, beyond the point where he required listeners, a single listener, anyone.

An off-duty academic, down from Cambridge on a jolly, moon-lighting as a tour guide, one of three jobs he needed to keep himself in Walter Benjamin reissues, told Norton about a set of examination papers he'd been called on to assess. A student from the Middle East, offering his response to the usual sneaky stuff about Beowulf, *The Pardoner's Tale*, Jane Austen, racial stereotypes in Conrad, Harry Potter, came up with precisely the same essay, copied out five times. The stratagem had been discovered by accident. The man was sailing through quite nicely. 'Very respectable upper 2/1,' breezed the don, taking a refill, one for the road, before the dash to King's Cross. 'He'd hit on the perfect form. Content doesn't matter. A smooth passage between relevant bullet points.'

Early light in Fortune Street soothed him, soothed Norton; leaf-patterns carpeting the grey tarmac, fish-shadows, movement. The voices of girls singing behind the fence of the primary school, singing as they skipped. Like a newsreel from the lost Fifties.

Ring-a-bell, Ring-a-bell,
Mamma's belly's going to swell.

'It's a privilege to be here, at all, don't you think?' the young woman, Katie Harwood, asked. 'Before it disappears.' Give her credit, she could put away a decent plate of meat, two kinds of sausage, a couple of kidneys, liver black as treacle, nestling on a bed of refried potato, a bright wink of egg. She passed on the stout, the whisky chaser Norton offered – to collect from the bar. Katie was paying, picking up the tab for her employers to process.

Norton liked her warmth, the moist heat of a woman who enjoyed a good walk, knocking off twenty miles every weekend. She was in bloom, hair shining, catching the best of the neon strips, the fluctuating inter-ference in that fan-cooled dungeon beneath Smithfield meat-market. A pale-gold moustache added distinction to the modelling of that interesting area above the upper lip. What do they call it? Not labium. You could use the term for the lip itself, but it might give the wrong impression. Good word though. Evocative, but inaccurate.

John Major – remember him? – horribly misnamed, was a man defined by this apparently insignificant area of his physiognomy. Major had a swelling beneath the vertical trench that runs from lip to nose. It looked like a gumshield that had slipped, a moustache growing on the inside. The way the ridge bounced artificial light was his undoing. Nobody listened to what he had to say, the Librium drone of a peevish man keeping his rage in check, vanity in a solemn disguise. You could see them at cabinet meetings, the Lamonts and Lawsons, leonine Heseltine, baggy Ken, pantingly ambitious Portillo, sniggering behind their hands. The PM has a prow like the *Titanic*, so who cares what he wants us not to do? Better fix up something in the City, sketch out the slimming books, before the whole mess goes public; before the punters get another chance to check out that inflexible philtrum.

That's the word, one of the best. Pure music. Philtrum with philtral ridge. Katie's was a beauty. Especially when she talked, flicked her hair back, told Norton what she had in mind: a follow-up to a book he'd managed to get his name on, years before, a Jewish girl's research into a Whitechapel cabbalist who had disappeared from a cluttered room. Except that he hadn't and he wasn't: magician or golem or golem-maker. Just a sad survivor, the last of his family, swept away by social reform. Plenty of stuff had been liberated from the garret, the weavers' attic, books and manuscripts, real and fraudulent and really fraudulent, surfacing now with boring frequency in rare book-dealers' catalogues. The synagogue itself was so well preserved nobody had set foot in it for years, except for kosher artists, names who did things with installations and pretty lights.

'Rodinsky's mirror has been traced. It was photographed aeons ago in some book we're still trying to locate,' said Katie. 'But it seems to have acquired, in the years of its disappearance, a rather sinister reputation. Stare into it long enough and you see his room. As it was. What *really* happened. The mirror never learnt to lie. It's fixed in a perpetual present tense, the moment when the room was sealed, the window boarded over, and the light died.'

'Fine,' said Norton, disguising a yawn in a swipe of eggy bread. He'd heard it all before and was weary of these Gothic retrievals, now that they'd run with the tide to Chelsea, Fulham, Putney and points west. The whole business had been heritaged, art-streamed, given a provisional blessing by lottery sponsors with a sharp eye for the way a good yarn can underwrite development; tents on swamps, fairground rides rebranded as futurist architecture and operated by airlines looking for a way to get out of hardware. What better than wingless modules attached to a bicycle wheel, a journey that never leaves the terminal? Great views, plenty of point-of-sale merchandising, minimal upkeep. We were back, all unknowingly, to those two-quid flights around the bay. A glimpse of the pier, a quick chuck in the brown bag, and home for tea.

Norton blamed himself. He couldn't keep shtum, didn't know when to leave well alone. He had to worry at, tease out, secrets that were better left untold: vanishing caretakers, patterns of malign energy that linked eighteenth-century churches, labyrinths, temples, plague pits. Now they were far too loudly on the map, or trashed by attention. All he ever wanted was to write himself out, to fade into the masonry, become one of the revenants someone else would track. But there wasn't enough of him to interest even the most desperate bounty hunter. Biography? The guy had never done anything, been anywhere, said anything memorable. He was a material ghost. An addict of the city, not of smack or booze, women or whips. He couldn't even offer family interest, a monster father or a mum who put it about.

'Men were buried with their weapons, women with mirrors. Polished copper ovals – like ping-pong bats with a touch of mange. Super examples in the museum at Heraklion,' Katie gushed. 'Been to Crete lately?'

'I had a kebab once,' Norton replied. 'Didn't care for it. Like gnawing your way through a mummified arm.'

'It's just that I was thinking of, you know, the famous Phaistos Disk. The patterns of dust in Rodinsky's mirror, silvered flakes, where the backing has chipped away, seem to make up, if you want to see it, a sort of serpentine path. With mysterious figures or letters from an alphabet nobody has cracked.'

I've cracked it, Norton thought. I know what I am: a set of Scottish teeth. That is to say, an absence that nags; phantom pains, aching gums to remind you that something was once there. It was like sex. He'd been dreaming lately of pleasures he hadn't experienced in thirty years. The taste of good food. Being able to bite back in a friendly domestic tussle. He relished nightmares involving an underground bunker, passages opening from passages, an earthy chill. And how, as his flickering candle failed, spilling hot wax on his trembling hand, he located the magic box, arm at full stretch, in a spidery aperture. Opening it, his fingers traced the solid tines of a Celtic comb, king brooch or miniature diadem. Before the light failed, leaving him disorientated, prematurely incarcerated in a vacant tomb, he saw what he'd found: some hermit's upper set, a denture put aside against the lucky day when meat would be back on the menu.

'Why I suggested the Cock for our meeting,' said Katie, discreetly sliding an envelope across the wreckage of the table, 'was that the market porters drink here when they've finished their shift. What with the new Euro regulations and all the silly fuss about beef on the bone, Smithfield's a shrunken operation. Clean as a whistle, no blood in the sawdust, no trolleys of cows' heads…'

'Talking of which,' Norton suggested, 'they do a very nice bubble and squeak, if you could go another round. And a Guinness to wash it down.'

'Look over there, but discreetly,' she whispered, as Norton, feigning interest, was up on his toes. 'The two old boys in that booth. Know who they are? Last of the bummarees. They still haul *fantastic* weights. Some of those carts weigh five hundred pounds, empty. George is nearly seventy years old, ex-boxer, friend of all the villains. But he's sweet as pie. Keeps going, so they say, on alcohol.'

Norton expected creatures from the lower depths (not unlike himself), but in greasy leather aprons. And discovered instead two elderly gentlemen in business suits and wing collars being served with enormous tact and deference by the guv'nor. Two or three bone-helmet lads, with tattoos and prominent veins, stood back from the table, showing off their cross of St George T-shirts as if auditioning for entry to a Templar Lodge.

'It's what they call their "Parliament". They meet here every morning after they've punched their cards,' Katie said. 'The bummarees, a few of the security chaps – ex-military police – and skinhead footsoldiers from Dagenham, BNP, putting the world to rights. Old George is married to a tax lawyer, has a flat in the Barbican.'

'Mosley was a prince,' George was telling them. 'Toffs don't move like the rest of us. Brought up with horses, born in the saddle, so to speak. And dancing lessons…'

'Buggered rigid in all them schools,' his friend chipped in, approvingly.

'Discipline. Top-drawer personal hygiene. You've seen the films of Cable Street, Ned, rank and file like a load of bleedin' ants, rushing and jerky, with old Oz still as a statue. Hand on hip. He always put me in mind of Robert Donat, or Cary Grant, white tie and tails, stuck with the Keystone Kops.'

Katie led Norton over to George's table. This parliament, the hack thought, isn't much different from the one in Westminster. They all talk as if they've got too much tongue in the mouth. They yawn and scratch like monkeys. The old boys, it's true, have better manners, less ego. They don't have to disguise their opinions and they've put in a proper morning's graft before they let their prejudices out for an airing.

'Please don't get up, no, really, George,' Katie fluttered, laying a cool hand on the pinstriped sleeve. 'We don't want to interrupt your meal. It's just that my friend is trying to get in touch with your friend, the one who works in the burial ground.'

'Who's she on about?' Ned wanted to know. Women weren't welcome on the wrong side of the bar, unless plates needed shifting, or an ashtray was beginning to spill.

'You know, the lovely old chap who hurt his back and had to find a less demanding occupation. I don't know *how* you pull those weights. Carts are so unstable on cobbles and slippery floors. You're both so frightfully fit.'

'Bent Les,' Ned shouted. 'The bint means Bent Les. He's only gone and got 'isself webbed up with a Jew Boy. Whossit? Marks? Spencer? Lew Grade?'

'Sorry, Miss,' George said. 'We've lost touch with Leslie since he transferred east. I believe he found employment taking care of the tomb of one of them banking families. Usurers, money-grubbing scum, but they take care of their own. Respect for the dead. And beautifully polished shoes.'

'Could you tell us *which* burial ground?'

'It's a foreign country down there now, Miss. I couldn't say. Try Brady Street. There was a few nice little boozers round that way, before they sent the Twins down.'

'Thanks so much,' Katie said. 'So helpful.' And she signalled the guv'nor to bring another round. The parliament went back to giving the single European currency, regulations governing the transportation of livestock, a bit of a going over.

Back at their table, Katie showed her delight by squeezing Norton's hand. He caught a nostalgic whiff of coconut butter. It seemed that Katie's hunch was confirmed, the whispers that her researcher (a man called Kaporal) was trying to punt: Bent Les, the supposed keeper of Rodinsky's mirror, was hiding out in a Jewish burial ground, just off the Whitechapel Road, within a stone's throw of the Royal London Hospital. You'd catch a great view of the stone slabs, lined up on an east/ west orientation, and hidden among scraggy trees, as they choppered you in after a major road accident. Norton, in his wanderings, had often paused, near the new Sainsbury's, to watch the latest Glasgow wet-brain being elbowed by security guards. Despite the Dalgleish-impenetrable curses and the waving arms, these demented Jocks never spilled a drop of their industrial-strength Tennents. Then there was the noise. You didn't see the red helicopters making for the hospital roof, you saw trees sway, windows rattle in the flats. The uncut grass of the burial ground, behind walls, glimpsed through a locked gate, was woven into crop circles. Weed-trees, sycamore and London Plane, lost bark, felt their root-anchors give: as if the Day of Judgement had come early, the Whitechapel Apocalypse when the parched ground gives up its dead.

'... have to fly, late for my appointment at the clinic.'

Norton had drifted off on his East London heritage trail; decom-missioned synagogues, chirpy Marxists disputing the pavement, old Jack conducting his experiment in social engineering, a premature National Health gynaecologist. The word 'clinic' brought him up sharp. He wasn't a fastidious man, but he broke off his attempt to spear Katie's leftover rind.

'Anything... serious?'

'I'm pregnant. We, I, both of us... absolutely chuffed. Due on Midsummer's Day. My first.'

Useless at noticing these things, or knowing what to say, Norton chewed his fingers. He'd read some stuff about the Transit of Venus, a shift in the cosmological gears that was having a devastating effect. Women, in Norton's experience, conceived to ward off bad karma. One of his wives hadn't been able to go within five miles of Glastonbury without getting knocked up. 'An evil place,' she'd mutter, as he embarked on his circumnavigation of the Tor. She couldn't read John Cowper Powys without breaking out in hives. 'I'm not pregnant,' she would reply to impertinent questions. 'I'm having a baby.'

'Go down there. See if you can persuade this man, Leslie, to show you the mirror. Keep it under 2,000 words. We're not the *LRB*. No digressions, nothing heavy. Bit of a mystery, blah-de-blah. Like opening a Pharaonic tomb or the Palace of King Midas. Facilitate him, if you have to. And we'll arrange to send a photographer. That's *important*. The story has to be picture led.'

On the street, abandoned, left to a fractured narrative of self, Norton searched out potential parentheses. He was being paid in millennial increments: grave-robber, mirror, morbid frisson wasn't much to be going on with. He'd never been able to sculpt a page with dialogue (it came out like Pinter slumming). He couldn't work out where to leave those lovely white spaces the Sexton Blake gang exploited to polyfill their 30,000-word novellas.

He got out of the sun and into a medieval church, strolled the crescent, the shady stone forest, as if he had a perfect right to the cloisters. He admired the stills from *Shakespeare in Love*, read verses dedicated to men whose lives were reduced to polished heads, ruffed and chill, in wall safes with a bit of text.

Then he retraced his steps through laneways with perfect Elizabethan proportions, wine bars that serviced futures traders, victims who had signed up to the Net – and, consequently, weren't there, not really. You saw them walking with things clamped to their heads like battery chargers. Their lips never rested, driving, eating, lounging alfresco, chatting to their mates. They talked while they were talking, talked over themselves, contributed to the universal babble that formed a permanent electric cloud over the city. Norton had been in bars and heard them yelp, 'Where are you?', to someone sitting at the next table. And still they were happy to carry a spit-stick against the cheek. Like an electric-razor that chats back.

The last time Katie had called him, caught him in his favourite grease caff, Norton thought she was on the job. She was panting so much he could barely hear what she had to say. It turned out she was running for a bus.

Nothing in the slog through Clerkenwell, Shoreditch, Tower Hamlets took Norton's eye. If he'd had a camera, he would have left it in the bag. London was a book with no surprises. It knew itself too well. When self-consciousness turns into art, art into fashion, fashion into property, it's time to pull the plug. If that were an option. London, for Norton, was like life: unremittingly grim, until you considered the alternatives.

They were putting up a fresh poster outside a newsagent's shop on Bethnal Green Road: CHERIE, IT'S A BOY! Didn't she know?

For a week or more, Norton hung around Mocatta House, ducking into the Bangladeshi minimart to buy a bottle of milk and a packet of brightly coloured dust that looked like broken biscuits and burnt a hole in his tongue. He'd been all round the Brady Street burial ground and hadn't found a way in. Most of the original doors had been bricked up. Norton didn't want to lurk in such a way that the CCTV cameras picked him up. He waited and he watched.

A child, male, one of the dusky ones, a local, had a key. Either that or he knew how to pick a lock. Early, every third day, he would heft a clinking carrier bag, leaning heavily against the bias of its weight, into the burial ground. Norton positioned himself to track where the lad went, when he passed through the gate. But that didn't help. He saw the blackened memorial slabs, the shell of a gatehouse, several grassy mounds and an unnecessary profusion of trees. The place was half wilderness. It had been let go, sealed, willed towards erasure. As if someone wanted to wipe the slate, overdraw the memory bank: the stones here were mute. The sounds of the city ran around the perimeter wall, cracking bricks, but didn't penetrate the ash-garden within. Norton refuted Bishop Berkeley: here was a tree in the forest that fell unseen, and still experienced a profound existence. An otherness. The places, people, buildings that weren't there were the ones that affected Norton most. Chain the doors, cover hospitals with plastic sheeting, plant a crop of screening bushes and the ghosts must sing. It was the bits you couldn't see, black holes on the map, unlisted bunkers and disregarded lives that made most noise. When an old tin street sign was chucked in the skip, Norton withered, felt the wind from the steppes creep into his bones.

The boy with the bag walked up to a black marble monument and vanished. Maybe it was the shock of finding one memorial in perfect nick, ready for inspection at any time. Norton stayed on watch until he reappeared, bag empty, rolled into a truncheon with which he swiped the heads from dandelions.

Outside Tyler House (Masonic implications noted), Norton tried to suborn the lad. 'Oi, baldy. Fuck off, you. Pervert,' shouted a squad of his older mates, mobhanded but slender. They saw enough in Norton's eye, the way he ignored them, to appreciate that the designer vagrant was still capable of inflicting collateral damage. 'Oi, wanker. Oi oi oi,' they taunted, moving off in search of better turf; reverting to the old language, bird-swift, choral, provoking laughter. Neat as knives.

For the price of a couple of dozen Pokemon figures from a machine outside the minimart, a deal was struck. Bad habits dying hard, the pedant Norton worried about the plural of Pokemon (obviously, in his jellied brain-computer, he was writing this as he went along, translating life into language). Pokemons? Pokemen? Or the one that sounds like a Jamaican menu, 'Poke, mon. Poke and beans.'

Next time up, when the kid delivered his groceries to the man in the burial ground, the one who might be Bent Les, Norton would shadow him; make his play.

Norton was waiting outside Mocatta House at dawn, looking at the lion. And it was worth the trouble. There was a plaque set into the wall above the bit that said: 'Erected 1905. Modernised 1980.' The plaque had been dosed so heavily with emulsion that it was almost drowned, but you could still make out the Lion of St Mark, the wreaths forming the inner rim of a mandala, a botched labyrinth. Jewish mysticism of some kind, Norton supposed. He owed a lot, more than he cared to admit, to Jewish patrons who emerged from time to time to underwrite some of his crazier projects, like publishing books. Through these relationships, practical wisdom that ran deep, he had defined himself, found out who he was: a void, a man without family, tribe or allegiance. An outsider to outsiders.

The kid plucked at his shirt-tails, rattled the keys. He moved fast, effortlessly, barely seeming to touch the ground. They were through the gate and locked inside this secret garden before Norton had time to register the drop in temperature, the coldness of his hands.

The black marble tomb was a magnificent thing, belonging to various Rothensteins. 'Vessels of Wrath,' Norton punned. Someone had been busy with the weedkiller and the polish. What made this grandiloquent sepulchre stand out, like a Rodin dropped amongst bits of coloured string and beanbags in the Tate Modern, was the unloved bleakness that surrounded it. Dead stones. Half-eradicated histories. An angry form of black pollution, part crustose lichen, part soot, crept from the ground like a living shadow to swallow memory.

'Come on, mate. Hurry up then,' the kid called. Norton couldn't see him. He'd done his trick again and disappeared into thin air. Norton tapped the Rothenstein tomb till his knuckles bled: solid as an invest-ment portfolio. He was glad that, in respect, he'd covered his head – by cutting the peak from a baseball cap. He felt exposed, watched. He'd been turfed out of graveyards too many times; asked what he wanted, who he was looking for, if he knew where he was: the difficult ones.

There were glass snails on the stone slabs, eyes without pupils, oval shapes you might find in Italy or Greece with photographs of the officially dead. Such things, Norton reckoned, didn't belong in a Jewish burial ground. He was niggling at this anomaly when a hand tugged his trouser cuff. The kid was in a hole in the ground.

Les had done the crypt out quite nicely. Nobody knew who he was. Nobody knew he was there. Money was paid to an associate by an unknown intermediary for the upkeep of a single tomb. Les was bare-headed, silvery-pale with a black mouth. Like a burnt-out light bulb. He was shifty, rocking his shoulders in a constant sparring action, dry-popping his lips.

He'd got a mattress, a table, a couple of chairs, a paraffin lamp and a battery-driven TV set that flickered and faded as a constant irritant in the shadowy depths of the chamber. There was also a cat, an albino that looked as if it had never seen the light of day.

'My brother,' Les said, 'was in the demolition. Had first call on every fucking church in the East End. He done Princelet Street. Fetched out this mirror. Old, he reckoned. What you call it, Gregorian, Georgian? The business, John. I told him to run it up Camden Passage of a Wednesday.'

Down here, under Whitechapel, under poignant earth, Norton was in no hurry. The kid left his carrier bag and skipped. Norton had waited through sixty lifetimes to broach this dark reservoir of time, he wasn't going to jeopardise the possibility of shifting dimensions, accessing a parallel world, by arguing the toss with a pensioned member of Mosley's legions. He let Les drag out cases of gas masks, bundles of newspapers, boots with brown labels, ceremonial robes. The longer this went on, the more time would coalesce overhead. There might, at last, be a way out of his fix. A way of quitting London, definitively, without taking another step. The crypt, Norton imagined, ran into other crypts, other passageways. His dream of the dripping candle and the treasure hidden in an alcove began to seem prophetic. A bad sign.

Rustling the cashmoney from Katie Harwood's envelope under Les's nose was like belling one of Pavlov's dogs. Les was keen to be shot of this inopportune intruder, keen to return to silence and the oracle of the TV monitor (so old it played programmes that had decayed *before* they could be repeated).

'A oncer in the hand. Give me a receipt and I'll take it away,' Norton grunted. And, muttering, Les shuffled off into the darkness, the inner sanctum; where he scratched about, searching for a pen.

Picking up the mirror, the terrible thing that once hung on the wall of the hermit Rodinsky's attic, Norton lost his breath. There wasn't, as promised, a room frozen in time, but a face! Vague, dolorous, tragic. Shaped from pain. Hair gone, mouth creased; toothless, with sunken cheeks. Norton. He was staring at himself. His first emotion was relief. He balanced the mirror against a stack of books and stepped back like a connoisseur. The face stayed where it was. An X-ray of the Turin shroud, a flash of white heat. A negative. That made sense. Fear projected into the silver surface like elective alchemy.

This wasn't Norton. This was the *back* of the mirror. Sacking and wood with the vague imprint of a man who had turned the mirror, long ago, to face the wall.

You could scam Norton once, scam him again, as often as you liked if you were female, but this contract smelt iffy. With Les still cursing and stumbling, Norton pulled back the oilcloth and looked under the table: a dozen mirrors, wreckers' plunder picked up for a couple of bob in Club Row. Naughty Les was pulling a flanker, raising funds for the party and the bummarees; an irony they would appreciate as they gummed a hunk of bull. An immigrant myth was being exploited to fund stiffer immigration laws, alien expulsions, detention camps. Les was punting his final solution to the Princelet Street mystery wholesale.

Very neat. Norton called Les out to congratulate him, before he smashed his ribs. But Les was gone. The TV had stuck on mob footage, face after face, accusing Norton, screaming their approval in a silent paroxysm of hero worship. He was alone. He sat at Les's table. He thought he heard the cat once, then nothing for hours. Days. He reversed the mirror. And there *was* a room. Like this. Exactly like this: mattress, table, lamp. With one minor difference: no Norton. An empty room with darkening shadows. A mortality Polaroid quietly transmuting into oil. Darkness that lapped around his ankles, threatening to rise.

Some time later, when Norton realised, and accepted, that he would never leave this place, he brought out the other mirrors. Each one contained a different room, a crypt. Unfurnished chambers with slabs for beds. Frames of film from a bureaucratic catalogue, a monumental library of the dead. Beneath London was an untenanted necropolis. While up above, pale sunlight glinted on the glass snails, those small oval frames that had attached themselves with sticky secretions to the gravestones. In each frame now was a face, one of the sleepers from limbo, involuntary zombies; one of those who had to know how the story turned out.

Rapprochement

Maureen Freely

I was glad to see him. It is strange to say, but I must not deny it. After twenty-six years, seven months and three days of relishing this man's absence, of drawing dripping guns next to his head in old photographs, of assassinating him nightly with spikes and spears in my dreams, here he was again, the Reptile. In the flesh, at the Savoy, in the same room at the Savoy, racing across the room no less, calling me by name. And yes, I was glad. No, even more than that. The truth is that I was close to ecstatic.

The occasion was a fund-raiser on behalf of the Byzantine and Ottoman Society. As you may not have heard of this obscure organisation, allow me to explain. The B and O, as we members like to call it, was founded in the early '80s by group of London-based architects, historians and other hopeless visionaries with ties to the Near East, with a view to saving important heritage sites from the wrecker's ball. Not much had been achieved since its spirited inception, with most projects being nipped in the bud for the usual panoply of historical grievances. However, the sentiments of the board had moved up to a higher plane in the wake of the Istanbul and Athens earthquakes. As indeed had my own musings.

In fact, the gathering on the night in question had the aura of a homecoming for me. For it was with no little gratitude that I was noticing many others in the room who, like me, had had to absorb the horror of the twin calamities and the happy shock of the rapprochement that followed in the company of English wives who did not grasp its full significance.

My own wife had been particularly impervious. In retrospect I cannot find it in my heart to blame her. But at the time her opacity pained and perplexed me, and as this pertains to my behaviour later on, I shall pause here to give chapter and verse. Even on the day of the Turkish catastrophe, when we were watching the first pictures of men and women pulling their dead relatives from the rubble with their bare hands, Jennie's response to my involuntary but heart-felt cry of recognition had been, 'But of course they're humans just like us. Why on earth would you have ever thought otherwise?'

And then, the next day, when we were watching those young Greek soldiers filing out of an airforce jet on to Turkish soil – sober, wild-eyed, wanting only to know how they could be of assistance to a people that they might have dismissed as devils only the day before. When I turned to Jennie and said, 'What must it have been like for them, circling in the air over Aghia Sophia? What must it have been like for their mothers?' Without even looking up from her marking, she had pressed her lips into an infinitesimally English smile and said, 'I expect they were happy that their sons were making themselves useful.'

Come what may, she refused to take any interest in the historical ironies of the situation. This was never so apparent as when I showed her a banner headline in a Turkish newspaper bearing the Greek words for 'Thank you, friends'. When I asked her, 'Did you ever think this day would come?' all she did was shrug her shoulders and turn back to the proverbial stove.

The most hurtful remark had come several weeks later, in the aftermath of the second earthquake, the one in Athens. I was explaining to Alex and Constantine, our six- and seven-year-old sons, why it was politically significant for a Turkish rescue team working alongside Greek colleagues to pull survivors out of a collapsed factory. I was trying to express my thoughts in concrete terms they could appreciate. So I had been repeating to them the things I had been taught at home and school about the Terrible Turk. Following this I was encouraging them to imagine the tumult in the heads of the Greek rescue workers came to the electrifying discovery that, for all these years, on the other side of this impenetrable fence that had divided the two countries for the better part of a century, their Turkish counterparts had been eating the same foods and dancing the same dances and singing the same songs. And Jennie had interrupted my soliloquy to say, 'But how could that be, my love? It just doesn't add up. If you share a common culture, surely it follows that you can't have been entirely separate. You must have spent some time together, and since you all look so much alike, presumably some of that time was spent in bed.'

She could not have known how her clever little quip pained me. However, she cannot be blamed, for I did not want her to know. I did not want to know it myself! Nevertheless, it was an intense comfort to find myself later that week in this back-of-beyond ballroom at the Savoy, surrounded by so many others who showed signs of having been similarly afflicted.

Where there would once have been smoky smiles and pulse-taking handshakes there was now a torrent of alarmed questions. 'Have you spoken to your parents? Your aunt? Your uncle? Your cousins? Your friends?' 'Where did you say your family lived? Kipseli? Kifissia? Halandri?' I remember in particular how a coterie had formed around a professor who had just flown in from Athens. With rapid, abrupt hand gestures that invigorated me as much, if I had just taken the opposite trajectory, this man described how he had been sitting at his desk only moments before the tremors began but had then quit the chair without a logical pretext to take a breath of air in the garden. When the shaking had stopped and he had gone back into his study, there had been a big chunk of the ceiling sitting on his chair. The professor had paused here to meet our eyes. 'Yes, my friends, this is how close I came.' There was, I recall, a chorus of emotive ahs. One man put his arms out and looked up at the sturdy ceiling above us and said, 'Saved by an angel.' Another said, 'I have heard so many similar stories from my family in Istanbul. And then others involving apparitions that bore a greater resemblance to the denizens of the nether regions.'

A third man nodded in agreement. 'And we've not heard the last of them, either. The long-term psychosocial effects are yet to be tallied.' 'All the more reason to open up more channels of exchange,' said a fourth. This was followed by murmurs of approbation. And in spite of the sombre subject, my spirits lifted. As I surveyed my motley group of sudden soulmates, the following thoughts passed through my mind. 'I will never belong in this country.' 'I will continue to resist the idea of British citizenship.' 'I will pursue the Athens University possibility.' 'I will do whatever is necessary to make my sons understand what it means to be Greek.' 'If not Athens, then perhaps Thessaloniki. If not that, then perhaps my uncle's offer.' I looked across the room, at a huddle of dignitaries whom I would normally have detested for the fact that they were Tories. Today I was hating them for no other reason than that they were English.

It was in this spirit then, that I opened my arms to welcome the already open arms of the Reptile. I had recognised him instantly, even though the Reptile's face was browner, smoother, larger, and in every way more Turkish than it had been before. His student jeans had made way for a suit so sharp it hurt my eyes, but the bright, boyish, slightly bulging eyes were the same, and it was the same jubilant, insouciant, gravel-mixer-in-a-megaphone voice. 'It's really you, isn't it?' he bellowed, not caring a whit how many fragile attempts at stiff, English small talk he shattered with his decibels. 'Yes it is! Yes! It's really you! My great good god, after all these years, who would believe it? My good men,' said the Reptile, as he turned around to the two rather rattled looking stuffed shirts who had followed in his wake. 'Allow me to introduce you to the most formative experience of my youth. My great friend and former co-conspirator, sometimes known as Stellio Hadzoglou, distinguished professor of industrial sociology at the LSE, but to me and to all those with a more intimate knowledge of him, there is a preferred term of endearment which I cannot stop myself from sharing with you.' He clapped a warm and friendly hand on my shoulder, and said, 'Ladies and gentlemen, allow me to introduce you to the Goat!'

I did not at the time ask himself how it was that the Reptile, aka Sami Tekir, heir to one of the biggest industrialist fortunes of Turkey, could have been so surprised to see me, when he already seemed to know my curriculum vitae backwards and forwards. If I can look back now, I can ask myself, if our reunion was not entirely by chance, then for what purpose was it engineered? However, this was one of many questions that may have flicked through the forefront of my mind at the time, only to be lost in the fast-forward rush of events and emotions. What Sami said to me was this: he had caught a glimpse of me while en route to another appointment. But as he himself put it with his playful, I-won't-take-no-for-an-answer smile: he was not about to let his long-lost friend slip through the net again so easily! Almost at once, I found myself whisked out of my dull drinks do and into a neighbouring room where a fabulous banquet was already in full swing.

The host was a familiar face, but I have to tell you I could not put a name to him, so in this regard at least I am an innocent. I vaguely recalled a link with the MoD, and half remembered that he had left under a cloud, possibly during the Westland Affair. Or was it the *Belgrano*? If he had decamped to Ankara to run this shadowy and dubious think tank about which we have now been hearing so much, I was none the wiser on the evening in question. However, I could hardly fail to note that this man, whoever he was, knew who buttered his bread for him. He was all teeth and snapping fingers when Sami asked if he might find it in his heart to make room for just one more at the head table. And neither was there dissension from the other diners.

It was a stellar cast. The woman seated to my eventual left was the wife of someone in British Aerospace, while the man on my right was the owner of an engineering company that specialised in roads and damns. This was as close as I had ever come in my adult life to eating with the enemy, but I am afraid to report that I made precious little of this rare opportunity. In order to keep a balance to my account, I must readily admit that I descended cravenly to their level, asking the woman about her children and enthusing over the Greek island on which she had spent her summer holiday, expressing interest in the road- and damn-builder's myriad projects in the Eastern Mediterranean without once asking about kickbacks or union bashing, or unlawful displacement of indigent peoples, leave alone the ravaging of the environment. When the time came for me to explain my own research, I must even have made it sound like an apologia for global capitalism, instead of the scathing critique I now more sincerely than ever hope it can become.

And perhaps if we had stayed the distance my conscience would have compelled me to clarify my position. But no sooner had the main course been cleared than Sami was whisking me off again, in a white limousine no less, to a second gala. This one was in a swank Covent Garden restaurant that had been decorated to conform to a Hollywood set designer's vision of the Casbah. It was all satin drapes, carpets, hanging lamps, copper trays and waiters and waitresses dressed to look like houris and eunuchs. The guests of honour were two singers, one Greek and one Turk. The Greek, Marinoula, had been a household name in my life since early middle age. I was close to being struck dumb when Sami introduced me to her. She and her Turkish counterpart, who enjoyed a comparable degree of celebrity in his native country, were in London at the behest of a disaster relief fund. They were to appear together at the Hackney Empire that very Tuesday. One of the many promises Sami extracted from me that night was that I cancel my Tuesday evening seminar so that Jennie and I could attend the concert. Tickets or the lack of same were not to deter us. We would be joining Sami and his party, who would be taking over the three front rows. 'Or more, perhaps, if we can dig out a few more co-conspirators.'

Rapprochement

If anonymous and unsubstantiated reports are to be believed, these were in overabundance already. Also in alleged attendance at this gala, and at the casino to which a fleet of limousines later decamped us, were the owners of three football clubs (one Turkish and two Greek) plus an assortment of the more unsavoury variety of MPs and disgraced former police chiefs, mostly but far from exclusively Turkish. Little as it says for my powers of perspicacity, I am sorry to say that I met no one who conformed to these stereotypes. Equally, I regret to confirm that I cannot report a sighting of the notorious pro-government Kurd whom the tabloid press has dubbed King Casino. And I can I find nothing to add to what has already been said about 'Wolf Boy', the assassin who had been travelling on a diplomatic passport even though (as we now know) he was officially dead.

As to the suggestion that I myself had become a de facto guest of honour of Tekir and Co by virtue of a mistaken identity, this too is possible. It is true (as you have no doubt heard by now) that there is an unsavoury owner of many Panamanian-registered vessels who bears the same last name as I. Also there is another who is a minister of no little influence. I am happy to report that neither is a relative of mine. If, on the other hand, King Casino and 'Wolf Boy' had been led to believe that these men were my uncles, they would have been wanting to shake my hand with the possibility of oiling it later on, when they were taking advantage of the newly warm relations between their nation and mine to expand their business operations into Greece. All this is possible. However, I recall no such advances.

I do recall looking into this corner from time to time and seeing here and there a cluster of big burly men wearing black leather jackets that were too small for them. I discounted them then and I still do so, for they had no eyes for anyone except the listless, sloe-eyed, off-duty lap dancers they'd brought with them. Far be it from me to judge them for their inattention to their environment: my own span of attention was no wider. It is not, after all, every day you met the man who has ruined your life, only to discover that you can still have warm feelings for him.

If you will remember that I had been burning this man in mental effigy for a quarter-century. But every time Sami threw back his head in laughter and said, 'And do you remember the time when we…?' it was an event that had not so much as crossed my thoughts since the day our prior association had ended. It was as if I had put all the good things I knew about the fellow and filed them away in ice or aspic. But now they came tumbling back as fresh as the day it happened: the private vocabulary, the lost weekends, the card games, the pranks, some playful and some that carried in their tale the sting of history.

One game in particular had provided us with our common thread. It was an elaboration of a genuine conflict between us on the occasion of our first meeting, when we found ourselves being opponents at an LSE bridge table. Our friendship had flowered from our mutual decision (perilously far into the proceedings) to see our exchange in a humourous light. I feel obliged to pause here to explain this game, for reasons that will become clear in due course.

The rules were simple. I would begin, always in front of an audience, by pointing at Sami, who would be at the time in the midst of, let us say, employing a toothpick. I would say, 'Only a Turk would hold a toothpick in that miserly fashion.' Then he would put down the toothpick in apparent anger and say, 'Only a Greek would use a toothpick on his balls.' To which I would say, 'Only a Turk would sell his grandmother to save face.' To which he would say, 'Only a Greek would be able to stick an umbrella into his grandmother's vagina and then open it.' The trick of the game was to convince our audience that we were on the verge of coming to blows. The challenge was to respond to each insult with a graver insult without giving an exterior sign of how many of the other person's slings and arrows were hitting their mark. The game ended at the moment one of our outside observers expressed their distress. At this point, I would say to Sami, or Sami would say to me, 'But how can you even show your face in public, with that great red bloodstain on your shirt?' And he would say, 'What stain?' and look down, at which point I would flick the underside of his nose with my forefinger and then squeeze it between this and my thumb, in the manner of affectionate adults with young children. With this our audience would know that all they had witnessed had been in jest.

To have such experiences in common is to share for life a form of shorthand. And so it was at four in the morning, after we had left the casino and retired with the other stragglers of the evening to a hole in the wall in the Essex Road for a few bowls of tripe soup. I had just brought to a close an unpleasant chat on my mobile with Jennie, whom I had forgotten to advise of my change of plans, and whom I had now unnecessarily roused from her sleep. Then Sami leaned across the table with a portentous smile and said, 'Only a Greek would allow a wife to attach him to her skirt'.

My first instinct was to cry for joy at the recovered memory. My second was to rediscover a well of anger, which grew exponentially when Sami went on to say, 'So, while we await a suitable riposte, let us move on. Let us see this woman and what only she could have given you.' Still at a loss for words, I duly took out a photograph of Jennie and the boys, for which all in attendance expressed due admiration. After I had restored the photograph to the safety of my wallet, Sami turned to me with a special smile, to say, 'And now, my friend, it is time for me to surprise as well as warm your heart.' He drew out a photograph of two young boys with a Turkish version Barbie woman, complete with fake blonde hair and wraparound designer sunglasses. 'My wife and sons,' he said proudly. 'Tell me, Stellio, are you surprised?' In fact, I was not surprised. This was, after all, the sort of woman for whom he had always been destined. Even so, I could not stop myself from asking the question which now sprang to my lips: 'Sami, tell me honestly. Have you no regrets about the one you left behind?' To which he said, 'None. Absolutely none. It has not been easy, but that said, the alternative would have been unthinkable.'

. His words pierced me like a knife. It was without forethought that I suddenly found myself saying, 'Which brings us back to the question of a riposte. Only a Greek would tie himself to his wife's apron strings. However, only a Turk would rather let a woman waste away than accept her as an equal.' He met my words with a puzzled smile, as if he was unable to discern my veiled meaning. However, as this expression had always been part and parcel of our game, I was certain that – in sharp contrast to our audience – he understood it exactly.

My meaning was this: she was still there, the unfinished business standing between us. The new spirit of détente could make her fade but never utterly dispel her. So perhaps the time has come for me to restore her to her proper place in this sad account.

I would like to begin by describing her as she could have been. So allow me to introduce you to Sera Rabinovich, the most celebrated physicist of her generation, alone of her sex to be in the running for the ultimate Nobel Prize. If you have never heard her name mentioned in the halls of power, it has largely to do with our friend the Reptile. Or, to be fair, with Sera's hopeless infatuation for him. The only child of elderly White Russian parents, Sera had first set eyes on her nemesis at a dance while a high school student in Istanbul. In spite of also being the great white hope of every teacher who had had the good fortune to work with her, she had apparently decided after this one short evening that this charming but careless and superficial playboy was the man to whom she wished to give her life.

And so when she had the news that Sami was destined for the LSE, she had rejected offers and scholarships to Harvard, Stanford, and MIT in favour of UCL – just for the privilege to being close to the boy who had continued to shower her with his promises in spite of having never fewer than half a dozen other girlfriends on the go.

If I had balked at the wasting of this fine intellect with her flowing chestnut locks and her ethereal eyes, and if I had felt especial revulsion at her willingness to play Sami's 'good luck charm' during his Saturday night poker games, there was always, I will have to admit, a racial element. In spite of my own friendship with Sami, and in spite of the fact that Sera was herself most emphatic about her own patriotism to her native Turkey, it was galling to me to see a Moslem Turk having such a sway over a good Orthodox girl, over 'one of ours.' But I am sure I would have overcome the problem had Sami treated her with the respect that was her due.

However, he treated her as he did all the others with whom he carried on his careless dalliances. At best she was a toy, at worst an expendable accessory. It was perhaps inevitable that push should come to shove. Unhappily for Sera, this moment arrived after she had cast the die and once again turned down generous post-graduate fellow-ships at all the top universities of the Western world, for the privilege of following Sami back to Istanbul. It was immediately following this momentous decision that he had come to me confessing to a quandary. On a recent flying visit home, he now confessed to me, he had become engaged to a former Miss Turkey. This match was blessed by his family, and in fact they had playing a large part in arranging it. Although he had not found it in his heart to advise Sera of this development, he was now going to have to keep her out of his way, as this fiancée was arriving in London for an extended visit. In spite of my entreaties to level with the poor girl, Sami did not come forward. Instead he remained on the arm of this poor imitation of a Barbie with her shrill and brainless voice and her endless prattling about the superiorities of Paris fashion. And so it was I who, after the fact, was forced to be the bearer of the ill tidings. It was I who held Sera's hand during her grief. If I am going to be frank, I will have to admit that there was a part of me that hoped she would raise herself from her tears and see me with new eyes, perhaps understand a new future in which I could be her salvation. Alas, this never came to pass. Instead, she devoted her first opportunity of solitude to cutting her wrists.

Happily, I was able to apprehend and save her. However, I was far from being thanked by her family when, at the request of the hospital, I advised them of developments. When they had arrived to take her home, I had acceded to Sera's desperate plea that I imposture myself as the offending lover. She did not wish them to know of the true liaison that she had always hidden from them. Caught as I was in the exigencies of the moment, I failed to see how this act of kindness would make it impossible to remain in contact with Sera following her return to Istanbul. Indeed, every letter I attempted to send to her afterwards was returned unopened.

To add to my conundrum, I was unable to avail upon Sami to make enquiries on my behalf. With his connections, it could have been easy for him to discover if she was alive or dead. However, I was unable even to discern in him the merest concern for her livelihood. When I made what would become my final plea to him, beginning with the assertion that that he owed it to me, it was as if a cloak had fallen over his eyes. 'It will help no one to reopen this matter,' he had said coldly. 'She is best left where she belongs.'

This is the moment at which we had words. But I did not speak well. The good remarks came to me afterwards, as they so often do. Needless to say, it was on this note that our friendship met its ultimate Waterloo.

And now, eight hours into our chance reunion, after revisiting so many of the good moments we had shared, we had returned, in the manner of Roman roads, to the crux of the matter. A shadow passed across his face as he had digested my barbed words, and for a moment I thought he was entertaining the idea of an open discussion. Then he recouped himself. He took my hand and in a heartfelt voice he said, 'You cannot have known this in light of our long silence, but I would like to assure you that our last conversation all those years ago did not go unheeded. There were some things that were said that survived my initial anger to reveal themselves as true, and for this, my friend, I thank you. For the rest, I have long been willing to let bygones be bygones. I cannot claim to be a saint – what man can? – and I cannot claim to have made my wife a happy woman. But our children,' he said with renewed vigour. 'Our precious children! They would be worth a million days of married misery, would they not? Just look at them again, I beg of you. See for yourself!' At which he brought out another photograph, this one a studio portrait of his two sons, who were aged about two and five, he now told us, and whose names, rather preposterously as it would happen, were Attila and Timur. Imagine naming your children after Attila and Timberlane! Of course I did not say this to his face. I told him what was also true, how delightful they looked, and how very fair. And he said, 'Do you know, my friend? I do not regret a single moment of my past up to the moment of the birth of Timur, for if I had changed a single second, they would not exist. And now, following the catastrophe, I am experiencing such an even more pronounced and dramatic change in attitude. Life can be snuffed out, just like that, at any minute. I could step outside and the earth could move and a boulder appear from thin air to crush my skull. Or I could be stung by a bee and I could die of an allergic reaction in the manner of a beloved friend and business associate, and this would be that. Forgive me if I sound callous or paradoxical – but the tragic events of the 17th August have given me a new zest for life. Live and let live, I say, but not for tomorrow.'

In this way he brought us back, for the moment at least, from the brink. Having salvaged our reunion, he insisted that we celebrate our pyrrhic victory with another bottle of raki. So it was not until six in the morning that I finally tiptoed shoeless back into the silence of my home. What hit me in the face was how small it was. A man could not open his arms to receive an old friend in his front vestibule without sustaining heavy injuries. To add to this insult, it soon became clear that Jennie had channelled her anger by putting every piece of clothing in our possession through the wash cycle. Her refusal to make proper use of our perfectly amenable dryer meant that there was now not a square inch of the kitchen that was not adrift with stiffening trousers or slightly damp socks. Even with my superior knowledge of the geography, I was unable to make my way amidst the cluttered chairs and ubiquitous racks without tripping.

Rapprochement

Much the same could be said of my attempts to navigate my memories when I woke up just after noon the next day. The sequence of events together with my responses to them no longer seemed plausible. My old feelings about Sami swirled around my revised and updated mental image of the man like a pernicious mist. With them came shards of Sera. It was almost in a trance that I drank my coffee, performed my ablutions, and prepared my briefcase for what was left of the day. Even when I remembered, halfway up the escalator at Holborn station, that I had dug myself a far greater hole than necessary by failing to leave Jennie a note of abject apology on the kitchen notepad, I still could not bring himself to panic.

It was in a similarly disconnected spirit that I found myself leaving my normal route to cross Kingsway and wander into Covent Garden. It wasn't long before my aimless meanderings took me past the swank Casbah-esque restaurant where only hours earlier I had shaken the hand of Marinoula. In the dull glow of mid-afternoon, it was, however, stripped of its glory. The limousines and doormen and tuxedos and bejewelled evening gowns had disappeared to make way for an orange street cleaning machine and a man in a tattered lumber jacket who was selling the *Big Issue*. My memories thus denuded of their glamour, I had to ask myself: 'Stellio, what exactly has happened to you during this long night? Have you allowed yourself to be seduced? And if so for what?'

These, in any event, were the questions that dogged my thoughts during the interminable Library Committee meeting that afternoon, and following that the stultifying seminar on incomes policy. They preoccupied me even during my efforts to ingratiate myself that evening with a frosty Jennie. And they culminated that night in a dream in which I found myself in a tent with my grandmother and a bulbous Sultan, whose favour I was desperately attempting to curry, as for some reason my and my grandmother's lives depended on it. So I was continually bringing him things, and, having set them on the table, asking, will this do? Have I done enough? My first offerings were in the order of jewels and embroidered sheets, the stuff of dowry chests. But when the bulbous Sultan was still not sated, I moved on to gorier and even sacrilegious offerings. These began with the head of John the Baptist and finished up with a miniature but perfect replica of Aghia Sophia. At the sight of each offering, my grandmother, who was dressed in mourning, shook her head and shed a larger tear.

When I revisited the dream in the light of midday, it seemed to me that I should take it as a sign that I should stop my new friendship with Sami in its tracks, at least until we could speak frankly about the matter still between us. It was in this spirit that I rang him to say that we should find a way to meet, just the two of us. His response was, 'Yes, I was thinking the same thing. There are some proposals that I would like to put to you. So let us think what to do. You are of course coming to the supper after the concert on Tuesday, as for this I am not taking no as an answer. Once we have brought our wives together, we shall surely find the moment we need.'

The prospect of sharing a supper table with the former Miss Turkey filled me with dread. But there was of course the prospect of seeing Marinoula live to counterbalance that foreboding, and furthermore I would be having a chance to level with Sami later on. However, it was with the heaviest of trepidation that I walked into the Hackney Empire the following Tuesday evening. And there they were, beckoning to us from the front row, Sami and, on his arm, this woman with her fake socialite smile and her out-of-season tan and her tight golden bun and her Parisian dress that would be worth twice the GDP of Togo and Sierra Leone combined, and in addition to this, so many bracelets and necklaces dangling that she was having to stand as stiffly as a shop-floor mannequin. The first thought that came into my head at the sight of this preening wife was, 'What would happen to your smile if I told you that your good fortune is founded on the funeral pyre of another?' It was only when she came towards me, with that same swaying walk I had once loved so dearly, that I understood my mistake.

For it was not Miss Turkey who was holding out her hand to me. It was Sera. Or should I say, Sera reformed to reflect another's image. But what had happened to those flowing chestnut locks? Those ethereal blue eyes? What had she done to herself? Why had she been willing to give away her unique and priceless gifts for the sake of a man who could never be worthy of her? Of course I said none of this. My first words to Sera were, 'What are you doing here?' At this she looked startled. 'Didn't you know? Didn't Sami tell you I would be coming? And any-way for that matter, why would I not be coming?' Slowly slowly, the terrible truth dawned on me. For not only had Sami told me, he had also shown me her picture. It was I who had failed to recognise her, and who had been misreading so many remarks and signals ever since.

Rapprochement

And now I had to go over the events of the past few days and reinter-
pret every detail. A tall order when one is also in the front row of the
Hackney Empire. My every attempt at logical thought was muddied
by the swirl of unknowns – at what point had this ill-fated reconciliation between Sami and Sera had occurred? And why, when this
had occurred, had he considered her great intellectual gifts to be less
important than his own need for a conventional wife? Finally – what
were his motives in parading her thus before me, when he knew my
feelings? If his aim was not to rub my face in the dirt in full view of
my wife and so many others, then what was this humanform devil
hoping to achieve? As my mind scurried this way and that, doing cart-
wheels between the possible permutations, I was unfortunately unable
to take an enjoyment from the incomparable Marinoula. And it was
the same at the gala dinner at the Dorchester that followed on the heels
of the concert.

No expense had been spared for the two-hundred-plus guests. But
I could hardly think, could only go through the motions of nicety at
this hell-on-legs that was our supper table. Even the polite banter was
close to being beyond me. I only had eyes for Sera, and yet I could not
dare look at her. I could not bear hearing Sami beginning so many
sentences with the word, 'we'. 'We' were having a house renovated in
Tarabya. 'We' were deliberating about whether or not to sell our house
in Bodrum. 'We' had a wonderful new yacht that could sleep twenty.
When 'we' took a Blue Journey in July, would Jennie and I do them
the honour of joining 'us'? And then Sera would echo his words. Yes,
'we' would be so happy if you could come, if you could bring your
sons, if your sons could become friends with 'our' sons. When the
waiters came out bearing platters of Baked Alaska, it was as if all twelve
were parading pieces of my chopped and burning heart.

So when Sami stood up after coffee and said, 'My friend, is this
perhaps a time for us to retire to the mezzanine for cigars?' I begged
off, claiming an upset stomach and made an alternative arrangement
to see him at Claridges the following day at five. My feigned illness
gave me the opportunity to bow out of the tortuous evening before
the scars began to show.

But you can imagine how difficult it was for me to concentrate the
next day, and how my dread increased as my assignation with Sami
drew closer. For by now I was no longer sure what it was that I had

to say to him. As for Sera, it seemed to me that if she was indeed happy with her choices in life, it was not for me to question them. And yet there was something about the glimpses I had had of her face at the candlelit table that made me wonder about a possible gap between her true feelings and the façade she had been intent on showing me. It was this doubt, I think, that caused me to forget to turn off my mobile when entering the Special Cases Committee after lunch. And strange as it may sound, I was not surprised when it rang, and when the voice that emerged from it when I had scurried from the room turned out to belong to her. 'We need to meet,' was all she said. I recovered my equanimity just enough to explain where she had found me, and why I would be confined in this small space for at least another hour. But I was no match for her plaintive tones when she murmured, 'Am I not a special case, too?'

I hope it is not to hard for you to imagine why, when she asked me to find a way of extricating myself, I succumbed.

Now that we are coming closer to the events that went on to become tabloid fodder, allow me to paint the scene for you when I entered the DKNY juice bar at half past three that afternoon. It had taken me longer than anticipated to reach my destination, the nether regions of Old Bond Street being so far away from my usual beaten tracks. I had had to run the final distance to make up for lost time, so my heart was beating not just from anticipation when I swung open the door. It was a store I had never visited before, and I was somewhat taken aback by the film that was playing itself out on the wall over the counter. It portrayed the passage of larger-than-life but lifeless sylphs along a catwalk. In keeping with the attempt to remove all character from their persons, they were dressed head to toe in beige. So when my eyes descended to eye-level to find Sera leaning against the counter, surrounded by more shopping bags than I ever hope to have to count, all I could see were the sorrows that life had written on her face.

The calm collection of the previous evening was gone. The woman who now jumped to her feet at the sight of me had spent the previous night crying into her pillow. My suspicions were only further aroused when, after her initial embrace, she refused to look me in the eye. For a few painful minutes, I attempted banter. Finally, I said, 'Sera, I can't bear this any more. You must answer me honestly. In the final analysis, how do you describe your life?' If at first she balked at my intrusive words, she caved in after only a few nominal reproaches. Bursting into sobs, she said, 'Oh Stellio, how can I lie to you of all people? My life with Sami – it is the same.'

She went on to explain, in detail that I would feel indelicate to share with you. Suffice it to say that her miseries were far from being unusual for a woman of her age and position. But this is not to underplay in a way the pain they caused her, or the distress I felt at hearing of them. I am obliged to admit that this distress was not entirely disinterested. Married man that I now was, there was still part of me that wished to jump up and say, 'You have only yourself to blame! You could have prevented this hell, if only you had chosen me! It was clear from the very start that this man was going to throw you away. Whereas I, I would have taken your dreams and nurtured them like precious orchids!'

However, honour forbad me the true expression of my feelings. After I had said my goodbye and turned to beat my heavy-hearted path in the direction of Claridges, I could see only one honourable course of action that was open to me. I could no longer struggle to wrest her away from the father of her children, any more than I could wrest myself away from the mother of mine. I could only do a better job of what I had done already once before. I could prevail upon Sami to meet his responsibilities, which in this case would mean giving up mistresses as opposed to girlfriends, and urge him to give his heart instead to the job of becoming an honest husband.

And on this, my second attempt at reasoning with Sami, I managed to speak judiciously. Even so, Sami's surprise was palpable. He began by insisting that Sera had no right to complain, as she had her sons and everything a woman could want. It was clear to me that he had been drinking all afternoon, so he was not at his most coherent. However, his cumulative intake may also explain why, even before we had ordered our second whiskeys, he, too caved in and began to express his own miseries.

Again, I shall draw a veil over the ignominious details, stopping only to say that it is not always a boon to be the bankroller of a virtual harem, and also that such an apparently envious arrangement allows little opportunity for trust or true intimacy. In spite of my initial anger, I could not fail to pity him at least to a small degree. And it was when I expressed this thought that he, too, burst into tears and said, 'My friend, shall I tell you the most shaming thing of all? When we met again, my wish was to show you how I was a larger man than the one you knew, and to prove to you that I had indeed honoured my obligations. I wanted you to look at Sera with her head on my arm and congratulate yourself at a job well done! But now it seems that even this small vindication will forever be denied me.'

Of course I felt obliged to reassure him. Having succeeded in this endeavour, it may not come as a surprise that he resolved to seal our reconciliation with a bottle of Veuve Cliquot. It was only at this juncture that our conversation began to inch away from the past and into the future. However, I hope I do not need to explain why, even if Sami had been nurturing dreams of a joint venture, he would not have chosen this moment to unfold them, nor, had he done so, would he have succeeded in making much sense.

How much did I notice of the scene unravelling around us as we revelled? Only that there were a number of elderly and stiff-backed couples whom our sometimes raised voices were failing to amuse. I was not surprised to learn after the fact that most of these were en route to a function in honour of a lesser member of the Princess Margaret set. This would be entirely consistent with the vignettes I glimpsed through the corners of my eyes. It is, I think, inevitable that such types would have balked at our failure to conduct our conversation in whispers. However, it is unlikely that their disapproval would have amounted to more than looks askance had I not made the fatal mistake of insisting that it was my turn to pay the bill.

In and of itself, my failure to find a single credit or debit card to accept the charge was a minor and reversible mishap. I was embarrassed, of course, and the sight of Sami saving the day with his superior credit rating only underlined the gulf that had always existed between us. But this was the way it was. Ultimately, it was a fact I had to live with. However, it was while Sami was still hot with the pleasure of his one-upmanship that he chose to advance his lead with a joke too far.

I will repeat now what he said to me.

His exact words were, 'Only a Greek would impose himself as a marriage guidance counsellor and then make the object of his stern lectures foot the bill.'

My response, which I phrased without forethought, was this: 'Only a Turk would marry a Christian and then still insist on naming his sons after the world's most infamous and bloodthirsty barbarians.'

Rapprochement

The Maginot line crossed, there were then other things said. I will take them to my grave, as I hope he does, too, and as I am sure he would agree, if we have never seen each other in the interim, it will not be a moment too soon. It was inevitable that the escalation of insults would lead sooner or later to blows, so I can hardly complain if the management of Claridges saw fit to intervene before the first one was delivered. That said, it is undeniably true that I had a bleeding nose, and with it a large stain on the front of my shirt, by the time the police arrived on the scene. I am sure that we made an unruly sight as we were escorted from our seats and into the waiting police car. Certainly, the picture that ran on the front pages of every tabloid on the following day suggested this and more.

But you can just imagine my horror when I read the headlines. I will tell you — I saw these first in billboard form, without the picture, and when I did I never dreamed that they could possibly have anything to do with me. My first thought was, how strange that I should be at Claridges on the same night when there seems to have been a 'gangland brawl'. And then, to open these scandal sheets and read that it was I! To find myself described as Stellio 'the Goat' Hadzoglou, scion of a corrupt family of Greek shipbuilders! To be reading a list of Sami's business associates and dealings, involving not just the Turkish and Kurdish mafias and their counterparts in Eastern Europe, but also large swathes of the Tory other ranks! Worst of all, to find myself lumped in with the same crowd!

Not knowing what to believe, I was tempted to dismiss all of it. What in these revelations could I trust, when my own small contretemps involving a well-heeled friend and three credit cards that were over their limit became a falling-out between two warring godfathers from the Eastern Mediterranean underworld, over the subject of a prostitute and 'casino cash'?

And then the leaders. Asking the question, why had 'we' allowed 'our' capital city to be taken over by foreign criminals? As if there were no difference between me and the common or garden daytripper. As if I were not the husband of an English wife and the father of two English sons, and a university lecturer with a good list of publications and (until the professional humiliation brought upon me by these unfortunate events) a reputation as a rising star. As if these distinctions did not matter, because all foreigners were the same.

Did I tell you that I dream in English? But enough of that. I have shared enough pain. I have only one more corrective point to make. It may seem small to you, but to me it means the world, and so I shall ask you to listen carefully. The main point is this: in the altercation between Sami and myself, I was not the loser. I may have been the one who was the worst for wear in the physical sense. However, I was the one who had the last word. I will even go so far as to say that this was as it should have been. It may be the prerogative of the Turk to throw his weight around, but it is perhaps the consolation of the Greek to abscond with the poetic licence.

My parting shot could not have been more different from the quotation in the papers. I said something far, far deeper, something that spoke only too deeply about the dangers of becoming too close to people who eat the same foods and dance the same dances and sing the same songs. You think you can live together on the same patch of earth because half the time they are so much like you, but then your every attempt ends in cruel disappointment because they can never be Greek. And yet you try again, and then again. The longing never goes away, and neither the dream.

Because the dream has a basis. Because we need each other if we are to survive, because when we turn away from each other to face the world, we suffer under a common indifference, and a universal refusal to hear what we have to say. This is my greatest regret. It pertains both to Sami, who will never be forgiven for the things he said that night about my mother and my religion, and also to Sera, who has now receded back into the folds of her life and will be lost to me for ever. I am sorry that they were not able to pick up a paper on the morning after the altercation and at least see my words quoted exactly. For it is perhaps they and they alone who could have understood my meaning and appreciated the deft way in which I took my grief and humiliation and used my wits to set them alight. So finally, let me set the record straight. This is what happened when the police constable asked me what my altercation with Sami was all about. Far from saying that it had come about because I had called my former friend a 'reproach to humanity', I said the following. I said we had been embroiled in a most painful rendition of the human comedy, bearing the title 'Rapprochement'.

Touching base

Jacqueline Lucas

I'm walking down the Portobello Road in a shopper's daze when I see him. There's time to turn to duck, to wander off my path, but I've been waiting for this moment for years, so I carry on walking. I feel my face colour up, unsure what expression to set. Cool and unfriendly, chirpy yet casual. Warm and intense. Cool yet intense. There's that many variations and he's in my face by the time I've checked them out. I don't think I have a handle on it. It's more like a mishmash of cool and confused.

Hi! He stops in his tracks as if it's a welcome surprise, like he wants to check me out in detail. So we check each other out in detail. *You're looking well,* I say, which is one of those neutral messages you could use with your gran. *How are the girls?* I ask, another. He gives me a semi-smile semi-embarrassed semi-raise-of-the-eyebrows. *How's life with you?* Well, he wouldn't mention him, and he's not sure what's happened to me in five years or more.

This isn't my beat, I tell him, like I want him to know I'm not remotely wandering these parts imagining I'll see him again. *I live in Crouch End.* That's the phrase that says there's been a change of considerable momentum, but I'm not going to say I live alone. If he wants to hear that he'll have to ask. Put himself on the line. Not likely. *Yes. It's really nice to see you. Likewise,* I reply. It's that awkward moment when we should say goodbye and leave it at that.

Do you fancy a coffee? I ask with a shrug like it's no big deal, like it's so cool bumping into each other why not do that banal thing and share a hot drink while we're at it. Pass some polite conversation back and forth. He nods coolly, like it's not a bad idea, when we both know it's shocking, as we move off towards our old haunt on the Golborne Road. This is already a mistake 'cause as we wander up the road making hollow attempts at conversation like *Do you still shop at Ceres?* and *That's an amazing pair of shoes,* our bodies are slipping into an old routine and the years since evaporate as we mosey down the Portobello Road. If anyone could see us, I can feel us both thinking after all that blood, snot and drama. But I clear my mind and concentrate on the feel of my feet hitting pavement, which my yoga teacher says is like staying with the breath, and I use it often to keep me from the edge. When I think of the anger and bitterness, the years and months I would have paid to bump into him like this, smash his head on the pavement, lay the boot in, pay two or three hard men to do it.

We acknowledge some changes on the stalls and the shops and our bodies. You've put on some weight, I suggest, a smile in my eyes. Lost some hair. I'm the one with the observations, luckily. I know I've kept my end up, 'cause that's part of living alone and avoiding happy families. It's all those communal meals and snacks in between. I'm pretty careful. When we hit the Lisboa I make a point of not ordering the speciality custard tart that was our favourite, but I light up to illustrate some things never change.

So what are you doing these days? Though I know he'll say he's still flogging antiques, which is a kind and liberal term for them, I can tell you. And to think I never knew the difference, but now I know he's more Steptoe than Sotheby's. So I pretend I believe him when he says things are really ticking over, he's had a couple of good years. *In the same place?* I ask, and he says, *yes. Work-wise.* But they've moved house and they're out of the area, just off the Finchley Road. *Nice*, I lie. *How are your girls?* I ask again. This time he warms to the attention and drops his guard, and he's so busy complimenting his genes I feel the anger rising, the desire to say, let's stop this, what are we doing? To think I might be remotely interested in his kids when we might have had *ours*. *My* kids. Cunt.

I light up again and he stops abruptly, he can see I've lost my front. That's the strange thing. We've not set eyes on each other for years, but I know exactly what's going through his head and he mine. I know what makes him tick, how to turn him on in a second. I know the dramas he's had with his wife and mother. The fall-out with his brother and the fact he's always felt inferior, a loser all round. I know he'd like to be warmer and more generous but there's a mean spot where his heart used to be. I know he's that vulnerable that I could make him cry his eyes out at this table in this cafe if I chose to. Even if *he's* pretending to chat. It makes me go heady just thinking about the mendacity.

It would have been healthier if I was ramming his forehead on to the edge of this marble-topped table. *No, tell me about you*, I ask. *Are you happy?* And at first he doesn't answer, like I'm being hostile. But I don't mean to. *As happy as I'll ever be, I reckon. I've got my girls.* Enough with the girls, I say to myself. *What about her?* I ask? I'll not say her name even five years later. He nods his head up and down repetitively. *Yes,* he says. *I can't complain. What about you, are you happy?* I still won't tell him it's over with Bruce, I can hardly say it. *I've got a very different life now,* I tell him, out in Crouch End. I talk about my new job with kids. *That's a new development,* he says. He seems surprised, and that's when I want to say, You moron, what do you expect after we got rid of our child and I'm on my own?

He's ordering more coffee. I wonder if he's going to pay for a change. He has another cake. Not too clever at his age. Our eyes keep catching each other's and our minds aren't on job descriptions. Do you remember the things we used to get up to just round the corner at your place in the daytime when you were playing antique dealer? *Do you miss smoking?* I ask, while my eyes ask, do you miss leaning over in a café whispering something filthy in my ear that has us so aroused we can hardly continue our errands?

He goes to the loo and leaves me to my X-rated flashbacks, while I note my bladder's also in better shape. It's the sort of trip that always brings you to your senses. I always wondered what brought him back to his senses.

Those wild plans of upping to Spain or somewhere equally not here and away from the mess we both made of our lives. The people we hurt.

He pootles back with a sheepish grin. I try to return the gesture. It's nice just to sit here like it never happened. The pain and the emptiness. The loss of confidence. When you're loved, really loved like I was twice over, it's a shock to find yourself making do with a cuddle in a kindergarten in Crouch End.

We test total recall, reel off friends we knew, and that takes the lid off it. A giggle that confirms nothing changes. People unhappy together are still unhappy together. People struggling are still struggling. Lonely people are still knocking around, though they may have done some uncharacteristic searches in the lonely hearts. Some babies arrived or on their way. That's when I look at him. *Are you not going to ask if I have a baby? If I still live with Bruce?* The smile goes and he says he heard something from Linda not long ago and he's sorry. He hangs his head and asks for a cigarette. I can't believe it. *Thought you gave up for a good clean home.* He takes it and doesn't respond to that one.

We blow smoke at each other and say little, our bodies revisiting hot summer all-nighters. I better be heading off soon. I can tell there's nothing for it unless I want to start a witch hunt. And we both know it's too late for that. *Well, it's been great to see you.* He looks a touch moved. Maybe it's guilt. I just nod back at him. The look's definitely sad and intense now.

I suddenly feel exhausted a need to lie down. I know I'll not see him for another five years. *We might be fifty next time,* I smile. And that's when I lean over and stroke his head. This is a mistake 'cause we've turned things about and he has tears in his eyes and takes my hand off to squeeze it. And I've no idea what we must look like. Teenagers or something. But it's had the effect of the filthy whispers, I can feel it. I can see our expressions change from nostalgia to lust and desire and I grab his hand tighter and we get up together and walk hand in hand, squeezing each other till it hurts, thinking of nothing but this moment as we head down Golborne into Portobello, and cut across the back of the mews into his place, and we can hardly get inside the door before we tear at each other's clothes like they do in movies and devour each other sucking hungrily at each other's mouths and genitals like a couple of chimps.

I remember to do all his favourite things and I've forgotten nothing. The way he likes me to cradle his head and to squat down on him and take him inside me, the words we use over and over like a Buddhist chant till we're coming in unison and crying at the same time.

We lie like that for maybe an hour and I know he's got to go fetch the girls.

It hits me now. My loneliness. How I miss what we have but what we'll never attempt to have again. And I'm whimpering now like a lost kiddie and I can see he wishes to god he'd never seen me, that we've done something worse this time than all the terrible things we did then. 'Cause this time we know there's no future and no going back and then we could kid ourselves.

And instead of leaving him with the sexy memory of our special communication, I leave on hands and knees knowing there's profundity in banality and destiny too, but one I guess I can't figure. And two people approach me as I howl down the road, which shows community isn't over, and that's what I hang on to as the 28 no doubt passes his home off the Finchley Road and the fruit and veg and bustle of Portobello is something I'm planning to do without for as long as I'm able.

Bone orchards

Paul J McAuley

Cemeteries are fine, private, quiet places, for it is the living, not the dead, who make ghosts. It is the living who slough shells of anger or terror, shed shivers of joy or ooze sullen residues of hate, sticky as spilled crude oil. Only the living, at the crucial moment of transition, cast off yearning or puzzled phantoms, and because most ghosts do not know they are dead, they do not often stray into the gardens of the dead. And so it is that I go to cemeteries to find respite from the blooming, buzzing confusion of the city.

Usually my clients must seek me out, and I make sure that I am not easy to find because I am their last hope, not their first. But, rarely, I discover someone I can help, and this was one such affair, begun in the peace of a bone orchard.

It was in the spring of 199–. Collective manias and delusions at the end of this dreadful century had set loose a host of strange and wild things. I had taken to walking about the city, trying to understand the redrawn maps of influence. It was a transformation as slow but sure as the yielding of winter to spring, but more profound, more permanent. It was as if the climate was changing.

My walks were not entirely random. I made a point of stopping for an hour or two of peaceful contemplation in the sanctuary of one or another of the city's cemeteries. The secret garden of the Moravian cemetery, entered by an unmarked door next to a public house off the King's Road. Kensal Green Cemetery, with its great Doric arch and gravelled roads wide enough for carriages. The ordered plots of Brompton Cemetery, radiating from the central octagonal chapel. The City of London Cemetery, its drained lake now a valley of catacombs. Even Bunhill Cemetery, its weathered tombs protected by prissy green municipal railings, could afford a little tranquillity as long as one avoided the lunchtime crowds of office workers.

That day, I had walked north up the Kingsland Road, past the new mosque (although my family has a long and honourable tradition in the matter of the dead, I am not a religious man, but any sign of communal faith gives me hope), through the brawl and tacky commerciality of Dalston (the Santería shop was closed down; I wondered if that had been caused by a minor fluctuation of the new climate), to Stoke Newington and Abney Park Cemetery.

Abney Park:

Beyond the modest entrance off Church Street, hard by the fire station, beyond the imposing graves of Salvation Army generals, paths divide and divide again, leading you away from city noise. The place is thick with trees, and saplings push up between close-set graves or are even rooted in the graves themselves, as if the dead are sprouting at skull or ribs or thigh. There are angels and pyramids and obelisks and hundreds of ordinary headstones. There is a lion. There are anchors cast on a rough boulder. Many graves are tilted, as if the dead, restless for Judgement Day, have been pounding on the roofs of their tombs. At the centre is the derelict chapel of rest, a Gothic ruin surprisingly free of graffiti, its windows boarded up or covered in bright new corrugated iron, every bit of glass smashed from the rose at the apex of the square tower. Boards have been prised away from one window; the scraps of the trespassers' spent lust curl within like exhausted snakes.

That day, yellow daffodils nodded in the mild breeze above some graves – the last land our lives leave, our final plot, is a garden the size of our bodies – and others were bright with rainwashed silk flowers. I wandered the paths, munching chocolate bourbons from the packet I had purchased at a Turkish corner shop. The blue sky was netted by a web of bare branches. Birds sang, defining their territories. A man in a grubby T-shirt and a wrinkled leather jacket led an eager mongrel on a string and carried a can of strong beer; imps hid from me in the tangled rat-tails of his hair. An art student in black was hunched on a bench, sketching one of the angels (its left arm had been broken off at the elbow; fresh stone showed as shockingly white as bone against its weathered grey skin). A man and a woman in identical shell suits sat at another bench, talking quietly. A young woman pushed her baby in an old-fashioned perambulator.

And an old woman in a shabby grey anorak knelt like a penitent at a grave. Something about her made me stop and sit at a bench nearby. I took out my book (a badly foxed copy of Abellio's *La Fin de l'ésotérisme*), and pretended to ruffle through its pages while raking her with covert glances. She was bathed in sunlight that fell at an angle between close-laced branches, like a saint in a medieval woodcut. A quite unremarkable woman in her late sixties, with a pinched, exhausted face devoid of make-up, coarse grey hair caught under a flowery scarf. Her anorak, her rayon trousers and her cheap flat shoes had all been bought in the same high street emporium. She was tidying the grave with slow, painful care, raking its green gravel, straightening the silk roses in their brass pot, washing city dirt from the white headstone. She did not see me; nor did she see what seemed to be a small child running about the old graves in the distance.

No one could see it but me.

At last, the woman pulled a shiny black purse from the pocket of her anorak, opened it, and took out a piece of paper. She lifted up a smooth beach pebble, removed something, and tucked the paper underneath. Then she laboriously got to her feet, one hand on the small of her back, dusted her hands, and hobbled away down the path.

I shut my book and went to the grave and retrieved the paper. It was a sheet torn from a cheap, lined writing pad, as soft as newspulp, folded twice into a square. I was about to unfold it when something said, 'That's mine.'

It presented as a girl of ten or eleven, thin, determined, petulant, in a pale dress fifty years out of date. A scarf was knotted at her skinny neck. Eyes that were no more than dark smudges were half-hidden by tangled hair that stirred in a breeze I could not feel. It stamped ineffectively and said again, 'That's mine.'

I held out the folded sheet of paper.

'I don't want it now, not now you've touched it, you smelly old thing.'

'I will read it for you, if you like.'

'Smelly old fat thing,' it said spitefully, and turned and took a few steps along the path the old woman had taken before stopping and looking at me over its shoulder, hesitant, unsure.

'I can read it for you,' I said again. 'I am not like the others. I speak for people like you.'

The pale child ran up to me and swiped at the paper with fingers crooked into talons. It failed to take it, of course, and was suddenly dancing in fury. 'Fat fucker! Smelly fat fucking fucker!'

The sun seemed to darken, and the child grew in definition, as a candle flame steadies after it has been lit. Branches moved overhead like bony fingers rubbing together.

'You fucking fat smelly fuck!'

Stuff like drool slicked the child's chin, dripped on to the path.

I waited, holding out the paper. When the child was quiet again, I said, 'I can read it for you. I do not think you can.'

'Fuck you.'

Quieter now.

'Is she your mother?'

'She's mine. She's always been mine. You can't have her.'

And then the child was chasing away through the trees after the old woman like smoke blown from a gun. There was a wetness on the path, frothy as the mucus shed by a salted slug.

I unfolded the sheet of paper, read the few lines written in painstaking copperplate, then looked at the headstone of the grave.

> *Jennifer Burton*
> *28th November 1933 – 28th November 1944*
> *Taken from us, she sleeps in peace.*

I had thought the grave only a few years old. It had been faithfully tended for over 50 years.

I wrote down the particulars in the flyleaf of my book, copied the lines on the sheet of paper, and tucked it back under the pebble.

'She was murdered,' Detective-Superintendent Rawles told me. 'Strangled by the scarf her mother gave her for her birthday. Murdered, but not sexually assaulted. Her sister was found wandering the streets nearby, with scratches on her arms and face. She had been attacked too, but she must have managed to get away when her sister was strangled, and she couldn't remember anything. You don't think of ordinary crimes happening then, with the war going on, but there it is. The case is still open.'

'Like a wound,' I said, remembering the scarf around the little girl's neck.

We were sitting in the snug of The Seven Stars, the comfortable old pub just around the corner from Lincoln's Inn Fields. Rawles was due to give evidence at a murder trial in an hour. He was uncharacteristically nervous, and had kept stealing glances at his watch as I described my encounter and worked my way through a steak and kidney pie.

Around us, sleek lawyers in dark suits talked loudly about chambers gossip and old and forthcoming cases. The sad quiet shade of a pot boy was drifting about a dark corner of the bar; out of courtesy, we pretended to ignore each other.

Rawles passed a hand over his close-cropped white hair and sighed. My old friend and ally looked worn out. There were deep lines either side of his mouth, and nests of hair in his ears. The skin on the backs of his hands was as loose as a lizard's, and crazed with a diamond pattern. He said, 'Do you really think you should be prying into this, Carlyle?'

'How long is it until you retire, Robert?'

'Three months, as you know very well. I'm dreading it.'

'The bungalow in Essex? Your roses?'

'I can't wait to get out of the city. What I dread is the party they're going to give me.'

'I will be there in spirit.'

Rawles drained his pint glass and said, 'The bungalow is brand new. No ghosts at all.'

'There are ghosts everywhere, Rawles. I can look at your bungalow, if you like. You might be surprised.'

'I'd rather live in ignorant bliss. That's going to be my motto from now on. See nothing, hear nothing. What about you, Carlyle? Why the interest in this?'

'Think of it as spring cleaning. It is the time of year when you do all those little jobs that in the depths of winter you always meant to get around to but never quite did. Now the world wakes, and you do too.'

'I've seen your place,' Rawles said. 'I don't think you've ever dusted in your life.'

'It is merely a metaphor. In these strange times, a small bit of work like this will do me some good. Think of it as a charitable case.'

Rawles said, 'I'm going to be out of it soon, thank Christ,' and pushed the brown folder across the table. It was tied with faded green string. 'I'll want this back. And if the animal that killed her is still alive, I suppose I'll have to do something about it.'

Jennifer Burton had been murdered a few streets from where she lived, on a bombsite where, according to the police report, the local kids had made a kind of camp or den. She had been found amidst candle stubs and broken bits of furniture, strangled by her birthday scarf.

It was amongst the anonymous streets just to the east of the British Museum and Bloomsbury, where cheap tourist hotels, student hostels, council blocks, red-brick mansion blocks and university offices crowd together along treeless streets where the sun never quite reaches. There was a block of flats – white concrete and metal-framed windows – where the bombsite had been. I rang bells at random. When at last someone answered, I said, 'It's me,' and shouldered aside the door when it was buzzed open.

I found a stair down to the basement, and stood a while in the dim light that seeped from a pavement grille, amongst bicycles and boxes of discarded belongings, under pipes that snaked across the ceiling. There was nothing there, but I had not expected anything. The ghost of the murdered girl had fled with her sister, I thought, and she had carried that burden ever since.

My Darling Jennifer, the old woman had written. *It is a lovely spring day and so I came to visit you, and see that you were nice and tidy. It will soon be the next century, the new millennium, and I wonder how it is that I am still alive. I carry you with me always, my darling.*

The fierce deep anguish that burned through these banal sentiments!

I had learned little from the old police files. Jennifer Burton had been eleven when she had died, older by a half-hour than her twin, Joan. The police had interviewed known sex offenders and every soldier arrested in London for drunkenness or desertion in the weeks following the murder, but with no result. Joan had been interviewed three times, but remembered nothing of that day. The case had gone cold.

I left that quiet basement and found the address where the two girls had been living with their mother. They had only recently returned from the village in Devon to which they had been evacuated at the beginning of the Blitz. The building had been made over into offices, with a stark modern foyer behind big plate-glass windows. A security guard sat behind a bleached oak desk. I could have worked up some plausible bluff, but someone who could help me was nearby, and I went to find him instead.

Coram's Fields, in the middle of the parish of St Pancras, is one of the happiest places I know. There is a playground where the only adults allowed in are those who bring their children, and there is an adjoining park, St George's Gardens, where I sometimes sit for a while. The playground is built on the site of the Foundling Hospital; the gardens are laid out on what was once a cemetery. I know only too well how much of London is built on her dead.

That the park and playground are unmarked by darkness is due in large part to its unofficial and unacknowledged guardian. Harry Wright was a pacifist who became a volunteer fireman during the war. He was killed at the height of the Blitz, when the front of a burning house collapsed on him as he went in to rescue three children trapped inside. I sat on a bench amongst clipped, mulched rose beds in cold sunlight. The shrieks and laughter of children at play was clear and sharp. Presently Harry drifted over, tentative and curious.

'It's you, Mr Carlyle,' he said, smiling with relief. 'For a moment, I thought it might be trouble.'

'I am afraid that I have brought a little trouble, Harry. Sit down, and I will tell you about it.'

'I'll keep watch if you don't mind, Mr Carlyle, and I do it better standing.'

He was a small, tough, bantam-rooster of a man in his mid-thirties, in shirt and braces, his honest face smudged and indistinct, like a half-erased sketch. He drifted around the bench, head cocked for any trouble, as I explained my encounter at Abney Park Cemetery.

'Oh, I couldn't go all the way up there,' he said, when I had finished. 'I have enough of a job here.'

'I understand. What I have in mind is much closer to home.'

'I don't know if I could, Mr Carlyle.'

'There is a child to be helped, Harry, and it will take only a little of your time.'

'Still,' he said doubtfully, 'things are difficult at the moment. It all seems so hopeless sometimes, as if the whole world is bearing down on me and my little patch.'

'Things are changing, Harry. We all feel it.'

'I saw that librarian chap a while ago,' Harry said. He was still patrolling my bench, keeping watch on the perimeters of the park. 'Was it last week? Anyway, he felt the same thing.'

Like many of his kind, Harry was vague about time. I knew it must have been at least several months ago, for that was when the librarian had been devoured. It had been my fault. I had sent him against something whose strength I had underestimated. I still carried the guilt, like an ink stain on my soul.

I said, 'I am afraid that he has passed on.'

'That's a shame. Him and me, we had some interesting talks. Very well educated, he was, and polite as anyone I've met. Perhaps it was for the best, Mr Carlyle. I don't suppose he would have liked the changes to his place.'

The old Reading Room of the British Library was closed; its books had been transferred to the new red-brick building on Euston Road. When I had last been there, I had stood a while in the wood-panelled room where the autograph manuscripts had once been on view, and where display boards and glass-cased models of the new extension now stood, mantled with a fine layer of concrete dust from the building works, disturbed only by the occasional tourist who had taken a wrong turning. I had waited a long time, but he had not come.

I told Harry Wright's restlessly circling ghost, 'You are quite right. He would have hated it.'

'He was a man of his time, Mr Carlyle. Now, I think I can help you, but I'll have to be quick. Even the day isn't safe any more.'

I was glad that I did not have to compel him. I waited outside the office building while Harry made his search. I waited more than an hour, pretending to read my book under the gaze of security cameras, and I grew so anxious that I almost cried out in amazement when at last Harry appeared with his burden.

'We'll take the poor mite to my place,' he said, brisk and matter of fact. 'Safer that way.'

I lost him when I had to wait for a gap in the traffic shuddering angrily down Judd Street, but he was waiting for me in the rose garden. He was still holding the child he had rescued. Her face was pressed against his shoulder. There was a scarf around her neck, and she wore the same dress as the venomously angry thing I had confronted in Abney Park.

'She's scared,' Harry said. 'She was hiding in a cupboard. It's all right now, darling,' he added, speaking softly to the child. 'You're safe here.'

It took a while to coax her round. At last, Harry set her on her feet and resumed his patrol while she scampered about, stopping every minute to look up at the sky. I waited until she drifted back to me, shy and sidelong.

'You're a funny man,' she said.

She stood on one foot, twisting the other behind her calf. A breeze could have blown her away.

'I know I am,' I said.

A woman walking her dog glanced at me as she went past; I suppose she would have seen an overweight man in a black raincoat, hunched over and talking to himself. Hardly an uncommon sight in these troubled times.

The girl said, 'So many people came at first, and they were making such a fuss, that I hid. But then they went away and after that I couldn't make anyone hear me. I thought Joan would find me. I waited and waited. Will you take me to her?'

'I cannot do that. But I can help you, if you will help me. I want to know what happened to you. Do you understand?'

She nodded. She said, 'It was like being filled with black boxes. The dark came flying in, and it had corners. It filled me up.'

'Did you see who brought the dark, Jennifer?'

The child's hands had gone to her throat, plucking at the knotted scarf. She said, 'I don't want to cause trouble.'

'None of that matters, not any more.'

'That's what the nice man told me,' the child said, and added, 'He said that he was a fireman.'

'So he is. And a very good one. We both want to help you, Jennifer. I think that I know what happened, but I need to be sure. Will you tell me?'

'Joan was cross. She wanted my scarf because she said that it was nicer than hers. She said I always got nicer things because I was older. She wanted it, and I wouldn't give it to her because it was mine!'

She ran then. I did not try to follow her, and at last Harry brought her back. She would not talk, but it did not matter, because I knew now how wrong I had been. I told the little girl that she could rest. That she could sleep. And then I sent her away.

Harry said, 'Is it like that, Mr Carlyle? Like going to sleep?'

'I do not know,' I said. 'But that is what everyone wants to believe.'

Harry brushed his hands together. 'There's no rest for the wicked, as my gran used to say. I'll be back to work. It's getting dark, and there can be trouble, after dark.'

★

A week later, I was sitting on the bench in Abney Park Cemetery, near Jennifer Burton's grave. I had been coming here every day, waiting for Jennifer's sister, and her burden. Every day, at dusk, when I knew that the old woman would not come, I had passed by her mean little basement flat in Albion Road on my way home. I once saw her coming up the steps in her grey coat and her neat scarf, moving slowly and painfully, bowed under the weight of her burden, which had hissed like a cat when it had spied me across the street.

It was another sunny day. The buds were beginning to break on the trees, so that the stark outlines of their branches were blurred by a ghostly scantling of green. The old woman came just after noon, and her burden came with her, circling us both at a distance, hardly more than broken shadow and sunlight. At last, the old woman finished tidying her sister's grave. She took out a piece of folded paper and tucked it under the pebble, and crumpled up the note I had carefully replaced.

The ghost circled through the trees as the old woman went away down the path. I called its name and told it to come to me and it did, glaring at me through the tangle of its hair.

'You fat old fucker,' it said. 'You don't scare me.'

'I know why you did it, Joan. You wanted the scarf. You did not realise that you had hurt your sister so badly.'

'She messed her knickers,' the thing said, with a vicious smile. 'She made a funny sound and messed her knickers, the smelly silly.'

It was the ghost Joan Burton had cast off in a moment of sudden and intense anger. It was the memory that she could never acknowledge, the memory of murdering her own sister. She had been imprisoned by it ever since, a longer sentence than any court would have imposed.

It glared at me through its tangled hair and hissed, 'Keep away from me, you fat fucker. I'll hurt you. I will.'

'Enough,' I said, and gathered it to me. It was like lifting up an armful of icy briars, but only for a moment.

'So you found nothing,' Detective-Superintendent Rawles said. 'That's not like you, Carlyle. You usually like to see things through to the end.'

Once again, we had met in The Seven Stars. Once again, Rawles was stealing glances at his watch. The jury in his case was expected to announce its verdict that afternoon.

I said, 'Times are changing.'

'Times change, Carlyle, but you don't. You're more or less the same as when I met you back in '64.'

'Ah, but I was already old then.'

'You do have a bit of a spring in your step today,' Rawles said. 'I noticed when I came in.'

'I did? I suppose it is the season. Everything seems hopeful at this time of year.'

I had passed Joan Burton on the way out of the cemetery. She was still stooped, but I think it was out of habit, not necessity. I said, 'A nice day, is it not?'

She glanced at me and smiled, and I saw in that smile the pretty girl she had once been. 'I hadn't noticed,' she said, 'but yes, you're right. Isn't it beautiful?'

The cookery lesson

Michèle Roberts

London is the city where anything is possible. Where you can reinvent your self and your life. London's alchemy lets you dissolve into the crucible of the crowd and then be reborn. The dull skin of the suburbs or the provinces sloughed off, the new creature emerges, eager and radiant. London transforms a person, just as love does. The streets of London are paved with the gold of dreams and of love.

I began to love you when I met you in the flesh, as opposed to merely watching you on television, and noticed your hands, their deftness and strength, your blunt-tipped fingers and very clean fingernails. On TV it was often only your face that the camera lingered over in closeup. Fair enough, because you are so beautiful, but I was frustrated; I wanted to see the rest of you and understand more intimately how you worked. I wanted to focus on how you dealt with gutting fish, preparing kidneys and liver, hooking the giblets out of ducks. But of course TV cooks aren't shown performing such acts; the audience might become upset at so much gloppy mess and blood.

Nonetheless, noting you insouciantly swirl crêpe mixture across your pan, give it just a second to set over the flame, then twist your wrist and flip the brown lace disc into the air, learning from your nonchalant demonstrations how to produce perfectly risen and crusted prawn soufflés and sweetbread-stuffed vols-au-vent, I began to dream of meeting you. It was difficult to achieve this ambition. For years you'd run your own tiny restaurant in Kensington Park Road. But, now, I discovered, you'd got fed up with chasing Michelin stars and had sold Chez Larry to a burger chain. You were no longer to be found, night after night, dishing up lobster à l'armoricaine and tossing up your trademark towers of foie gras mille-feuilles; you'd moved on. You were no longer readily available in public to your fans. Only on TV. You were a celebrity wrapped in privacy like a fillet of beef in pastry. Then I read in a food magazine that you taught regular classes in the cookery school you had founded at your home in west London. Holland Park sang to me and summoned me. Number six Claridge Gardens said Come.

The cookery lesson

Holland Park. Hang-out of the rich. Palazzi with Venetian-style windows and pastel plaster façades, elaborate wrought-iron gates. Tiny front gardens crammed with roses, wisteria and vines, fleets of estate cars parked outside. Your house sparkled as though carved from sugar. A big white villa festooned with balconies, columns, cornices. I trod gaily up the cream and grey marble steps and rang the bell.

Ten of us shuffled from the mirror-hung hall into the enormous, steel-clad kitchen in the basement, twitching our new overalls into place, adjusting our caps. We were not precisely beginners, having signed up for the cordon bleu class, but nonetheless we were nervous. You, my darling, didn't bother trying to put us at our ease. You were brisk and professional and just got on with the job. You shrugged at our clumsiness as we cracked eggs and dripped hot stock on to whisked yolks. You shouted at us when we dropped ladles or curdled our infusions of butter and meat juice. You gave us credit for not needing to be babied like the TV viewers and I liked you even better for it.

At the end of that first afternoon, I remember, you carved a chicken while we watched. How elegantly you dismembered it, parting muscle from bone with flicks of your razor-sharp knife, while we clustered around you and admired your unerring aim, your exactitude. So I fell in love, at that precise moment, with your hands, that knew just what to do. With your hands' capability and skill. And then with the rest of you.

When the class was over, I weaved across Holland Park Avenue, dodging the rush-hour traffic, ran along Lansdowne Road with its Dutch-look houses, washed lemon, strawberry and sky, its long windows barred by grilles, crossed over Ladbroke Grove just below the lift of the hill, dived into Portobello Road. I got to the butcher's there just before it closed. The butcher I remembered so well from my squatting days in Powis Terrace, before the landlords got rid of tenants like me and the owner-occupier yuppies moved in. Breast of lamb or veal pie, that's what I ate on Saturday nights. Now the shop was decked with trussed game, rabbits hung up by their heels, strings of saucisses de Toulouse. I bought a free-range organic chicken and carried it home with me on the bus, nursing it on my lap like a baby, and poached it according to your recipe. Then I cut it up, just as you had, darting my knife into the tender joints. I ate it, every last scrap, thinking of you meanwhile. As though I were kissing your flesh and tasting your fragrance. I licked up lemon, tarragon, white wine and cream. Then I made stock from the bones.

I haven't got a proper kitchen here in Camden Road, only a shelf with a two-ring cooker and a tiny free-standing oven, and a small fridge underneath, but it doesn't matter. My kitchen, such as it is, has become transformed, like the rest of my life, by the power of love. My kitchen glows and is beautiful. While I cook I gaze out of the little dormer window, past the restless frieze of pigeons and seagulls strutting and pecking at the crusts I've put out for them on the sooty parapet of the roof, out over London rooftops. I can look westwards towards Holland Park as I patiently stir my bowl of thickening sauce Béarnaise over a pan of bubbling water, or as I knead and pleat brioche dough, and think of you.

I'm making a chestnut pâté for supper tonight, no, not a nut roast, darling, what a tease you are, a proper pâté, composed of minced pork and veal mixed with crumbled chestnuts, bound with butter, flavoured with thyme and juniper berries, that I'll cook in the oven in a proper earthenware terrine I picked up cheap in Holloway Road car-boot sale because the lid is chipped, and I am making a proper tomato sauce, just as you taught us, with finely chopped celery, onion, parsley, carrot and garlic sweated in olive oil to start it off, to go with the delicious mound of scented, chestnut-studded meat. Afterwards I'll serve a curly green salad tossed with a few roast hazelnuts and dressed with walnut oil, and a cone of goat's cheese. To finish: a plate of navy figs, that I picked out from my favourite stall in Berwick Street, the one with the man who sings out incomprehensible cockney sales patter and tosses up the brown paper bags of vegetables by their twisted ears for the customers to catch. He'd make you laugh, darling. I'll take you there one Saturday and we'll buy purple-veined globe artichokes and thin haricots verts, and then we'll go round the corner to Lina's and stock up on fresh focaccia and rocks of parmesan and home-made pumpkin-stuffed ravioli. Arm in arm we'll wander along to the French pub in Dean Street for an apéritif, and then we'll have lunch at the Escargot before lugging all our goodies home.

Yes, you've guessed right, I wish you were here to eat this modest feast with me. Here in my little garret bedsit, perched opposite me by candlelight, smiling at me, smoking a Gauloise and drinking Ricard while I test the pâté with the point of my knife. I want to cook for you. I want to feed you the most exquisite dishes I can possibly make. That I learned in your class. That's one way of saying I miss you, now that the class has ended and I've found a temp job and I haven't seen you for weeks, to imagine cooking for you and to imagine writing this long letter to tell you so.

I was your favourite student because I was the most promising cook. You said I had talent. You singled me out for praise. All my life I had been so lonely and shy, so starving and desperate, and suddenly there you were, like the land of plenty, feeding me kind words, promises of affection, hints of a future together. Even when you were brusque and gruff I could still feel the warmth simmering underneath. You didn't want all the others to know how you felt. Sometimes you stopped to chat after class but quite often you didn't. It was a signal to me, to warn me we had to be discreet.

I love you.

You haunt me. Whether I'm waiting at the bus-stop in the morning for the 253 to Tottenham Court Road or whether I'm home again in the evening, cutting carrots into julienne strips or watering my herbs on the windowsill or washing my tights in the sink, I'm aware of your presence. You're with me, in spirit, all day long. So I talk to you. I can't not talk to you. The words bubble and run in my head and roll over my tongue like rich gravy. If only you were with me here now and I could actually tell you all the things I feel. It is truly terrible not to be able to touch you. I caress the flesh of carrots and chestnuts instead.

I dreamed of you last night, darling, as I dream of you almost every night. We were in company together, at a TV chefs party of some kind, on the pavement outside the TV studios in White City, and then you turned your back on me and walked away. Please don't do that to me, darling. Can't you see it hurts? I don't think you understand how terrible rejection feels and that I can't bear the pain.

You see you light up my life and give it meaning. Before you came I had nothing and now you give me everything. London flushes with excitement, a suddenly magical city impregnated with images of you, inscribed everywhere with your name. As though all of London is your body, so that you surround me at every turn. As though you fly before me along these shabby streets, whistling just ahead of me around corners, leaving secret messages written in our private language for me to find. I translate the code of love on brick walls, uneven pavements.

Paint splashes, chalk marks, graffiti. The tuft of feathery weed in the crevice of the neighbours' gatepost reminds me of your eyelashes. I saw your name – Spode – written up on a card in a china-shop window. The wholesalers in Old Compton Street sells checked chef's trousers exactly like yours. Tonight the radio is playing songs from that Paris Blues CD I want to send you for your birthday. It's uncanny, how you are everywhere I look.

Tonight, remembering how you once told us in class you loved the beignets they make in those small, authentic bistros you can still find in Paris, I have got out the deep-fat-fryer because after supper I am going to practise cooking fritters. While the oil heats up I shall whisk together the batter of milk, flour, egg white, a dash of white wine. It's very light, not stodgy at all, the thinnest and crispest of golden coats puffing up in the smoking bath.

Those unlucky Christian martyrs tortured in vats of boiling oil – however did they bear it? I suppose God performed a miracle and saved them, to show how holy they were. I wouldn't want you ever to come to any harm, my precious one. Not the least touch of hot iron ever to blister your beautiful skin. If you were ever in danger of being harmed I'd rescue you. My love for you is also a miracle, because it makes me very brave and strong. There's nothing I wouldn't do for you and you know it.

Love is the power. So simple, isn't it? I cook well for you because I love you. Supposing you were here, supposing that you turned up after supper, very hungry, well, as an *amuse-gueule* I shall serve you deep-fried battered sage leaves, perfumed with just a drop of lemon, and deep-fried spoonfuls of egg white lightly mixed with grated gruyère, fluffy golden clouds perched on tiny rounds of toasted baguette, and then afterwards deep-fried battered courgette flowers stuffed with minced mushrooms and chicken bound with cream.

London supermarkets these days are vast halls gleaming with treasure, even grubby old Holloway Road and Seven Sisters Road now have five between them, in which you can buy anything from anywhere in the world. The seasons no longer exist; time and space have been annihilated. Every desire can be satisfied, whether you want Korean red pepper paste and pickled cabbage, Mexican *mole* sauce of chocolate and spices, black pastaciutta dyed with squid ink, sesame-scattered Turkish loaves of bread as round and thick as your arm, or sweetmeats from the Lebanon dusted with honey crystals and flecks of brilliant pistachio.

I go shopping for you, my darling. I bring you home carrier bags full of gifts, spilling with scent and colour. Bouquets of emerald coriander and wreaths of pearly black grapes and alabaster curls of the very best prosciutto money can buy. I lug my sacks of food up five flights of stairs but I don't mind the weight. I fly upwards as though I were an angel, to my heaven-kitchen where you wait for me.

So what else can I offer you? After these rather rich delicacies that we started with, how about a good, bitter salad of red chicory leaves, and perhaps a slice of camembert served on a toothed chestnut leaf, and then a dish of pears poached in spices and red wine? And of course if you were here with me I'd get out the very best Beaujolais in my cupboard. The two bottles I've been saving for a special occasion.

Wouldn't you like to come and eat these treats with me? Oh please come and see me soon. Please ring me up. Please answer the telephone when I ring you. Please reply to my phone messages. Please acknowledge the gifts I post to you, and the emails I send you from work, desperately hoping my boss won't find out I'm using the computer to write love-letters not invoices. I take risks for you, darling, but love makes me reckless. Even if I got the sack for wasting the firm's time I wouldn't care.

I can't believe you don't love me as much as I love you. I imagine it's just that things are difficult for you right now. I do understand that. You've got to act cool, to seem to hold back. But in your thoughts it's a different matter. I've always been able to read your thoughts and I know how desperately you desire me. It's just that at the moment you're not able to say. I understand that and I respect your attitude. Your message conveys itself to me through our special telepathy; mind to mind. On the surface you behave with complete indifference but deep down inside I know you long for me.

It helps me very much to repeat all this quietly to myself while I fold shavings of pale cheese into egg white and test the heat of the oil with a crumb of bread, dropping it in then watching it turn rapidly gold. Rehearsing how I feel, well in advance of seeing you again, means my mind will be clear and calm when we do meet. I'll have cleared out all the junk and got rid of it, I shall be floaty and light as a fritter, friendly and normal, and you'll realise how much you do love me after all because you'll feel so good in my company. You won't be able to resist me.

You see I do know an awful lot about men, having observed them carefully, from a little distance, for, oh I don't want to admit for how long. I still reel just like a young girl inside, and I look like one too. Because I haven't let experience sour or wither me. I'm still an optimist, an idealist even, and it shows on my face. I still look fresh and pretty. I know because I've seen this in the mirror. I'm not boasting. It's true. Every morning I look at myself and I realise I'm still young. My life can begin all over again. There's still time for you to admit you love me and for us to be happy together. We could move to Hampstead, a little Georgian cottage with a white-fenced garden and an apple tree.

What I meant was, I know men don't like women to show too much emotion. You don't like it if we laugh or cry too much and particularly if we just do it and we haven't clearly explained to you why. You don't understand that if we could explain then we wouldn't be crying or laughing. But we appreciate you for being so clever and secure and successful and able to take everything so lightly.

With you I can relax and not worry about laughing or crying too much because you don't rub things in by discussing them. You and I are so close we hardly need to talk. We communicate through glances. I intuitively know how deeply you really love me.

Now, that's the problem with thinking too much while you cook. You almost burn things. I caught that sage leaf just in time. So I'm going to finish preparing supper, my angel, and then I'm going to open a bottle of Sancerre and eat. Please forgive me if I carry on talking to you, though, as I carry each delicious forkful to my mouth.

How I do love eating. There is no greater bliss: the tastes of salt and hot olive oil coating this cloud of deep-fried egg white melting inside with gruyère, each mouthful sliding over my tongue and down my throat, filling me up deep inside until at long last I am sated and can finally stop. Heavy with pleasure. Food like a sack of gold in my belly. My barn of harvest grain; my treasure store against the years of famine. I'll never starve again, for there is always more, as much as I want. I lick my lips, greased with olive oil, my lovely drug, the only one I need. It soothes me. I'd never be able to go on a diet and give it up. Olive oil tastes of summer and happiness and tranquillity and hope.

I used to be quite slim, as a girl, but I've become a plump woman, in fact I am what some people call a nice armful and others call fat. And yet I want to be more insubstantial than the paper of an imaginary letter, a ghost. Some people yearn to see ghosts but I yearn to be one. If I can't be with you, can't touch your arm as I talk to you, can't kiss and embrace you, then I'd like to nudge you in spirit instead. I want to be the invisible presence in the corner of your room, the object to which your thoughts obsessively return, the image you glimpse when you first open your eyes in the morning. I want to be there when you wake and see you look at me.

Love has made me unashamed and bold. At first I contented myself with trying to catch a glimpse of you after work, getting off the tube in Notting Hill, walking down Holland Park Avenue and hovering about outside the posh bakery where I know you buy your croissants for breakfast the following day. Just on the off-chance that you might appear. Might spot me, greet me with pleased surprise, suggest we go for a drink. Somewhere intimate and quiet, with a certain bohemian charm, somewhere like Julie's Bar. I rehearsed what to say, what funny stories to tell you, anecdotes to amuse you. I had it all prepared, my conversation, to offer you like a fine dish of *hors d'oeuvres variés*, arranged with a flourish and served with a light hand, just as Elizabeth David says in *French Provincial Cooking*.

Then I grew more daring. I drew nearer to your house. I couldn't wait until dusk. I came to visit you in the mornings, before going to work.

I played fair. First thing, I went into Holland Park and had my run, then did my meditation on the bench near the gate, so that if you'd been out for an early walk and encountered me on your way home it would have been a genuine accident, I'd have been able to say with perfect truth that I came here every day for exercise. Then, I strolled up and down the pavement outside your house, admiring the little bay trees in their terracotta pots adorning the steps, the ferns clustering to one side, the discreet iron hood over the cellar door. I was quite happily just waiting for you to wake up. Loitering with intent. To give you my love in person.

If you'd looked down into the street first thing yesterday, darling, when you got up, as you should have done, you'd have seen me there again, patiently attending on your pleasure, holding the bunch of mixed pink and red carnations and roses I bought for you in the 24-hour supermarket next to the tube. But, without warning me first, you changed your signal. You changed your routine. You didn't draw the curtains, open the window and lean out to sniff the frosty autumnal air, as you've done all week. You didn't look out and spot me. I spied the lights go on behind the grey curtains – damask, I think, gleaming and heavy – but you weren't to be seen. In the end I was forced to leave the flowers on your front step. I hadn't got all day, my darling. I couldn't hang about waiting for you on the off-chance indefinitely. I knew you'd realise immediately the flowers were from me. Pink and red are your favourite colours, chopped veal awaiting its transformation into sauté de veau Marengo, and you know I'd never forget you telling me something like that. I walked through to Ladbroke Grove and ate breakfast in the greasy spoon at the corner of Elgin Crescent. Amazing it's still there, really, and not turned into a tapas bar. I celebrated the enduring nature of greasy spoons by ordering fried eggs and bacon, fried bread, sausage, mushrooms, baked beans, tomato, a side portion of toast.

I said to the girl who served me: that's a fry-up worthy of Larry Spode himself!

She looked a bit blank then her brow cleared: oh, the bloke on telly, yeah, right.

Oh with what cunning I invent new ways to mention your name. At least once a day I gently insert you into my conversations with bus conductors, dry cleaners, my fellow clerks at work, the waitresses in greasy spoons. I thread you in like lardons into chicken skin before roasting. I rock you with my words, my darling, I hold you in the hands of my language, and I caress you with my tongue, all over. At the same time no one must suspect. It's my secret. Ours. You're my secret. My prisoner. I keep you captive inside my mouth and belly. I swallow you down with bites of mushroom and fried egg.

You're mine you're mine you're mine. People pity fat girls like me. They assume we must be suffering torments not being skinny rakes. They don't understand how sometimes you really need and want to be fat. What a comfort fat is. A padding that insulates you from the cold, harsh world. A cushion generous as a mother's breast. When you're fat you know you can survive for the next couple of hours. You've got enough wadded round you to know you'll last for a bit. Until the next meal. No more starving and screaming for food, no more hunger pangs tearing your insides apart, no more desperate terror that nourishment will never ever come. That the bough will break and the baby will fall and will die starving and screaming. I have learned to feed myself and feed myself is what I do. No junk food, mind. Only the best and freshest ingredients. You taught me that. You taught me that cookery is a form of love, and that for the beloved only perfection will suffice.

So, my darling, goodnight. Until tomorrow, then.

I'll see you even earlier than usual, long before you're expecting me. I'll tiptoe into your house by the cellar door under the front steps, which you carelessly left unlocked yesterday and whose key I was able to purloin, have copied, and replace, all in the space of twenty minutes. I don't like stealing and deceit, sweetheart, but you left me with no choice. You stopped communicating with me and thus threatened to deprive me of all I hold most dear: your love, my reason for living. I've told you before that I can't stand rejection, being dropped into the bottomless black pit, where there is only the starving monster tearing with its fangs at its human prey, where there is only mouth and teeth and biting and death. You must not send me there, darling. I shouldn't be able to survive. Not after I have known this love. So I'll creep into your bedroom while you're still asleep. Out of my handbag I'll take my Sabatier knife, the one you recommended, that I use for carving. You won't feel a thing, I promise you. I'm your apt pupil. I shall be accurate. I shall be swift. I'll hold you in my arms and kiss your beautiful hands and then I'll cut you up and cook you and eat you and we'll never be parted again, oh no nevermore, my sweet angel, you'll be mine for ever and you won't be able to leave me, darling flesh of my flesh, not this time, oh no never again.

Known

Conrad Williams

Povey watched white paint unfurl in chains along riveted steel shanks bordering the tracks. The Network South-East from Lee had been late again this morning and there had been no unoccupied seats. He'd stood hunched against the door, slow fire moving through his back, looking out at a colourless skyline as veils of rain hung motionless against the thin wash of buildings.

One word – KNOWN – endlessly repeated, blurred by broken obliques of moisture on the windows. The capital letters formed harsh angles which bracketed the soft middle 'O'. He couldn't decide whether it was the result of a brainless ego, or an attempt to impart something more significant. Whatever, he felt drawn to the uniformity of the letters as they dogged the train across Hungerford Bridge.

Only since leaving the centre of London in favour of commuting in from the limbo of its outer districts had Povey begun to appreciate the ingenuity of its engineers and construction workers. Any available space was filled in with new flats, shops, entertainment arcades. Staying with his uncle, in a grim conurbation on the South Circular, he yearned to be in the heart of the city once more, to feel its pulse through his feet. That way his present, drab thread in the city's fabric might find a little lustre. He was looking forward to viewing the flat that evening. It seemed to call at him from over the rooftops, across the miles, like a desperate request from a distant lover.

Povey walked the Strand to Aldwych where he turned left. He liked the rain, the way it cleansed the buildings and turned them into glittering spires and domes. He imagined the city's detritus being washed into the Thames. The rats drowning, the pissy alleyways and door recesses polished. All those channels and creases scrubbed clean.

But not the graffiti. Somehow it clung, tenacious as tattoos. Even in this fresh, burnished light, the crude slogans and signatures looked vital and new.

At work, the feeling fell away from him, as if this office was somehow insulated against the banal miracles of the city. He discussed layouts with Lynn and blithely complimented every letters page and fashion spread she showed him. He wondered if his apathy shone through. Lynn was the editor of a 'secret' magazine project. She had contacted Povey via a chief sub-editor from the parent company. He had done some work for her last summer and even though it was interminably dull – subbing real-life tragedy stories offset by 'humorous' articles and tips to make household chores that much more bearable – it paid well. He'd leapt at the chance of five weeks' employment, an opportunity to be nestled in London's centre, even though Lynn's overtures to him on the phone prior to his first day were almost comical.

'So can we book you until the end of March?' she had said, having explained that this was all hush-hush and that he would need to sign a document guaranteeing his lips to be sealed.

'Certainly,' he had said. 'What will I be doing?'

'Can't tell you,' she had replied, 'it's a secret.'

It turned out the magazine was a downmarket version of their market leader. Called *Goss*, it was aimed at a teenage readership, hence the appearance of words such as 'shag' and 'willy' and 'cum'. The problem pages were a lifesaver amid the tedious copy-proofing and fact-checking. MEN ONLY screamed the banner in 108pt Soupbone. *My little man bends the wrong way… am I abnormal?* And the Top Tips: *Clean venetian blinds with L-shaped pieces of crusty bread.*

They were based at the top of a building in Holborn, in an office big enough to host a game of five-a-side. Golf. Along with Jill and Lynn, there was Yvonne on features and Sally and Fran designing the pages. Friday lunchtimes they nipped down to the Sun Tavern on Long Acre and talked about dreadful magazines they had worked on in the past. All the same as this one, save the name.

An hour or so into his work, Povey received a phone call from Sutton, his best friend. He had moved down to the Smoke a year before, at around the same time as Povey, and did similar work for a finance magazine. He was living in a studio flat off the Edgware Road. They had made noises about meeting to compare subbing notes in recent months, and to try out some of the bars that were mentioned in the listings magazines, but nothing had been firmed up yet. Now Sutton sounded strangely on edge and asked Povey if they could meet that evening – he'd be in the pub from about three-thirty. By four o'clock, the skittish nature of Sutton's call had infected him and, in a mild panic, he went to the toilet, affecting a pained look and rubbing his stomach. In the mirror, he was surprised to find that he did not look well.

The colour had fled from his cheeks, giving him a greasy complexion. His eyes seemed to have sunk away from the flesh of their sockets: red filled in the gaps. He felt as though the real version of him hadn't caught up yet, that he was just a ghost, a sliver of the real Clive Povey. The real Clive Povey was stuck on a train staring at the codes and tag-lines sprayed on the portals to the capital.

'Lynn?' he said, cracking his voice just right. Jill, the assistant editor, looked up too, which was fine by Povey. He knew she liked him and the concern that darkened her face told him that he'd pitched this correctly, even though he was only partly acting. 'I'm going to have to go home. Sorry. I feel dreadful.'

Lynn looked aggrieved that she was losing him, clearly of the opinion that freelances sold their souls when they agreed to work and had to sit at their desks even if they were to suffer an arterial bleed.

'OK,' she sighed, finally. And then: 'Hope you feel better, tomorrow,' with a smile that didn't reach her eyes. Hardly reached her lips either.

Povey limped back to his workstation and closed the file he had been using before copying it back on to the server from his hard drive. The dummy layouts he returned to their trays.

'See you tomorrow,' he said. Sally looked at him acidly as if he had just stolen her plan for the day.

In the lift, Povey felt stitches of guilt about bunking off early and stared at the graffiti on the doors. He hadn't taken his lunch hour, so that supported him in mitigation but didn't stop him feeling like a school truant. They needed him; there was no need to worry about being sacked.

He seemed to descend too far, further than usual, but when the doors opened, there was the sliding glass entrance and, beyond, Kingsway's mad rush.

Although it was barely half past four, the sky had blackened and the rain angling in over the forbidding roofs showed no sign of stopping. Bruised light loitered behind the thinnest junctions between clouds; the streetlamps were off and the cars on the road drove blind.

He plugged his ears with a pair of headphones and depressed the play button on his Walkman. An epic loop of sound instantly drew something immanent from the deflated sky, the constant traffic. Holborn tube was closed off; a huge scrum of commuters stood with their backs to him, staring bovinely at the concertina gates and the ticket barrier beyond. Two fire engines ticked over in the centre of Kingsway, lights flashing.

Povey made a series of turns into ever diminishing streets – High Holborn, Southampton Place, Bloomsbury Way, Bury Place, Little Russell Street, Streatham Street – until the traffic's voice was toned down to an asthmatic gurgle. A crocodile of diners spilled out of Wagamama, thickening his sense of claustrophobia. Snazzy fucks in soft leather pants and white T-shirts and linen jackets. Fifty-pound haircuts. A woman fingering her pearl necklace while talking to some pinstriped goatee who made expansive gestures with his Nokia. Everyone seemed to be travelling somewhere and never arriving. He brushed past and ghosts followed: cK One, Fahrenheit, Dolce & Gabbana. Stuff he recognised from the peel-off strips in his magazines.

He caught the tube at Tottenham Court Road and travelled north, imagining his colleagues belittling him behind his back. His lack of spine. Such an insular man, a cold man. He bristled, imagining them, and jolted the arm of a woman reading a newspaper. She clucked her tongue and rattled the pages. He remembered acutely the embarrassment he'd known as a child when everyone's attention had been reluctantly drawn to him. He pressed himself against the seat, reining in his claustrophobia as it tried to deal with his distance underground, the way the train was just big enough for the tunnel, the optimum exploitation of space.

At Kentish Town he surfaced, gulping air. At the tube exit he watched the rain splinter the white and red exchange of car lights as people trundled home. A bus crawled by, its windows misted with condensation. Dark lumps filled every square of light. Each seat taken, every foot of Tarmac used, shoes secured pavement slabs as far as he could see.

The nest of lights on the underbelly of a jet shone through the barrier of cloud; through his feet he felt the chunter of trains worming north and south. By the time he crashed through the doors of the Academy Rooms, a hundred feet away, he was exhausted. It was as though there was no space for him to move. Every umbrella had wanted to do for his eyes; every briefcase clouted his knees.

He found Sutton squeezed on to a settee near the pool tables. He signalled: a pint. Povey bought drinks and moved unsteadily towards his friend, casting a glance at the pool tables where a woman was playing a leather–clad boyfriend. Behind them, a huge screen formed a backdrop: footballers glistening under floodlights in a derby match.

'Hello Frank,' said Povey, 'have a drink.'

Conversation tumbled around them. Povey perched on the edge of a stool that was being used as a footrest by a heavy piece of beef wearing sunglasses and combat fatigues. He heard the word 'known' used twice in quick succession by different people, and tried not to let his anxiety show.

The girl at the pool table pirouetted around her opponent, tipping him over with her thigh as he lined up his shot.

'You sounded a little bit wired when you called me this morning,' said Povey. 'What's up?'

Sutton flattened his lips together and shrugged. 'I'm having a bad time of it, Clive. I needed to see someone I know. Someone who would look at me instead of through me. Jesus, one of those days I've had, when everyone tries to walk over you like you're not there.' He took a long swig of his pint. Povey wasn't sure how many of the empty glasses arranged around him were his, but he bet it was a fair few.

'Another thing,' said his friend, staring blearily at the football match. 'Perhaps the main thing. I tried to do a few things yesterday – simple things.' He huffed what might have been sour laughter. 'Sort myself a loan and find out why I wasn't sent a voting form for the local by-election. Same response on both occasions. Didn't know anything about me, couldn't track down anything to do with my history. They were very apologetic but it sounded like they were talking to someone who wasn't there. Who didn't exist.' Sutton leaned over and whispered the last three words conspiratorially.

'Come on, Frank, you're just having a shit day. I'll send you an application form to join the club. You might have to hang on a while though, there's a fuck of a long waiting list.'

Sutton was shaking his head now. 'No, Clive,' he slurred, 'you are not yet in full possession of the facts. Today I opened the newspaper and found this bastard.'

He passed Povey a crumpled copy of that day's *Guardian*. Sutton had ringed a section and Povey had to put his glass down before he poured it into his lap. Below the strapline 'Death Notices' he read:

> **SUTTON, Frank Stanley** died sadly on 31st March
> 19– aged 34. Fondly remembered by many friends and
> family. Beloved father of Gillian. Funeral at Broadclyst
> Parish Church, Exeter, 24th April, 2pm. Family flowers.

'My God, Frank. But this is a joke, surely?'

'Yeah, I'm splitting my sides over it.'

'This is awful,' Povey said. 'I'm really sorry. What are you going to do? I mean, you must go to the funeral, sort this out. Imagine their faces!'

Sutton seemed to have withdrawn from the animation of the crowd and Povey blinked to bring his edges back into focus. Too much smoke and heat. He watched the girl playing pool as she appraised the table. Standing over her shot, bouclé grip, her right breast collapsed around her cue like the slow unhinging of a snake's jaws as it envelops a rabbit's hip. She looked up at him through a dirty blonde fringe and took her tongue for a trip around the waxed O of her mouth. Flecks of white ringed her jumper sleeve.

'Not sure if that's a good idea, Clive,' mused Frank. 'I might turn up and spoil everyone's day. But I suppose there are some advantages. If I don't exist, I can't be harmed, can I?'

Povey smiled. 'I suppose you're right. Strangest thing I've ever seen though.'

'Right.' He drifted into his own thoughts and Povey had to reach out to steady him when it seemed he was about to lean back against a couple reading *Time Out*.

'I don't know how we stick it in this place, Clive, I really don't. Everyone I see here looks pasty and frightened. They look like... you know those transfers we had as kids? You rubbed them with a pencil and they came off the tracing paper? Well, it's like that. People having their essence crushed out of them as they enter the capital so that all that remains are features, the husk.'

'Yes, Frank,' Povey smiled, patting his hand. 'Have another drink, won't you? I have to go and view a flat.' Povey tried to affect non-chalance as he waved goodbye to his friend and forced his way into the teeming night, but his hands were shaking. *I know what you mean*, he should have said. But he was worried that Frank's left-field logic might insinuate itself. He felt vulnerable and unsupported. He didn't like the drifting aspect to his life, the way he could sometimes believe he was a ghost trapped on the conditioning thermals of a dull prior existence, doomed to live every day as an exact replica of the one that went before. Commuting now took up so much of his time that his life seemed to be truncating. Every day was like standing on a succession of edges. His nerves were permanently tensed and shrieking: a slew of violins in a Bernard Herrmann score.

It was happening to everyone around him, this thing they labelled routine but which deserved a less innocent name.

Rain had slapped the city awake. It pinched her cheeks and cleared snot from her nostrils; showered the rheum from tired eyes, rouged her cheeks. London in a night-black cocktail dress: sleek and sexy and switched on. Eschewing the bus, Povey walked up Fortess Road past tired shops flagged with hopeful FOR SALE signs. Accommodation blocks sat squat in the misting rain; pale squares of light played hopscotch into the sky. Ceaselessly motile, the traffic zipped closed the tracts of the road, barring his view of the opposite pavement. He wondered if he should have asked Sutton to come with him.

Povey had received the details of the property – a converted one-bedroom flat – on Crayford Road that morning. The thought of moving back to north London spurred him on, despite his fatigue and the prospect of an awkward trip back to Lewisham. He paced the orange-blue street to Tufnell Park Tube where he turned on to its namesake road leading down to Holloway. The fifth turning on the right, according to the estate agent, was Anson Road. First left off that was Crayford Road. He wished he'd remembered to bring his *A-Z*.

The neon streetlamps fizzed, teasing his shadow. Broad streets spliced with the arterial road; Povey counted them off. It took longer than he'd anticipated, the blocks of houses between each turn-off proving to be substantial. Maybe he'd miscounted, because this, the fifth, was Carleton Road, not Anson. He spent the next twenty minutes trying his luck down various side streets until, by chance, he found Anson Road. But the first turning on the left was not Crayford, it was Dalmeny Avenue. The first left at the other end of Anson, just in case he'd got it arse about tit, was Melvyn Close.

OK, he calmed himself, *you're late now. Stop panicking and just ask someone.*

But there was nobody to ask. Povey found his way back to the main road, intending to hail the first taxi he saw when he spotted an old man with a carrier bag walking on the other side of the street.

'Excuse me!' Povey called, trotting across the road. The man lowered his head, bringing the rim of his hat across his face, and hurried away.

Another man came out of his front door, saw Povey and hesitated, as if caught red-handed.

'Do you know where Crayford Road is?' asked Povey, before the man could retreat.

'No, sorry,' he said, 'I don't know this area.' He slipped back behind the door.

Povey stared after him, confounded by what was happening. He returned along Anson Road, hoping he'd made a mistake and Crayford Road would reveal itself to him, although he was late for the viewing now and the occupants might have gone out for the evening.

He rejoined Carleton Road and asked a woman wearing earphones if she could help. She seemed affronted, as if the earphones were a signal not to be disturbed, but waved vaguely in the direction of Tufnell Park Road with an umbrella speckled with white. Without bothering to thank her, Povey stalked away. It was as if he'd failed some test that prospective home-owners had to take before being accepted into the neighbourhood.

Now he could see how the estate agents had got it wrong. They had mistaken Anson Road as the junction road with the main drag, when in fact it forked off Carleton. The fools. Here was Crayford Road, first turning off Carleton Road. Carleton. He dug in his bag, which was beginning to put a strain on his shoulder, and pulled out the property details. He underscored their false directions savagely. If he lost this flat it would be down to them. Should he hurry, he might catch the incumbent residents before they went out.

Povey ran past an estate on his right, all low, red-brick balconies and strip lighting. There was a figure moving slowly in the stairwell's dark pools. Povey glimpsed a whitish inverted cone flicker past the frosted glass where a head ought to be. Then it was forgotten as he reached the row of Victorian houses where he might set up and be happy. The light was on; his hopes soared. A woman's voice crackled over the intercom when he rang the bell. He tried to apologise when the buzzing of the lock drowned him out.

On the second floor he smoothed his hair and was attempting to dry his face with the sodden sleeve of his mac when the door opened.

'I'm glad to catch you in,' he said. 'My name's Clive Povey. I'm sorry I'm late.'

The woman blocking the wedge of light stepped back, although her eyes seemed to be fixed on a spot behind him. As he stepped through, her face set in a basic mode of recognition.

'Sorry,' she said, 'the stairwell is so dark. I didn't see you for a second.' She led him into the living room where a swarthy man was drinking from a huge mug. Povey raised a hand and the man swivelled his eyes just as steam from his drink clouded the lenses of his spectacles.

'As you can see,' said the woman, who, Povey now saw, was heavily pregnant, 'it's quite small.'

I wouldn't say that, he suddenly wanted to blurt, and clamped his teeth against a shock of laughter. It was very hot in the room; every bar of an electric fire glared. On a stuttering television, a newsreader told of a royal visit to Kuala Lumpur. It must be the faded screen that caused the cuffs of the waving Prince to appear stained white.

'Through here,' said the woman, 'is the kitchen, which, as you can see, is a bit tired but there's a surprising amount of storage space. The bathroom's just next door. Don't worry about the cracks, they're superficial. Nothing a dab of Polyfilla can't handle. And here,' she gestured with her hand; the other rested against her tummy, 'is the bedroom.'

Giddy with the warp and tilt of the flat, Povey ducked into a bizarre room that seemed to taper away from him in terms of height and width; not so much the Cabinet as the Cubby-hole of Dr Caligari. The far end was little more than a sharply angled recess. To sleep in this room, it would be necessary to evolve a needle-shaped head. He tried to mask his disappointment and mumbled something about being in touch. The television mumbled something about 'suicide' and 'train delays' as the door snicked shut on him.

Outside, the rain was muscling more intensely against the houses. It stung his face as he returned to the main road. The figure in the stairwell was across the street from him now, the cone shape revealing itself as the peaked hood of a grey tracksuit. He was spraying white paint from an aerosol on to the side of a black van and had got as far as the middle 'O' before stopping, his head twitching at the sound of Povey's gritting footsteps. Povey felt breath snatched from his lungs as the figure began to turn. He did not want to hang around to see the vandal's face. He sprinted towards the road, trying to ignore the tattoo of following feet.

'Taxi!' he yelled, hurtling into the path of a black cab. The driver seemed to take an eternity to set off for Charing Cross once Povey had blundered into the back seat. As soon as they were away, he chanced a look behind him, but the drenched street had diffused the light spilling from the lamps to such an extent that the entire avenue was concealed by a core of liquid fire.

He lay in bed listening to the uncertain squish of valves in his chest. It was hard to believe there was any blood in his veins for the coldness, the enervation he felt. He was scared to close his eyes in case he faded completely away. At least while he was awake he exerted some kind of physicality, despite the illusion of the blankets reducing his body to two dimensions.

His uncle was in the bedroom next to his; a muffled radio play moved through the wall by Povey's ear. Over dinner his uncle had twice looked up startled, as if surprised to see his nephew sitting across from him. His uncle told him, as Povey had flapped his way out of his soaked clothes in the bathroom, that a body had been found by the delta spread of tracks leading into the depot at King's Cross. There had been some consternation when the authorities had been unable to find its head, his uncle explained, somewhat tactlessly Povey thought. Initially, they believed it to be a murder. But then someone had discovered the head rammed deep inside the chest cavity, which suggested that the victim had been kneeling on all fours, facing the oncoming train. A witness had since confirmed this theory.

Povey slept fitfully until his uncle brought a cup of tea in for him at 7am. He had already decided not to go into work. Rather than wait until Lynn was in the office, he rang and left a message on the answerphone. If they wanted to find someone else to do the work, he couldn't lose any more sleep over it than he was already.

After breakfast, tired of his uncle's gory speculation as he scanned the newspapers and watched the morning news, Povey opted to go for a walk. He negotiated the lethal rush of traffic on the South Circular and headed north, the wink of Canary Wharf like a beacon ahead of him, pulling him into the heart of the city.

He reached Blackheath half an hour later and wandered without much conviction among the shops and across the fields where, even in the rain, kite enthusiasts attempted to launch their vivid array of wings, boxes and scimitars. At least here there was space to think. On three occasions he caught sight of that simple, wise word: an expression of vigilance or the boast of an omniscient entity. He saw it sprayed on the coping stones of a bridge wall, on the back of a road sign, a bench. Almost everyone he saw was streaked with white. What was going on? Was it paint? Those that weren't daubed seemed to be like windmills without sails; all purpose drained from them. He saw faces in windows gazing at the totemic needle of Canary Wharf, flesh etiolated by a lack of association. Povey sat on a bench, numb to the seepage of rain through his trousers. Terrible thoughts were gravitating towards him since he'd heard about the suicide. He had once believed that the culmination of all his love and ambition would manifest itself in his nurturing of a child. But the compulsion behind this need had mutated recently. It might be because he had failed to establish any precious links with the women he met, but he suspected it was more a crisis of identity. The fear that he might look into the mirror one day and not recognise the face staring out came from the same black source as the voice persuading him that giving birth was nothing more than the laying down of an eventual death sentence.

The rain had stopped. He watched the band of mist retreat across the greensward and tear the wrapper of shade from the towers ranged across the capital. His jacket smelled musty and his shoes rested in a thin gruel of pigeon droppings. Maybe he would feel better if he took a long bath and rang some more estate agents. Invigorated with a plan, he caught the bus back to his uncle's flat. There, he took a copy of *Loot* and had a long soak, circling possible flats with a red pen.

By the time his uncle returned from market, Povey was clean-shaven and dressed in a fresh suit, a list of addresses and accompanying times clasped in his hand. At the top, enclosed in a box, he'd written: *Clive Povey – potential accommodation*.

'I'm off flat-hunting,' he said, as his uncle pushed by, dropping an *Evening Standard* on his armchair. Povey saw the words: 'TRAGEDY OF LOST SOUL'.

'Right you are, lad,' his uncle said, picking at a blotch of white on his coat. 'Although, by the look of you, you might as well be off courting royalty.' He laughed thickly and set about making a pot of tea.

Povey was tempted to read the lead story in the newspaper, but he would be late for his first appointment. He trotted to the station and made the platform just as the train pulled up. At this time of day it was empty and Povey enjoyed the luxury of sitting wherever he pleased.

In the aisle, the pattern of cleats from a pair of trainers took a journey in white paint towards the front carriage.

Soon, he was spotting fresh instances of the graffito. Now it was in black paint, now red. Sometimes it appeared with a suffix: a colon or an arrow flying away from the final 'N' as though an urgency had developed in the author's craftsmanship, a need to convey the promise of something to follow. It lifted Povey. His reading of the signs came as an epiphany, much like the sudden break in the weather. For the first time in weeks, his flesh seemed to sing and his nerves were attuned to every twitch of his clothes, each minute change of tack in the breezes that swept through the window vents.

Approaching London Bridge, he saw, plastered against the brick-work of a defunct printers, Known's acme of achievement. An oblique of lemon-lime letters, each three feet high, parallel to the fire escape's slant. The evidence of such industry seemed to match the sprawl of the city and the commitment to obliterate the concept of space. Povey had to believe that the word existed elsewhere in the country, and for many other people, not just the glut of girders and bridge panels here or the isolated jottings north and south of the city centre. He wasn't sure he could cope with the possibility that the word was for his benefit alone.

At the terminus he passed through to the station concourse and checked the clock against his watch. He had half an hour to get to Finsbury Park. There wasn't much of a wait for a northbound train. Quick change at Warren Street for the Victoria Line and he'd be at the first address on his list with time to kill.

He sat opposite a man in orange tartan bondage pants and wrap-around shades. He was reading the *Standard* and Povey stared for a long time at the photograph on the front page. It showed, beneath the same headline he'd read at his uncle's flat, a picture of railway lines. To the right was a cluster of policemen and railway staff in reflective clothing. To the left, stark and arresting, a white blanket failed to cover a body: its left arm poked out from beneath, the hand upturned and relaxed. It wasn't this that shocked Povey, nor was it the faint but legible word punctuating the carriages of a commuter train as it travelled out of the borders of the shot. It was the inset picture of Sutton.

Povey couldn't move his eyes from the page. When finally, the man folded his newspaper and stood up, Povey was left with the negative flare of the words on his retina, a red shriek of truth to jolt him from the black and white sobriety of the newsprint. A streak of white paint flashed before him as the train slowed for the platform; he'd overshot. This was Camden Town.

In no mood for the task he'd set out to achieve, Povey took the escalator, barely feeling the other passengers as they barged past him. On Camden High Street he was sandwiched by two men running to catch the same bus. His notes were knocked from his hand into a puddle. He watched as his name was washed away before moving off towards the Lock. Dusk was mottling the sky over the canal. He plodded down to the towpath, ignoring the street vendors as they plied him with stained-glass light bulbs and kaleidoscopic knitwear. The buildings hunched their shoulders against him. Blocks of life piled on top of each other. No space left on the ground, take to the skies. High-rise and basement, purpose-built and luxury, maisonette and houseboat. Real-life soap in length and width and depth. If Povey had deviated by half a dozen steps from any roads he'd walked upon today, he'd have ended up on somebody else's property.

Further along the towpath, where the bridge on Oval Road passed over the canal, a hushed gathering fluxed like a knot of snakes. He saw a grey hood slipping swiftly in between the limbs, keeping the crowd's energy motivated. As he approached, he heard the people hissing, as though condemning a theatrical villain. But then he realised what it really was. He truffled around the drifts of litter at the towpath's edge and grasped a thick blade of broken glass, in case he needed to defend himself. He moved forward and prepared himself for a battle against the tangle of bodies as they vied for position in front of the wall; there wasn't much virgin space left on the brickwork. But as he tensed himself to enter the fray, the limbs unlocked and moved away from him, allowing him passage. Eyes assessed him, gracing him with a respectful nod to his physicality. His foot kicked against an aerosol and he bent to pick it up. For the first time in what seemed like weeks, he felt his mouth trying on a smile. Was there real blood surging through his veins after all? Might there be a portion of this tired, knowing city that could be his?

He clenched the glass and readied himself with the aerosol as white palms fed him to the wall. One way or the other, by God, he would reaffirm himself.

City of dreams

Rhonda Carrier

Spring

Day breaks, threading the sky with pink. I wake, as always, with the birds, my lips slick with dew, and watch as they unfold their wings and the trees unfurl their leaves. Together we preside over the still-sleeping city, and for a time she is ours alone; we are no longer under her spell. Then the tube exits begin gasping, spitting people out on to the streets, and we are effaced again, constrained to wait until night falls and London belongs to us once more.

Pulling blades of grass from my hair and shaking dreams from my head, I gather up my belongings and move along to my usual place, past the bright shiny shops and the office windows that glow through the mist and the sticky exhalations of the traffic. Once I'm there I sit down and break the bread brought to me by the lady from the café across the road, watching as the world comes back to life around me in a blur of human motion.

Some of them stop, the passers-by, and press cold metal into my mittened hands, their soft skin brushing my frost-reddened fingertips. Most of them merely look at me, or look just past me, to a point beside my head, with a mixture of fear and pity, but some of them can't help but ask what happened to me, how this came to be. When I don't reply, their faces darken with embarrassment or rage and they walk away muttering and shaking their heads.

Don't think I don't know what's going on here. The bastards want to buy my history, as if letting it inhabit their heads would justify their own, would make it more bearable. But maybe I would tell them if I could, perhaps I'd offer it up to them after all, like some kind of charm for warding off evil. Here's my life – may yours not turn out to be so terrible. What none of them realises, however, is that the past is dead to me and has been for as long as I know, a bad joke that I sloughed off with my old skin and left heaped in a corner, rotting to a pulp along with the sodden mattresses and vegetal detritus of the city. It's a land for which I no longer have a map.

So fuck you. That's right – fuck you all. I can't remember how I got here, OK? Nor do I know how long I've lived in this place, or how long I've lived. No more questions, please. Just hand over your money, if it makes you feel any better, and leave me in peace.

The call of the birds and the lengthening of the light are the clocks by which I live, but I can also gauge the passing of time from the activity that surrounds me and its subtle rhythms and tempos. Now, for instance, though the human drama follows its usual evening course, people bursting forth from doorways with the wide-eyed vacancy of wooden cuckoos emerging as the hour strikes, the light is beginning to dim more slowly than it has for months, and it's clear that spring is here.

It's at this time of the day, when the world starts to fold back in on itself like a bloom that opens and closes with the daylight, that I feel most invisible, most prey to the crush of heels and the onward surge, aware that I could be trodden underfoot at any moment. It's almost as if these streets have claimed me, have made me part of them through the years – I feel as grey and hard as they are, a chameleon with a hide as tough as that of an elephant.

I don't, for better or for worse, remember like elephants do, but I'd be lying if I said I didn't sometimes try to figure out how long I've been here. When I catch my reflection in the glass of the bus shelter or in shop windows, I feel older than time itself, yet I also feel timeless. In my eyes, in the bruise-like pits where my eyes should be, there's nothing to remind me of who I am, or where I came from.

Perhaps, after all, it is better that way.

Summer

The sun stains the sky red and a thousand birds open swollen throats to welcome in another new day. I lie still and feel the grass warm beneath me and listen to the insects drone drunkenly among the flower-heads, indolent as sated lovers. The ground beneath me seems to seethe with a life more ferocious still than that of the metropolis as it awakens around me. Yet little by little the city takes the ascendant once more, stifling nature's voluptuous undertow with its stenches and its sounds, and it's then that I get to my feet and head back to my usual place.

There's a mad onslaught of people, arms bare, faces feverish, already exhausted by the effort of getting from A to B. Checking their watches, they curse under their breath and move faster, ever faster, suffocating beneath skins choked with sweat and fumes. Anxious puppets hurling themselves along parched pavements, their eyes are haunted by the hours to come, by everything that needs to be pressed into them, all that must be extracted from them. An eternal calculation of sums that never quite add up, and never can, buzzes in their brains.

Me? I push crumbs into my mouth and then lean back to let the sun beat down on my eyelids. A wash of orange floods my brain, as bright as the ice lollies I used to eat when... when was that? I grasp at the memory, almost against my will, but it's gone, leaving nothing behind but a blood-sugar rush of vain longing.

Confused, heat-filled, I feel myself begin to slide into sleep. The world will carry on without me. I have nothing to give it anyway. I live outside of time, you see, in a frozen world where the past and the future are mere words, as insubstantial as a flash of spring rain.

I doze on and off until the lights in the shops begin to go down and others fizz into life, washing the city in blue neon. People disappear and reappear like stars winking in the sky. Some look sad and alone, their course through the city aimless and haphazard, others shriek and leap with wild inebriation, bunched together like pack animals. From time to time lovers walk by, too, arms entwined, faces congealed in expressions of happiness whose end is inscribed within them from the start.

There are seven million souls in Greater London, I read on a scrap of newspaper that I pulled from a bin, each of whom experience about one and a half hours of slow-wave sleep per night. That's, let's see... ten and a half million hours or twelve hundred years of dream-time every night, more or less, in this vast city (for simplicity's sake we'll forget the nightworkers, the insomniacs and the other lost souls). Sometimes I think, as I lie awake on my bed of leaves, watching the constellations shift over the earth, that I can see all those dreams streaking the sky, crisscrossing one another like searchlights across the vast dark spaces. Often they'll intersect, these nocturnal voyages of the mind, flowing into one another or colliding in the blackness, knocking one another off course and sending sleepers spinning in their beds as plots twist, thicken or take on entirely new directions in their heads.

What do they dream of, all these people in their warm, womb-like houses, folded like infants into beds firm and white, clasping one another to their chests for fear of loss or sighing into their pillows with loneliness? Do they, like me, dream of casting off gravity like a worn-out coat and circling the stars? Do they swoon and stagger like drunks as they dance naked through imagined fields, the wet grass cool on their legs? Do delicious wines pass their lips, intoxicating them like gusts of headily perfumed air, and do snatches of divine music make their souls reel? Do the secrets that are only ever whispered during the black hours make them giddy with joy, or are their night-selves as fearful as their day-selves, rushing blindly through the same choked streets in the endless pursuit of...

Of what? What *is* it they are searching for, these people in their well-cut clothes with their little black boxes pressed to their ears? What is it their eyes seek in mine, in my sunken orbits, as they race by me, jabbering like fools, speaking in tongues? Why do they smile so little, and why are their rare smiles so sorrowful, so unconvincing? What is it they want?

My own dream-time is dwindling as I sleep ever less, constrained to keep watch for the robbers and the children of the darkness, their amber eyes glinting fierily in the light of the streetlamps. What have I got to steal, you might ask, and rightly so. A mouldering sleeping bag and two plastic sacks full of tin cans, empty bottles, filthy rags and husks of bread, their innards pocked green, that's what. It's what they imagine I have that draws them to me, as if all this were a feint, as if I were really a sidewalk princess weighed down by my stash of jewels, as if I asked for this. As if it were *preferable*. Or perhaps they simply find a kind of mindless pleasure in battering my weary limbs and spilling my possessions back into the gutter and the rank bins from which I so carefully and so lovingly rescued them.

But I must prefer this, after all, must have chosen this over something, a long time ago, before forgetfulness ambushed me. Must, in some terrible moment, have reasoned that even this life, this almost-life, was better than whatever it was that I fled from.

Autumn

I wake with the smell of decay in my nostrils and find myself shrouded in brown where leaves have hurled themselves from the trees, borne on the gusts and sighs of night. Sadness pervades the air like a virus, and I feel a kind of melancholy I can't quite define, as if I'm homesick for a place I can't even remember.

I leave the square, my chest constricted, and return to my daytime spot, where I sit and let the pigeons alight on my shoulders and snap at crumbs that fall on to my great oilskin coat as I eat my daily bread. The coffee the café proprietress has brought me scalds my tongue, but it doesn't matter because I have no need of talk. What would I have to say to the men and women at the bus stop nearby, who cast me looks of reproach or incomprehension, or to the schoolchildren who point and giggle as they observe the stain on the building behind me where the black of my coat seeps into the wall day after day? How unjust of them it is to begrudge me my mark, the only one I'll ever leave on this world, the one thing that will remain when my flesh is rotted, my bones burned. But if I tried to tell them how I feel I know they'd only laugh in my face.

What do they do with people like me, I often ask myself, when we die? Do they load us into their clanking, stinking rubbish vans and throw us into some huge pit out by the city tips, or do they burn us en masse in some monstrous municipal incinerator and throw our silvery ashes to the wind?

I wonder this more and more, but there's never anyone to ask.

The people come out again at night, restless as automata run wild. Just recently, in the last few days, or perhaps weeks, some of them have begun to appear familiar – it's not so much that I am beginning to recognise them from seeing them pass me day after day, I think, as an apparent reawakening of memories in me, as if they're sparking off echoes across the lost and empty years. Could it really be true, as some claim, that as death grows closer we're deluged by memories we believed long forgotten, that our childhoods are returned to us piece by piece, in all their intensity, only to taunt us with their irretrievability? Am I now, after all this time, going to remember? And what happens if I don't want to remember?

I place my head down against the pavement and try to white out the world and all the people in it, but I can feel the beat of their feet against my ear and hear the traffic helicopters circling overhead like assiduous, outscale bees. I'm starting to feel afraid now. I thought the past was dead, but it's beginning to seem as if I spoke too soon. I struggle to contain my panic but my mind is racing, my breath quickening, as the fight to keep the memories at bay shows signs of foundering. And just when I think I've pushed the past away, the crowds press in on me still more fervently, eyes, noses, mouths standing out like the grotesque features of cartoon characters. Fleeting, desultory glances prick me, set me on fire, and inside me scenes both alien and familiar, conversations forgotten but now reheard, flare up like a thousand matches struck at a single moment in time.

I'm going up in flames. I struggle to remove my coat, but it's been welded to me by the pressure of years. That woman over there, the one with the kind face, she just looked over at me. Perhaps she will help me. Madam, Madam! Please stop! My God, could it be true? Her eyes are fixed on me, electrifying me, blazing tunnels back through the years like wormholes in space. Her face hovers above mine, a pale oval radiating unfathomable, unconditional love, and in my nostrils I catch the scent of mother's milk. Is it really you? Could it really be you?

Oh, I'm very sorry, Madam. I thought for a moment you were someone I once knew. I didn't mean to touch your arm like that. Please forgive me. Madam... Please, Madam, come ba–

It's no good, she's gone. The face of a stranger dissolves back into the crowd, leaving behind nothing but a void inside me, and a scorchmark around my heart.

I return to the square, avid for sleep.

Winter

My breath is ice-white against morning's blue haze and my eyes water from the world's brightness. I know as I sit up and scrape the frost from my coat that I've dreamed long and hard again, and I close my eyes once more to freeze the images in my mind. She's as beautiful as ever, and so radiant, like an angel illuminated from the inside. Is she still alive, and if so, where is she now? And why did I ever leave her, this mother of mine? A flood of love makes my heart skip a beat and impels me to my feet and back on to the streets.

It's a long day, the cold eating through my sleeping bag and my coat to numb the flesh within and draw out each hour like a needle being slowly extracted from a vein. I interrogate each face that passes me, as I have every day since I saw her, but it's never her, never the one whose face is inscribed on the inside of my eyelids, the one who might be able to tell me who, and why, I am, and why I ran away.

But of course it can't ever be her; it can only be a counterfeit whose face has unlocked the door to the past, allowing me the most fleeting of glimpses into a room that's remained long unlit.

The day passes in a dream of warm holding and sweet words, and when I open my eyes again the light has dimmed. I stay where I am, watching the people pass me by, until darkness deepens further and neon starts to sputter and die. It's nearly time to go now. It's getting very late, and she's not coming, that much is clear. Another day is done. I'd so much like for someone – anyone – to hold me tonight, to take me in their arms and enfold me, but I wouldn't dare to hope that such a thing will ever happen to me again. There'll never be anyone to sing me to sleep like Mama used to do, never anyone to cradle me in their arms and rock me back into forgetfulness. Instead I can only hold my hands against my ribs and try to ride the wave of dream-images for as long as I can, humming softly to myself as if I were my own child.

Warmth spreads through my body. I can feel my blood sloshing through my veins like amniotic fluid lapping against a foetus, can hear my pulse ticking in my ear like a heartbeat in miniature, and slowly my hands loosen their hold on my bags. My eyelids flutter and fall, as heavy as unwanted memories. I desperately want to sleep, but I'm afraid to do so here in case they think I'm finished and drag me away from everything I know. I'm anchored to this earth only by these streets I call home. But I'm so tired. I'm so very... so... I'm so...

I'm brought back to the world by a click of heels and the clink of a coin as it falls to the pavement before me. I glance up and my chest leaps and bounds as I look into his eyes. The world seems to slide and buckle around me as I'm pulled backwards in time, tumbling down the years like rain falling from a sky bleached white with clouds.

It's you, I stammer, and the face I seem to recognise becomes perplexed, fearful. A hand reaches down to me, slowly, hesitantly, and I find myself recoiling, backed up against the wall with a blade of ice shooting up through my core, my arms flailing in front of me like the tentacles of some creature roused from a deep-sea slumber.

Get away from me, I hear myself hissing. I told you before, I won't let you touch me again. Not ever. I'll tell her, I promise you. Next time I'll tell her. Or I'll run away and never come back. And what will you tell her then? How will you explain that to her? Oh God, just leave me alone – please. Let go of me.

The man withdraws his hand and begins to run, looking over his shoulder as he recedes into the distance, his face no more than a white smudge now. I take up my bags quickly and move away, homewards, to the tiny square where I haul my lumpen form nightly over the railings and fall to sleep beneath the trees, the thrum of the trains in the tunnels beneath me rattling up through my bones and the wail of sirens in my ears. My heart is growing calmer now, its beat less wild and disordered, and suddenly I'm weary. I don't think I can make it back just yet, after all. I'll rest here for a short time, in this narrow alley where the pigeons, my only friends, strut and coo, oblivious to the past and the future, to their own births and deaths and everything in-between. I'll only stay for a while, till I can make it the rest of the way. Just a second or two, to catch my breath, that's all I need.

And so I lay me down to sleep. Below me the pavement yields, as soft as pillows filled with the finest down, as welcoming as my mother's smile, as warm as my father's beard when he pulled me to his face, his lips parted, his breath hot and vile. I feel its pull, and I can no longer resist. I'm falling, and it feels so good. My heart is slowing, my body is blueing. But I don't feel the cold any more, and there's no more pain.

Night falls. Let the dream-life begin.

The hard shoulder

Chris Petit

There she was, proud and tall, heels at nine in the morning, shopping in the big new American-style supermarket, just as O'Grady had guessed. When he saw her he knew at a glance, from the way she stood and the tilt of her head. It felt like some long dead connection was being made inside him that his body couldn't take.

Feeling dizzy enough to fall over, he followed from a distance, wondering what he would do if he was spotted and telling himself that he was fretting for nothing. Maggie as always was caught up with herself. Seeing her again he marvelled at what he had thrown away. She was a fine-looking woman, tall and beautifully boned, and immaculately turned out, her make-up just so. Dressed to kill, he thought. From the sensuousness of her walk he guessed the underwear was silk. She looked like she was got up for a date, or a play, for something outside the normal scope of things. No tins of baked beans for her. The items she placed in her cart were carefully middle class. She loitered in front of the fancy olive oils, and in the dairy section took a low-fat spread. Even in his day, he remembered, Maggie had refused to buy margarine like everyone else. 'Too many airs and graces for her own good,' was his mother's verdict.

His own cart stayed more or less empty as he forgot to fill it. Maggie's purchases seemed idle compared to most shoppers', nothing so vulgar as bulk buying. Her bored saunter announced that she had time and money to spare.

He loitered in the drinks section while she queued and paid and he watched her push her cart over to a sporty hatchback Golf. He left his own shopping in the aisle and hurried to his car once she was in hers. He watched her leave then immediately lost her. There were no cars on the slip road. He could not understand where she had gone.

Then he saw she had turned off into the filling station and was getting out of the Golf. She seemed to be looking straight at him as he drove past, which started his heart banging again, but as she showed no surprise he thought he was probably safe. He came to one of the new small roundabouts and looped round the garage and back into the car park. He got out and watched from a distance, with a hedge for a screen. She came back from paying, putting her purse in her handbag.

He was thirty yards behind her by the time she got to the little round-about and he tried to keep that distance, following her on to the North Circular then off at Wembley. After Wembley he recognised the road as one he had driven down before. It was a faster road, straight and with common land on either side and a camp of gypsy caravans. There were a couple of cars between them, which meant less chance of being spotted. He was probably safe enough anyway. Maggie had never been one for looking back. That they had once shared a life now seemed beyond the shores of remotest possibility.

He guessed correctly that she would carry on north to Stanmore. The road after the Kingsbury roundabout he remembered was called Honeypot Lane and eventually he found himself in streets he recognised from his previous drives.

Maggie's house was on a modern estate in a cul-de-sac. He watched her turn in, and drove past, turned himself and slowly drove back. The hatch of Maggie's car was up and she was unloading her shop-ping. The house was smart, what was called executive style. The estate was deserted, as empty as a dream. Either it was so new that half the houses were still unsold or the inhabitants were so discreet that their homes gave nothing away.

Although he kept telling himself he was keeping everything normal he knew he was not.

Breaking into his old flat was not normal.

Making the normal bits seem even more normal created enough space for him do what he needed to do, then pretend to himself he wasn't doing them. The logic of it worked after several drinks but fell apart soon after that. He persuaded himself that he was drinking less. The ones he had at night in his room watching the television he didn't count.

The afternoon he broke into the flat had started as a walk, down the High Road and over to Swiss Cottage. There he decided it was the open space of Primrose Hill he was after. From the top of the hill he could see Bethlehem House. It was where he and Maggie had lived after marrying and it was Lily's first home. He remembered the humiliation of his last visit, being told to fuck off by the old woman. He decided to give her another go. But when he was there he did nothing. He got as far as her door but didn't ring her bell. Instead he went and sat on the back stairs and wondered what he was doing. He must have sat there several hours, listening to the sounds of the building and the noise of the lift going up and down. It was working again. He reckoned a couple more hours of daylight. He would give it until dark because she wouldn't go out after that.

He had always liked the flat. It had been difficult living there with Maggie because what she wanted, even on the simplest day-to-day level, clashed with him. She was always looking ahead and planning while he was happy to go along with things. She wanted better and complained all the time about the state of the building – the shit on the stairs and the graffiti and so on. But O'Grady never minded particularly because he liked living so high up. He had once tried to explain to Maggie, saying how it made him feel like he was on top of everything, and she had snorted and hadn't understood. Up there it felt like nobody could touch them, and he wanted that to be clearer to her. Then maybe in return he would learn to accept the idea of what she meant by a home.

It grew dark and O'Grady slunk back to Kilburn, telling himself that it wouldn't happen like this on one of those police shows on television. He went back once more, with no expectations. Some time in the middle of the afternoon he heard the woman's door open and shut, and through the crack in the fire door he watched her take the lift.

He gave her five minutes. He had bought a metal nail file in Boot's, which had earned him an odd look from the sales girl. He tried it on the lock without success. Picking locks had never been a skill of his. He checked the other front doors for sounds of life in the neighbouring flats, then gave the old woman's door a good sharp kick. It flew open at the first attempt and O'Grady felt like he was in a television show all of his own. He went back and waited on the back stairs, ready to run if anyone came, but no one did and he walked into his old flat, pushing the door to behind him.

It was exactly as he remembered apart from the furniture. Even the kitchen cupboards were the same green and the doors to the rooms were blue like they always had been. He sat for a moment in the living room, wanting to stay there watching the clouds drift. There was rain to the east. The television had been left on with the sound up.

There were two bedrooms. The bigger, where he and Maggie had slept, was empty. The old woman had her bed in the narrow room that had been Lily's. It smelt of old age and talcum powder. O'Grady remembered how fresh Lily had always smelt as a baby. It used to make him feel sad in a sentimental way. There had been talcum powder in the room then too, but with none of the sense of collapse that now hung in the air.

He took a chair from the kitchen and placed it in the hall under a small trapdoor that led to the loft, and hauled himself up into the tight space. There was still no proper light. From what he could see, the old woman had none of her stuff up there and there were just a couple of old cardboard boxes. He crawled forward, checking them on his way past. It felt like clothes inside. He used the light of the trapdoor to see what they were – children's clothes, a little girl's. They would have been Lily's. The other box was a mix of his and Maggie's. It made him uncomfortable, thinking of a part of themselves still being accidentally together all those years.

He knew he was taking too long. The woman had probably only gone to the corner shop. He crawled forward to the cistern, which was on the far side. It was too dark to see and he had to work by feel. He pushed up his sleeve to the elbow. The coldness of the water made him feel for a second that he was deep underground.

The package wasn't there.

Nobody else knew, so there was no reason for it not to be there. The cistern was bigger than he remembered and he had to put his arm in up to the shoulder. He walked his fingers along the bottom of the tank, hurrying at the thought of the old woman already being in the lift.

He stirred the water as his search became more urgent. He couldn't imagine Maggie stumbling across it. She would not have gone up in the loft had her life depended on it. Perhaps it had been found during some routine maintenance. It was a long time ago.

He was on the point of giving up when he found it, standing up against the side of the tank and not flat on the bottom as he remembered.

The package had been carefully waterproofed and he hoped it had kept out the wet after all this time. He squeezed his own clothing dry as best he could, and on his way back collected the boxes without giving a second's thought as to why.

The hard shoulder

He closed the hatch behind him and returned the chair to the kitchen and left by the stairs. As he was going out of the building he saw the old woman paying a minicab. The boxes helped hide his wet sleeve. He wondered what she would make of her wonky lock.

He walked around till he felt normal. He pretended it was still fifteen years ago and he was taking some old clothes to the charity shop. This would normally be Maggie's job, but with Lily ill she wasn't able to go.

He sat on a bench and sorted through the boxes. The smaller one was just the child's clothes, tiny brightly coloured cardigans and T-shirts with pictures on. Maggie had always bought expensively. He remembered asking her the point of spending so much money on them when she was growing so fast. The other box was mainly Maggie's, apart from an old shirt and trousers of his. He tried to picture the boxes lying there undisturbed and forgotten all those years, like ghosts of the family they had once been.

The box with his and Maggie's clothes he left in a charity shop on Camden High Street. Lily's he took home, along with the package, which he placed unopened at the back of a drawer, and tried not to think about it or what he had done.

Wittgenstein's mattress

Geoff Nicholson

I ate my breakfast at the Savoy Grill today. I walked in and went straight to the best table in the house. I had my pick. The place was empty. Completely. No other diners. And there weren't any waiters, no maître d', and there weren't any chefs either, so obviously I had to go into the kitchen and serve myself.

Of course, there's no gas or electricity in there any more so I had to make do with what I could find; some crackers, half a pound of caviar and a magnum of Dom Perignon, which was a bit warm actually, but what else can you expect?

I enjoyed myself well enough at the Savoy, but let's face it, the place has seen better days. And when I went up into the hotel to sleep off my breakfast, I had to search through a couple of floors before I found a room that was habitable, and it was up on the sixth floor. Most of them are a big mess, beds not made, still full of other people's gear. Frankly, it could have been a bit depressing, but I wasn't depressed. I'm not like that. Not any more.

And it's the same everywhere these days; the Pharmacy, Sheekey's, the Ivy, Simpson's in the Strand, the Hard Rock. There's never any problem getting in. I'm always the only one who's ever there. I'm always the only one who's ever anywhere.

Anyway, after I'd had my little doze in the Savoy, I got up and then I chucked the bed out of a sixth-floor window. I had my reasons. Believe me.

I'm not exactly sure how I came to be the last man alive in London. I know I was in the hospital because I'd been having the old problems again, and I remember the psychiatrist telling me they were going to try out a radical new therapy on me, and I imagine I must have signed some consent forms before they gave me all the injections.

After that it gets a bit confusing. I don't really remember going to sleep, but I do remember waking up, and I know I felt as though I'd been out of it for a really, really long time. I also remember feeling better than I had in years. Everything was very quiet: the ward, the hospital, the inside of my head. Everything felt very peaceful and ordered and sane, so I wasn't going to knock it.

Even without getting out of bed I could tell that I was the only one left on the ward. And when I got up and wandered about I soon worked out that I was the only one left in the whole hospital. After that, and obviously it took a bit of time to get to grips with it all, I eventually sussed that I was the only one left in the whole of London. My pain had been obliterated and so too had the entire population of London. Bit weird maybe, but basically it seemed a small price to pay, really.

Now, I know some people might have thought, blimey, I'm the last man alive in London and they'd have got all gloomy about it, what with the loss of all that life and humanity and civilisation and hope for the future and what have you. But not me. Personally I could see possibilities.

When I say I'm the last man alive in London, I don't want you to think the place is full of a lot of dead people. It's not. There aren't corpses piled up on street corners, like there's been some kind of apocalypse or holocaust or angel of death or something. No, everybody's just gone. I don't know where, obviously, and although it'd be nice to think they'd gone to a better place, like outer space or Florida or somewhere, there's not much future in wondering about it, is there? Even if I think I've got it sussed there's not going to be any way to prove I'm right, is there? So what's the point? If you don't know what you're talking about then shut the fuck up, that's my motto.

At first I was a bit reluctant to move out of the hospital. I was comfortable there, and I had a bed and food and access to most of the drugs I needed, but then obviously I realised I had access to every bed, every bit of food, every kind of drug, every kind of comfort that London had to offer. So I decided to go for it. I decided to live a little.

I did pop in to my crappy old flat in Peckham, and I did spend a couple of nights there recuperating, but basically it just did my head in. When you know you've got your pick of every gaff in London, you're not going to stay in a one-bedroom scum-hole above a laundry for long, are you now?

These days I live all over the place. I sleep around, in other people's flats and houses, in other people's beds, and sometimes in posh hotels like the Savoy and sometimes, once in a while, in a palace or penthouse or houseboat, and once in a rock band's luxury tour bus that was parked outside Wembley Arena. I've had stays in Kensington and Mayfair and Chelsea, which are places I once wouldn't have felt very at home in, but they're a lot better now that they're not full of poncey, stuck-up, rich bastards.

And now and again I take a walk on the wild side and spend a night or two in Kennington or the Isle of Dogs or Plaistow, and they're all right too. In the old days I wouldn't have been seen dead in these places, but you have to ask yourself why I wouldn't have, and the answer is obviously because of the people there. Once the people are gone, everywhere's a lot better. Lot safer too. There's no muggers, no burglars, no crack dealers, no coppers. You can't knock it.

Obviously one of the first things I did was break into a few houses, see how the other half lives, or used to live; not that there was very much breaking in required. You'd be amazed how many doors and windows had been left unlocked, like people had legged it in a hurry.

Going into somebody's house and going through their stuff is always a good laugh, but obviously it's more fun if the people are a bit famous. So I broke into Paul McCartney's place in Abbey Road, and Keith Richard's in Cheyne Walk, and Madonna's gaff in Little Venice, and into 10 Downing Street, and Jeffrey Archer's pad in Greenwich, and I had a good root through Buckingham Palace. Well you would, wouldn't you?

And it was all pretty good, looking through famous people's underwear and their photograph albums and diaries, and seeing what drugs they had stashed away, and necking their best booze, and seeing their stashes of mucky Polaroids and all that. And I know some people would think there was also something a bit creepy about it, knowing that Paul and Keith and Madonna and Tony and Jeff and Sweaty Betty weren't there and didn't look as though they be coming back, but me, I thought good riddance.

And sometimes I think it'd be nice to be able to tell somebody about it, to say that I'd mucked about with Zoe Ball's knickers, and that I'd had my breakfast sitting in Chris Evans' kitchenette, and that

I'd practised trick shots on Liam Gallagher's snooker table, but I suppose that if there was anybody to tell I probably wouldn't be doing it. Funny that.

Like anyone would, I did a bit of looting. Obviously. I went down to the Tower, and I tried on a few crowns and robes and what have you but they weren't really me. I looked a twat.

So I went down to Saville Row looking for a suit, but you know, hand-tailored suits aren't much cop when you've got nobody to handtailor them.

In the end I settled for a few off-the-peg, Paul Smith charcoal-grey three-buttoned numbers. Simple elegance. There's no need to go mad is there? And frankly, looting's not that big a deal when you can have every-thing you want whenever you want it. Most looters like to grab their stuff and leg it home before they get caught. Doesn't really apply in my case.

I'm not saying that everything in London's mine, like I think I own it all or anything, but the fact is, I can have the use of it any time I like, and in some ways that's much better.

Like I had the use of Wembley Stadium and Stamford Bridge and Loftus Road, so I went in all of them and kicked a football around. Then I went and kicked a football around on Centre Court at Wimbledon and then in the middle of Hyde Park Corner. And I also did a bit of ten pin bowl-ing on Tower Bridge, but that wasn't as much fun as I'd been expecting.

There used to be those jokes, didn't there, about 'Will the last man in London please turn out the lights?' Well, in my London there aren't any lights to turn off, because there's no electricity, which means that a lot of the stuff you might think about nicking isn't much good to you.

There's still petrol about, at garages and in the tanks of all the thou-sands of abandoned cars all over the place, so I suppose it'd be possi-ble to rig something up with a portable generator and have electricity that way, but I've never been very mechanically minded, so basically if a thing can't run off batteries then I say sod it.

Obviously there's no television or radio, and no satellite broadcasts, and the phones aren't working, and there's no planes or helicopters up in the air, so that might make you think it's not only London that's empty. Either that or the rest of the world is giving London, which is to say me, a very wide berth. Well, fuck 'em if they want to be like that.

Every now and then I think I might get in one of these abandoned cars and try to get out of London, because loads of them are just sitting there, keys in the ignition, petrol in the tanks, and in fact I do drive them from time to time. In the last few weeks, for instance, I've driven a Roller, a Ferrari and a London bus. But the problem is you can't drive very far before you come across some other abandoned cars blocking the road.

I suppose you could take one of these other cars and drive that until you came to the next blockage, then change cars again and so on until you eventually got somewhere, but it'd be a balls-aching job. And actually riding a bike makes a lot more sense, and it's even better when you know you're not going to get run down by some prick in a Roller or a Ferrari or a London bus.

But the fact is, even if there is some sort of life going on out there in Hungerford or Surbiton or Caversham or God knows where, I'll be buggered if I'd want to go there. You know what Londoners are like, the rest of the world doesn't exist for them at the best of times.

Actually the best laugh I had with a motor was when I found this cool old Jag and I hammered it up and down the Mall a few times, avoiding abandoned cars as and when necessary, and, when I got fed up with that, I set the car going, jammed the accelerator, then leapt out and watched the Jag explode in flames as it crashed into the statue of Queen Victoria, yeah, that was a good night.

You could call it vandalism, but I wouldn't. I'd call it self-expression, the same as when I smashed a few thousand panes of glass in the greenhouses at Kew, and when I went into the National Gallery and drew moustaches on some of the paintings, and when I sprayed 'Mandelson Sucks' on the side of Waterloo Bridge.

And I had a right blast in Madame Tussaud's. I went in there with a blow lamp and I melted down the faces of Adolf Hitler and Michael Jackson and the Queen Mother. You'd have pissed yourself if you'd seen it.

Which brings me to another big improvement that's happened in London. I always thought London was really badly off for public loos. These days I can have a pee just about anywhere I like. And there's no need to be shy about it. If I want to have a slash in the fountains in Trafalgar Square, I just let rip. I've strained the greens down the steps of the Members' Pavilion at Lord's, done it off the Spectators' Gallery in the House of Commons, from off the top of the London Monument, to name but a few.

So one day I'm sitting there and I suddenly think to myself, what about the animals in London Zoo? What are they up to? Obviously nobody's been feeding them. Are they starving? Are they eating each other? And actually I must admit I did think that if they weren't all dead or disappeared they might be a good source of fresh meat. I always wondered what zebra tastes like.

But I got there and the place was empty, so I had to make do with smashing beer bottles against the ramps in the penguin pool. And that was when I had a bit of an epiphany. You can't just be a vandal all your life, I thought. No, what you want to be is an artist.

And I thought to myself, well, what sort of artist? And obviously I can't paint or play a musical instrument or do ballet dancing, and I'm not likely to learn since there's nobody around to teach me, so I thought I'd better create my own art form, based on the skills and interests I already had. So I did.

What I do as my art form is drop things off, and on to, other things. Like I went into Harrod's and got a few sets of their best china plates and then I went up to the roof and chucked 'em off like frisbees. It was great. Sound, light, movement, drama, the whole thing.

It was the same with chucking Egyptian mummies down the stairs of the British Museum – I thought that said a lot about life and death and that. And dropping early Roman glass artefacts from a great height on to the Rosetta Stone; well, it speaks for itself, doesn't it?

And then I went into Somerset House, where they keep all the wills, and the birth and death certificates, and I threw them out of the windows and they got blown about and some of them landed in the river, and that was quite a subtle one, and in some ways it was better than when I pushed a piano off the stage at the Albert Hall, because that seemed a bit obvious in retrospect.

And I was especially proud of the thing I did when I got this box of Cadbury's Creme Eggs and I went up in the Whispering Gallery in the dome of St Paul's and I unwrapped all the eggs and threw them up in the air and watched them rise and then fall and then smash down on to the floor below. It was amazing.

But my greatest artistic triumph to date was, I think, in the Trellick Tower. I went up to the top floor, dragged all the mattresses off people's beds and threw them out the windows. Then, when the mattresses were on the ground, I started tossing out other things, stereos, mirrors, television sets, bits of furniture; and some of them landed on the mattresses and bounced around a bit in an aesthetically pleasing way, and then some of them missed and smashed to pieces on the concrete and that was even better. Really. Take my word for it.

Now, you could argue that an artist needs an audience, but from what I've heard about artists and audiences I'm probably better off without one. And it's definitely good to know I won't ever have to sell out and pander to the masses.

Obviously I do miss certain members of the masses; not many, but one or two. My old mother obviously, not that we were close. And there's my mate Brian who I used to have a few jars with on a Friday night. And there's Andrea, who was this bird I fancied. I mean, she didn't fancy me; in fact, she didn't even know I existed, but I was working on it.

Actually I broke into her place recently and I had a look through her things, her clothes and her make up and her condoms and her vibrator and some letters from ex-boyfriends, and basically I think I was better off without her.

Her flat was up on the fourth floor of a mansion block, so dropping all her stuff out the window wasn't as good as it would have been if she'd been up higher, but when I tossed out her laptop and it smashed into the windscreen of a parked Ford Capri, well, that was quite a moving experience. Really.

You know, I always used to think that somewhere among all the millions of women in London one of them might be right for me. And you might think that the fact there are now absolutely no women at all in London would make things worse, but the fact is I have exactly the same number of girlfriends, exactly the same amount of sex these days as I did when London was fully populated; ie none.

Wittgenstein's mattress

*

Even though I said I try not to think what it's all about, I do some-times wonder if maybe it's some really amazing experiment with me as the guinea pig, and the real London is going on somewhere else just like before but they've built this superb replica complete in every detail, in one-to-one scale, and they've put me in it to see how I'll react. Sounds a bit bonkers, but you know what some of these scientists are like. They want to watch how I cope with the isolation and loneliness and all that.

And frankly, I think I'm coping pretty well. Some people would go mad with all this, but not me. I suppose London has always turned some people insane, but in my case it's turned me into an artist. Funny that.

Author's note: this story is a pastiche or appropriation of a very serious novel by David Markson, called Wittgenstein's Mistress, *which is about a woman who may or may not be mad and may or may not be the last person left on earth, and she goes around musing about classical civilisation, high art and linguistic philosophy; and it just seems to me that the last person left in London might be a little less highbrow than that.*

London blood

Michael Moorcock

There are certain memories that never really reach your brain. They stay in your blood like a dormant virus. Then something triggers them and you don't remember the moment; instead you relive every detail. It's the reliving, not the original experience, that your brain registers. I think this happens to you more as you get older. And you don't always welcome it, either, however ordinary. Last week I was just looking out of the window and suddenly I was back at Gloria's funeral, with all the family there and Mum still alive. It's when it stays on as a memory that it hurts. Nine of us survived childhood out of thirteen. Three boys and six girls. Little Jimmy, named after Dad, Freddy, Ellie, Sammy, Nora, Lily, Nellie, me and Gloria. Everyone but Mum and Gloria is still with us. We're a bit too crochety to travel much; but we stay in touch on the phone.

I had a flashback the other day of what we called Mum's grieving chair. It was a funny name for such a big, comfortable bit of furniture, but usually she only sat there when somebody had died. An old-fashioned, Victorian easy with dark flower patterns and enclosing wings. You could divide a chair like that into flats, these days. Of course, there'd be nowhere to put it in a place this size. The chair survived the Blitz but not the '50s. Mum's buildings were knocked down as part of the Battersea project and we sold everything to a dealer. Ellie, who was staying at Mum's then, didn't want it. She was moving to Australia to live with her son.

Gloria died of cancer in Bournemouth within a year of her husband. It was a real shock. We'd never had anyone with cancer before. It was just before Mum moved to Lily's, so it was probably the last time she used her chair.

We were all sorry Ellie missed the Coronation and the Festival of Britain. Mum visited the South Bank eventually, though she blamed it for knocking down her flats. She really enjoyed herself when she got there, especially at the funfair, but outside the Skylon she helped an old man. He'd collapsed with heatstroke and she looked after him till the St John Ambulance Brigade turned up. She took care of every-thing. She did all the right things. They said she probably saved his life. We couldn't help feeling proud of her, even though we were a bit embarrassed by all the attention. And then, of course, it was too late to do anything else. We never did get to the Dome of Discovery.

Lily's kids adored Mum. She was a perfect grandma. She couldn't have done better than Lily, who was married to a GP. They made her a lovely little flat of her own in their really posh old house looking out over the common. But she still missed her chair. It's one of my first memories, that chair.

I couldn't have been more than six, 1924 at the latest, when our little Gus went down with TB. After Gus's final illness, when all the funeral arrangements had been made and the rest of the formalities were over, Mum sat in that chair for five days. Hardly spoke a word. Most of us were still at home. We knew what to expect. We were all old enough by then to look after ourselves.

Of course, she didn't sit for five days solid. She ate a bit and slept a bit and so on. She was very sweet to us when we had to speak. But distant. She sat there nights, too, with her favourite cat on her lap.

Tizer was a massive green-eyed African orange brindle Mr Simpson the missionary gave Mum when he had to go into Sunnydales. Tizer loved her as much as she loved him. He'd mope when she was away and he'd shake with a deep vibrant purr whenever she came back. He was the boss cat but he had a kind, dignified nature.

Half our cats were from other homes, not always with their owners' knowledge. Mum would send us out to find them; then she'd pick the best and make us put the others back. It was the only crime she'd condone. Of course, she didn't see it as crime. She knew she could look after cats better than anyone. She could double their lifespans. She understood them. Everything about them. She'd always talk to them in her ordinary voice and you had the feeling they answered back the same. She could tell you if a cat was going to get sick or leave or pine. And she wouldn't have it she was psychic.

Another ordinary memory. A family story, really. One frosty Boxing Day we were out on Tooting Common with Sammy's new roller skates and we found this skinny dog we took home. Mum was horrified. 'Look at his poor ribcage!' She offered him a huge plate of goose and chicken scraps. He wolfed them down, grinning and wagging and panting for more. So, while Tizer twitched his tail in outrage, she gave the dog seconds. Eventually the owner was found and arrived glad to see his dog again, if a bit glum.

Mum was relieved. He seemed a decent sort of bloke. The animal clearly liked him. 'He was so hungry when he got here.' Looking fondly down at the contented dog, Mum folded her arms in a gesture of self-satisfaction. Mum was tall, with a nose that could cut concrete, thick raven hair and blue x-ray eyes. People didn't often argue with her. 'He must have been lost for days. I bet you're glad to have him back. You keep him well. Greyhound, is he?'

'Yes,' the man replied sadly. 'He was due to run at Summerstown this afternoon. We rather fancied he'd win.'

Mum didn't say anything then but after she closed the door on him she said she thought it was wicked to starve animals for sport. Let the skinny little bugger have a good sleep instead. It was Christmas, wasn't it? Nobody should have to work over Christmas. She offered me a secret wink. God, I loved my Mum.

She could pick horses, too, even though she had a feeling steeple-chasing might be cruel. When she got the chance she'd have a couple of bob each way on the National and she'd always win. She'd never put too much on, and she never told Dad. I often took her bets to Mr Phelps in the greengrocer's, there being no betting shops in those days. He was what they used to call a bookie's runner. But only a couple of bob. Always each way. She felt it would break her luck otherwise. Dad used to try to get her to pick a name off his card, but she wouldn't.

Mum's room was the long narrow one at the back. It was the nois-iest but that didn't matter too much to her since she was going a bit deaf and she had the wireless by then. She'd made the room her own after Jim married. Nellie, Gloria and me all got her big bedroom to share. Me and Nellie were best friends. We loved it. But Gloria thought we were horrible tomboys and kept her little bed neatly to herself in the corner. Nellie got prissy like that. Lives in Hove. Won't relax and have a laugh. All health food and perms, these days. Disapproves when I have a gin.

People thought we were Irish because we had red hair and green eyes like Nellie or black hair and blue eyes, like me. They always described us as vivacious or full of life. They'd have called us slappers if we'd been ugly. But we were the famous Lee girls. We were never short of mashers.

And Mum saw to it we didn't fall in love with anyone unsuitable. My first husband was a civil engineer. More engineer than civil, I must say. While I was entertaining the troops, he was entertaining the girls they'd left behind.

After our Gus died I was the youngest but one. I was born at Stone Cottages, Mitcham, when there was a village green and one pump, and the tram link with Streatham went across lavender fields. That was at the end of the first German war. But I was brought up in Tooting, which we thought of as proper south London. You could take the tram direct to Vauxhall.

Ours was a big flat. We had the first and second floors above a furniture showroom. Their warehouse was over in Figges Marsh, so most of the flat was never too noisy. We were at the pointed end of a parade of shops, handy for the market. Our building was wedge-shaped because it was on the corner where the trams turned down towards Mitcham Cricketers. 'The prow' Dad called it. 'Ahoy, ahoy, I'm captain of the clipper,' he'd sing in a good mood. Then Mum would tell him off when he mumbled the rest of the words and he'd laugh that infectious, dirty laugh of his. He drew you in to stuff like that, even if you didn't like it much.

When I lay in bed I could see the spider's web of tramlines reflecting the light of the shops sparkling through our net curtains. I thought those lines were roads through fairyland. On the whole we weren't very imaginative as a family. Probably that's why almost everyone but me went into politics. I used to lie there, hearing Mum and Dad in hissing argument. I'd actually teach myself to go somewhere else – into a fantasy so vivid I almost remembered it as real. I kept it all to myself, even from Nellie. Dad would have laughed himself silly if he'd have guessed. Especially if he'd had a few of his 'noggins'.

Even early on Mum would sometimes lock Dad out until his pleading and oaths threatened to involve the neighbours. Then she'd let him back in on promises to stop drinking and playing the horses. He'd cheer up for a few days and stay around the house. 'Bai jove, bai jove,' he'd sing, 'Our Jimmy's a jolly old cove!' But sooner or later the kids would drive him out to the pub or the racecourse. He complained she didn't discipline us.

Mum kept us in order all right. I don't remember her ever raising her hand. And when she was grieving you didn't feel you had to behave any differently. You only heard her going to the lavatory or having a wash, but you were always aware of her, there in her room, sitting in her chair. Doing nothing but staring and thinking. It was her way of praying. And the respect we automatically gave her was our way of joining in.

She wasn't a religious woman. Though she'd been a suffragette, her hero was still Lloyd George, whom she saw as the people's prime minister. She believed fiercely – and fierce was the word if she heard you putting down some underdog – in equality, liberty and all that other stuff. With a couple of exceptions, she bred a family of men and women who could stand rock-solid on their own feet and look anyone in the eye as an equal. But natural arguers. We had the lot from Trots to Tories.

Tooting's changed since our day, naturally, because of the bombing. What you see now that isn't concrete is a collection of ancient and modern; the old blood-red brick of south London or that new hard-fired pale brick which they used so much in the '50s, when they thought it looked clean and contemporary. There's no warmth to it, except what you can write with a spray-can. The people who painted messages on walls in my day were communists and fascists. This new stuff's prettier and wittier.

We're now in our nineties except for Ellie and Nora who are 104 and 105 respectively. That's London blood for you. You can't find a gene pool like that any more. Antibiotics is what I blame. Wiping out the cheap and natural and replacing it with the pricey and artificial. You see it everywhere, don't you? The only time you looked for bottled water when I was a kid was when there was a cholera scare. And a scare was all it was.

I've had two penicillin shots in my life and benefited from both of them. And apart from the junior aspirin I take every day now, that's all I've ever needed or wanted. I've got kids, grand-kids and great-grand-kids and we're all the same in the main: healthy as horses. Four of them are actors now, all doing well. Better than me. I still do some radio stuff and get good offers, and I'm in that new red grapefruit commercial. Apart from the home help once a week I'm completely self-sufficient, as ever. At this rate our family will survive a nuclear holocaust. It's survived most other kinds.

Anyone the gypsies admired they'd say had gypsy blood. It was their way of praising you. My mother used to say that you had to give yourself deep roots. If you didn't know what your original roots were, if they were lost somehow, you made up a set of rules and a history to go with them. Find them in a book. A novel. Anything. The best you could be. The best your people could have been. People you admired. You invented your ancestors if you didn't have any. And those were the roots you kept alive and they kept you alive. It was nothing to do with staying in the same place, she said, though that helped. It was to do with being the same, whatever else changed. Listening to your blood, Mum called it. Being yourself and as good as you could be. It sounded like gypsy lore to us, so we took it seriously. You stuck to your word for your own sake, she said. You didn't let anyone tell your story for you. You trusted yourself because your private behaviour matched your public conversation. She told us never to lie knowingly, except sometimes to authority, and never to give too much away either. Sometimes a little white lie was all right because it wasn't so much the lie in that case as who you told it to.

By the time Jim came back from the war, she had four lots of money coming in. Jim's, Freddy's, Ellie's and Sammy's. Ellie was a book-keeper at the Home and Colonial. The boys went into the civil service and all did very well. The depression was looming. They kept jobs that were certain and steady and unaffected by lay-offs and bankruptcies. They could give Mum money regularly. And she was still manageress at the Sunlight Laundry.

For a while she must have taken over Dad's money, too, when he earned at all. He was a master tailor, but he couldn't hold a job. She'd told him enough times about his drinking and gambling. You could say she waited until she was no longer in any way financially dependent on him before exerting her power. The boys were leaving home, getting married, and she'd come to rely on them. She was probably a bit scared of what might happen. Though my brothers all worshipped her, they knew she wouldn't have wanted them to stay. They had their own lives.

She worked late on Mondays and sometimes Fridays to pay for her pleasures. She liked the pictures but would never go in seats any more expensive than the one-and-threes. She also went to the music hall once a month in the evening. She complained about the new acts but loved Max Miller, of all people. She thought it was narrow-minded of the BBC to keep banning him. She'd always insisted on her nights out. Which meant sometimes only Dad was home when we got back from school.

Dad said I was his favourite, and I think it was true. I couldn't easily resist his crooked charm any more than Mum had been able to. He could make me squirm, half embarrassed, half delighted. Like her I was a bit unsure of him. There was something aggressive and needy under the jokes. He said I was the only one who understood him. I knew he wasn't really misunderstood. I'd noticed the difference between him and ordinary people. And when he was away, life became more secure, more predictable. The house cheered up quietly.

Mum never seemed to miss him. To be honest, I missed his attention, the flattery. I knew he was a drunkard, a gambler and a conman, and nasty sometimes, too. As Mum grimly said to me around the time Gloria died, it wasn't his charm that gave her thirteen kids.

When they were courting, my Dad promised her the earth. Jimmy Lee was considered a catch. He was finishing his tailoring apprenticeship. Nothing safer than the rag trade, he said. He'd told her he was well-connected. Marks and Spencer's, I think. Of course, all he was really attached to was the track and the saloon bar.

Dad had inherited half a gent's outfitters in Streatham Hill. The family he sold it to kept the name. You could see it for years. Lee and Green, Bespoke Tailor. Green was his cousin who went to America. My brother Jimmy, who wound up in the Foreign Office, met him out there.

Mum saved what she could from the sale. She had three boys to educate into good jobs and six girls that had to be properly schooled so as to be married to professional men. That was six weddings just there. And six dowries. She hid the money from Dad, of course. He never knew, as he worried how to pay his bookie, that he was sleeping over a chest of sovereigns.

There's a story how later, when Dad had gone and Nellie was thinking of getting married, there was some dispute between the families. Someone had suggested Nellie was marrying for money. Mum dragged her box out and showed it to the intended in-laws to prove we weren't poor just because we didn't live in a road with trees. 'That's my Jewish side,' she said. 'Romany, too, I suppose.'

Mum had an insurance policy to pay for her funeral, small endowments for us when we were twenty-one, but nothing else. She nurtured a deep suspicion of 'paper promises'. She and her family had been through what they called the Great Depression, which had lasted well into the 1890s. When she'd met my Dad she was reluctantly going into service.

She was too much of an egalitarian to show respect for authority just for the sake of it, and she defied respectability, too. From the first year she was married, she regularly took the tram up to the Corinthians in New Jewry. Mostly to see Marie Lloyd, whom she adored. She always went on her own. I suspect she reckoned it wasn't right to take kids. They had a Ladies Only bar by then. And she'd always have a pint of Guinness in the course of the evening, coming home a little jolly. Otherwise she generally drank half a pint, but no more, at suppertime. To keep up her strength, she said.

We ate well. Most of our stuff was homemade. Mum was a dedicated putter-up of pickles, pies and preserves. She had routines. We always knew when the time came round for beetroot jars or saltbeef or apple butter or plum puddings. And we had a huge pantry, which she tended to keep locked, to stop us pinching the pickles and crystallised fruit. She refused to use the butcher two doors down because she'd seen rats in their yard. The same went for the baker's. She wouldn't accept that most yards had rats. Ours didn't, she said, because she kept enough cats.

Really she just had a passion for moggies. When Tizer died of kidney failure, she sat in her chair with him in her lap for over twenty-four hours, then took him to the pet cemetery at Streatham and had him buried. It wasn't cheap. His stone said TIZER: Born Nairobi, 1909. Died Tooting, 1930. You can go and see it. It's still there, if it hasn't been vandalised. He was a wonderful old cat, that Tizer.

One day I came home and Dad was sitting in Mum's room, on his own, drunk. It was probably Monday. Everyone else was out doing something, including Nellie, who was round at Aunty Rachel's getting her piano lesson. The worst thing was he was sitting in Mum's grieving chair.

'And how's my little princess?' he said. He knew he shouldn't be in that chair. I was alarmed, but fascinated by his affrontery, what might be his courage. He told me to come and give my old Dad a peck on the cheek. Then he sat me up on his knee and bounced me and kissed me and I was a bit startled, because I was too old for it and he'd never done it much before. I wanted to go to the lavatory. I was praying I wouldn't pee on his leg. Then Mum bustled into the hall with Nellie, shouting for me, saw him and he turned very funny. Very placatory. Put me down with his hands round my waist. It hurt. I stood there for a moment in the silence. Then I was sent out with Nellie to get some butter Mum had forgotten.

Next day Dad was gone for good. Almost without trace. I don't think it had anything to do with me. I knew he'd overstepped the mark at last, sitting in her special chair. She had the locks changed right away. I heard her talking to her sister, who had come up from Brighton. 'I sometimes think I prefer the company of the dead,' she said. 'It's the peace. They stop struggling.' I didn't understand her. I probably heard wrong. But she'd sat out her share of death, one way or another.

Not many remember the big tram crash of 1929, partly because of the City news. The tram came off the rails on the corner and almost smashed through our front windows. It was a terrible accident. Mum had been on her way home. She was one of the first there. She helped a dozen people until the ambulances started turning up. This old lady died in her arms, blood running down her head. Mum said she couldn't get the stench of death out of her nostrils for months, though Freddy said it was probably the butcher's she was smelling.

Mum wouldn't let us come near. There were two dead little boys whose heads had been crushed. Twins. Nobody in Tooting saw worse in the war. It was pretty gruesome. Sammy told me the details later. It made me queasy. I nearly passed out. I've always had a weak stomach. I can't watch the news. I won't let people tell me things like that any more. Why fill your head with horror you can't do anything about? You just worry all the time. Mum sat through her personal storms in her chair, I suppose. I'd need a drink at that point. But Mum didn't drink except for her usual Guinness. Nora said Dad had done enough boozing for all of us.

I was the only one who occasionally missed Dad. Mum joked that I was always flirting, but I don't think I really was. I just didn't like to offend anyone. Everyone said I was highly strung. It wasn't attention I needed, it was approval, security to be left alone. So I don't think I loved him. I just trusted him in a way. It was as if I could make a deal with him. I've tried to explain it in the past. As if I could buy privacy by giving in to him for a little while. He wanted to know the old smile worked for him. I wanted to be daydreaming in my own world. But the reality was nasty.

When he left we were all upset. Mum told us under no circumstances to let him in if he came round to the flat. And he did come round. Usually in the evening when he'd had a few. She instructed us not to answer the door and went into her room. Can you imagine? Not answering the door to your own Dad? But Mum wouldn't have it different, and we cared a lot more for her approval than his.

Do you know how hard it is to disobey your Dad? Particularly back in those days. I remember shivering on the other side of the big, curtained door and crying. 'I can't, Dad. I can't. Don't, Dad. Don't.' I didn't dare shout at him to go away and leave me in peace.

'Come on, darling, open it for me. It's just your Daddy.'

My stomach turned over and I continued to cry silently as he cajoled me through the letter box. 'Come on, princess. Come on, little 'un.' I used to dread it and would try to be somewhere else in the house at any time he was likely to arrive, just so I wouldn't have to say no to him. Mum would let Nellie off, but I was part of her anti-Dad guard. I never blamed her. I was always on her side. But I just hated doing it.

I was congratulating myself that I'd got avoiding him down to a fine art when I came out of school one day after gym, and there he was, all glittering false teeth and cosmetic dash. He was wearing that cream suit of his with a straw hat. His new moustache gave him a bit of a Ronald Coleman look from a distance. He said he was passing and did I mind if he joined me on the tram home? What could I say? Apart from his face, which, close-up, was a map of Mars, he looked dapper and genial as ever. He always wore a fresh pink rosebud in his lapel. On Armistice Day he wore a poppy. 'Call me old-fashioned,' he'd say, 'but I'm a bit of a patriot.'

When the tram came he bowed me aboard like a lady. He knew the tram conductor by name. He paid my fare. I was already in profit. He made a friendly enquiry about the conductor's wife. I loved those trams, rattling, bouncing, sparking and swaying, with their scarlet and brass, their reversible wooden seats varnished almost orange. There was always a chance they'd go somewhere new. When the tram reached the terminus you ran along the grooved wooden floors thumping the seats back on their big oiled brass hinges. All the metal was worn and golden, and everything had that strange metallic smell of electricity.

I got off at the usual stop and he went on. And that was all. Of course, he told me not to tell Mum, but that suited me. I'd rather feel a bit guilty and still be able to see them both. I cheered up. He started taking the tram with me a couple of times a week.

Once he bought me a quarter of toffees, which I had to stuff down before I got home. Then I couldn't eat my tea and was sick, and Mum was worried and let me have the next morning off. Dad had that way of 'not wanting to worry people' with too much information. Soon he'd meet me almost every day. I had to make up delayed trams and late chats with teachers at school to explain the odd half-hour. Once or twice she noticed chocolate on me, and I said another kid had given me some. I remember my first conscious lie to her and how easy it was and how she believed me and there were no consequences. It worked. Life became easier.

One Monday Dad said he was going to show me where he lived. Would I like that? I was really curious. It might put the picture together for me, I thought. Maybe explain why he'd left. He said he'd have me home in an hour, long before Mum got back. My knees were knocking, but I felt excited, too. I'd know something even Mum didn't know about him.

So we stayed on the tram for another two stops and got off at Mitcham Road. His road was called Undine Street and he was about halfway down on the left. A nice road, I thought, with trees in it. I was impressed when we went into a proper garden but then wondered why we had to go up so many stairs to the top of the house. 'My little hide-away,' he laughed. 'Bai Jove, Bai Jove, Ai'hm a comical cove!'

I think it was what they used to call a bed-dinette. All one room with a kitchen area curtained off. It had a cold feel and stank of grease, tobacco and beer. There was a big wardrobe, a single bed covered with a green silk counterpane, a table and chair and an old horsehair sofa. A bit of faded carpet on cracked lino. Mum wouldn't have tolerated it. She set high store by appearances. Sporting papers and race cards were everywhere. And empty bottles. I didn't want to stay, but he said I'd hurt his feelings if I didn't accept his hospitality. So I sat on the edge of his bed and drank some tea I didn't like and ate a piece of stale buttered bun that looked as if he'd brought it home from a Lyons tea shop in his pocket.

Dad was in a very sentimental mood. I knew from the familiar smell that his cup didn't have tea in it. That smell made me feel sick, and it was so close and nasty in there. I got a headache. I think I must have fainted. My weak stomach was always my worst enemy. I probably threw up. The next thing is I'm going out his door and I'm in Garratt Lane, still feeling weak, while he tells me I need some fresh air. Maybe a glass of lemonade? I say I want Mum. He thinks there must be a gas-leak in his room. Just say I met you from school, he keeps telling me. Say you were sick before I saw you.

I remember him delivering me back home and Mum not talking much to him. He didn't seem to want to come in.

I'm not sure what she said, because she went out on to the landing to say it, but I never saw him at my school or on the tram again. I think I caught a glimpse of him once or twice in the street. I waved but he never said hello.

The next day there was a funny question about my clothes. Mum'd found a spot of blood and wanted to know if I'd been scratching myself. I couldn't remember, I said. I really couldn't. She started asking more questions. And then I lied. I don't know why. I said, Oh, yes, I'd been climbing a tree. I'd put some iodine on it. But this time she didn't seem reassured. I said I had to go to the toilet. I used a pin to scrape my leg in case she wanted to see it. But I never really knew why she'd mentioned the blood.

Funnily enough she sat in her chair for a day or two after that, even though nobody was dead. It was more like she was thinking, as well as praying. Something about Dad, maybe? She was nice to me, so it couldn't have been the lies. Later she talked to me a bit about telling the truth sometimes being harder than not. And the difference between pretending and deceiving. For instance, she said, Dad didn't know the difference between a game and reality. It meant nothing much to me, although it probably helped me think of going into the theatre.

By then I'd started reading those *Playgoer* magazines Lily gave me, and it was dreamland for years and years. I got in with a crowd Nellie knew. They did local theatricals and things. I told them all sorts of stuff and they believed me. I told them I'd been schooled by nuns in Portugal. That my father was an exiled Spanish count. I fell out with Nellie for a while, because she wouldn't back me up. It was only for fun. Just white lies. They didn't do anyone any harm.

I was married and twenty when I got my first real job in Dicky Diamond's Pierrots. At first Mum wasn't sure about it, but she spoke to Dicky himself who offered all sorts of guarantees and contracts. No mixed accommodation or facilities, I heard him tell her. Entertainers were in demand. It paid to stay wholesome. I'd hear him say that a few times in the coming years. Les was all right about it, too. Of course, I didn't know why. Then I got into films and was offered the Jessie

Mathews parts she didn't want, because I looked quite a lot like her apparently, though I could only see it when dressers posed me in her style. I could dance like her, that sort of slinky stepping and kicking that went out when American dancing came in.

Like Jessie, I didn't have luck with men. I expected too much of them, I suppose. All I've wanted for years is my cats and my little garden. A comfortable easy chair. Something decent on the telly. I think it's really all Mum ever wanted, too. Most of my career, though, there was something in me that really craved a chap's approval, even when I was starring in the West End. Well, obviously that kind of approval's the easiest thing in the world to get. So you wind up never valuing it for long. Chaps aren't a lot different, are they?

We were touring the South Coast that wonderful summer of 1939 and I was still married to Les Andrews when I heard that Dad had died. It was a stroke, apparently. They found him on the steps of the Horse and Groom. We were finishing the season, so I was able to pop up from Worthing to see Mum and help with the arrangements. I stayed two or three nights in my old room. What surprised me was that while she was withdrawn and briskly sad, she never once sat in her chair. It was as if she was avoiding it.

After we buried him in Streatham Cemetery with the other Lees, Mum didn't want to go home. We were with her, all nine of us. Jimmy was over from Washington. Ellie came on the boat train from Paris, where she was living with an Italian count who couldn't get a divorce. Everyone else still lived nearby, then, in Norbury and Streatham. Sammy was furthest away in West Kensington. We had a brief reception at Aunty Rachel's in Khartoum Road. Then we were all expecting to go back to the flat. We thought that was where Mum would want to be. But she took us up to Streatham Hill on the tram. We were mystified. Her treat, she said. We were going to the pictures. Not the old ABC or the State, but the new Astoria. These days they'd call it a luxury cinema. They charged top prices because the posh films were shown there first after they left the West End. Mum had a big white five-pound note. She paid for everything, including ice creams. It was like being kids again, only better. This time we sat in the half-crown seats, which were wonderful, almost like sitting at home. We watched *Dark Victory* with Bette Davis, George Brent and Humphrey Bogart.

Mum cried all the way through.

Watcher

Tamara Smith

He's there again. I close my eyes in the dark, click my heels together and say, *There's no such thing as paranoia.* At times like this, it's quiet enough to hear the dust settling on the floorboards.

Ridiculously, I managed to reach the age of fifteen before discovering that seahorses actually exist in nature. In spite of all potential exposures to the truth, I had assigned them to the realm of childhood fantasy along with flying. Then, one day, here in this flat for no apparent reason, a little seahorse popped into my consciousness, as a photograph mysteriously dropped through my letterbox in an unmarked white envelope. It was like a diamond, a little gift of magic pulled back into the real world. A consolation prize for all the other disappointments of growing up. Alchemy.

Now, I believe that anything can happen. I hear they are using leeches as computers now, and cucumbers as conductors of light. When I open my eyes again, the lone security guard has disappeared, to patrol the deeper workings of the massive mock-Egyptian monstrosity opposite my flat. At night, this one, anonymous, black-uniformed figure fills that entire, deserted building with more presence than hundreds of daytime office workers. Sometimes, he stands squarely at the window and just looks at me, for all the world as if I couldn't see him in that brightly lit space. He never makes a sign, and doesn't seem to care that I see him staring directly at me.

It feels like New York here, because the buildings are tall and the streets are narrow. But this is the eastern edge of the City of London, where the ghosts of Victorian prostitutes in Leman Street, E1, sidle up to the plastic shine of company headquarters not quite prestigious enough to have landed the granite and steel of an EC1 address. Living across from these offices is like peering out from the nineteenth-century squalor, the rotting bricks of Jack the Ripper territory, on to a Vegas theme hotel. There is a large family who live on the floor above mine, who have never quite worked out how to use the trash disposal system in the building. I often see dirty nappies hurtling past my window, and wonder what the office workers make of their being located here.

While you can't see the pavements from this height, the two build-ings are just close enough that you could actually shout across to all those bad suits hardwired to their computers. If you wanted to. At night, you are just close enough to see the features of a single face, an expression. Close enough to read his lips, to watch the rise and fall of his shoulders as he breathes. And just far away enough to keep the intimacy insubstantial.

Scanning the acres of empty desks to track him down makes this game a two-way thrill. Who is watching whom? He is as unknown and threatening as a stalker, but increasingly I feel defined by him more than anything else in my existence. He knows where I live, which frightens me, but still I'm drawn to him. In my hours of sleeplessness I indulge in perceiving him as benign, desirable. His presence makes the tenacious stench of death lessen for a little while in my room. I find myself hoping he is the one sending me the sea-horses. I touch the cold surface of the window with my fingertips and it feels like a come-on.

For a second, I catch sight of his figure moving between doorways at the rear of the building. I can't be sure though. Hundreds of softly glowing computer monitors sit and wait patiently through the night as their human owners fulfil their organic need for sleep. The screen-savers are like the dreams of each little pining machine. In their open-plan proximity, they have shared nightmares of running away through brick labyrinths. Sometimes, when the wind buffets the windows, I can see the monitors breathing gently in their sleep, short circuiting in wet dreams of exotic fish. Please touch screen to resume.

In those distorted window reflections, the night sky reveals a strange map of stars by which to navigate reality. My horoscope is determined by refraction. Closer to the ground, though not much, the reflection of Canary Wharf, like a bright star in the East, blinks at me benignly. If I take two steps back into the darkness, it looks like a fat and bloated semaphore; up close to the window it morphs through the uneven glass into the campanile in Piazza di San Marco. This is how I perceive everything these days. Mirrored, abstract truth, turned inside out by surveillance. Why not? What's the difference? On the shipping for cast from the radio in my bedroom, it is announced that another lighthouse station has lost its identity.

Watcher

In the morning, nothing is as enigmatic. Huge depths of perspective and light, within flat panes of glass, show wobbly Docklands Light Railway tracks stretching from Tower Gateway to infinity, with toy trains meandering through meeting rooms. The ultra-modern – the new world – reflects the old East End; the Promised Land remembering its cradle of immigrants through the centuries. Italians, Jews, hospitals, asylums, synagogues, mission houses, mosques, recordings atomised from redbrick minarets.

I feel bold again in the daylight and miss my security guard. He knows I exist, and this makes him a great comfort to me. Lately it feels like nothing I do has an effect on the physical world. I can't even get rid of the dust in my apartment. I try to imagine what my watcher is like as a person, what he does in the daytime. Maybe he has the power to become invisible, or transform himself into another beast. Perhaps he sleeps with arms crossed over his chest in a corporate catacomb.

Paranoia remains persistent through the day, however, and pursues me like a stalker. Outside my flat, a little harmony of car-door bells follows me as I go about my business. Your door is open; your lights are on; you aren't wearing your seat belt; don't forget to exist. The invasion of technology feels personal. Intrusive like a mother, invasive like an assault. On the splendrous tips and domes of the Egyptian plastic cladding, I notice a surprisingly large crow patrolling the office rooftop. A sharp black against the cold blue sky, he looks ridiculously out of place. Starlings better suit this area of infinite migration. Like a sentry strayed from the Bloody Tower, the crow circumvents the closed-circuit cameras trained on my window. He is the only element from nature on my horizon. A familiar.

The window washer's cradle also squats on the roof, a big metal trough for two men. Its enormous crane arms look long enough to swivel across the street to my window and pick me up, and I imagine the security guard sending it over to get me in the middle of the night. Bringing me back to him. I step out and he helps me on to the carpet tiles. Now that I am over here glancing back on my room across the street, it looks shockingly revealing, like a goldfish bowl. I am close enough now to distinguish his smell amongst the photocopier chemicals, plastic and stationery. I've touched his warm, living hand. Nothing is said, and it feels right to retain the silent way we have communicated until now.

I follow his heavy frame under the bright spotlights towards an end wall. There, we are still in full view of my room and I feel as if I am judging myself from my windowsill. Like a Caspar David Friedrich painting, I see myself from behind, with my hair in a bun, looking wistfully past my old wooden window on to a sea of great sailing ships, and off into the future.

We are also in full view of hundreds of computer monitors. Every one of them is monitoring us. Tiny little cameras on top of each screen record us, and send us out on to the internet like a virus. He takes my wrist and lifts it to the wall above my shoulder. With his other hand he gently pulls open my shirt, bends down and takes the very tip of my right nipple between his teeth. His tongue flicks across me quickly as he leans into my wrist, and I feel a needle line of sensation from right there in the deep centre of my breast all the way down to the pit of my stomach.

As I focus absentmindedly on my own window again, two palm prints outlined in a trace of sweat begin to fade from the glass. I run my finger along the shapes, but the moisture is on the outside. There is an enormous thud as the post hits the wooden floor in the hall, and my palms tingle at the shock.

More images in an unmarked white envelope. I must be careful what I wish, but I do find myself wishing that he is sending me all this. His way of communicating. There are drawings of Execution Dock in Wapping just to the south of here, where pirates were hung and then left pinned to the dock wall for three tides to wash over them. I look over to the empty flagpoles on top of the Egyptian temple and laugh to imagine the Jolly Roger flapping merrily in the breeze as the company's corporate branding.

Next, dozens of strange photographs of a dingy basement with arched openings radiating out from it. Close-ups of the individual arches show that all but one is blocked with detritus, bricks and rubbish. One opening has been cleared, and more images show a long passage leading from it towards a white space. Photos of the inside of the room show that it is igloo-shaped and covered from floor to ceiling with white tiles. Bolted into the walls at regular intervals are heavy, rusted chains connected to iron manacles. The horror of the space is not about death; for some reason it feels to be more about waiting, imprisonment, fading away into weakness.

Watcher

I've heard that there are basements in the houses in Fournier Street, in Spitalfields just north of here, where buried rivers still run. If there are heavy storms, the old Fleet River still floods the cellars in Farringdon Street. Once-mighty watercourses carried drowning cows and bedsteads from the hills north of London all the way to the Thames. Escaping from imprisonment in that white-tiled room along an incarcerated river, and to be gushed into the Thames, must have been the mortally dangerous part. One will have been spat out like a dead dog. For those drowned souls lucky enough to be identifiable and reunited with their families, a flat table-like tombstone was advisable, so that relatives could sleep on top to protect the body from nightly grave robbers.

Yet more post. The Last Post. As if intended to connect me with the Jewish past of this area, information leaflets about Cabbalism and Jewish mysticism. The old concept of the Watcher in Judaism hits me like a wave. The Watcher was the person appointed to take care of the soul of the deceased, until the Kaddish could be spoken and the soul allowed to find its final resting place. All this is from him, and I know that if I dash downstairs, and run across the road now to hold him, thank him, he won't be there any more.

I close my eyes one more time in the darkness of my room, lay my arms across my chest, click my heels together, and let the dark waters of an underground river carry me to the mouth of the Thames. There I am whole, released into nothingness. The silvery meandering expanses of the broad Thames breathe me out past the monolith of Canary Wharf, the factories of Silvertown where they used to crush and boil horses to make soap, and on past row upon row of caravans lining the Isle of Sheppey. I will myself across the early-evening flats of the estuary to find a better resting place, perhaps like the pirates wished themselves back to the Caribbean on their third tide, where millions of seahorses are mother, father, lover, and beautiful.

Suicide note

Courttia Newland

> *'What reason weaves, by Passion is undone'*
> Alexander Pope

Hot water cascaded from shiny metal taps, to foam, bubble and churn in the bath. Steam rose, swirled, made the air around him hot and moist, heightening his feeling of sensuality, caressing his pores. Welling stuck out his tongue and could feel the tiny particles landing gently, as they'd already landed on his naked arms, shoulders, and buttocks. He closed his eyes and arched his head back, giving in to the moment, relishing the moisture's light touch on his body, like a thousand lips kissing him all over.

He ran his own hands over himself slowly. Over his meaty chest, flat stomach, then down to his penis. Fingers splayed, he stroked the coarse and curly pubic hair, rubbing his balls lovingly, moving along the hard, veined ridges of his member until he reached the head. He pulled his uncircumcised foreskin back as far as he could; the action made him moan, low beneath his breath. His warm fingers curled into a fist, sliding his foreskin over the head; it disappeared, then returned as he repeated his actions. Slowly at first, then more rapidly as feeling grew inside him. Soon his fist was a blur, his breathing laboured.

The water had risen too high. He forced himself to stop and return his attentions to the bath, shutting off the taps. For a moment Welling stared at the steaming water as if it were a mirror and he could see some reflection of himself within its depths. His chest still rose and fell. He gripped the bath sides as he had his penis – firmly, possessively, as though unable to let go. When he realised what he was doing, he laughed to himself and climbed in.

Soap, flannel, pumice stone, razor blade. They were all there, sitting at the side of the tub. He picked up the soap and flannel, then washed himself methodically, making sure every crevice and pore was clean. When he was satisfied, the pumice stone had its turn, and he proceeded to scrub roughly at the hard bits of flesh on his toes and heels. Soon he'd smoothed them down. He put the grey piece of volcanic rock back, next to the soap and flannel.

Now for the razor blade.

He lay back as far as he could, knees in the air, toes just below the twin taps. The blade between the fingers of his right hand glinted like a devilish eye. He raised his left arm out of the water, staring in wonder at the map of veins, arteries and tendons. He'd always been a veiny person. Whenever his doctor needed a sample of blood, they used the needle without a garrote, as his veins were that obvious. He flexed his fingers up and down. The tendons moved in compliance, like pulleys. He smiled, then relaxed in the bath.

It was time.

Breathing lightly, he moved his right hand closer to his left. If he'd had an extra hand, it would have been holding his penis; he was excited, and his excitement grew the closer the blade got to skin. When the sharp corner touched his wrist he gasped with pent-up tension; then brought the blade across in one swift movement. He watched. For a moment there was nothing.

Then the skin went pale and blood abruptly came rushing to the surface.

Quickly, he did the same to his right wrist, then put both wrists in the tub and lay back. His hardened penis protruded from the water as though watching proceedings.

After fifteen minutes he knew it wasn't working.

The bath was getting cold and his blood wasn't filling the tub. There was a little bit of pink water where his arms were resting, but apart from that, nothing to mark what he'd done. He lifted them up, critically inspecting the slashes on each wrist. Wounds as fatal as paper cuts adorned them. They'd long stopped bleeding and were starting to sting from their introduction to the air. His penis sank back beneath the water, bored by the display.

He couldn't do it. As much as he wanted to, he simply couldn't do it. He didn't know if it was because of his Catholic upbringing or his love of pain – but every time that he tried, it just wouldn't work. Welling knew that he wanted to die. Had wanted it far too long, as he was fed up with being an outcast, different from the rest, a freak. Every quest to meet this end became another chance to explore his strange sexuality, rather than a real attempt at death. But he wanted to die. It had to happen before he went too far. Last week only served to prove him right. He didn't deserve to live, but loved himself too much to do the necessary thing.

That was him he supposed. Selfish to the last.

He'd known he was sick long before last week; course he had, it was too obvious to miss. But his time with Corelle was like sedative to a madman. She made him forget, made him docile, made him believe he was normal. This was an act he found increasingly hard to maintain before she came into his life.

Then he saw Suzanne, and he knew he couldn't kid himself any longer. He'd been at a coffee shop in Soho, his favourite prowling ground. He loved the place; it was all of his deepest thoughts embodied in dank staircases, neon lights, black rubber boots, whips and chains. He could stroll from street to street, his face blank, his mind whirring. He could enter the shops, the staircases, and nobody cared.

The girl appeared on the opposite corner of the street. He immediately noticed her and paused mid-sip, the rim of his coffee mug lightly touching his lower lip. Her skin was darker than ink, and she was tall, mature, dignified. Her hair was tied back, resting loosely against her neck. A broad red bag packed with books and girlie fanzines hung from her shoulder. Her grey school skirt was short, exposing smoothly curved legs to his gaze.

The girl was exquisite.

He watched as she talked with her gathering of school friends. She was easily the tallest of the group, the most physically mature, and also a ringleader judging by the other girls' actions – which, through the window of the bar, proved as entertaining as a mime show. They laughed and gossiped, mini-caricatures of grown women, loud and raucous, oblivious to glances of Soho passers-by. Fifteen minutes later they were still there, him watching her every move, entranced by the unconscious fluidity of her girlhood. She was aware of her growing body, but her awareness was detached somehow – the way she played with her ponytail, ran a hand absently along her thigh, and licked her lips before she spoke; all constant accompaniment to words he could not hear. After a further twenty minutes by his watch, the group of girls said their reluctant goodbyes and went off in different directions. Suzanne (although he didn't know that was her name yet) shouldered her bag in a weary manner and walked right past his window seat, on the opposite side of the road. She was alone. Quickly, without any thoughts over his actions, he downed the cold coffee he'd been nursing and rapidly left the shop.

As he'd walked behind the girl, Welling recognised that his behaviour at this point could be classified as highly irrational. Such thoughts were rare, mostly confined to early morning hours alone in bed, when things that he'd done over the years sunk in, saturating his brain. She was a schoolgirl. A little older than fifteen, possibly as young as twelve. As for him… He was pushing forty. Pushing forty, his mind full of lurid scenarios involving a teenage girl who could almost be his daughter. Forty years old, filled with a sickness he couldn't control. Harbouring feelings that leaked down his inside thigh as he walked.

It only took one look at the girl to dispel his misgivings, as surely as a broom dispels dust. She strode proudly, head high, weaving through the crowd of commuters with a mature confidence that he found all the more enticing.

Sometimes, somehow, this was the most exciting part. When they didn't know him, hadn't met him, and were open to his unshielded gaze. He cast his eyes over calves that tensed athletically as she walked. Up to the back of her thighs, which did the same, rippling smoothly. Further upward, to the hemline of her brief skirt, tightening over rounded bum cheeks that rolled left, right, left… He grew harder at the sight, his lower stomach crying out in pain, his want all consuming. It was impossible to suppress. He walked faster, caught her up, and placed a hand just above her elbow. Startled, she turned around to face him.

He knew he'd be all right when she took in his features; her shock was quickly replaced with curiosity. She raised her eyebrows in a silent question.

'Oh…' he stuttered. 'I thought –'

She continued to stare, amused by his seeming discomfort.

'I thought –' he continued stiltedly. The timing had to be right. 'Are you – you're a singer aren't you?'

She put her hands on curving hips, smiling coyly and displaying perfect white teeth. He was stunned. She was even more gorgeous close up.

'Why, do I look like a singer?' she replied.

'You're that girl from that R&B group ain' you? Fierce or suttin' like that. You sing the lead, right?'

She giggled and shook her head.

'Everybody says that, says I look like her. It ain' me though. I can sing but I ain' in a group yet.'

They looked each other over and Welling could see was sizing him up. Teenage girls loved the fact that older men were interested in them, but at the end of the day, you couldn't look too old. He was a bit wrinkly around the eyes and mouth, and had found some grey hairs over the last few months; but he jogged, worked out, and ate well, so he knew he looked more than adequate.

Suzanne seemed to agree, as she was looking him boldly in the eye, closing the space between them until there was barely any left. Although she was tall for her age, she still had to look up to achieve this task. Sweat burst out on his forehead as her warm breath caressed his chin.

'Why, are you a music manager or suttin'?'

She's got to be kidding, he thought wryly.

'Nah… I'm an artist. I paint pictures and I think you're quite beautiful. I'd like to paint your portrait. Please.'

She giggled again, playing her coy act once more, stepping from foot to foot before gazing back up at him.

'Thank you,' she breathed, mouth open, lips glistening from apricot balm, the odour surrounding her like an aura. Her eyes were dark and slanted, blinking at him openly. She was standing so close he could see his reflection in them.

It was easy as that.

Over the next few weeks, Suzanne became a regular visitor to his west London towerblock home, which doubled as the studio where he exercised his craft. He took his time painting her, using pencils to sketch an outline, then expensive oils to colour and define her further. Suzanne was quick-witted and feisty. She was a willing model who refused to pose, instead sitting in a relaxed and natural manner, eagerly obeying his commands to turn and hold still. They talked as he worked, and got to know each other's minds as he familiarised himself with her body, learning more with each line he painted.

Their once-a-week meeting grew into twice, then three times. Sessions became longer, stretching far into the night. On these occasions, he'd call for a cab to drive the girl to her Harlesden home; and though he wondered what she told her parents, he never dared to ask for fear of the answer. He knew she hadn't told her friends about him, for when they called on her mobile phone, she was furtive and vague about her whereabouts.

They smiled and touched a lot, more often recently. He liked her quietly assured confidence, her very real maturity; and somewhere inside, he began to believe Corelle's absence was really a good thing.

During one particular late night session, an unusual silence had fallen between them, comfortable despite its length. Welling concentrated on Suzanne's portrait, which framed her head and shoulders, irradiating clear eyes, high cheekbones, baby-smooth skin. Frowning, he flicked his paintbrush over the cleft of the painted Suzanne's chin, before standing back and thinking for a second, comparing his subject with her likeness.

Suzanne was sitting with a hand against her head, teeth clenched and wincing with pain. The glass of Holsten Pils she'd asked for when she arrived still sat by her feet where she'd placed it, untouched. His concern was instant.

'You OK?'

Suzanne looked up morosely. 'I got a headache. It's killin' me, man.'

'I got some painkillers in the bathroom if you want 'em.'

'Yeah, all right. Thanks.'

She got to her feet shakily, walking past him and out into the bathroom. He continued to paint a little longer, then gave up and took another three steps back. The painting was looking very good. He was so obviously inspired it frightened him somehow – as if here, with Suzanne, he'd crossed some boundary, never to return. Welling sighed and placed his brush in a pot of water by his easel, then walked over to his window, staring at the expanse of lights and streets that made up London.

Maybe things *were* getting too deep. He was supposed to be trying to stop, trying to change the way he looked at the world. Corelle leaving him was the test he'd been sure he could pass – then he'd seen Suzanne and found himself mesmerised by her beauty. Now her eyes took him in deeply, while he fantasised about her in return. He'd thought he was stronger than that.

It was going to happen and there was nothing he could do about it.

Welling sat staring into the night for almost half an hour longer, before he suddenly realised that Suzanne hadn't returned. Going after her, he found the teenager sitting on the edge of the bath, crying silently but passionately into her hands. A quick glance around the bathroom informed his eager eye of the cause – the open cabinet, with its contents of deodorants, painkillers, Listerine, and an open box of Corelle's tampons. He looked from the open cabinet to the girl, then back again. Gently, he perched beside Suzanne on the bath rim, reaching out a hand.

'Suzanne, don't get like that –'

'I thought you said you was single!' she blubbered through her tears, pushing him away with a wet hand. He slid closer to the taps and stayed where she'd pushed him, replying calmly.

'I am single…'

'Then what's that?'

She pointed at the offending blue box. They craned their necks upwards, then looked down at the lino.

'That's my ex girlfriend's. She hasn't lived here for three months.'

Actually, she'd moved out three weeks prior to him meeting Suzanne, but telling her that wouldn't make her feel any better. The schoolgirl had been meticulously determined to hide any real feelings for him, though she could flirt with the best of them. They'd hugged, kissed and she'd even massaged him once (clothes on), yet throughout she'd upheld a healthy distance between them. All at once, he was faced with what he'd been fantasising about. As if he'd called it into being, here was his final test.

Welling looked over her curves and he knew he'd failed.

'You must think I'm jus' a stoopid little kid,' Suzanne was complaining tearfully. 'All my friends told me you'd be like dis, and they was right.'

'Don't say that.' He took her hand. She allowed this contact, still refusing to hold his imploring gaze. 'If I did have a girlfriend, don't you think you would have seen her? After all, you've bin here four or five times a week, the past four weeks. If my ex had was living here, you would've met by now, don't you reckon? What d'you think?'

'I've only bin 'ere three times a week,' she replied haughtily.

He laughed, unable to stop himself lightly touching her hair. Suzanne stiffened, but still defied his attention, eyes latched to the aqua blue tiled walls. His fingers strayed from her hair, to her cheekbones, then her lips, caressing their softness tentatively, his eager mind loosely tethered by a last link with morality – which was, in turn, further diminished by the actions of this girl-child sat before him. Suzanne abruptly closed her eyes, leant her head back, and let her dark-tinged lips fall open, tongue exploring the roughened ridges of his digits. Surprised, but not unwilling, he allowed her to continue, part of him wondering if this was the way she sucked ice poles on her way home from school – and while he was shocked at the thought, he was also aroused – undeniably aroused. He slid his way along the bath, moving closer to the girl, who turned to him blindly, lips parted, eyes still closed.

Their kiss began clothed in innocence, but was quickly stripped bare until their passion was exposed in the dim light of the room. Her youthful probing was filled with confidence of maturity, though her imitations of his lust belied how much she had yet to learn. Welling parted her legs with the same fingers that had been pressed between her lips – though now they squeezed and kneaded warm thighs, sure in their quest, ceaseless in their journey.

She opened her legs wider to ease his passage. He traced the hem-line of her knickers, then rubbed the fleshy mound. She rested one foot up on the toilet bowl. He moved the knickers to one side, know-ing he'd found what he sought when Suzanne cried out – a keening exhalation of breath that had her clutching his shoulder in response. She was tight, creamily wet, her pleasure dampening her inner thighs. He rubbed harder as she became moister, deeper as her hips writhed in pleasure, faster as she sucked hard on his tongue.

He felt orgasm flood her body and knew Suzanne was his. She kissed him soulfully and he lifted her into his bedroom.

Their relationship took a new turn, became more intense and demand-ing. Though he'd wanted her to fall for him, Welling hadn't been able to foresee exactly how hard Suzanne would hit the ground – and what the effects would be. Within two months, the happy-go-lucky, sassy young thing had changed into a brooding, paranoid girlfriend, ever watchful of her man. Admittedly, he didn't handle this transition well. He stopped calling so often, snapped at her when she complained about his lack of attention, and openly spoke of other women he knew. Suzanne, whose die-hard attitude had been reined in, but not quite captured, found herself backed into a corner from which she came out fighting. She screamed at him, smashed plates in fury, and when all of this went unheeded, she committed the ultimate sin – destroying his painting of her, first by using his oils to deface it, then grabbing a knife from the kitchen and puncturing the picture in several places. All of this because a female friend had rung the flat, asking Suzanne if Welling was ready to paint her portrait. He'd been out at the shops when this happened, and the teenager's actions finally pushed him past the point of no return. The sight of the torn canvas, as thin and fragile as human skin, ignited his anger in a way that she'd never seen. He hit her, many times, until she was a bawling heap on his studio floor, mouth and nose streaming with blood. He noted the thick, glassy redness a moment before shock rolled in. Then it was: 'Suzanne, I'm so sorry, Suzanne please forgive me…'

She stared up at him in disbelief, allowing herself to be helped to her feet, allowing him to move her to a chair, sit her down, and run into the bathroom for the first-aid kit. When he returned, the seat where he'd placed Suzanne was empty – apart from a scrap of paper that shuddered in the breeze from an open window, as though alive and feeling the cold. First-aid kit in hand, he walked towards the message slowly, lifted it with a heavy heart, and looked down. Two words were scrawled with what looked like one of his 4B pencils – two words, no more, no less.

I'm pregnant.

And that was the last time he ever saw Suzanne.

Fate eventually led him to the lonely BT telephone box, on that windy Soho street where he'd met with destiny. He'd taken his failed suicide attempt as a sign that he should force some contact with Suzanne, if only for the sake of his child. When his numerous phone calls provided no joy and he tired of her repeated answer phone message, he took to sitting in the coffee shop where he'd first laid eyes on her – day in, day out, with no reprieve or success. He drank so many cappuccinos his nights were as lengthy as his days and his eyes grew dark rings that emphasised his stress.

Prowling the dingy side streets was a tiring task. He saw many school-girls in those lonely days, none Suzanne.

Then one afternoon, out of the corner of his eye, Welling saw her – that head-high, confident walk and swinging black ponytail. He jumped out of his seat, pushed past an elderly foreign couple just entering the shop and ran recklessly after her. When he reached the corner of the block, it was apparent he'd lost her. He swore in a frus-tration and desperate anger, startling suits and shoppers alike. Looking wildly from side to side, he saw the BT telephone box standing like a beacon – a signal pulsing for him alone.

An idea quickly took root. If she was in Soho, her mobile might be on. He could call and get her to meet him. They could make amends.

He crossed the road and fairly flew into the box, inserting his change and dialling as soon as he could; then waiting, breath held deep inside his lungs. Two beats and nothing. Four, and still that empty static of an electronic world. Five, and he received the deafening three tones that indicated a disconnected line. He slumped against the glass of the box in defeat, the handset falling by his side. Suzanne's number had been the only real link he'd had. If that was gone it meant that he'd surely lost her.

Agony for his unseen child – his only child – consumed him, as wholly as a killer whale consumes a seal. He sobbed in stomach-wrenching pain, then looked up at the box ceiling as if in silent protest to the Most High.

There was a card on that ceiling. Fluorescent pink, stuck with Blu-tak, hanging like ripened fruit, demanding to be picked. At first he mistook it for the calling card of a prostitute, and he looked back down at his feet, recapturing his pain. He closed his eyes. The words he'd seen for the tenth of a second flashed in his mind – now he saw them with the clarity of a Golden Eagle. Shocked, in one fluid movement, he looked back up, reaching for the pink card and holding it close. He hadn't been mistaken. It said what he had seen.

SUICIDE NOTE
020 8932 2005

The words kept replaying in his head. Suicide Note. What did that mean? Could he dare to believe it was what he thought? That, at the very moment where hope had seemed useless, there was a glimmer of light?

He didn't know the answer to any of those questions, but his finger found NEXT CALL, and he dialled the number on that pink card all the same.

The office was on the tenth floor of a towerblock in Farringdon. The block seemed to house a myriad of small businesses in a rabbit warren of passages and doors. The receptionist on the other end of the line had given him an address and door number, both of which he'd scribbled on to the back of the pink card. When he reached room D-474, he stopped and looked at the rectangle of bright colour once more, then back at the door. It was a plain, unpainted wood-brown colour, devoid even of varnish, bearing only two letters – one S, one N. Welling took these letters to mean that he was in the right place, and knocked once, entering when requested.

The reception area was kitted out in more wood-brown colours – pine, mahogany, oak, beech. The woman that he assumed had spoken to him on the phone got to her feet and crossed the room to greet him, arm outstretched.

'Mr Welling?'

'Yes…'

'Glad you could make it!'

She was an Oriental beauty with features close to perfection, long black hair, and a calm enthusiasm that surprised, yet comforted him. He saw that she had one grey eye and a brown one, which gave her face the feline look of a tiger. *She'd be amazing to paint*, he told himself. Welling hadn't touched his paintbrush since he'd hit Suzanne, which seemed like years ago. He wanted to ask the receptionist to pose for him, but settled for shaking her hand.

'Ms Grantham has just finished with another client – you can go right through,' she offered warmly, guiding him gently towards another doorway. He was jarred by the fact that this door, unlike any of the others in the office, was painted a glossy black, dark enough to see his reflection. A gold plaque told him that this was the office of Toby Grantham, Managing Director.

He was suddenly, inexplicably, very afraid.

'Thank you.'

It seemed to take for ever to reach the door, but before he could register that fact, he was there. He knocked. A muffled voice called for him to enter. He turned the gold doorknob and did as he was asked.

This office had a colour scheme that matched the reception room, though black and gold was mixed in amongst the wood panels. A huge bay window provided a panoramic view of London, and an equally large black and gold desk stood proudly in front. Sitting behind the desk with her back to the window, was a middle-aged white woman, full of smiles and attractively dressed in a lime-green suit. She got to her feet, her classy attire moulding itself to the curves of her body as she stood – he noticed that she was quite sexy, in a mature, dignified way. Her features were more attractive than pretty. A straight, pointed nose, chiselled jaw, ocean-blue eyes. Where the receptionist's orbs were friendly, Grantham's showed nothing but curiosity. He took her smooth, baby-soft hand within his own.

'Mr Welling…'

'Yes, that's right.'

'I'm Toby Grantham, Managing Director of Suicide Note. Sit down, make yourself comfortable. Would you like tea, coffee, orange juice?'

'Coffee please.'

He sat in the expansive black leather seat beside him, then looked around the office while Grantham spoke into a desk intercom, ordering their drinks. Books of all kinds lined the wall, on shelves that looked as though they were straining with their weight. Most seemed like hardback non-fiction, apart from a book sitting on the desk in front of him. He frowned, leaning closer to inspect the spine – yes, he knew it; this was a book he'd read. *The Five Gates of Hell* by Rupert Thomson. It was about a town that thrived on the business of funerals and death. He wondered if Grantham had read it yet, and whether that accounted for the cold gaze in her eyes.

'Coffee's on the way,' she told him, a tiny smile at the corner of her lips. She motioned at the book. 'Have you read it?'

'Yes, I have.'

'Good?'

'Not bad. Did you like it?'

'I did.' She beamed a perfect smile over the desk at him. 'You could say it was right up my street.'

He smiled vaguely, nothing to say to that. The woman had a creepy air that made any words he might have voiced die somewhere deep inside his throat. She watched him like an anxious baker waiting for bread to rise.

'Where did you come from?'

'The West End. Soho,' he replied, cursing himself for getting specific. 'I saw your card in one of the phone boxes.'

The woman smiled at him. 'That's great, really great.'

There was a long silence, in which he looked everywhere but at her, and she appraised him unashamedly. The Oriental receptionist knocked on the door, put their drinks down on the desk, then exited wordlessly. The rich smell of fresh coffee filled the room, its odour relaxing him somehow. He reached for a mug as if it were a lifeline and sipped eagerly.

'So, Mr Welling... How can we help you?'

Welling started right at the beginning – when he first discovered his passion for young girls, working up to the point where he'd met Suzanne. He was deeply embarrassed, especially having to tell a woman these things – but Toby Grantham's encouraging nods urged him on; pretty soon, he lost himself in the telling of the story. By the time he got to his failed suicide attempt, he was talking faster, more passionately, his penis a hard rod inside his jeans. He shifted a little, then stuttered to a halt, realising where he was once more.

'It's OK, Mr Welling, you don't have to say any more. Let me explain what Suicide Note is about.'

He nodded and sipped at his cooling coffee, anticipation adding to his desire.

'Suicide Note was founded by my father in 1980, who very sadly passed away in '92. The idea came from that old argument about euthanasia – you know, if a man or woman wants to take their life, is it right or wrong for someone to help them? My father thought the laws concerning this type of thing were antiquated, and completely irrelevant in some cases – such as yours. He founded this company to present a human way to provide such a service, and allow decent people the dignity of choice.

'Suicide Note works like this. We have an in-house psychiatrist who looks you over mentally, and a doctor to check the physical side of things. They're basically making sure you're of sound body and mind. When you've been passed and you're still sure you want to go through with things, you sign a contract with us to that effect, which bonds you to suicide. Think very carefully before you make that decision, Mr Welling – you can't turn the clock back once you've signed. We send all the papers to outside contractors after that. Once they receive your documents, you can't change things. They finish the job within two weeks.'

Finish the job, his mind repeated frostily. He gulped back the sudden lump that had formed in his throat.

'You said outside contractors – does that mean hit men?'

Grantham made a disgusted face.

'No – not hit men at all, Mr Welling. They're too humane to be called anything like that. Much of our staff is made up of ex-professional doctors and their like. There are certainly no guns or other weapons involved – death is usually painlessly achieved by lethal injection or a pill of some kind.'

She smiled again when she said that, then sat back and watched his reaction. Welling blinked, rubbing his head fitfully. When he closed his eyes, he saw Suzanne laying on his studio floor, mouth and nose streaming, hands on her lower stomach. He wanted to cry out to Grantham, tell her he never meant the girl any harm, he only wanted to love her; but she'd destroyed his art, and he'd reacted instinctively to that. It took another quick moment, but thinking back over all the young girls he'd seduced helped him put that particular episode into perspective. Suzanne, truth be told, wasn't the first he'd hit. There'd been others, for many other reasons.

Melanie had been sleeping with a boy from her school. Nadine had caught him going out of the house with Corelle. Tashee made a disparaging comment about his art one evening, and that had set him off once more. When he looked at his back catalogue, things were worse than he'd ever been able to admit.

Now this woman and her company urged him to accept what he was, make a decision about how to deal with it. He had to grab the lifeline he'd been offered. Either that, or drown in his own shit, taking every innocent girl he was destined to meet in future with him.

To her credit, Grantham waited patiently before speaking again. When she did, there was no pressure, no goading in her voice. Instead, it was tinged with curiosity and gentle caring, all rolled into one. He found himself eased by her pleasant tone.

'What do you think?'

Welling looked up with dampened orbs that glistened from tears.

'Do it,' he whispered to the woman. 'Do it.'

So they did.

He saw the physical doctor first, then, afterwards, the head doctor. When both were finished, he sat in the reception area reading a magazine, vainly attempting not to stare at the receptionist's legs. It took forty-five minutes, but he was eventually called back into Grantham's office, where he sat rubbing his sweaty palm against his thighs. He'd passed – and was legally certified in perfect physical and mental health – or at least well enough to die. His contract, a piece of A4 paper the exact shade of Grantham's ocean-blue eyes, sat on the desk in front of him, his full name neatly typed at the top. Grantham nodded and motioned for him to look it over. He took the contract and scanned the words, blurred vision and legal speak making the terms that much harder to read.

> PH Welling hereafter to be known as (THE CLIENT), being of sound mind and body, grants Suicide Note, hereafter to be known as (THE COMPANY) the divine right to perform an act of artificial suicide on behalf of THE CLIENT within two weeks, beginning from the date specified below...
>
> 15th June 2000

There was more, but none of the rest made any difference. He had to stop himself before he seriously hurt one of the girls that so innocently trusted in him. He signed his name at the bottom of the contract, then handed it over to Grantham with a tiny portion of relief lodged in his heart.

Welling arrived at the foyer of his towerblock less than three hours later. After leaving Farringdon, he'd found himself travelling back west – not to Soho, but to the South Bank – packed with as many tourists, but calmer, sedated, more serene. He walked the Thames, along a pathway that took him past Tower Bridge, London Bridge and others, until his legs could take him no further. From there he took a taxi home, thinking that he may as well spend the money – after all, he had no more need for pounds and pence.

Thoughts like those were victors in the fight for attention within his mind, whirling like kites caught by the strength of a blustery wind.

No more would he watch London lights under nightfall. No more would he marvel at female forms that graced grimy streets. No late-night Garage pirate stations, hot summers lazing in Hyde Park, or Sunday dinners with *EastEnders* on TV. It was all denied him now, never to be given back. There was no getting used to that fact. His copy of the ocean-blue contract burned a hole though his inside pocket; he knew why he'd signed, but the sight of his familiar scrawl on that paper had created a void he could never have imagined – and wouldn't wish on an enemy.

Welling was suddenly scared to die.

He stepped blindly through the foyer and over to a trio of lifts, pressing the call button almost in a trance. His hand was trembling. He looked at it, entranced by its gyrations, which were completely out of his control. The lift's bell pinged and the metal doors opened. He stepped inside.

'Paul…' came a hesitant voice behind him.

It's her, the voice inside him croaked in a whisper. He turned slowly, his heart leaping, almost unable to believe. But it was true. Corelle stood there, all five feet five of her, beautiful hazel eyes narrowed in concern.

She'd cut her hair; it curled in a short bob around her head, framing her face like open and closed brackets. The style suited her. Welling had to admit she was even more stunning than before.

'I came earlier, but you weren't home, so I waited… Do you mind?'

He shook his head mutely. If he spoke… If he spoke, it would all come tumbling out – everything he'd done, every backward step he'd taken.

'It's been so long. I missed you, Paul… I couldn't do it any longer. I forgive you. D'you get me? It doesn't matter any more, I forgive you.'

Welling gaped at her, unable to voice his emotions – unable to admit he'd been convinced he'd never see her again. Too many things had happened, too many girls, he'd messed up too many times… Surely he didn't deserve her back in his life. Corelle was one in a million, everybody said as much – she managed to touch everyone she came in contact with. She had one of those personalities – the kind that was loved by all. A woman like Corelle was almost too good to exist in a world as corrupt as the one he inhabited.

He wasn't good enough, but without her he was nothing – Welling had proved that beyond any doubt. Plus he needed her around him, now more than ever.

Whether he'd tell her about Suzanne, or the subsequent fall-out from that latest incident, was another, deeper matter.

'I'm… glad you came back… I missed you,' he stumbled, eyes cast down at the lift floor. She lifted his head with a light finger, he relishing her touch, Corelle staring into his eyes. They hugged tightly. She turned and pressed the button for his floor, guiding him, taking control almost as soon as she had appeared.

Luck and love had visited him in one fell swoop – he immersed himself in both, secure in the feeling. On that first night, they made up with a combination of Indian takeaway, bottles of beer and fierce love making, just as they'd done many times, all those months ago. It was good for him to get back into the world he knew, the woman he knew – his rightful space in time. They lay in bed for almost two days, catching up on all the things they'd experienced while apart – or reliving special moments they'd shared.

Corelle had given up her nursing job and found work as an assistant to a well-known male artist, attempting to gain experience by working with someone else. The sketches she showed him were of such a high standard, he wondered how close the relationship had been – but refrained from asking, his fear of knowledge defeating him once again. Instead, he told her of pictures he'd created in her absence, showing her abstract paintings of buildings, the woman who lived four floors down, and other indiscriminate things that had nothing to do with Suzanne, or the work he'd done with her.

The painting of the young girl was safely stashed at the bottom of a cupboard in his bedroom – gone, but not forgotten. His pact with Suicide Note was mentally treated in much the same fashion; pushed into a distant corner of his mind, unwanted for now, but never completely discarded.

On their fourth morning together, he awoke around five am to find Corelle snoring lightly next to him, low down on the mattress, arms clasping her head. He quietly slipped from beneath the duvet, padding across the room and selecting his varied brushes with a keen eye. Setting up his paints, palette and easel next to the bed, he proceeded eagerly to sketch his woman, brow furrowed in concentration, inspiration touching him once more.

If she turned or rolled over, he simply moved his workstation to the opposite side of the bed, continuing where he'd left off. It took six hours, but what he created was a bizarre mixture of real and surreal; a sleeping beauty crafted in Corelle's likeness, lying on a bed made up of the grimy London streets he'd reminisced about the night he'd signed that ocean-blue contract. Behind her was the London skyline at night, twinned with that of another country – Africa or the West Indies (he wasn't quite sure yet) – made up of huge trees, an orange/russet sun peeking out from behind rocky mountains. By the time she opened her eyes, he'd sketched it all, and had painted most of the background, calling his new piece *Sidewalk Princess*.

Corelle laughed with joy when she saw what he'd done; then wrapped her arms and legs around him, pulling him back to bed.

The following few days were like the blissful honeymoon period they'd enjoyed at the beginning of their relationship. They shopped, ate out, watched movies, went raving – and, in the space of a long weekend, found each other once more. Welling fell in love with Corelle all over again, finding the current deeper and stronger, moving him along at a speed that was relentless, but enjoyable nonetheless. At night, he found his muse again and again, painting pictures at the rate of one a day while his woman slept.

It was only at the end of the first week, when Corelle went back to work, that he gave Suicide Note any serious thought. Alone in his bedroom, staring at the cracked and plastered ceiling, he replayed his signing of the contract, clenching his fists and closing his eyes as he remembered. What had he done? The agreement had been signed with no idea of what would follow – without any inkling of Corelle's return. Now she was back...

He gulped back tears and forced himself to admit his feelings. Now his lover was back, he wanted to live – needed to live – suicide was something for a man with no hope. His hope was alive in the beautiful smile that greeted him in the mornings, the bronze hue of the skin he caressed as she slept. Even the fact that she returned was a sign that he could curb his sickening desire for underage girls – for when he was with her, around her, he had no need for their bodies or minds. He was devoted to Corelle, who had left, partly, as a test to see if he could really change for good. Welling had slipped – he knew that – but she didn't know; and he saw no reason that she should. The only fly in the ointment was his pact with Suicide Note. He had to get the contract legally nullified, and then he'd be free...

Welling leapt from his bed, frantically bounding across the room to his wardrobe, searching through the pockets of his jeans and jackets like a man possessed. He retrieved the pink card from a pocket of his jacket, kissing it like a lost child and jumping for joy. Wasting no more time, he picked up the phone and dialled the Suicide Note number, holding his breath while he waited for the connection.

There was nothing, then the dull burr of a disconnected landline – a sound he'd been completely unprepared for. Welling looked down at the phone handset in shock, concluding that he'd dialled a wrong number. He tried again, with the same result. Then again, hearing that burr once more. Panic gripped his gut on his fourth and final attempt. He slammed down the phone, feeling his heart gallop in his chest, every sound and colour in the room vividly real and alive.

'They finish the job within two weeks.'

Grantham's calm voice was the catalyst for his terror. He jumped to his feet, dressed without washing and left the flat, heading back to Farringdon, his terror etched into the lines on his face.

He couldn't believe it. After buzzing the bell at the building entrance for near to ten minutes, he eventually got inside when someone came out and held the door open. He'd fairly run through corridors until he found room D–474, with that blank unvarnished wood he remembered so well. Knocking on the door tentatively provided no immediate answer – louder knocks had the same effect. Welling's panic increased until he was eventually pounding the door as hard as he could, screaming at someone to answer. Locks clicked and turned. He stepped back, taking huge gulps of breath and feeling relieved until he realised he'd been joined by someone from the next office along.

'Can I help?'

It was a thirty-something white man – black loafers, 501s, Ben Sherman shirt tucked in at the waist – who was looking at his sweaty features suspiciously, eyebrows arched in that eternal question he knew so well – *what the hell are you doing here?* Welling stared back at him, his panic forcing him not to react to the man's assumption that he must be up to no good.

'I'm looking for…' He quickly realised how little he should expose about his business, and took his words back before they left his lips. '… the company that used to be based here. I have some unfinished business with them.'

'You and the rest of London,' the man returned with arched eyebrows. 'You're about the fifth person to come knocking on that door today. I don't know what's going on, and we never had much dealings with those guys, but they moved out almost a week ago.'

His heart sank like a dinghy in troubled waters.

'Didn't they leave any forwarding address?'

Welling's voice was a featureless monotone, cold and formless, chilling the air between himself and the man, who now gazed at him curiously.

'No, they didn't. We didn't even realise they'd gone until those people started turning up,' he said, looking him up and down as he began to back away. 'Can I pass on a message?'

Welling shook his head, hopeless fear invading him, before he turned and ran back down the corridor. The man watched him flee until he ran down the emergency stairs.

'Crazy people,' he muttered, then went into his office and forgot he'd ever met Welling.

Unadulterated horror spurred his feet into movement, his eyes into panicked concentration, his mind into terrified visions of death. Every car, every person, every face on the street was out to get him – danger haunted him from every angle. He stumbled along the pavement, jumping at the sound of loud voices and car horns; then, on the tube, he sat with his back against the sliding doors, eyes moving furtively from left to right, scanning the crowd of commuters with an almost psychopathic gaze. Others felt his tense air and moved away, until he was alone at his end of the carriage. Of course, this only worsened his desolate feeling of isolation, and he slid to the floor whimpering with his arms clasped around his head, oblivious to the stares. When the amplified woman's voice informed him that he'd reached his station, he ran off the train, up the escalator, and jogged a complex route to his estate, full of twists and turns, so as to confuse anyone that might be following. He entered the towerblock from the fire exit at the back of the building, taking the stairs until a woman came down with her laundry, scaring the shit out of him. From that floor, he took the first empty lift he could find, arriving at his front door drenched in cold sweat.

Once inside, he closed and locked the door behind him, then ran around the flat bolting the windows and patio door that led to his balcony.

When he got to the bedroom Corelle was already there, painting a potted Asiatic lily that had just begun to bloom. He stopped in his tracks, but was unable to hide the beads of perspiration coursing down his head and body, saturating the thin T-shirt he wore. She smiled in greeting, then frowned into the silence, which was broken only by the harsh sounds of his breath. Her smile faded, replaced by equal measures of concern and worry.

She got to her feet, paintbrush in hand.

'What's up?'

Welling had to think fast – he couldn't let her know what was happening.

She'd leave him for sure if she did.

'Nothing... I think I'm comin' down with flu or somethin' – I feel so weak...'

He staggered to the bed, laying down and closing his eyes, while Corelle watched him carefully, then sat herself down beside him. The cool hand she laid on his forehead was a welcome respite from the heat that threatened to set his brain alight and combust his body. She felt both sides of his neck with the same careful attention that had been part of her former job at the hospital. He opened his eyes and nearly cried when he saw the pity in hers.

'You've got a real bad temperature, Paul, it really does feel like flu. Come on, get those clothes off, you're going straight to bed.'

He willingly complied, stripping to his boxers awkwardly, faintly annoyed at himself for lying to her again. She wrapped him up, then disappeared into the kitchen, saying she was going to boil the kettle for some Beecham's flu remedy. When she was gone, Welling quickly checked the window locks, making sure they were closed tight before jumping back into bed. Unable to stop himself, he began to shake in fear once more, teeth chattering, fingers clutching the duvet as though rigor mortis had claimed him already.

Corelle came back with a steaming mug of lemon mix, then stopped dead when she saw the discomfort her man was in. He tried desperately to stop his shaking limbs from jerking, but only made things that much worse. His body shook with suppressed convulsions. Corelle came closer, her pretty hazel eyes narrowed into thin slits of disquiet.

'Wow Paulie – you really *are* sick aren't you?'

He couldn't reply to such a precise and ironic statement. She sat on the edge of the bed and made him sit up, then handed him the mug of Beecham's.

'It might be a bit hot, but I put some cold water in. Make sure you drink it down in one go.'

He nodded, playing along with the charade, taking the mug and knocking the warm mixture back, then stopping for breath before finishing the rest. When he was done he thumped the mug on to the bedside cabinet, falling back on to the bed, wiping his lips and wincing at the taste. Corelle stroked his head, looking down warmly on him. He blinked at her, feeling minutely better. At least he had Corelle in his life. A lot of men never even had that much.

'OK?' she asked. He nodded silently and she smiled radiantly once again. 'I love you to death, you big baby,' she continued, leaning over him to kiss his clammy head. He twitched involuntarily at her words, but she stroked his temple until he calmed down, her soothing touch as light as a cool breeze.

'Now sleep,' she ordered, still massaging him softly.

He nodded in return and closed his eyes.

A deep, painful sting in his arm awakened him, intense enough to make him cry out in pain. He tried to open his gummy eyes, but they were stuck together as if bonded by Super Glue; it took all of his effort to achieve this task. When he managed, the first thing he noticed was the darkness of the room – it took a moment more to realise this was due to the tightly closed curtains, coupled with the absence of lights. He felt drained of energy, but somehow strangely formless and free enough to soar like a bird.

He realised why a second later, when he tried to sit up in the bed. He couldn't move, couldn't feel his arms or legs. Both were completely numb.

He was paralysed.

'Fuh… fuh…'

He was trying to scream out the word *fuck*, but he couldn't even do that. His mouth was hanging open, and he had no control over its movements. He tried to turn his head. Nothing. He put all of his energy into what had been a simple thing hours ago, straining the tendons and using all the will he possessed. Once again, nothing happened at first – but slowly, he got some power, and his head began to twist to the right. It was the single hardest thing he'd ever done in his life, but he managed to turn enough to see his right arm.

When he saw what he was doing, the fear returned in a flood that threatened to drown him alive where he lay.

An arm gripped his by the wrist. Another covered his fingers, which were wrapped around a pen, scribbling something on to the bottom of an A4 sheet of paper. He squinted, thinking back, before realising the sheet was ocean blue – like the eyes of someone he'd once met – and another sheet of A4 he'd once seen. Focusing harder, he saw that the scribble he was witnessing was his signature.

PH Wellin

He took in the gentle curve of a 'g' being formed, then his fingers and arm were released, to fall back on to the mattress with a thump. With effort, he turned his head to find that he was sitting up, the duvet cover around his knees. Corelle moved from behind him, placing his back against the headboard, then walked in front of the bed, hazel eyes cast with a critical gaze. Her pretty features were set like concrete, the ocean-blue contract clutched in her hand like the pelt of a dangerous beast she'd slain herself. In her other hand, she held a large hypodermic needle, its barrel fully emptied of its contents. She held both up in front his eyes so he could see them for what they were. All trace of pity had left her eyes.

'Just a formality,' she said in a crisp tone devoid of emotion, strictly business. 'We needed your last signature as confirmation that I finished the job, as intended.'

Welling opened his mouth to scream, but the injection she'd given him had done its work. His body shuddered in spasms until his spirit finally fled.

The author would like to thank Riggs O'Hara, Sanchita Islam, bLACKmALE, and Jade McCubbin for the inspiration.

Jonesing: the end

Elizabeth Young

25/1/99

*8 stone 2lbs, half gram Cocaine, third gram Heroin (snorted & smoked) –
20mgs. Prozac, 1 beta blocker, Intal asthma inhaler, 15 mgs Valium, 1 green
Temazepam (these are mainly prescription drugs), 25 cigarettes. (Won't count
calories – someone told me that they don't exist. Nor protein either.)*

'I think I ate your ashtray.' Marsh had the door open before I'd started
fishing for my keys. It was pouring wet and I'd left the brolly somewhere. Stood like a zombie in a downpour, wheezing from the stairs,
while Marsh unwound my sodden, non-rainproof outer clothes; scarf,
velvet hat, velvet coat. Drip, drip. Felt totally relieved to be home.

'Which ashtray then?'

'I'm aw'fy sorry, hen. It was that wee 'un with the lid. The one you
could clap in your pocket. Painted very bright. Your friend made it in
her pottery class.'

'And you thought it was some extra-large, economy-size pill, then?'

'I wasnae thinkin', that's all. Now away upstairs and get warm. You're
soaked through, you'll get your death.'

'Oh well, at least you got some roughage, then.' Laughed as I started
up the stairs. Junkies are always constipated. Most of them manage to
hang on to a bit of gear for the morning but then they unfailingly have
it first thing when they wake up as a reward for their far-sightedness.
I always figured I must be the most middle-class junkie in the world
'cause I never had mine until after I'd been to the loo.

Leant over the banisters, trying not to topple the tower of paper-
backs at each side of the thin stair-carpet.

'Marshal, did you see anyone... nice today?'

He'd hung up my coat and was brushing the water off, straightening
and petting the folds like it was some small, sick animal.

'Oh no. It's been verra quiet. Dead quiet the whole day.'

He has a good poker face expression but I know when he's teasing.

'Kettle's boiling. Dry that hair now. I'll follow ye up.'

Brief skirmish with Manda over occupation of the big, comfy sofa under my platform bed. (Diamanda is a horrendously expensive red Persian, hard as a diamond and just as beautiful; definitely the prettiest girl in this house. She was a birthday prezzie.) Anyway, I win. Manda shoots out the door. Snarl. Tail doing the bottle-brush bit.

Exhausted, I sink into the cushions and draw my old patchwork quilt over me. It is worn through and scarred by burns and cigarette holes. The gas fire has been lit and the red velvet curtains drawn. My two pink-shaded lamps are on. You can't see the dirt like this, or the walls, patched brown and yellow from nicotine and the damp.

Marsh comes in with a tray and a towel folded over one arm like a waiter. He puts the try down carefully on a miniature wooden table by the couch, unpins my hair and rubs it thoroughly. On the tray are two mugs of tea, one Marks and Sparks roast-beef sandwich – for me – and a pile of chocolate-filled Hit! biscuits. Their brand name amuses Marsh. There is also – for me – a mirror with a pile of cocaine on the right side, and a pile of heroin on the left. If Marsh hadn't seen someone, there would have been much less powder. Marsh even provides a tube made from foil, a razor and a new Clipper lighter. I grope beneath the sofa for the roll of foil, tear off a strip and smoke some heroin. OK, I know it's boring written down like this but straightaway I feel a lot less panicky and shaky. Marsh switches on the television. He doesn't start work till 8pm.

3/2/99

8st 4, half gram Heroin, half gram Cocaine, 2 joints, Valium, Temazepam, Domperidone, Prozac. (Prescription stuff too dull for detail.) 36 cigs.

I don't think I'm doing this right; I mean I'm not designing a stage set here. What *does* one put in a diary? Private thoughts, I suppose. I don't like writing about drugs – am too paranoid, scared that the police might get hold of it. It has a lock but that's so frail and dinky that even Manda could unpick it with one claw. Today, well, same old same old. Oh, don't be so dull, Alice. (Actually I was christened Alison but no one knows. It is such a damp handshake of a name. Alice Colefax sounds better. Anyway, there's a secret.) Although no one else is likely to read this, I should still try and write properly. I am more likely to clarify things for myself that way. Although if anyone did read it I bet they'd go, 'Oh no! Not drugs again! Yawn... tedium.' And I would have to agree. Writing about taking drugs is indeed deadly dull. I suppose it's because it is an entirely subjective, selfish and internal experience, which loosens one's ties to the world, rather than, in the case of most episodes, strengthening them. Drug-taking – serious drug-taking – has no context. Well, none beyond a faint drizzle of pain, poverty and self-hatred.

Male writers seem to have completely hijacked the subject of drugs. Not very surprising as, along with the music biz, drugs are the last hold-out of unreconstructed sexism. In boy's books and films, doing drugs is all action and attitude – Rip off your friends and run! Rob a chemist and run! See your friends overdose and save the day with your quick thinking! Become a gun-toting, hard-eyed drug lord and shred competitors with your Mac 10. See Dick Score. See Jane Beg. See Dick Hit Jane. See Dick Run. See Jane Find the Stash. Watch Dick Run Back Home. Watch Dick Shoot Up. I am not saying that all this Boy's Own melodrama is false. It's just that it implies that drugs are *about* something, even if it's only betrayal and treachery, rather than being the big nothing that they really are. Of course, things *do* happen sometimes, but never to an Iggy Pop soundtrack.

It's odd – girls very rarely write about hard drugs. Dissolution is no prisoner of gender – I know some female users who are rapacious in their greed. Unlike the men who enjoy pissing around with weights and scales and chemical experiments, girls keep their eyes on the drugs, always.

My friend Anya is a writer and she goes on about how much she wants to be all decadent. But she never *does* anything. I think many women writers feel like that, but know, on some level, that writing books requires a degree of sanity and order that is rare in the drug sub-culture. Those, like me, who have abandoned themselves, are exhausted by living out a deviancy that is, even now, harder for women to choose than men.

So, bad girls don't write books. And boys glamorise it all. And film, by its nature, glamorises everything. Addiction is not glamorous; it's dreary and monotonous and everyone's too listless and ground-down to have... adventures.

25/2/99

8st 9, half gram H, 3/4s gram C, Prozac, Valium, beta blocker, 15 cigs.

Because I don't drink, a tiny corner of my mind harbours the arche-
typal image of the drunk – some sort of WC Fields character reeling
about – even though I must know dozens of alcoholics and they are
nothing like that. I suppose it' s the same with junkies – I wonder if
ordinary people imagine junkies having commonplace lives like mine?
Or do they just envisage skeletal, wild-eyed wrecks, rifling through
their mum's handbag or knocking pensioners down lift shafts? I have
never stolen anything to get drugs. Prostitution? Well. It depends on
how you define it. I have often had boyfriends who shared their drugs.
I didn't always love them. Love is too painful. I don't even love Marsh,
although I like him better than almost anyone. Is that prostitution? I'm
not sure. And what will happen when I'm too old to appeal to anyone? I'm already in my mid-thirties and have been seriously addicted
for about six years. This thought makes me so panicky that I have to
take lots of extra drugs to make it go away.

23/3/99

*8st 13, half gram H, 1 gram C, 1 joint, Valium, Prozac, Temazepam,
Mefenamic acid, 20 cigs.*

Get up in the morning, same thing for breakfast... I have to get up
really early, about 6am, to get to work. We live in what must be the
only area left in central London that is wholly impervious to gentrifi-
cation. Somers Town is like an undigested lump of the dreariest part
of Leicester or Nottingham which has landed – splat! – behind King's
Cross and Euston, as if God had gone in for a bit of projectile vomiting. Old GLC low- rise blocks, deserted playgrounds, brown grass, dog
turd heaven, off-licences wrapped in harsh parcels of corrugated iron.
And we are near to the two dreariest streets in London – Hampstead
Road and Gower Street.

Marsh gets up when I do and tries to make me eat porridge or eggs.
Yuk. Then he goes back to bed. We have separate bedrooms, although
sometimes we sleep together. Occasionally we even do some sex but

there is a constraint between us. We are too polite, too solicitous of the other's pleasure. Sex has to be a bit selfish before one can enjoy it. Really we just do it because we think we ought to. Sex is hardly a priority with either one of us. Marsh's whole personality inclines towards caring and nurture. My temperament is one of avoidance and secrecy. We are both far more interested in drugs than sex – anyway, heroin depresses the libido so completely that one never even thinks about sex. I think you'd have to be very much in love with a junkie partner in order to permanently share a bed. Inevitably there are times when no gear can be found and you start withdrawing. Who wants to share a bed with someone who can't keep still, who soaks the duvet in sweat, who farts continually and vomits into a washing-up bowl? Gross. Marsh and I have never reached that degree of intimacy. Our relationship is courteous, even slightly formal. We do need each other, though. Marsh needs someone helpless to protect and I need to be looked after as I am so hopeless at everything. In the drug world, Marsh appreciates the modest status that living with a pretty girl in a reasonably ordered household confers. I am his per-manent excuse – 'Och no, thanks all the same, but Ali's expecting me home'; I can also, if necessary, dispose of evidence, get down to a police station at night, find lawyers and, if it should come to that, take care of him in prison. (And that really is a full-time job – visit-ing, smuggling drugs in, sending endless packages, handling the appeal and providing the 'stable home environment' so vital to early release.) Reciprocally Marsh can play the Glasgow hard man and shelter me from the menace implicit in crime. A lone girl can be vulnerable if she is forced to deal drugs.

I've got completely off the track, haven't I? I was describing going to work. We're equidistant from King's Cross and Euston stations. Either way, winter or summer, it's a long, pitiless walk. I have to make a couple of changes on the tube and then get a bus. I teach at a college in the far frontiers of the London suburbs.

Actually tonight, when I got home, as shagged out as ever, Marsh said suddenly, 'For fuck's sake, Ali, do us a favour and jack that job in. You hate it. I hate it. They pay shite wages an' all.' I couldn't explain how much his suggestion agitated and scared me. If I didn't have the job, I would be nothing. Well, I'd be a junkie, but that's the same as being nothing. If someone asks what you do you can hardly say that you're totally committed to your career as a junkie. You might as well just say, 'Oh, I'm a full-time failure.'

So all I said to Marsh was that I was a bit rundown since becoming vegetarian and probably needed more vitamins and less drugs and I'd be fine. Not that I used the word 'drugs'. No one ever does. There are countless face-saving and self-deceiving euphemisms for every part of the drug life and they are all invoked continually, subject to a complex and necessary etiquette that prevents anyone having to confront the realities of their behaviour.

Without a job I'd just spend lots more time waiting and worrying while Marsh is out on business. And then I'd use more stuff. Will make a big effort to cut down anyway. After the weekend.

14/4/99

9st 2, 1 gram H, half gram C, 2 pipes freebase, Prozac, Rohypnol, Valium, Domperidone, 30 cigs.

Well, I tried. I really tried. I tried hypnosis and confronted the valley of the acupuncturists in Stoke Newington. I phoned Narcotics Anonymous and went to the nearest meeting. It was in a church basement and it was just awful. First they tried to make me drink industrial-strength coffee and then they tried to throw me out because I was only trying to stop taking drugs and hadn't actually stopped. I asked what counted as 'stopping' because even if I stopped illegal drugs I'd still be taking all this prescription medication. This was evidently a poser that taxed them too far, so they let me into the meeting. In there everyone seemed to love me, although they didn't know me. They all had that slightly unfocused intensity that you get with religious fundamentalists – as if they were talking to someone hiding behind you. During the meeeting (I'll use terms from Lit Crit rather than names) one after the other kept bounding to their feet. 'I'm Aporia and I'm an addict'. 'Hi, Aporia,' everyone chorused. 'I'm Codex and I'm an addict.' 'Hi Codex' – well, you get the drift. Even though some of these people apparently hadn't used narcotics for years, they all insisted in reiterating lasciviously every detail of their addiction and how they hit 'Rock Bottom'. What is this 'Rock Bottom'? Should I be expecting it? When it turned up, why didn't they just kill themselves? Afterwards I was given a lilac piece of plastic – a bit like a gambling chip – and urged to read the Big Book, which proved unreadable. Everyone kept saying 'Go to a meeting, go to a meeting, go to a meeting' three times over as if repetition improved it. Then, to complete the horror, these people wanted me to go somewhere else with them and Drink More Coffee. It was quite late. Didn't any of them have jobs to go to in the morning? I think not. NA seemed to define their lives, to provide boundaries and structures. There were definitely a couple of blokes nodding out in the back row: I've been told that NA is the best place to score in a strange town. Anyway, what with everyone droning on for hours about drugs, I was gagging for a smoke, so I went home and had some. Quite a lot.

I did feel a bit guilty – I know this method *has* helped people, so I went back a couple of times. Still awful. I proved incapable of turning myself over to another Power, Higher or not. Of course I know that addiction fucks me up but this is my own responsibility. I am aware of my faults and, well, they're not so terrible that I need to make all this fuss about them. I read a letter meant for someone else once – like, hea-vy. Oh, a couple of times I nicked a bit of Marsh's stash in the clock. That was wrong, though I told him. In general I just don't want strangers mucking about in my life and acting like I'm their good friend. Sure I'd like to take less drugs, but listening to others go on about it has the opposite effect; I can't even read books about drugs when I'm trying to cut down. I *will* take less. I'll start cutting down again tomorrow.

6/5/99

9st 4, half-gram H, 3/4s gram C, 2 joints, Prozac, Valium, Rohypnol, beta blockers, 27 cigs.

Why are so many dealers called Dave? There's Big Dave, Little Dave, Skinny Dave, Essex Dave, Sussex Dave, Dave the Dog, Tattoo Dave, Miser Dave, Shoplifter Dave, Alky Dave, Mental Dave. I can't really focus on any of them, not that I see them or any of Marsh's business people much. He doesn't want them around either. In a glow of malicious self-righteousness, the neighbours will turn a suspected dealer over to the local police in an instant. Marsh works – roughly – from midday till 4pm, then 8pm–1am. He prefers to deliver, it's safer that way, and, as he has a motorbike, he could be a courier. No one gets our home phone, only the mobile number. He usually has a couple of runners to help out, boys in their early twenties, and they have mobiles too. Marsh worries about them; if he picks a boy who's into drugs, then he is unlikely to be trustworthy, but if the boy doesn't use, Marsh is concerned that he might get into it. So he tries to find kids who are into the drugs Marsh doesn't often sell – dope, speed, Es. And you thought addicts had no ethics? Some do and some don't – just like everybody else.

A favoured few people come to the maisonette and Marsh sees them in the downstairs sitting room. Marsh has made the room as un-welcoming as possible. The window blinds are pulled down tight, the carpet is all sticky and gummy. There is a television on a wooden crate, a sort of sofa made from old car seats, and two huge pub ashtrays. There is nothing whatsoever to steal. The whole room seems to shout, 'Please Don't Let Me Detain You a Moment Longer.' Even Manda won't go in there. We had to move her lit-box outside, to the hall.

I was cuddling Manda today, despite the drifting clouds of moult which fill my mouth with fur, kissing her neat, pink nose and admiring the precision elegance of her tiny teeth. Marsh was fixing yet another deadbolt to the front door. He turned the new key – click, clunk – and straightened up, rubbing his back. 'I was thinking – should I put a reinforced steel door on the outside?' 'I thought you didn't keep large amounts here?' 'I try not to, but sometimes, ye ken, there's nae alter-native.' Manda scrabbled on to my shoulder and leapt free. 'Fuck's sake, no steel door,' I say. 'You might as well make tannoy announcements to the neighbourhood: "Big Drugs sale! Everything Must Go!"' Marsh laughed. 'Fair enough. Let's have that wee smoke now.'

24/5/99

9st 5, 3/4s gram H, 1 gram C, Rohypnol, Valium, Prozac, Asthma thing, 14 cigs.

Thinking about why people get addicted. It's like that old maths debate – is one revealing something already there but not previously known, or actually creating something new? Often wonder why I let that boyfriend long ago get me so deep into drugs – I even let him inject me, as I have no visible veins. I suppose I wanted to look cool and brave. It takes so long to learn that no one is cool until they don't care whether they are or not. The concept of Cool started in America, where it acted as a status system for those who had nothing – urban black people. By inverting and parodying the American success story of prosperity and acquisition, their disadvantages became potent status signifiers in the ranking of prestige. Notably explicit within the doubly deviant netherworld of jazz, blues and drugs, the construct of Cool eventually seduced white kids and ultimately subsumed the world.

4/6/99

9st 8, 1 gram H, 1 gram C, 8 pipes freebase, Prozac, Valium, Rohypnol, Benadryl, Corsodyl, Gaviscon, 35 cigs.

Marsh doesn't work on Fridays because that's the day the police like to arrest druggies. Then they can keep them in the cells all weekend, apparently hoping – rather cinematically – that the withdrawals will drive the poor sods into naming all the big importers. As if. The prisoner, down at street level, knows absolutely fuck all. Drug barons keep their hands clean. They also keep their distance, as they heap their coffers with the spoils of desolation.

So, on Fridays Marsh says, 'Well, we can have a wee holiday from life now.' And he cooks up some coke with ammonia to make it into smokeable freebase and we smoke it through his glass pipes and cuddle up on the sofa and talk gibberish about all the places we'll go to when we have enough money. Of course we can't go anywhere. We are chained to London by our addiction. So it's all nonsense, but nice nonsense.

28/6/99

9st 9, half-gram H, 3/4s gram C, 2 joints, 4 pipes freebase, Rohypnol, Valium, Domperidone, 17 cigs.

Finally ditched the job. Did so for such a silly reason that I couldn't tell anyone, not even Marsh. When you're using H, for some reason, even a small amount of exertion makes you sweat. Remember Elvis at his later Las Vegas concerts? He'd be dripping and handing out truckloads of tatty scarves annointed with his precious bodily fluids? Well, there's no demand for my used Little Mermaid tissues and I just couldn't go on lecturing with sweat beading my hairline and coursing down my face. It was just too embarrassing.

Have been thinking about drug terminology and how weird it is. Most of it is US in origin and self-explanatory: 'scoring', for example, 'getting high' or 'doing cold turkey/turkeying/clucking', a reference to the shivery gooseflesh of withdrawal. But why is it a 'monkey' on one's back? Shouldn't it be a sloth? And why is having a habit called 'a jones'? 'Junk' is pretty obvious, but why 'smack'? Who knows? Who cares?

25/11/99

(Too hot to write all summer, then I couldn't be bothered.) 1/3 gram H, half-gram C, 5 pipes freebase, 3 joints, Zopiclone, Valium, Prozac, Rohypnol, Gamolenic acid, Mefenamic acid, 32 cigs.

Oh God, it's always the same. The Xmas drought. Everybody wants to get completely out of it for the holidays, so the drugs vanish around the end of November and reappear – heavily cut and more expensive – a few days before Xmas and everyone is so relieved they buy them all anyway. There is usually no problem with heroin again until early summer when last year's crop runs out and the new one still has to be imported. Actually, apart from Xmas, the price for gear has been falling and falling.

4/12/99

10st 2, 1 and a half grams H, half gram C, 2 pipes base, 5 joints, Valium, Prozac, Rohypnol, Zopiclone, Gaviscon, 43 cigs.

Oh no! Oh Christ! I hadn't noticed until today, when I couldn't zip up my jeans, I have been gradually packing on weight. Now I'm a monster, a manatee. I haven't bought new clothes in ages. Robert Elms once wrote that you can tell when someone became an addict by the degree to which their clothes are out of date. I tried not to let that happen, although it did. But I went on wearing jewellery and perfume and doing my hair (still black) in lots of tiny, tight plaits when it was wet so that it rippled like Pre-Raphaelite wavelets when dried and hanging down my back. I bathe all the time in scented water – I like almond and coconut oils. (It's not true that junkies don't like baths. It's just that they don't like doing *anything*.) But there's no point now if I'm just a repulsive blimp. I've heard (and noticed) that some long-term users, mainly women, but a few men, eventually start to retain water and bloat. Am I going to be like that? Yes – my ankles are all puffy and I can't get some of my rings to fit – my fingers and hands have swollen up. There's not even anyone I can talk to about it – my non-drug friends have drifted away – I was always late for appointments. On smack one is invariably late – often feel like I'm moving through toffee. I can't replace them with drug friends – there are no drug friends, only fellow travellers. I feel as if, one by one, the frail filaments anchoring me to the real world are shrivelling up. And when they're gone I'll just fall away and swoop into endless, timeless space and darkness. 'The Wind that blows between the Worlds/It cut him like a knife.' Like that, see? God, am *so* depressed, I will just swell and swell like an angry puffer fish. I must find the drugs.

21/12/99

10st 5, 1 and a half grams H, 1 gram C, 5 pipes base, 1 joint, Prozac, Valium, Zopiclone, Rohypnol, Domperidone, 30 cigs.

Xmas is always bad. Of course I had a family once, although we never really became a 'family'. My Dad was an electrician, often away for long periods wiring public buildings. My Mum was a doctor's recep-tionist. They were both shy and reserved, but it came across as indif-ference. They moved from Basildon to Southgate to Wimbledon and finally retired to Devon. Onwards and upwards. My sister is a social worker somewhere in the north. No one stays in touch. One of my boyfriends was raided once. I was there and had to get a psychiatrist's report for court. This shrink kept on about 'Anhedonia' (sounds like it should be sung to 'The Hallelujah Chorus') and dithsymia, so I go, 'What?' and he says, 'Depression. You're depressed.' Well, give the man a dog-biscuit, everyone's fucking depressed. They gave me pills, later changed to Prozac. Prozac is slightly like smack in that you become an amiable blob. But smack is better at keeping all your troubles locked up tight and losing the key. It's more fun too.

Marsh always goes up to Glasgow around now. 'Mainly for the New Year,' he says, 'and I like to see my ma an' my sister Isa and the weans.' He always asks me along, specially this year. But I can't face quite that much Scottishness and whisky, both undiluted. This time, however, he says that a friend he met in prison is just about due back from Thailand and might drop by. 'Fine. *No es problema.*' I'm barely concentrating. Marsh hesitates. 'He's a bit… big-headed, kind of. But beneath the blether he's nae bad.'

2/1/2000

10st 8, 2 grams H, 10 pipes rock (crack), 7 joints, 2 Es, Rohypnol, Valium, Zopiclone, Prozac, Daktacort, 9 cigs.

Well, the Ego has landed. He turned up on Xmas Eve. I was feeling sorry for myself. I kept hearing that song on the radio, something like 'So now it's Xmas/And what have you done?' (Fuck all.) It ends balefully – 'the Xmas you get you deserve' – *so* reassuring. I almost didn't get up, but when I did, I thought I might as well do it right. I put on a raspberry frou-frou short skirt (elasticated waist) and a Victorian silk blouse with a high neck, lots of pins and tucks and heavy, frilly lace cuffs, sheer black tights and stiletto suede ankle boots. Took some drugs. Brooded. Put on some of my make-up from Space NK – Xmas present from Marsh, as requested. Then the doorbell code went. We never answer unless someone rings it right. It was Marsh's friend, Alan. There were snowflakes on his eyelashes. He had one of those long coats they wear in cowboy films – a duster coat, that's it, or a Drizabone – and a leather satchel over his shoulder. Took him up to my room, as it was the nicest. He had a grey ponytail (bad, very bad) but a good face, hard and spare, like how you'd imagine a war photographer would look. It was difficult to give him anything as he said he was a vegan. (It is amazing how many druggies fuss about healthy foods when they're pumping themselves full of poison that's been up someone's bum.) Marsh was right, Alan did large it – you know, dealer to the stars, red-carpet treatment in Bolivia and such like crap – but he was generous. He had some uncut Thai smack. He said the bulk had come through with mules and he was just carrying his 'personal'. His idea of 'personal' was my idea of feeding the five thousand enough drugs to ensure their collective wipe-out.

He unwrapped a white rock from some foil. 'Is that coke?' 'Nah.
Rock. You know, crack. I got it here, in London.' I knew. Marsh hated
it, called it 'debased freebase' and he preferred to base his own from the
powder you snort, the cocaine hydrochloride. Marsh had taken his freebase pipe with him, so Alan showed me how to take a small plastic bottle
– Evian I think it was. Keeping about a third of the water, push an empty
biro tube through the side, cover the empty top with foil and make
pinpricks in it. He mixed some cigarette ash with some of the crack
and put it on the foil. He held a lighter to this while I inhaled through
the tube. You could see the smoke billowing about in the bottle. It isn't
really like freebase – it's cruder, nervier, less subtle. Then he had some.
And I had some. And so on. We talked the usual bollocks. Alan said
he'd been 'seriously getting into Aleister Crowley' and Lovecraft made
sense to him now and did I want to see his first edition of Austin Osman
Spare's demonic artwork? I said that Enochian magick with a 'k' was
as stupid and commonplace as adultery.

After a bit it became obvious that he felt it would be discourteous
not to try and fuck me. I let him. Perhaps I had some vague idea about
insurance for the future or something. He unzipped and produced
one of those thick red and purple cocks with huge veins like winding
tendrils. I took off my boots and tights. In the bathroom I put some
coconut moisturiser up me, cos I was drizabone. We stayed on the sofa
– it's hard to be uninhibited and fall back casually on to a platform bed.
Like most blokes on a huge drug cocktail, he couldn't come. He just
pumped away till I was flayed and raw, then fell asleep on top of me.
Actually I let him – and his drugs – stay over the millennium, then
when he got too much I said Marsh was coming back.

12/1/00

*10st 12, 1 and a half grams H, 11 pipes rock, 6 joints, Prozac, Temazepam,
Rohypnol, Erythromycin, 5 cigs.*

'I am a black, falling, empty unfamous star.' Some murderer wrote that.
That's what I feel like. I told Marsh about Alan. He shrugged. I am on
a sort of perpetual fast – never liked food anyway. I exercise for hours
but I just puff up more. It's the drugs. If I stop them the weight will go.
I refuse to go to a Drug Dependency Unit where they openly despise

and condescend to you. I hate telling people that I'm a junkie – people like doctors. At first they act all nice but if you tell them their whole face snaps shut and they start thinking you're going to pinch their paperweight or prescription forms. And I wouldn't mention it if I was in hospital because then they don't care if you die. This isn't hysteria – I had a friend, obviously a junkie, and the doctors managed to ignore the fact that she had throat cancer for six years. Then it killed her.

2/2/00

11st 2, 1 & three-quarter grams H, 9 pipes rock, 4 joints, Valium, Rohypnol, Zopiclone, Gamolenic acid, Prozac, 14 cigs.

I've started quite liking crack, although I never saw any rock as good as Alan's again. Marsh has stopped me using a pipe, just like ages ago he stopped me injecting – each was screwing me up too much, he said. Smoking rock on foil shows up what vile stuff it is – made with bicarbonate and stepped on heavily, death by a thousand cuts. They're gonna step on it again. And again. A few years ago the media had this massive panic – Shock, Horror! Crack is coming over from America. Woe, Wailing, Gnashing of Teeth. So everyone was ready, the drugs squads straining to go and – nothing happened. They had to do the best they could with Es – a deadly threat, oh sure. Then when crack sidled in the back door later the powerbrokers were too embarrassed to mention it. Even Marsh has to get it sometimes now – it's becoming harder and harder to find cocaine powder and the quality has taken a real dive. Rock has taken over everywhere. So, beam me up…

23/2/00

11st 6, 2 grams H, £30 rock, 5 joints, Zopiclone, Valium, Rohypnol, Prozac, Gaviscon, Mefenamic acid, 21 cigs.

A hedge came to the door today. It was attached to a dog so I knew it was really Dave the Dog. His supplier had buried an ounce in with all this potted greenery and Dave couldn't find it, so could he dig through properly at our place? Oh, absolutely, come in and make a complete tip of our house. So he did. Manda had a good time, stalking the shrubs.

10/3/99

11st 12, 1 & half grams H, £60 rock, 6 joints, Zopiclone, Temazepam, Rohypnol, Prozac, beta blockers, 15 cigs.

Obviously, rock has been around for ages, but it's suddenly taken a big leap forward. Gresham's law – the bad drives out the good. Everything seems destabilised; for example, the drought went on long after Xmas. There's nothing disorganised about the crime – test marketing, loss leaders and all. The Drug Lords have had decades now to buy up chemists who can approximate virtually any drug. Coke and rock are particularly easy, what with mannitol, inositol, lidocaine, procaine, any-caine, ketamine, strychnine and a whole rat's nest of shit you didn't mean to buy. When the police say that drugs seized are something ridiculous, like seventy per cent pure, they're lying to justify their waste of public resources. London is carved up between rival drug gangs – the Irish control one bit, the Turks and Iranians another, and the Cockneys yet another. The West Indians control virtually all the crack trade, from west London. The black dealers throw middle-class druggies into a spin. It's against their psychic law to even *think* critically about… people of colour, and all these guys act as if their white punters had personally shackled their great-great-great-grandmas into a slave coffle and now they're demanding total financial restitution Some people get racially bewildered – at that recent big demo this bloke was prevented from getting through a police cordon and he was shouting at them, 'It's cos I'se black, innit?' – and he was a white guy. Some punter of Marsh's told us. Anya says soon we'll be able to change our pigmentation, just for fashion. Roll on…

7/5/00

12st 1, 2 grams H, £35 rock, 5 joints, Prozac, Rohypnol, Valium, Asthma thing, 23 cigs.

The drugs don't work. Neither do I. Am so horrendously huge that I use more and more stuff, trying to blot it all out. Mostly I hide away in my room, wearing my nightdress. Sometimes at dusk I put on a big coat and scuttle round to the library. There is no future. I have a pamphlet from EXIT on how to kill yourself efficiently – I don't want to wake up in some hospital and see Jimmy Savile. The drugs get weaker and weaker. There's a whole new generation now who have never had proper drugs but have insanely high expectations. So they can cut the rock with dirt-cheap Ice or Crank – smokeable methamphetamine. The kids get that big flash and everyone's happy, albeit quite, quite wrong. Only old losers like me moan. Anyway, I hate saying 'I remember when a twenty quid bag lasted two days', or whatever, cos it reminds me of old soldiers reminiscing about the Somme, whereas I am only a veteran of my own limitations.

23/4/00

12st 5, 2 grams H, £60 rock, 8 joints/Rohypnol, Valium, Prozac, Domperidone, beta blockers.

I really think it's over. Even the good times are bad. The drugs are crap and all the tensions are driving Marsh crazy – the fluctuating prices, the guns, robberies and rivalries, the endless waiting, which went away when things were running smoothly. I could buy some methadone off someone with a script and cut myself down to nothing. Would Marsh and I even like each other off drugs? I've no idea.

Essex Dave came by wearing carpet slippers. His feet were all bound up in grimy, seeping bandages. He said he had hepatitis C and it makes his feet itch till he claws the flesh off. They discovered the virus not long ago. He says junkies get it, but so do lots of other people – at the dentist or tattooist; the virus is such a hardy bugger that it lives through normal disinfectant measures. There's no cure. That's all we need now – a really hideous plague. Perhaps that's why I'm always so exhausted.

How does that hymn go? 'Change and decay in all around I see…' Right. I should get that methadone and some extra sleepers and come off. I know I should.

I'll start tomorrow.

Trompe l'oeil

Marc Werner

'How long have you known Toby?'

I don't know. How long *have* I known Toby? Six years? Seven? I've
known him as long as we've been working together. I've known him
almost as long as I've known Mandy and as long as I've been working
with her. As long as we've been publishing the magazine. We've
worked hard at this magazine to get where we are today – just about
scraping by. Which, for an art magazine produced by three people in
what are generally recognised to be tough times, is not bad going.

Tough in general terms perhaps, but the art scene in London has
expanded phenomenally in the last few years and our magazine has
grown in size and stature to reflect that. It's a crowded marketplace,
but by continuing to limit our staff and staying in the same hole-in-the-
wall office, we keep our overheads down and manage to survive. The
fact is that without Mandy, and, more to the point, Toby, this magazine would not exist. My name might appear next to 'Editor' on the
masthead, but I'm under no illusions. It's a joint venture. We're a team.

We share certain duties, but retain our areas of specific responsibility.
Toby writes the copy and Mandy designs the pages, which I then edit.
I'll do a bit of writing and Mandy will chip in with the odd headline,
and fortunately Toby is pretty clued up on the marketing front. Half
the time, though, Toby is hitting the streets, checking out the galleries,
coming into the office to write up his reviews. We're located down a
narrow little alleyway north of Oxford Street. Up on the third floor
above a specialist bookshop. When the window is open we get smells
wafting up from one of three places – the Italian sandwich bar, the
newly opened coffee shop or the pub on the corner – depending on
which way the wind's blowing. We used to get our lunch from the
Italian place. They did the largest ciabattas in London and it cost something like £1.50 to get one stuffed with mozzarella, fresh tomato and
black pepper. The guy running the place was a Neapolitan. He and
his wife and daughters were very friendly and by one o'clock every
weekday the queue was out the door and halfway down to Oxford Street.

But the family packed up and returned to Naples and the business was taken over. The ciabattas are now half the size and twice the price. We go elsewhere for lunch.

That year, as always, everyone kept writing off the summer. It had happened. We had missed it. Just because of a drop of rain. It was always hot in the office, whatever the temperature outside. Air-conditioning was a distant dream. One morning Toby came in all excited at having just seen the actress Joely Richardson walking down the street.

'Where?' Mandy asked.

'Some place off the Bayswater Road – Leinster Terrace, Leinster Gardens?'

I looked up at that.

'Did you see the *trompe l'oeil* house?' she asked.

Toby did his baffled look – beetled brows, narrowed eyes, shoulders hunched forward – which I had once found so charming.

'You like *trompe l'oeil*, don't you?' she asked.

'You know I do,' he said, then added, extravagantly, 'It's the essence of all great art.'

He had written a good piece about Cornelius Gijsbrechts, the master of *trompe l'oeil*, for the magazine, I had to admit.

'There's a house there, part of a stuccoed terrace, that looks exactly like the houses on either side, but it's just a façade. Eighteen inches thick.'

'Cool,' Toby remarked. 'I'm going back to take a look the first chance I get.'

'What were you doing on Leinster Gardens anyway?' Mandy asked.

Mandy was wearing a tight white top. It seemed especially hot in the office that morning. She had her long auburn hair tied up in a loose knot, pierced by a Wagamama chopstick. By lunch time she would remove the chopstick and her hair would settle on her bare, freckled shoulders.

'I walked part of the way in,' Toby explained. 'Delays on the Circle line. Person under a train between Bayswater and Paddington. And there she was, just walking down the street – Joely Richardson.'

'Just like a real person?' I kidded him.

He took this at face value. 'Just like a real person – exactly.'

'How d'you know it was her?' asked Mandy, returning her gaze to her screen.

'I wasn't sure at first. It's so hard to tell sometimes. But there was something about her walk and the way she was dressed.'

'Glamorous? Look-at-me sort of thing?'

'Quite the reverse. She was so casual, completely relaxed. Wearing some kind of vest top and old jogging pants.'

'Amazing,' I said. 'It really does sound like she's just a regular person.'

'It was her,' he said. 'I'm sure of it.'

A day or so later I was flicking through a back copy of *ES Magazine*, deploring its recent trashy redesign and the fact they'd dropped Andrew Martin's 'Tube Talk' column and never seemed to do any more interesting, quirky features, when I came across the 'My London' column with, as its subject for that week, the actress Joely Richardson. Asked in what part of London she lived, she answered, 'Bayswater.' She liked it because it was transitory, she said. So I guessed Toby was right. He *had* seen her walking down the street, whether Leinster Terrace or Leinster Gardens. One of them feeds into the other.

Toby was out having a look at the latest Fig-1 exhibition in Fareham Street. I had asked him to do a big piece about the gallery, which was mounting a different show every week. Since the start of the year, there had been some interesting stuff and some rubbish as well. I'd be a liar if I said that all the art being produced and shown in London in the wake of the whole YBA explosion was any good. You can't park a car in Hoxton and Shoreditch these days for skips, as more and more old houses are stripped and turned into galleries with bare-brick walls and bare-boards floors. At least half the art they show should be dumped straight in the skip outside by the art removal guys. Save you the trouble of having to go and look at it, us the effort of writing about it.

One advantage of the tide of crap was that the islands of good stuff really stood out. Hayley Skipper's installation at the Clerk's House – in which she cleared out the attic, painted it white, hung tiny pink curtains over the windows and placed a child's musical box in the corner, then covered the floor with broken glass – was powerful. Douglas Gordon's *Feature Film* made exciting use of the huge Atlantis Building on Brick Lane. Marc Quinn's work was always worth seeking out, likewise Gavin Turk's, two self-referentialists whose work *did* seem to have something to say beyond 'Hey, look at me'. The Wilson Twins showed some interesting video work at the Serpentine. Mike Nelson's *Coral Reef* at Matt's Gallery was the strongest, most stimulating installation I'd seen since Jim Whiting's refit of a Basel nightclub, *Bimbotown*.

It was after he'd been to Matt's to look at *Coral Reef* for the first time that Toby first talked to me about what was going on. He leaned around his screen to catch my eye and asked if I had time for a quick drink. Aware of Mandy picking up on our exchange but not joining in, I nodded quickly.

'Won't be long,' I said to Mandy as we exited the office.

'Whatever.'

When we reached the street I started walking towards the pub, but Toby indicated the coffee shop.

As soon as we were sat down with a 'small decaf cap' and a 'tall skinny latte', Toby started talking about Mike Nelson's installation.

'It's fantastic,' he said. I let him get away with the incorrect usage; we weren't in the office now; this wasn't his review, although I was aware that it was his run-up to it. 'It's completely disorienting. Atmospheric, spooky, mischievous. It's just so *bold*.'

'Save it for the magazine,' I advised. I'd been out to Mile End to see the piece myself a few days prior to Toby's visit.

'It's just so *good*,' he went on. 'It completely wrong-foots you. The guy genuinely is, *must* be, a genius.'

He clearly wasn't going to shut up about it, so I let him go on. He was fighting something of a losing battle against piped Mozart and the regular metallic thud of coffee dregs being binned. *Coral Reef*, Toby explained – clearly under the impression, which I didn't correct, that I hadn't seen it – had transformed Matt's Gallery into a warren of plywood corridors and hardboard partitions. One room was a mini-cab office with an old phone, a wire-mesh grille, a set of playing cards and an Islamic calendar, another a waiting room with a pastoral scene on the wall and drugs paraphernalia on the floor next to a dirty sleeping bag. You worked your way around the various rooms, through a workshop full of oily tyres and a hotel lobby complete with sinister clown's mask, and eventually back to the minicab office with the phone, the wire-mesh grille, the playing cards and the Islamic calendar. You exited the minicab office, leaving the installation by the way you came in, and you got the shock of your life. You weren't set upon by an actor wielding a chainsaw (as you were at Scarborough's Terror Tower, which isn't thought to be art but perhaps should be); the shock was less visceral, but more profound. It throws you off track and under-mines your concept of reality and your faith in your perceptions. It throws you straight back into the art at the same time as giving you reason to doubt everything you imagine to be true about the real world. It is, without doubt, a masterpiece, finished off with the simplest of devices executed with sly panache. I'm not going to tell you what it is, because if Nicholas Serota knows what he's doing, *Coral Reef* will end up as a permanent exhibit at the Tate – Modern *or* Britain – and you'll get to see it, if you haven't already.

'Do you know you can get ninety-six permutations of coffee here?' I asked facetiously. 'And, as far as I can tell, sixteen flavours of muffin.'

'Fuck off, Andy,' Toby said equably.

'Is this really what you wanted to talk to me about?' I asked.

'Not exactly,' Toby admitted. 'But it's sort of connected.'

He was silent for a moment, staring into his froth. Then, he said, 'I think I'm being followed.'

'Oh?'

A young guy in three-quarter-length combats wheeled a silver scooter into the coffee shop and amazingly no one seemed to mind.

'You know how most of these galleries have visitors' books?' He looked at me. I didn't reply; there was no need. 'I always sign it. It's just something I've always done, wherever I've been, whether it's a guest house in the Highlands or a church in the Cotswolds or an art gallery in the East End. I always sign the visitors' book. It's just something I do. They've gone to the trouble of providing one, so I might as well.'

'They've got to get their mailing lists together somehow,' I said.

'Yeah, well. Whatever the reason, I make a point of signing it. And as I sign, I suppose I glance at the names above mine. Now and again I'll turn back a page or two. And that's how I found out I was being followed.'

'I'm not with you,' I said.

'Every gallery I go to, there's one other name that appears in the visitors' book before mine. Not immediately before, but three or four names before.'

'Don't tell me,' I said. 'Joely Richardson.'

'Fuck you,' he responded tiredly.

'So who is it then? And how come *she's* following *you* when you are quite manifestly visiting the gallery after she has been and gone?'

'Because it's just too weird otherwise. Anyway, why do you assume it's a woman?'

'Grande decaf latte, triple shot,' yelled a camp male voice from behind the counter. The order was duly echoed by the girl standing eighteen inches away who would prepare the drinks.

'I suppose I always assume there's a woman involved where you're concerned.'

This earned me a dark look, but I wasn't going to retract it.

Toby was an attractive man, and I think he knew it, although he gave the opposite impression, taking little care over his appearance, dressing scruffily, rarely bothering to shave. He had what is often referred to as a shock of blond hair, and in his case the term is appropriate, since it grows away from his forehead in an alarming, apparently uncontrollable fashion. He's Christopher Walken without the fancy clothes. His threads are acquired secondhand at vintage clothing stores. His eyes are a soft greeny-blue, like opals resting in crinkly velvet. It's all too easy to imagine women gazing into them and becoming lost. All too easy.

'Her name is Anya Stern. At least, that's the name that appears in the visitors' books. I think she must be anticipating where I'm going next and making sure she gets there first.'

I put my paper cup down on the table. 'Why?' I asked, gesturing with upturned palms. 'To what end?'

'That's what I don't know. But if she's doing it to wind me up, she's going the right way about it.'

'When did this start?' I asked him, my tone becoming solicitous, since I could see that he was anxious.

'Well, I don't know, do I? It could have been going on for years without me knowing. I noticed her name for the first time only about a month ago, five or six weeks at the most. I was at that new place on Shoreditch High Street. I don't know what the space is called; the show's called "I Hate New York". Some terrible stuff. Especially the video. It was funny actually: some guy came down from one of the flats above the gallery and demanded they turn down the volume. He worked nights and couldn't get any peace. I mean, it *was* on pretty loud.' Toby looked away, at the corporate branding all around us, the uncomfortable, caramel-coloured armchairs, the overwhelmingly brown decor. 'I signed the visitors' book and saw her name on the same page, just three signatures above. It rang a bell and I instantly remembered having seen it but not particularly registered it at that café-gallery down Westland Place.'

'Sounds more like a case of you following her, if you ask me,' I argued.

'But you feel guilty about it. And with good reason. It doesn't look good. So you turn it around and make out she's following you. What's all this got to do with Matt's Gallery anyway? Had she been there too?'

'She wasn't far ahead of me. I might have seen her. I'm not sure.'

'If she's only four or five people before you in the book, it's quite likely she's visiting on the same day, when you think about it. What made you think it was her?'

'I don't know. There was someone there who was so nondescript, yet who seemed familiar, as if I'd seen her before and not realised it. Do you know what I mean?'

'Well,' I said, leaning back in my chair, 'I can't say I've had much experience of being pursued by women.'

Toby looked sharply at me. I'd drawn blood. I could feel it. See it in that look.

'I thought we'd finished with all that,' he said.

'*You* might have done,' I muttered.

Toby glared at me for a moment, then looked down at his half-empty cup. 'This is cold,' he said with a grimace. 'Let's go.'

Two more people on scooters arrived as we were leaving, but they were good enough to let us exit first.

'Are you going to stop going to galleries then?' I joked.

'Short black Americana!' shouted the camp guy in the coffee shop.

'How can I?' he replied bitterly. 'It's what I do.'

'I'm sure it's the same for her, this Anya Stern,' I tried to reassure him. 'It's what she does. You just share an interest. Shows open when they open and you're both keen to see them early.'

We walked back to the office. Toby picked at a loose thread on one of his shirt buttons. I watched to see what Mandy would do when we walked back in: she picked up the phone to call someone, for all the world as if she'd been intending to, and so didn't have to acknowledge our return. Toby left to check out White Cube[2]. Having been the day before, I could have told him what to look out for – Gavin Turk's Che Guevara, Marc Quinn's latest body cast, Mona Hatoum's beautifully made but somewhat cruel and ultimately pointless go-faster hospital wheelchair in stainless steel – but I didn't.

When Mandy and I were in the office alone together, working in silent contentment, it was possible to imagine it was three years earlier and that when we'd finished for the day we would wander down into the West End together and have a couple of drinks at the French, then dinner somewhere cheap. Pollo Bar, PizzaExpress, Kettners if we were feeling flash. But it wasn't three years ago. Those memories were painful for me. As for Mandy, I don't know if she even retained them as memories at all. Knowing her, I guessed she was able to erase memories as easily as dropping unwanted files in the Trash and selecting Empty Trash. In any case, I didn't blame Mandy for what happened. I blamed someone else.

Toby went back to Leinster Gardens. It took him a while to locate the *trompe l'oeil* house, since it had had such a good job done on it. When he did spot it, he stood and stared at it for a good ten minutes, studying it from all angles. It was from the back, he told Mandy and me later, that it most resembled something by Cornelius Gijsbrechts. When you saw the massive struts that held it in place, the tube tracks that ran beneath it. The façade disguised an air vent for the Circle and District lines.

'When I walked away,' he elaborated, 'everything else suddenly looked false – faux, if you like. All the other houses around it now seemed like façades as well. The people in the street all famous actors and actresses. It changed the way I see the world, which is a pretty good definition of art.'

He kept going back. As if to top up his art fix with a drop of the hard stuff. As I heard him explaining to Mandy one morning, while I hovered outside the office door, art became more powerful the further away from the gallery it was situated. Just as non-art only really became a force to be reckoned with when it was inside a gallery: he cited the paint pots and stepladders left lying about in an apparently unfinished room at Tate Modern.

But Toby also had his job to do, review pages to fill. He headed out east again. He was thinking it would make more sense to live out there than in Earls' Court. Except for the fact that rents were rocketing in Hoxton, and Spitalfields was already beyond reach. He was looking for the Construction gallery on Calvin Street and unusually he didn't have an *A–Z* with him. He was relying on his sense of direction, but all the new buildings around Broadgate played havoc with his interior compass and he overshot, ending up at the top of Shoreditch High Street and having to come back down. He constantly caught his reflection in mirrored glass and the funhouse windows of parked cars, and each time it happened he jumped. He thought it was the woman, Anya Stern. It was almost as if she was him and he was spooking himself.

Anya Stern. The name meant nothing to him. Nothing beyond the freight of foreboding it had acquired, possibly entirely innocently. He did acknowledge that, in respect of Anya Stern, he was losing it.

A convenience store, its fruit and veg a magnet for soot from the churning traffic, had an angled full-length mirror built into its fascia, so that he saw himself coming. He noticed someone behind him and wheeled around, but there was no one there, and when he turned back he'd gone beyond the point of being able to see his reflection but didn't realise it and thought he was watching the street receding behind him when in fact what he was seeing was the road unrolling ahead of him. Someone exiting the shop passed directly behind him, but Toby stopped dead, thinking the man wanted to pass in front of him, and so they collided and the man spat a stream of insults at Toby's back.

Toby staggered into Commercial Street, where even the tarts turned away as he approached.

Construction was showing five new photographic works by Sebastian Boyle, studies in reflection. Multiple reflections. Modern, glass buildings in Essen, Germany. Boyle had deliberately shot through as many layers of glass as he could, not forgetting the glass of the lens, and each layer threw up its own reflections. You could stare at them for several minutes and not realise that the part of the image you were focusing on was in fact a reflection. The conceit extended to the gallery itself, which was a work of concrete and glass, and to the way the photographs were framed and hung. They were positioned for maximum light interference, so that you would even get reflections off the glass in the frame. Anyone standing behind you in the gallery would appear to be a figure in the work.

For the second time that afternoon Toby spun around to check his back, adrenalin spiking his system, panic heightening yet distorting his perceptions. The gallery door was closing, a departing figure still visible. Toby crossed the floor to where the visitors' book lay open. He read the names, going back from the most recent: J Penrose, Nick Moore, Christina Marlowe, Anya Stern.

Anya Stern.

He pulled open the door and looked both ways. Seeing no one, he walked quickly back up to Commercial Street. Before he got there, he turned around and went back to the gallery, because he'd remembered something. There had been a space left for addresses, and there had been an address next to Anya Stern's name. He thought he knew what it said, but he wanted to go back to check and make sure.

Having done so, the next thing he did was call my number at the office, but I wasn't there. Mandy took the call and suggested he try my mobile. He did, and he got me. I wondered – as I always wondered – what passed between them when they were alone together, whether in the flesh or on the phone. Would there be any vestige of the passion that had suddenly caught fire three years ago and burnt out in a matter of weeks leaving devastation in its wake? Would there be a shared intimacy of the kind that I imagined I still had with Mandy but knew I did not? Or would there be embarrassment? Awkwardness? Was it, paradoxically, only when I was also present that they could relax with each other? Was I their foil, a straight man?

I didn't really need to know the answers to these questions.

I advised Toby to drop it, to forget about Anya Stern, but I could hear the agitation in his voice. The fact that he kept breaking up seemed to be a function of more than just unreliable technology. I heard him say he was going back to Leinster Gardens and, for the record, I advised him against it.

'How long have you known Toby?' the detective sergeant asked me again.

'Six or seven years,' I told him. 'Since we started working together.'

He'd been missing a week. The detective asked me if I could help piece together his last known movements. I told him that Toby made a habit of signing the visitors' books in small East End galleries and that to start there would perhaps make sense.

They came back with a name.

Anya Stern.

'Maybe she was the one he was convinced was following him?' I suggested.

'How could she be when her name consistently appears *before* his in the visitors' books?' the policeman asked, reasonably.

I could only shrug. 'I wish I could be of more help,' I said.

Unable immediately to locate Anya Stern, the police now wondered if they should focus their enquiries on searching for *her*, since it did seem as if she had been the one pursued. They were looking worried.

Trompe l'oeil

Toby was right. Art was more powerful taken out of the gallery and on to the streets. The police searched my flat, and they checked Mandy's place. They were curious to know why a single man kept some women's clothing in his wardrobe. I said I had nothing to hide. They had been left by my last girlfriend and I couldn't bring myself to get rid of them.

When they interviewed Mandy she didn't mention their affair, which seemed to consign it once and for all to the past as far as she was concerned, or as far as I could tell. But she did volunteer the information that Toby had shown a close interest in Leinster Gardens. They checked it out but didn't come up with anything. Their local history guy gave them some story about a hoax in the 1930s in which a conman sold charity ball tickets at ten guineas a throw. On the night in question, dozens of people arrived in Leinster Gardens all dressed up with nowhere to go.

I discussed with Mandy the possibility of taking on a freelance to tide us over until Toby turned up. Someone had to get round the galleries, I told her, cast a critical eye over the exhibitions. Just temporary. There had to be someone out there who fancied themselves as the next Jonathan Jones or Duncan McLaren. Just until Toby turned up.

We shared our concern for Toby. It felt good to share something again that was more than just the satisfaction of producing the magazine.

'He'll turn up,' I assured her. 'But, in the meantime, life – and art – must go on.'

Waste ground

Christopher Kenworthy

Some people think that London is held together by wires. Others say it's held together by gravity. Both sides agree that London is falling apart. So either there's something wrong with the wires, or there's something wrong with the gravity. It depends on which school of thought you subscribe to. Until the events of this year, I used to opt for the wires theory. How could you argue with it, when every crumbling building you see reveals a mesh of broken metal cable? You never see rubble without the shine of wires protruding from the shattered plaster. Some of those wires were put in there at the time of building, for power and reinforcement, but most of the metal is new. It migrated to London from elsewhere in the region. Whether the particles were transferred in the air or water isn't agreed upon either, but when bacterial metal found its way to street level, it leached into buildings and attached to the host structures. For years, nails, struts and wires had been going fibrous, spreading filaments into concrete and brick. The infections didn't do any damage themselves; if anything, they helped to hold those old walls together. It was only when the wires began to fracture that buildings let go of themselves. In a matter of months, London was going to pieces.

You'd know what I mean if you ever spent a night out in Shepherd's Bush. And I don't mean a night out in PizzaExpress or at the Empire. I mean a night wandering around outside, because you've been locked out of your own home. It only happened to me once, and it was my own fault for putting my trust in a metal lock. I should have fitted a plastic one ages ago, because the metal one kept sticking. I'd wanted to believe that constant use would prevent it from ever furring over, but that night there was no give in the lock at all.

I might have been upset, except that it happened on the first night that I'd been out for dinner with Ruth, after months of build-up. When you want to be with somebody, the anticipation can be half the pleasure, wondering what they will feel like. With Ruth it was different, because we'd already spent one night together, six months earlier.

Waste ground

At the time we met I was friends with Casper and Ian, brothers who still lived like students, even though they'd left college years before. They had a basement flat in Stockwell that felt more like a cellar, even though they could have afforded much better. They held parties at least once a month, where the two of them would sit on this big brown sofa for the entire night. They didn't put out any food or provide drinks. You rarely saw the same people twice at those parties, but they were always full. The ceiling in there was so low that people came in, sat down, and only moved if they needed to. Ruth was the last person to arrive, and her hair and face were wet with rain. She sat by me immediately, as though we already knew each other. She didn't tell me what she did that night, but I got the impression she was a geologist, because she kept telling me all these facts about rocks. She told me about the light they contain. There are certain rocks that, if smashed or cracked, let go of a tiny spark. 'When you break a powerful bond, it gives off energy,' she explained. She probably had no idea how moved I was by that.

'It even works with Kendal Mint Cake,' she said. 'Go into a dark room, and snap a piece in half. It's just sugar, but the fracture breaks into light.'

I could think of no better cue than that, so kissed her. It only lasted a few minutes. The party had wound down, and rather than going elsewhere, we slept in that corner, using cushions for comfort and each other for warmth.

In the morning, she woke me up because she was about to leave.

'I can't see you again,' she said. 'It was lovely, but there's somebody else.'

'You're already with somebody?'

'No, but I want to be.'

It was disappointing to be dropped so rapidly for a potential somebody, but it wasn't the end of the world. She saved that for the autumn.

During summer, there was a growing rumour that building decay was nothing to do with wires. It was more to do with gravity. I might have been excited by that, except that I'd seen ministers on the news standing their children next to wire-infested buildings to show how safe they were. They dismissed the wires theory altogether, saying migrant metal was much less common than people supposed. New metal didn't really make the buildings any more stable, they said, so even if it was eroding, it didn't matter. This disinformation made me think the wires theory probably was true.

The alternative theory was based around a belief in local gravity. There were some extremists who believed that even thoughts and emotions could affect gravity on a small scale. The reason, they said, was that consciousness extends backwards in time, ever so slightly. That's the only way you can account for our reaction times. The brain responds to situations much faster than impulses can actually travel through the nerves, but because that's inexplicable, most scientists tried to ignore it. Others came to believe that consciousness must exist slightly earlier in time than our bodies. We think, just before we exist. Wherever there's a thought, it shifts back in time, just a touch, and that disturbs the local gravity. It leaves a slight impression, a force of attraction. A really emotional moment can leave a heavy tension, which holds things together for a long time. These people claimed that London was held together by the aftermath of emotion. There were significant moments all over town, so there was plenty of local gravity. Most of the buildings would have fallen to pieces years ago, just through age, if it wasn't for the emotions that pulled them together.

All that gravity made London like a magnet, they said, which is why metal had migrated here in the first place. Elsewhere, England was re-establishing its natural history, becoming greener. It was a slow process, one you'd hardly notice. Some roads looked more like lawns, telegraph wires were strewn with moss, and spring had been unusually fecund, the hedgerows brimming with too much life and falling into the roads. What you couldn't see was that metal was being rejected, washed away as waste matter that eventually found its way to London.

Hardly anybody took this theory seriously, and neither would I have, except for the fact that it was invented by Ruth.

Her absence had bothered me more than it should, so that I was still thinking about her months after the party. We aren't attracted to people for who they are, but for what they bring out in us. I had no idea who she was, but knew that she made me feel better. I couldn't imagine ever getting mad with Ruth, or being in a bad mood around her. This feeling, of course, was based upon a few drunken hours at a party, but it was enough to make me hope I'd meet her again. I'd been unable to work out who'd invited her to the party, or find any way of tracking her down. As you might expect, she reappeared just as I gave up.

Waste ground

I was at another party, in Colliers Wood. It was quieter than usual, because the people downstairs had a baby, and the host kept shushing us. Pissed and bored, I decided that it would be good to kiss somebody, and ended up talking with a snub-nosed girl called Petra. She was wearing a yellow tank top and a white shirt, and her skin was flushed as though she was unwell. Her eyes were slits. It was a peculiar house, because they'd put fluorescent strip lights in the halls, and lampshades in the kitchen. We'd made the mistake of gathering in the hall, the blue fluorescent flare making everybody look weary, as though they were ready for bed. Petra was about to leave, and I asked if it was impossible for her to stay. She said it was, but kissed me, her jaw clicking throughout.

When she left, I saw that Ruth was standing close by, watching.

'Nothing like that ever happens to me at parties,' she complained.

We both laughed, no further introduction being necessary.

To excuse my actions, I pretended to be more drunk than I was, and she started looking after me, getting me water and helping me sit up straight.

'I wanted to see you again,' she said, 'but I didn't know where you were.'

'What about the other?'

'It's a long story.'

She wrote down her phone number, said I should take her out for dinner, and called me a cab. The last thing I wanted to do was go home, but it was important by then to keep up appearances. I resisted inviting her back with me.

When we went out for dinner, two days later, she came to Shepherd's Bush. It was one of those pine-and-glass restaurants that thinks it has atmosphere just because it's built on a street corner. All we talked about was her gravity theory. It came up early in the conversation, because I was still trying to work out what sort of geologist she was. I couldn't believe I'd met somebody who had a theory.

'But these buildings are undeniably falling apart,' I said, gesturing at London in general. I didn't want to be awkward, but nodding and being amazed by her all night would have been ridiculous. 'Your gravity can't account for that.'

'Nobody has an explanation. The wires–people think metal fatigue was to blame, but that's another word for the same thing, not an explanation.'

'And you think?'

'We're working on that.'

After a break, when I went to the toilet, I managed to ask her what happened with the other bloke, the one she'd left me for.

'We all just keep raising the stakes,' she said. 'I'm such a fickle bitch.'

It was too late for us to go on anywhere else, so as we left, I said I'd like to see her again, hoping she might invite herself back to mine. Instead, she hailed the first cab that came past, and was gone.

I was still wondering if I'd somehow offended her, when my key welded itself into the front door lock. I shared the house with my sister, Gill, but she spent most of her time staying with friends. After two minutes ringing the bell I knew she wasn't there. Breaking in to our house would have been an option if she hadn't spent so much money on reinforced glass and window locks. I tried feebly to lift one, just to see how secure it was, but soon gave up.

My money had all gone, and I hadn't taken my cards out with me, because we were just around the corner. I could reverse the charges and call other friends, but most lived so far away it would be pointless. And by now most of them would be in bed. Instead, I resolved to walk around until dawn. It couldn't take that long. The sun rises at about four in the morning, and London must wake up around five. I was feeling happy, after our night out, despite the way she'd left. In the morning, I'd be able to get help fixing the lock, and everything would be all right.

One of the most interesting things is how quickly my attitude changed. At first, I didn't want to cause anybody any trouble, by ringing them up so late. Two hours later I was considering breaking shop windows, so I could get arrested and spend the night in a prison cell. Anything would be better than the cold. London was colder these days, because of the metal. It drew the heat into walls, away from the air. If you were inside, you'd probably be warm enough, but outside, the air was thin and chilled.

In the early stages of the night, fear kept me walking briskly through better-lit areas, crossing the road every time I saw somebody coming in my direction. By three, though, London was deserted. Emptied of people, it became more interesting, because I was more willing to explore. It's incredible how much ground you can cover, and how many places there are near to your home that you never knew existed.

There were signs of decay once you got away from the main roads.

It was rare for buildings to collapse spontaneously, because they tended to rot from the roof downwards. Although I came across a few that had completely folded in on themselves, most were just giving up a few bricks and rafters.

Beneath the Westway – a road held up on concrete struts – there were many small areas of grass and scrub that could almost have been parks. In some of those were small old buildings of uncertain function; they might once have been toilets or storage rooms. Now they were chained up and left to rot. One of the larger buildings had been encased in scaffolding, which had insinuated its way into the walls, and couldn't be removed. The pipes and girders were frosted with oxide, webs of white rust gathering wherever water dripped.

Metal only gathers where it is dark or cold, which is why most homes were spared. Although the walls of your house might be riddled with wire, the power cables and phone lines in your skirting board were warm enough to be untouched. By the same token, people with piercings and fillings didn't clog with metal in the way that was first feared. Normally, these facts were reassuring, but given the amount of metal I was seeing, it only made me feel colder. It meant I was walking in locations that were dark and icy.

I kept moving along the underside of the road, looking for a building that might offer some form of shelter. Not because it would necessarily be warmer, but the thought of sleeping inside a building was better than more walking. The best I found was in one of the darker areas, surrounded by overgrown brambles. The walls felt moist, like the rocks you touch in caves. The roof was intact, but the north-facing wall had become chalky, dusting in the breeze. In places it had been sculpted down to the wire.

Having stopped walking, I couldn't face moving again, and crouched down. I decided to wait until it became light before setting off again. I might even be able to sleep. I arranged a few of the bricks and sat on them, leaning back against the wall. My arse went numb in about one minute and I began to shiver. My view consisted of the underside of the Westway, the sky beyond it a haze of streetlight. The only other colour came from a few high-rise flats on the horizon.

The bricks around me had a shimmer to them, but I couldn't tell whether that was because of the granular light, or moisture. They were old red bricks, the smooth kind. It made me remember the factory that used to be behind my school. We lived in one of those quiet villages that had one vile factory on the outskirts. For years we assumed it was a biscuit factory because of the sweet, toasted smell that came from the chimneys. To find out they were actually cooking bricks in the ovens, was one of the most startling moments of my childhood.

That memory, and the combination of exhaustion and cold, made me feel like crying. I thought about my room, and how good it would be to be sitting at the breakfast table. I'd never take it for granted again. Every bath I had from now on, I'd remember being this cold, and I'd appreciate every second. Once I was home, nothing could make me unhappy again.

Without even trying, I slept for about an hour. When I woke, the orange glow had gone, and although the sky was cloudy there was a strip of clear air on the horizon. Feeling that the night was over, I got up, enjoying the ache in my arms and legs. My hair felt dirty, but that just made me look forward to my bath even more. I'd been walking for about five minutes, when I realised I was still quite lost, and that it was only four o'clock in the morning. It might be another five hours until I was able to get a locksmith, so I wasn't even halfway through my ordeal. Soon, though, cafés would be opening. People would start walking around. That had to make me feel better. Even so, I decided to head home.

It took less than a quarter of an hour to make it home, but the key still didn't work. I didn't feel as frantic as I might have done, but decided I had to break into the house. If nothing else, it would give me something to do. The front way wouldn't be possible, but if I could scale the walls at the back, and make it to the rear door, I felt certain I'd think of some other way. That mild hope, without any logic or actual plan to back it up, was enough to get me started.

I'd not bothered with this earlier, because getting to the back of the house was so difficult. The walls at the back of the garden ran alongside an alley that used to be Shepherd's Bush Market, but had now been sealed off. The only way to get to that alley was via the raised brick ridge where the tube used to run. I once enjoyed watching the trains go past, because they were almost on the same level as my room, at the top of the house. It was one of the first lines to go down, with carriages fusing themselves into place. When the brick began to fracture, they'd closed the market as well.

Waste ground

The tube station was closed off, and I had to work my way round the back, to find a way to climb up. There were several options, but the best was to shinny up between a building and the wall. I scraped my back a bit, but managed to get up to the level of the tracks. The metal there looked ancient. Cables and wires were stretched along the length of the track, above head height, draped with translucent folds of metal. In places they looked like iron icicles. The wires were tight with the cold. If the day warmed up, they'd gradually sag, not much, but enough to make it feel as though the area was relaxing. I some-times thought it was as if the city spent each day heaving a single breath.

By the time I was alongside the house, it had clouded over again, going darker. That made me hurry, and I lowered myself off the edge of the ridge, and just as I decided it was much too large a drop, I let go. I landed badly, biting my tongue. Nothing was broken, which, having looked at the drop since, is quite surprising. Once I'd recov-ered, I walked over to the garden wall, which was eroded in a way that made climbing easy. This time, it was a shorter drop, and landing on grass in my own back garden was bliss.

The kitchen light came on, and I could see my sister in her dressing gown. She still had make-up on. I tapped on the window, and asked her to open the door. She looked wide-awake, considering it wasn't even six, and not all that surprised to see me. She looked warm and sleepy.

'I got locked out,' I said, as I stepped into the kitchen. I could smell washing powder and bread. The radiators were coming on. Grinning, I repeated myself and then said I had to have a bath. Gill complained about a hangover, said she couldn't sleep because she kept needing the toilet.

'Were you in all night?' I asked.

'From about ten, yeah.'

'Did you hear the door at all?'

'I was listening to music.'

I was less annoyed than I might have been, because she said there were all these messages for me on the answering machine. They were from Ruth.

After a brief phone call, Ruth and I rang in sick to work, and spent the day at my house. Ruth was calm in bed, but relentless, giving in to moments of gasping intensity. We talked, drowsed and occasionally dreamed. A few times I woke up, wondering if that night had really happened, or if we'd come straight here from the pub. The next time I was fully awake I asked her what had happened the night before.

Ruth explained that she had changed her mind about going home as soon as she'd left me, and had phoned, first from call boxes, then from her house. Eventually, Gill had come home and answered the phone, and told her I wasn't there. That had confused and worried Ruth. By the time we spoke in the morning, she had no doubt that she wanted to be with me.

When I tried to describe the walk to her, it was getting dark outside, and we were still in bed. It was difficult, but I managed to explain how potent the moment had been, sitting there alone.

'You probably left a gravity well there,' she said. 'I mean, if it mattered that much to you. And especially if you were tired.'

'So that building will stay there a while longer?'

'Yes,' she said, looking cross that I might doubt her.

She was giving a public lecture the next day, and said I should go along, to get an idea of what her work involved. She was trying to raise awareness of her project, hoping to obtain a research grant. I tried to listen to her, as she attempted to convince me, but I kept thinking about the space, and the impressions I might have left.

I went to most of Ruth's lectures that month, and afterwards she'd come round to my house. Things went well, because we were never bored and rarely argued.

The first sign of problems came in early autumn. The cloud that day was a meteorologist's nightmare, because it was so difficult to label, every level drifting into a confusion of mist and grey. The whole sky was washing itself out with strained rain, but sunlight and shadow came through it, so that everything was silvered. Most of the light settled on green things – leaves and grass – making them shine.

I rang Ruth at work, because I felt sure there was metal in the air.

'You're seeing things that aren't really there,' she said. She was busy trying to arrange contracts and funds. I said something about her being too busy with money to be bothered with real research.

'It's just a reflection,' she said. 'It's rain on grass. Nothing more.'

I claimed that I was only joking, and the conversation ended there. I think I knew, really, that it was only an effect of the light. I didn't believe that metal had become so insidious it was finding its way into plants.

Looking back, now, it's easy to say I was becoming obsessed at that point. Which is strange, because most of my friends thought that happened when Ruth left me, a week later.

I started going out again, at night. On the first night it was to walk off my anger, as much as anything. I hadn't planned to follow the Westway, or look for the place where I'd slept. All I wanted to do was stride angrily. If I hadn't, I'd have stayed in drinking.

Ruth had done it over the phone, refusing to see me. It was over, she'd said, and always would be. There was nothing else to talk about. 'We don't even get on,' she'd said. Sixteen hours earlier, I'd made her come. When I'd reminded her of that she'd called me pathetic.

I kept going over this in my head as I walked, barely taking in my surroundings.

It was still quite early, only just dark, when I located the building. I wasn't even sure if it was the same place now, because it felt more open and light. Only by looking up at the arches of the Westway could I be certain. The brambles had gone, revealing pale concrete, broken and coloured with rust-water. The building itself had gone to pieces, crumbling and washing away. In that light I wasn't sure if the concrete contained any metal, but something was glistening in the rubble.

That the building had decayed didn't worry me too much. I was more surprised by the surroundings. Not only had the brambles gone, but the nearby space seemed to have emptied itself of whatever large objects might have been there. I couldn't remember exactly what had been there, but it felt more open now. It was as though the place was converting itself into waste ground.

Despite her insistence that we never even meet again, Ruth came round a few times. She said we mustn't argue, only talk. We'd go to my room, to keep out of Gill's way. And then we'd have a drink, and I'd start feeling sorry for myself. She'd put my head on her chest, and it wouldn't be too difficult for us to end up in bed.

I locked into a cycle of grieving over her. Each time she'd leave I'd feel fine, and I knew I wasn't all that bothered, but whenever she was there, I'd be distraught, begging her to come back to me. It wasn't something I understood, or enjoyed, but it happened every time she came round.

I was flattered that she wanted the sex, but hoped that we might manage to be kind to each other, without me having to break down in front of her. I suggested a few times that we go out with each other. She'd have none of that, and I would end up crying again. My reward would be a cuddle, and then sex.

Ruth would never stay over, and that annoyed me. Even though we weren't going out with each other, we'd argue.

I kept saying that if we were friends, and sleeping with each other, it was a relationship.

'It's no good pretending it isn't,' I said, 'when it quite clearly is. If you like me and sleep with me, you're going out with me.'

'We're just going over old ground.'

'If we're friends who fuck, what's the difference between that and being lovers?'

'The difference is, there's no hope for the future.'

That was a self-fulfilling prophecy. Although she rang a few more times, I didn't invite her round.

Occasionally in a built-up area of town, roller doors are lifted, or gates opened in a wall, and you see that where you expected a warehouse or tunnel, there is empty space. These quadrangles are usually nothing but soily ground and sky, the brick walls patterned with the outlines of walls and floors that had adjoined them. In a few, there are iron stairwells, painted green, recessed into the wall, no longer leading anywhere.

I hadn't noticed these spaces until I'd created my own patch of waste ground. Now, I began to wonder what events had emptied these places, and went out at night, seeking them.

I refused to think of my discoveries as waste ground. What were they meant to be a waste of? Space? Because they didn't have shops on them?

Ruth was wrong. London isn't held together by the gravity of emotions. It's held together by easy television and tame shows. It's held together by bland drugs and dull dinner parties. When you see a part of London that's going to pieces, it's a good thing, because it shows that people still feel something. This is why multiplexes and McDonald's and Ikea are doing fine. Nothing happens there to harm those buildings so they remain pristine. It's the good buildings – the theatres, old cinemas, the homes where people fight – that have fractured. What appears to be desolation is just emotion making a home for itself. Making space.

When I tried to explain this to her, last week, she didn't know how to deal with me. I wasn't crying, or complaining, just letting her know how things are.

'Are you saying I did this to you?' she asked. 'That I reduced you to this?'

'I'm not reduced to anything. I'm all right.'

Ruth was looking for cracks that afternoon, in me, but there weren't any. What I felt for her could have happened with anybody. I didn't need to make myself miserable over her. She was just another girlfriend.

It's just difficult, sometimes, to justify your emotions, if all you've done is sat under a bridge and watched the sun rise. You can't believe you can feel that much by yourself, so you blame somebody else. It's tempting to collapse because of a person, to tell yourself that you've been damaged. In reality, you're probably doing fine.

Ultima Thule

Gareth Evans

1. *clear enough space to work without hindrance*

They are children without gardens, nameless because ignored, tenants in their own lives. Sharp as winter rain, they are the noise of their estates and a long way from the country. They parade the treeless Hackney streets – Narford, Northwold, Maury, Brooke – high on toxic nose fuel, bagged and sticking to their souls. Doorways, iron cuttings, lots as empty as the sky – from Dalston K to Rectory Road, small turf claiming the big picture and not a royal or vicar to be seen.

They break the windows in the flanks of phone booths (glass left at the edge like spray-on snow around a viewing absence), remove what channels out there might be left, feel that soon they'll be heading for the storm drains. They strip cars for audio and parts like surgeons on the wires for organs, with professional urgency; and corner travellers – Roma – from a distance with knife words and things sometimes thrown, not because they hate their horizon gaze, but because they long for it to touch *their* meagre shapes with light.

They are in simple speak adrift from any reason they can value, and on this Norcott morning, lead-hued weather their shoulder sack and future, are ready therefore to be overwhelmed.

2. *gather the necessary tools*

Something in them prompts a new direction, a further in. They know it's always been there, but the building's never surfaced in them until now. High gates near the school's locked own – fuck learning that you're useless, they do say – off Geldeston and spit from Alconbury – it rises like a dirty prow of ship above the dishes and the roofs. Warehouse dead for decades in the terraced triangle – merely garden view – once work in furniture for Clapton hands, now a site hot as a swollen asphalt night to up the prices. So say the suits that slide around the East sniffing out the useful vacancy. So they *would* say if they saw this one's tidy figure. Stack it full of desperates from the badlands. Shaft the voucher crowd *and* easy money from the ministry. Or claim its greenback loft potential – dizzy in their pupils, Friday night throughout the week. But they *haven't* seen it, and so it is the children's. It is theirs.

Perhaps it's just the dope need, thought of a new, another off-road shelter that pushes them in. Zero tolerance on their patch now. Stokey pigs bigoted as bullets sniffing out the small fry from their big pen on the High Road. Get inside the waste lot and laugh yourself stupid at the pork, feet away but blind to kids' transgression. Stirrup the palms and boot it, over. Pull up, swinging like a ledge scene, all in, well and good.

The yard is large as a mountain breath, doors all around its edge, and then the brick cliff rise of wall. Heap of rubble to the left but cleaned out otherwise. No trucks to ride down to the axle. No scrap to lift. Nothing to sell. Could rave it maybe one time, get the big boys in with sound to match the punters, but the getaway's not good. Look then, broken panes up towards the ridge, five floors maybe six, too far. Drop down to the level, delivery and personnel flaps, black teeth and sealed mouths. Entrances closed to history from back before the war, before the kids were even just a thought.

3. open the box

Try them anyhow. Jack all else to do. *Pour your blood straight down the sink*. Run and smash. Bang the doors like you're Stomp. An audience of ears across the weekday rooms. Zimmer surfers, students, webheads and the solitary poor. Watch the panels do their tight sail ripple, give a little at the hinge like a loosening fist. Shoulder at the far one, from a distance, nice, a touch of bruising, good to win the ladies, bit of story underneath the black. Here it goes, at it like you mean it. Hard meeting, numb of impact.

But it opens.

In without knowing it at first, face floored, grin of wound clefting the cheek, blood and grit, others piling after, scree and skid, ripped baggies and Nikes all fouled. Fast chest, confused, then calm it down. They gather themselves. Stand up. Look around. Poor visibles. Sure, some Jacob's drop-downs, skinny loft ladders of light from the high windows, and some bright spill from the door, but not a lot to go on. This is torch time, beams at chest level, held as if you're doing pull-ups. They brush down, form a wagon circle. Door already jemmied, could be company, needle jockeys from Nightingale or those Kurds who got kicked out of the corner empty. They're ready, alert at the knees for speed or assault. But there is nothing, not even the rat business they all know from the district dives, small scratch on the concrete like an itch in the skull. Maybe there's a bird, pigeon up in the vault, desperate feathers keening for the breeze. Rat with wings. You really need some noise OK so there's rodent action what do you want a medal let's check this out.

4. confirm that all the parts are present

They fan wide, ease forward from the doorway, dust galaxies still circling from the get-in, but nothing fine, it's heavy, like it's not moved for years, like it's the dust objects breathe out when they die, not the daily shedding but a vessel, like the hope of the thing is in its dust and it's given up except for that. There's a smell with it, again not just the must of shut-up, but something deeper, in the stomach, the odour of long aspiration, obsession. Fuck that perfume shit. No one's selling this one down on Oxford.

The building is altogether bigger than they could possibly have guessed from knowing its border streets. It appears to stretch away from them, a horror corridor, side doors to low-ceilinged offices lining the main drag. Above, it arcs stationwise, beams and curved supports and an umbilical caged ladder running up to iron balconies and crosswalks. It swells exponentially as they advance, lines on a graph mapping the increase. Following its course with their eyes, they realise that they cannot find the far end of the roof, where it should hit the down wall, even though the light is strongest at the height. They shuffle slowly on, old men suddenly, small in the great space. Shuffle until they see it.

5. arrange the parts in order of priority or need

It is ahead of them then, sudden as a tropical night, and at first they think it is something low and huge under a tarpaulin, the old assembly desks perhaps, shrouded in white like abandoned furniture. Its surface seems to glow with a dull burnish, as of mercury, holding light and letting it out over time. It is absolutely still and it stops them with its silence, even though they are more than a throw from it, and cannot clearly see what they're approaching. They move up as a group, until they are there, with it reaching out further than the afternoon, plexus high because they are still young, and for once they are all, as a single creature, without voice or sudden gesture. And they look, and look, and their sight runs out across it like water.

It is a model, but a model the like of which they never could have conjured. Crafted from the papers of all forests, so fine it barely is, as precise as gene reactions, it takes their breath as a simple wind from them. Loose planets, their eyes move past it, and their tongues are dry in their heads.

6. begin to assemble the model, following all relevant coding

It is London. Cut and shaped and firm and fragile, assembled out of card and pure desire, all of the London – every building, every street, every office, theatre, dock, bridge, bar, church and factory – they do not know. They do not know it because they are too narrow for its scale. Yes, they have been up west, lifted goods in shining Regent stores and run like exhilarated fire down alleys to escape, have pulled the bandits in Soho arcades, whistled at the selling girls off York Way and drunk White Lightning in the South Bank skateboard alley, under the switching neon of the wind sculpture, from discount bottles too large for their palms, but they have not pieced together these and a million other such locations, have not threaded them into a narrative that is the city and all its myriad prism being. They see as they are seen, zones of abuse, unanchored choreographies in the city's great dance, random jerks and twitches no part of the main body. Their lips cannot hold the sweet song of belonging and thus they pass on through, restless in their near streets, trouble in the too small territory, but nothing to the larger scheme and pattern.

So it is that they gaze upon this model as they would upon their first kill, with awe and not knowing and not understanding and no small revulsion together in the mix. Its sweep is female, a woman asleep on her side, and the dip from hip to waist the city's settled bed. From where they view, it reveals its genesis shape, its valley siting, and they can scan the strata of its building, in section as through a trunk or sliced torso, the workings. They stare from the East, from the Barrier, and it is only when they ground their sight in light of the compass that they realise the fact of the river. For it is there, but not of paper, stiffened with the gleam of varnish. It is glassy, a fixed flow of need, at permanent high, layered in sheets to give an idyll hue and shifting glint to its way. It shines out towards the group – they see their faces fairground-mirrored in it, as if they're not the same. And it is not alone. The buried streams, the hill offerings, all the fouled tributaries long since sealed, invaded or forgotten are present and sheened on the surface of the kit. They gift the river life in stained blue fragments, salvaged bottle and old church glaze. The Tyburn at Baker Street is freed from station piping; the Westbourne clears a path from Hampstead pond to Chelsea basin; its swelling as the Serpentine does not stop the journey. And Effra, Walbrook, Fleet also vein the miniature polis.

The kids do not know these utopian additions to be such. They cannot aye or no such fresh amendments. They go first for familiar acres, the pitch from Haggerston to Leyton Marsh, streets capillary in their old density. Run along the model's side for best view of the home strait, are ripe with infant marvel at the intricacy of it all, the precision of the wires and lamps, the peeled shop signs, the sidings, fast-food junctions and the dog track past the reservoirs. This keeps them fixed for a decent stretch, but soon they're drifting over, kings now of movement and the city theirs to chart. They take it in sweeps, pan first along the river, picking up the names left there by sailors; Cuba Street, Odessa, Norway Place, Russia Dock Road and on. Homesick monikers, the world in constant motion, small outposts of a larger vision.

This whets them, and they break off. Some stride north, others plummet south, ride each other's shoulders for the privilege of height, learn the city's lines of action, trace the carriage roads, the supply routes in and out, the green relax of parkland and the heath, the city's necessary lungs. Magpie the details, of the tram tunnel up from Holborn, where darkness drains away each commuter morning, the Knightsbridge tree, marker to the plague pits, and the glistening marble Mandir off the blasted Circular. Each makes their own excursions through the vast assembly, but all sense, the more they offer their attention, the secret story of the capital that is not shown at all. The gestures of the veiled Yemenis bargaining for fruit in Green Street market, the banter of the news vendor at Ravenscourt Park, the way that a girl stood while she was waiting in the trailer camp near the Westway, and the light upon her cheek. The secret seepage of stored human trace from the surrounding buildings into public air. The reason after all for all of it. They would and could not say it to themselves or to the others, that they are geared somehow by this into a new way, but...

Then one sparker shouts out, what about *this* place, is it here or not, and they all eagle in on the wedge for closer survey, almost thinking they might find themselves, a watching of the watching. But it is not and there is nothing in its place, just a slight extension of the backyards.

Their breath shifts again in their chests, and they are still with a new knowledge.

7. *note: do not attempt to deviate from the instructions – they are there to help you, not limit your expression*

And then when it is all seen, hours in all on the circuit, when there is perhaps nothing again that will change them like the witnessing of this, they glimpse the hand. The hand, out like a broken cup from underneath, down in the city's shadow, floored. They stoop and bend, it does not move, they are not thrown, they are beyond all the reasonable registers. They stoop and bend and pull it, out.

The hand is not alone. It is connected, it belongs to a body, but no, to the idea of a body. A pale man emerges dragged from the basement of the model, and it is so very clear to them, to them for all their brave chancing, their shout stuff and rage walking, fired cells kicking them to loudness, that he is long gone from them, from all of this and more. He is full of calm, it lines his lids like sleep, or experimental salt. His age at leaving they cannot guess. He is a white shadow, the cast of cherry blossom across the ground, a thin bruise, a hibakusha but without a trace of violation in his fade. It is as if all his blood has travelled elsewhere, has left him like the flow of refugees out of a beaten territory, has migrated into other forms, into the rivers of the model perhaps, into the contours of the valley; a new form of power, of generation.

They shall never know what road he took there, sheeted in dust underneath a table. How he closed a door behind himself, and stood quietly a moment, trying to find the solitude that would not hurt, a way to live alone and calmly across the great span of days. With the patience of a tree. Aiming for the larger picture. A branching into the future. Understanding the lessons of soil and sky, source and aspiration. This was how he built the model. He slipped like a thief into a different shape of time. He breathed out and held the absence. Forgot light as a place to be, and kept it only as a tool.

It was not a question of years, of clusters of years spent bent like a question over the desk, his own shadow on the surface sealed into the assembly. It was closer to the ticking of a faith. A Chartres cathedral schedule, building beyond the single life. Passing the wish on, faith rising like a great opaque wall around the warehouse, a hang of silvered mist, beyond which there was nothing except the reflection of his intention. He left the city and his body for an imagination, replaced his heart with the tokens of belief. Making the world with the ghost of wood, with slivers of match and glass. This was how he made the model. The rest was just bureaucracy: figures in an account, a phone call, authorisation, a tray each morning and another one in the evening; being left except for that.

8. note 2: try not to seek assistance, as the more you seek, the less the pleasure

They have never seen a body before, despite all their towerblock talk, their public blading, and certainly not one as altered as this. Perhaps it is the corpse that pushes them – like someone paid to help jumpers near the rocks, or euthanasia providers with a needle – shoves them afterhours-style into their result, what they do with all this crazy evidence. Perhaps this is why, and how one starts, tentatively at first, doubting the retina, to nudge at the thing with a boot end, like perhaps a cat found stiff with morning. Knock it a little, starting a motor, watching for it to take the hint and kick into the quiet hour. Nothing. Not a jack, not a blur. Again. Same. Again. Same. More. Yes, more. Into the ribswell, out to the room, into the breastbone, out to it, into it, out. Enjoying this now, this so familiar action. It's something real in all this strange perspective. Doesn't really matter that it's getting nowhere, that it's little more than stirring a heap of feathers smeared with passing. It stirs their blood all right, gets them working normal again, brings them back. And they like that, that six-month sailor feeling, back on terra f. In out in out, and he's gone, they're touching toecaps from either side, meeting in the middle, nothing in between them, but they've built up all this friction, like a tribe without a season, stoking a survival fire with not a hope of being saved. All the effort.

And so they turn, however many there are of them, little angers in matching shirts, and they turn first to what surrounds them, naturally, and what silenced them now fills them with a noise. And it is more, more than enough to be going on with. Voice in the foot and the fist, speaking in tongues. Losing it fast in the delirious evening. To the city that made them they address blows, and they are goliaths in the warehouse. When it comes to reckoning like this, it doesn't take much. The replica gives like a torture puppet. Westminster in a couple of kicks, Tear it down. They're on it now, running like giants through the falling districts. A sole removes a block that beat the Blitz. From Wanstead through to Kingsbury in a single arc of violence, and the ease of tearing down, the speed of it. Sharp brevities of action culling history in a savage instant.

The centre does not stand, and neither do the edges. The pendulum swing of the valley is stopped like a heart. Northern suburb sprawl – service points and car parks – becomes meaningless when torn from its origin, just a swathe of houses, a mess of neighbourhoods, mossy in their flattening and thrown wide like the wing from a crash. Wealth knows no safeguard, no insurance exit out of carnage; the kicks taken to Highgate, Dulwich and Belgravia will peal as long as rapture bells come judgement dawn. And poverty zones, the skinny east and south, fat only on the fruits of dereliction, they will not know justice while the hammers swing and swing; they fall slowly to the ground in the thickening air, as if they were savouring their final pulse of being one time more, on graceful rewind just to hold the feeling, any feeling.

9. *once completed, allow briefly to settle*

So it goes. From the gut to hands, wiry agents of coiled purpose through the gloom, until there is an eruption of dust and grit and a fog of going in the high vaulting. And the rasp of their breathings, their pumped blood sounding through the darkness of the warehouse. And when they are done, when nothing but the ruin is around them, they stop, feeling the night up and on them like damp, new skin, they stop in the long, slow settle of the maelstrom, and stand as men in the afterimage of a terrible gesture, a private wasting that is too close to be phrased, but which they know, in the far corner of knowing, shall demand a reckoning. A call to account, when they are all banked out. Perhaps tribunals in squares, the sun hot on their stalks of neck or, more expected, late calls to rented rooms, heels on the thin stair carpet, a determined knock on the doorframe, a knocking without cease.

But for now this thought is latent in them, a future, like wine in the hanging grape or the first stirrings of an end in the liver and bone. They stand, and fill like a flooded basement with exhaustion. Tired beyond all acts now. Tired only to fall, knees caving, concertinas of themselves, on to the churned floor. Ground like plough mad with debris. Fall, their time now, eyes dropping into sleep like coins down a well. Hear them reach the...

10. enjoy your completed model, comfortable in the knowledge that it could not exist without you

They wake separately but as part of a larger movement, like a body testing parts of itself for the rise. A dull cream of light runs through the hall. They have lost the clock, are running now on body time and hunger. They stand and brush themselves off. Look around. It is still here, the huge, smashed trace of it, but somehow it is smaller now, the way a highrise appears after blowdown. Stacked absence. Neat, but reduced, as if the only question is how it could ever have seemed so much when it was up.

And with it so the warehouse, so it feels, all shrunk or merely normal, the right proportions and them in it, if anything they the bigger, the changed. They laugh a little then, as if they are all thinking it through in tune with each other, unspoken, nervous, as if there is no other way it could be.

The light at the entrance takes their attention then, turns heads like taps, a cleaner brightness than from the smeared skypanes, and how close it is, the way out, nearer than they ever thought possible, given their previous pacing. They move as one towards the swinging door, daily questions in their mouths now, a fry up, table chatter and all of this can wait, this post-mortem of the wreck.

Walk the clutch of strides towards the door, and then, with easy banter, jostling and jokes, pass through and all step out.

And there is nothing.

There is nothing there.

Only white.

No compass point, no left or right, no back and on, no settling for the eye or brain, no horizon target, only white. It has all gone, everything beyond the door. Only a white, without distance because unending, without dimension because absolute, a white like fixed milk. Like being part of paint, like ceaseless snow, never to be trodden or thawed, with a sky that partners it. And no sound, not a sound under- foot or a sense of friction with the ground. No bird. No wind tree. No far-off road or river, no hum of labour and simple human busi- ness. No symmetry of things at all. Not even the sound of their hearts, building in them like a long runner, or their rubbing of eyes in doubt, or then, one by one, their opening of mouths into a fear. Only silence, like the silence after an explosion, the easing of breath. Blossom falling on blossom, and a sense, like a throb in the chest or the current running through water, of things passing away.

They have entered the white map; and they stumble as if concussed, double in vision and step while, without their notice, into this great enveloping the building is sinking, fading as into a pale quicksand.

They stand there then, thinking slowly, a pain opening in them they will not have breath to name, until, quietly, like rain against the hills, a print in falling winter, a few words on a page, they too soon are gone.